AFTER RIVER

AFTER RIVER

A Novel

DONNA MILNER

HARPER

An Imprint of HarperCollins*Publishers*
www.harpercollins.com

HarperCollins books may be purchased for educational, business,
or sales promotional use. For information, please write:
Special Markets Department, HarperCollins Publishers,
10 East 53rd Street, New York, NY 10022.

FIRST EDITION

Published in Great Britain in 2008 by Quercus.

Library of Congress Cataloging-in-Publication Data
is available upon request.

ISBN: 978-0-06-146299-3

08   09   10   11   12   OFF/RRD   10   9   8   7   6   5   4   3   2   1

For
Tom
Always

Geography has made us neighbours. History has made us friends ...
What unites us is far greater than what divides us.

John F. Kennedy: Address before the Canadian Parliament
Ottawa, May 17, 1961

Chapter One

He came on foot. Like a mirage, he rose in a shimmer of heat waves above the winding dirt road leading to our door. I watched him from the shadows of our enclosed porch.

I was fourteen on that hot July day in 1966, would be fifteen in less than a month. I leaned against the porch doorway and squinted into the sun while the last dregs of water drained from the wringer washer behind me. Outside, the week's laundry hung limp and motionless on the three clotheslines stretched across the yard. Sheets, hurtfully white in the brilliant sunshine, created a backdrop for the orderly procession of our family's attire. Mom stood out on the wooden laundry platform, her mouth full of clothes pegs, her back to the road. She reached down and plucked a denim shirt from the wicker basket at her feet, snapped out the garment with a crack of wet fabric and pegged it to the line.

There was something different about my mother that day. On washdays she usually wore a kerchief tied in a rolled knot in the middle of her forehead. That afternoon, bobby pins and combs held up her hair. Wayward blonde locks and wispy tendrils escaped around her face and at the nape of her neck. But it was more than that. She was distracted, flushed even. I was certain she had applied a touch of Avon rouge to her cheeks. Earlier, she had caught me studying her face as she fed my brothers' jeans through the wringer.

'Oh, this heat,' she said, then pushed back her hair and tucked it behind her ears.

Her attention was not on the road though, as she hung the last load, and I saw him before she did. I watched as he came around the bend by our bottom pasture. He crossed over the cattle guard, through the flickering shadows of poplar trees, and back into the naked glare of the day. He carried a large green duffel bag on one shoulder and a black object slung over the other. As he got closer I saw it was a guitar case bouncing against his back in the easy rhythm of his unhurried steps.

Hippie. It was a new word in my vocabulary. A foreign word. It meant oddly dressed young Americans marching beneath peace signs that urged, 'Make Love, Not War!' It meant Vietnam War protesters sticking flowers into the gun barrels of riot police. And it meant draft-dodgers. Some of whom, it was rumoured, were entering Canada through the border crossing a mile and a half south of our farm. Still they were nothing more than rumours. Rumours, and the snowy images from the hit and miss television reception in our mountain valley. I'd never seen one in the flesh. Until now.

'What's wrong?' Mom's voice broke my trance. She stepped in from the laundry platform and handed me the empty basket. Before I could answer she turned to look down the road. As she did, our cow dog, Buddy, lifted his head, then bolted off the bottom porch step where he had been sleeping in the afternoon sun. The border collie leapt over the picket fence and raced past the barn, a blur of black and white, barking a belated warning.

'Buddy!' Mom called after him. But by then the long-haired

stranger was kneeling in the dust on the road, murmuring quiet words to the growling dog. After a moment he stood and, with Buddy at his side, continued up to the yard. He smiled at us from the other side of the fence as the border collie licked his hand. Mom smiled back, smoothed her damp apron and started down the porch steps. I hesitated for only a moment before I put down the laundry basket and followed. We met him at the gate.

She was expecting him.

She wasn't expecting the heartache that would follow like a cold wind.

Chapter Two

I MUST HAVE known.

In all these years no one has ever said it out loud. But I could see the unasked question in their eyes. *How could I not have known?* Thirty-four years later, I still ask myself the same question.

Sometimes I catch myself falling back into memories. Back to the 'before' of my childhood. Before everything changed. Back to the time when it was unimaginable that my family would not always be together. To when my entire world was our family farm, four hundred acres carved out of a narrow mountain valley deep in the Cascade Mountains of British Columbia. Everything else, the town of Atwood three miles north, and its twenty-five hundred inhabitants, appeared to be only backdrop to our perfect lives. Or so it seemed until I was almost fifteen years old.

That's when the 'after' memories begin.

Sometimes I can stop them, those 'after' memories. Sometimes I can go for weeks, months, even years, pretending none of it ever happened. Sometimes I even believe it.

Still, it's impossible to forget that summer day in 1966. The day that marks the time when my family was whole and good and right, to the time when nothing would ever be the same again.

The beginning of the sequence of events that would change all our lives wasn't catastrophic or earth shattering. It even looked beautiful for a while.

Afterward, Mom would blame everything that happened on the world encroaching upon our little farm. New highways were being built; one would connect our town to the Trans-Canada. In the East Kootenays, valleys were being flooded and dams constructed to carry electricity to a growing province – and, my father said, 'to our power-hungry neighbour to the south.'

'There's too many jobs available,' Mom had worried out loud during dinner the evening Jake, the hired hand who had been with us for as long as I could remember, left without warning. 'Who's going to be interested in working on a small dairy farm in the middle of nowhere?'

'We'll get along,' Dad said between mouthfuls. 'Morgan and Carl will take up the slack and Natalie can help in the dairy. We'll be fine.' He leaned over and patted her hand.

'No,' Mom pulled away and stood up to get the coffeepot. 'You keep increasing the herd, and my boys keep quitting school. At least one of my sons is going to finish high school.' She didn't add, 'and go to university.' She never spoke this dream out loud any more. Carl was her last hope.

She hired the first and only person to call about her two-line ad in the *Atwood Weekly*. 'He has a nice voice,' she said after she announced it that July morning. She started to gather up the breakfast dishes. Then, as if it was an afterthought, she added, 'He's American.'

I glanced over at my father. His thick eyebrows lifted as he digested her words. I knew my parents held opposing views on the idea of young Americans fleeing the draft and seeking refuge in Canada. I wondered if, for the first time, I would see my parents have a real argument. Dad was seldom cross with Mom, but then he wasn't used to her taking it on herself to make a decision without talking it over with him first. And certainly not over an issue she knew he held a strong opinion on. He said nothing. Still, by the way he stood up and snatched his snap-brim fedora – his milk delivering hat – from the peg by the door then slammed it onto his head, I knew he was not pleased.

'Well,' Mom said after the kitchen door closed behind Dad and Carl, 'I think that went well, eh, Natalie?' Then her face turned serious as she snapped on her rubber gloves and said, 'I refuse to lose another son to this farm.'

From the moment they could carry a bucket, my three brothers were hostages to the milking schedule. Each morning they woke up in darkness to step onto the forever-cold linoleum floors of the upstairs bedroom and pulled on their overalls. I still believe Boyer slept with his clothes on.

Boyer, the eldest, had a room – more of a cubbyhole – to himself in the attic. When he was twelve years old he got tired of sharing his bedroom with Morgan and Carl. So he made himself a nest among the rafters above the two upstairs bedrooms. He hammered together a crude wooden ladder to climb through a hole in the hall ceiling. When he was fourteen he built a real set of stairs.

That narrow attic room was so cold on some winter days that you could see your breath. In the summers even the open window would not let the stifling air escape. Boyer never complained. The room was his sanctuary, and those of us privileged enough to be invited in, to share his company and the books that eventually filled every available space up there, envied the world he'd created under the eaves of the farmhouse built by my grandfather's hands at the turn of the century.

I was the only girl and so had a bedroom to myself. It had been Boyer's room before I came along and threw off the sleeping arrangements. If he ever resented me for it, he never showed it. I would have gladly shared the bedroom with him. I was too young to understand his need to have a room of his own. It was a long time before I stopped asking why he had to sleep with my brothers, and then way up in the attic.

Every morning Boyer was the first one to make his way down the enclosed stairway into the kitchen. For many years he would stir the embers, then add kindling, to re-light the hulking cast iron cook stove for Mom before he headed to the barn. After we got the electric range in 1959 he would go straight to the front porch where he pulled on knee-high rubber boots, winter or summer. And every morning, at exactly ten minutes before five, Boyer let the kitchen door slam behind him. His cue to let everyone know he was on his way to the barn. In the early darkness he and Jake, the hired man who lived above the dairy, herded the cows in from the pasture.

Morgan and Carl were never anxious to begin the day. Most mornings my father would holler up and threaten his youngest sons with ice water. 'Mutt and Jeff,' he called them. Morgan was two years older than Carl, but from the time they were toddlers Carl towered over him. The two of them were best friends, inseparable. Once Morgan stumbled down the stairs wiping the sleep from his eyes, we knew Carl would not be far behind, his heavy woollen socks flapping out in front of his feet like so much extra skin. Mom was forever scolding him to pull up his socks, and we all wondered that he didn't trip over them, especially in the dark of the stairway, but they were as much a part of him as his toes.

My brothers' morning parade was as regular and expected as my mother's prayers.

Mom prayed at every occasion. When we were growing up she made sure we did too. At each meal we bowed our heads before a fork ever clicked against a plate. Every night after the milking, beneath pictures of Mary and Jesus propped on the mantel, beads in hand, she gathered us all together in the parlour. 'Hail Mary, full of grace, the Lord is with thee,' she led the rosary while I knelt beside my brothers on the scratchy pink and grey flowered linoleum trying not to fidget. Mom believed wholeheartedly in the saying, 'the family that prays together stays together'.

When I was very young I would peek up at my mother's bowed head and moving lips as she fingered her beads and think that if praying made you that beautiful, then I wanted to be sure to do it right.

Mother grew up Protestant. When she and Dad married she converted. She embraced the Catholic Church with the enthusiasm of a hungry lover.

'I knew the first time I walked into St Anthony's with your father, that I belonged,' she once told me. 'It was the feeling,' she said, 'the feeling of permanence. As if the building, the statues, the paintings, and icons had been there – would be there – forever. The light streaming in through the stained glass windows, the rituals, the perpetually burning candles, the incense,' she mused as if talking to herself. 'It all felt natural, right somehow.'

The rosary beads were her comfort, something real, something solid to hold onto. They moved through her fingers as easily as breath through her lungs. 'Converting,' she said, 'was like coming home.'

She promised her future children to the Catholic Church. But the truth was, except perhaps for Boyer at one time, none of us ever became as devout as she was.

Even our father, who had been born Catholic, was not as pious.

Every Sunday, before he started his milk deliveries, he dropped us off at St Anthony's. When his route was complete he picked us up. If the weather and roads were good, and the chores were finished at home, he headed back into town for a later mass. Mom would return with him, attending twice on those Sundays.

She said nothing about his sporadic attendance. She knew the farm came first: before church, before friends, before family, before anything. Still, he joined us every evening for rosary in the parlour, and when my parents went to bed I often heard them murmur prayers in unison. I imagined them kneeling beside their quilt-covered four-poster bed like two picture-book children, their hands folded in reverence, their heads bowed.

Prayers were not all I heard.

My brothers, although we never spoke of it, must have heard too. The open ceiling grates that allowed heat to rise to the second-storey hallway also allowed the noises of the night to drift up. Noises not meant for children's ears. Later, as a mother myself, I often wondered at that.

They must have realized to some extent that sounds carried upstairs, because my parents seldom had conversations in their bedroom. The only words I ever heard were the perfunctory, 'Goodnight, Gus,' and, 'Goodnight, Nettie,' after their prayers. Then I'd hear the slow groaning of springs as they climbed into bed. And sometimes the rhythmic creaks and muffled animal sounds, followed by a few moments of silence before the night filled with my father's throat-catching snores and my mother's quick sneezes.

It was not until years later, as I watched my mother hold herself together during the days following my father's death, that I realized my mother gave three stifled sneezes whenever she was holding back tears. I don't think my father ever realized it.

He seemed as oblivious to her nocturnal wanderings.

Often, deep in the night, I would awaken to the protest of bedsprings, then hear my mother's footsteps as she left their bedroom. Sometimes, when I was a child, I crept down the stairs on the pretence of needing to use the bathroom. If Mom wasn't sitting at the kitchen table with a cup of tea and a book I went searching for her. I tiptoed around in the dark until I found her, either in the sunroom behind the parlour, or out on the front porch, staring into the night. Once I'd located her I slipped back upstairs before she realized I was there. I never once heard my father get up to join her or ask her to come back to bed.

During the day it was a different story. My parents were not above public displays of affection. They used any excuse to hold hands or put their arms around each other. Whenever they were within arm's length they touched. Like a teenage girl, Mom always sat right beside Dad in the truck. He would lift his chin and howl like an adolescent school boy – enjoying the embarrassment of whichever one of his children happened to be riding along – whenever he accidentally-on-purpose brushed Mom's bare leg with the gearshift. At the kitchen table, my mother constantly touched Dad's shoulder or stroked his arm while they discussed the business of the farm. And whenever they were outside together they walked hand in hand. Yet it seemed, when the day was done, as if all personal conversation was cut off at their bedroom door and they became intimate strangers. As if after settling in bed these two ceased to be, and whatever happened after that was not a part of who they were. I cannot imagine the strange couplings, which must have taken place through layers of nightclothes, leading to my mother giving birth to four children by the time she was twenty-six years old.

Years later, after my father died, my mother told me – in an unusual late-night, soul-baring conversation brought on by grief and wine – that she'd never seen my father without his clothes on, and that he'd never seen her fully naked. From the way she said it I understood this was not her choice, but just the way things were with him. I was left with the image of each of them in opposite corners of the room, their backs to each other, as they changed in the dim light. I imagined my mother, behind her wardrobe door, slipping out of her printed dress and pulling a floor-length cotton nightgown over her head. And in the other corner, I envisioned my father stripping down to his woollen underwear. Longjohns. He wore them like a second skin, winter and summer; the only time he was out of them was for his infrequent baths.

My father refused to take regular baths like the rest of us. He swore that every time he bathed he got a cold, or pneumonia. He avoided the deep, claw-foot tub that took up half of our bathroom. Every night after the evening milking we heard splashing behind the locked door as he sponge bathed at the bathroom sink. Once a month he risked death and disease and took his ritual bath. And sure enough, the next day he was hacking and coughing and swearing he would never climb back into the tub.

Dad said he didn't need baths; his longjohns soaked up his sweat. He had three pairs, which he rotated throughout the week. Despite his refusal to bathe, I never thought my father smelled any different from the rest of us. We all carried that same barn aroma of cow manure, sour milk, and hay. The acrid-sweet smell was everywhere, in our clothes, in the house; it was as much a part of us as the milk that was our livelihood. When other children held their noses in the schoolyard it never occurred to me that those odours, so natural to our lives, were offensive to others. I didn't realize the truth of their taunts until the first time I returned home after being away for two years. I can still remember how surprised I was when I walked in the door of our old farmhouse and inhaled memories.

But I couldn't help notice the odours on washday. Every Saturday morning my mother and I sorted the mountains of soiled clothes and linen on the floor of the enclosed front porch. Every week two pairs of father's longjohns ended up in a pile with my brothers' jockey shorts and T-shirts. My brothers refused to wear longjohns except in the worst of winter. Their underwear swished around with Dad's in the wringer washer, a grey swirl of man-and-barn smelling soup.

Mom once told me that it was interesting what you can tell about peoples' lives from their laundry. She knew my brothers' secrets from the state of their clothes and the contents of their pockets. Not that she ever used it against them. She adored her boys and was only surprised when she discovered some clue that betrayed they were human after all: the tobacco leaves stuck in the lining of their pockets, broken matches, snoose plugs and gopher tails. She read stains like a private diary.

Morgan was fifteen on the washday an unwrapped condom fell to the floor as Mom turned his jean pockets inside out for the last load. She leaned over and picked up the translucent coil of rubber. She glanced over at me with raised eyebrows as if she wondered if I knew what it was. I was twelve, old enough to have heard jokes at school and to piece it together in my own fashion. Growing up on a farm made animal mating as natural as grass growing, but human mating, well, that was another thing entirely, and certainly never spoken about out loud in our home. Still, I lifted my lip in a disgusted sneer as if I knew exactly what the foreign object was for. As my mother pocketed the wayward rubber in her apron along with the buttons, coins and other orphans of washday she said, 'Just wishful thinking, Natalie. That's all this is. Just wishful thinking.'

After all the laundry was pegged out on the clothes lines and flying in the wind, Mom opened the door at the bottom of the stairs in the kitchen. It was unusual for her to go upstairs except to change the sheets and we'd already done that. I waited a few minutes then followed her up. I slipped into my own bedroom. After she had gone back downstairs I peeked into my brothers' room. There, in the middle of the fresh pillow on Morgan's bed, was the condom.

I never heard Mom say a word to him about her discovery. Morgan was quieter than usual at dinner that evening. He left the table before dessert and headed down to the barn even before Boyer.

I'm sure Mom read my laundry as easily as she read my brothers'.

She knew whenever I had been up in the hayloft in the summer. Our mother had a morbid fear of fire, and even though she agreed with Dad that her fears were unwarranted, she paid attention to her instincts. Everyone did. So in the hot days of August, after all the hay was in, and the loft was full, we were forbidden to play up there. It was one of her few rules.

She knew it was me who had sneaked into the root cellar and polished off three jars of canned cherries when I was seven years old. She knew I almost drowned a piglet trying to make it swim in the water trough. And she knew when, at thirteen, I was about to start my monthly period. I paid no attention to the pink streaks in my cotton underpants. But she did. Before I knew I needed them, a large blue box and an elastic belt with metal tabs appeared on my bed one Saturday afternoon. When I realized what they were for, I thought she had read it in my tea leaves.

My mother read tea leaves for her women friends when they visited. Sometimes, in the afternoons, when Dad and my brothers were off haying or cutting firewood, she would say, 'Come on Nat, let's have a tea party.'

She would take out the good tea cups, her mother's china, from the glass-fronted cabinet in the parlour. I only call it a parlour because she did; it was really just a long room off the kitchen that served as both dining room and living room. She'd set our tea cups and cookies at the corner of the huge oak table and we 'girls' had our stolen afternoon while the 'men' worked. After I finished my cup of milked-down tea, she would have me flip the cup upside down in the saucer and turn it three times. Then she'd read my future and my secrets in the leaves.

Years later, when I had a daughter of my own, I realized it was really the laundry she read. The laundry gave away all our secrets.

So, when I think of everything that happened after that summer day, I wonder, how could *she* not have known?

Chapter Three

October 2003

MY MOTHER IS dying. She's been threatening to die for the last five years. This time I think she means it. I hear it in Boyer's words. 'She's asking for you, Natalie.'

Still half asleep, I am unprepared for the quiet gentleness of my brother's voice. I can't remember the last time we spoke on the phone. It takes a moment to relate voice and message. An uncomfortable silence fills the line while I search for a reply.

That's how it is with Boyer and me. Our conversations are stilted, stop and go, static. They've been that way for years. On the rare occasions when we're together, we constantly cut off each other's sentences. It's as if we fear any attempt to repair the damage; damage of wounds so old, scars so smooth, so healed over, that to pick at them would be like taking a knife to new flesh. So, whenever Boyer and I find ourselves together during my hit-and-run visits to Atwood, we fumble with safe words; we talk about the weather, the road conditions, my trip. Anything, except what stands between us.

'I think you'd better come,' he says now. It's the first time my brother has given me advice, or asked anything of me in over thirty-four years. His words are enough – too much.

'I'll be there tomorrow,' I say and we mumble our goodbyes. He doesn't invite me to stay out at the farm. I don't ask.

After I hang up Vern rolls over and places his hand on my back.

'It's my mother,' I say into the darkness. 'I have to go to Atwood.'

'I'll drive you.' Vern reaches up and turns on the lamp above the headboard. That's my husband. No hesitation, no questions, just a direct route to fixing whatever needs fixing.

I turn to him and attempt a smile. 'No, that's okay,' I say, then throw back the covers. 'I can take the bus.'

The plane is not an option, and not only because of my irrational fear of flying. We live near the city of Prince George, in the centre of British Columbia. Atwood lies in the southernmost part of the province. There are no direct flights. With an overnight connection in Vancouver it takes two days to get there.

Vern pulls himself up and sits back against the pillows as I get out of bed. I know what is coming. We have had this conversation before. Although Vern and I have been together for almost ten years he has never been to Atwood. Never met my mother. Or Boyer.

'I want to go with you Natalie,' he says, disappointment seeping into his words. 'John or Ralph can take over the crew for a few days.' Vern has a tree-planting business. Most of his planters have returned to university for the year. We both know how hard it would be for him to take time off, yet I know he means it. 'We can get there much quicker in the car,' he adds.

'No, really, it's better if I go alone.' I pull on my dressing gown. 'I don't know how long I'll have to stay. And I don't want to drive myself in case there's snow in the mountain passes. I don't mind the bus. It will give me time.'

Time? Time for what? For Mom to die?

With a sudden pang of guilt I wonder if I have deliberately

waited too long. We each have our own secrets and regrets, Mom and I. Is it too late for the confessions and questions that I have yearned to voice?

I pat Vern's shoulder. 'Go back to sleep,' I tell him. 'I'm going to go and check the Greyhound schedule.' As I reach up and turn out the lamp Vern's sigh is heavy with frustration but he does not argue.

In complete darkness I make my way around the bed to the bedroom door. It's an idiosyncrasy left over from childhood, feeling my way in the dark as if I were blind, counting the steps, and knowing exactly where each piece of furniture is. Lately when I catch myself doing it I wonder if I am preparing myself for old age. Does my body know something that I don't? After fifty everything is suspect.

Moonlight spills through the windows in my home-office. I sit down at the computer without switching on the lights. I'm frugal with electricity. Forced habits stay with you.

The screen flicks on as soon as I touch the mouse. There was a time when the only meaning 'mouse' had for me was the wet grey lumps outside the kitchen door; gifts left on our porch by the barn cats. Now after years of making my living as a free-lance journalist, this plastic namesake moves like an extension of my body. Writing, once done in longhand then typed on my Remington manual, now flows from fingertips to luminous screen; even my mistakes show up neat and clean.

The Greyhound schedule flashes up. The next bus is at six a.m. With transfers and waiting in stations the trip to Atwood takes fifteen hours. It seems all the roads of my life have led me further and further away from that remote West Kootenay town; as if distance alone is enough of an excuse not to visit, to stay away from my mother and brother. And now my daughter.

I glance down at my watch. Eleven-ten. Too late to call Jenny? No, like her grandmother, my daughter is a night owl. She always has been. Her nocturnal wanderings are only one of the many inherited traits that by-passed me.

She looks nothing like me, this daughter of mine. She is her grandmother's child. The ash-streaked hair, the high, wide cheekbones, the robin-blue eyes, the small bump on the nose, and the flawless skin that soaks up the sun so greedily, all have skipped a generation. At least with the women. Boyer inherited those same features, only with an increased intensity and stronger angles. The eyes, the profile, the smile, all the same handsomeness that was – still is – so uniquely my mother.

Over the years I have heard many people call her pretty, but that was far too dismissive a word for my mother's classic beauty. My daughter now wears that same beauty with grace, along with her grandmother's intoxicating smile, a birthright shared with her Uncle Boyer.

Even now, anyone meeting these three would know that they are family. Mom and Boyer have often been mistaken for brother and sister. And my daughter Jenny looks as if she could be the child of either of them.

I inherited my father's brown eyes and hair, his milk white skin and blunt features. I look like what I have become, an outsider, a stranger.

I was named after my mother. Although everyone calls her Nettie, Mom's given name is Natalie Rose. Our first name is where the similarities end. I might have suspected I was adopted if I had not heard the story from Dad – so many times that I thought I remembered being there – of how, while he was delivering milk on the day of my birth, my mother walked the three miles into town and up the hill to the hospital.

I was born on August 12, 1951. On the exact same day my grand-mother, Amanda Margaret Ward, was born sixty-two years before. She had been the first baby delivered in St Helena's, the brick and stone hospital whose windows overlook the main street of Atwood. Her great-grandchild would be the last. No one remembers this bit of trivia now except me and maybe, in her more lucid moments, my mother.

Tonight she lies in that same hospital, perhaps in the same room where I was born, and calls my name.

Chapter Four

Nettie

SHE HEARS THE baby crying.

The insistent mewing of a newborn drifts through the darkness and calls her from her unquiet sleep.

No, wait. That can't be right. The baby was stillborn. But he's crying. How can that be? The child is dead. He has gone to heaven. No. To purgatory.

Now she knows where she is. With him. In limbo. Forever. She has condemned the unbaptized child to spend eternity in this nothingness. She deserves to be here, but he doesn't. She must tell someone. Tell someone he's crying.

'Hush, Nettie,' a soft voice whispers, 'there are no babies on this ward any more.'

She feels a warm hand on her forehead, pushing back the strands of hair. For a moment she thinks it's Gus. Should she tell him?

She swims up, against the current of drugs flowing through her veins. She surfaces to meet familiar eyes looking down at her. Kind, caring, eyes. They belong to Barbara Mann, the granddaughter of an old friend. Now she knows where she is. She's in the hospital. In the extended care unit on the third floor.

Barbara is the night nurse. Nettie used to change her diapers.

The voice, the touch, pulls Nettie back, but the drugs are stronger.

She fights to stay for a moment longer. She tries to clasp hold of the nurse's arm. She needs to tell her, to tell someone.

'It's all right Nettie,' Barbara croons. 'Go back to sleep.'

And Nettie calls from a long spiralling tunnel, 'Natalie …'

But it's the nurse's voice that answers, a singsong lilt, 'Hush, dear, shhhh … It's okay, Nettie. Just let go now.'

And Nettie calls back, 'Not yet. Not yet.' But it's too late. She slips through an invisible trap door.

Somewhere the baby cries again, but now Nettie is standing in her kitchen at the farm.

This is real, she thinks, the rest was a dream.

Everything is so clear. She studies the green-speckled linoleum tabletop. Her fingers trace the familiar rings left by a thousand coffee mugs. This table, built by Gus's father, is large enough to seat a dozen people. It's solid, real, and as old as the farmhouse. Everything of importance to her family, to the farm, has been discussed and planned at this table. All the preparations of life. All the chopping, dicing, canning, and pickling; all the plucking, gutting, kneading, and baking was done here.

She surveys the array of vegetables spread out on the tabletop. The aroma of rich, loamy soil still clings to the potatoes, carrots and beets. She must hurry to prepare them. There are mountains of meat to be chopped and ground, chickens to be plucked. She will never finish before everyone arrives.

Natalie's footsteps sound behind her. Her daughter is leaving. Nettie wants to turn and tell her not to go, but there's too much to be done. Her hands are busy. Chop, chop, chop. A pile of cubed meat rises in front of her. She hears the creak of the screen door. She grabs a handful of wet meat and tosses it into the grinder clamped to the end of the table.

The kitchen door slams; still she does not turn. She wants to call out, but she needs to get this done. Footsteps sound, unhurried, hesitant, on the porch stairs. Nettie counts each footfall, each step. On the fourth tread, her daughter stops and waits – waits to be called back. Nettie opens her mouth but no sound comes. She wants to call out. She wants to tell Natalie she heard the baby cry, but she cannot form the words. Too late. The last footstep echoes and disappears.

The tabletop swirls before her. She dives into the green linoleum sea. It swallows her up and she drowns in the darkness, the nothingness.

Chapter Five

IN THE GLOW from the computer screen, I press the first speed dial on my phone. Jenny's home number.

'Hello?' Nick's voice answers after one ring. Only a man will pick up the phone on the first ring. I haven't met a woman yet who won't wait until at least the second ring before answering. Is it because we can't shake the old notion of being thought too anxious, too available?

'Hello, Nick. I hope it's not too late to call.'

'No, of course not,' he assures me, then asks, 'How are you, Mom?'

Mom, how easily he has taken to calling me that. We chat for a few moments with the small talk that is expected. Nick Mumford, my son-in-law of three years is much more at ease with me than I have ever been with him. But time has eroded my resistance – a resistance I felt before I even met him. Nick, whose grandfather was our family doctor when I was growing up, is one of life's little twists that show up with an ironic sense of inevitability. Just like the fact that Jenny chose to do her medical internship at St Helena's Hospital in Atwood. The moment she told me she was dating old Dr Allen Mumford's grandson, I knew she would end up with him. And I knew she would end up staying in the town I have spent most of my adult life avoiding.

'Here's Jenny.'

'Hi, Mom. How are you doing?' At the sound of my daughter's voice I am overwhelmed with how much I miss her.

'I'm fine. I just talked to Boyer.'

'Yes, I know. I saw him at the hospital earlier. I asked him to call you.'

I'm not surprised. Jenny is like a typical child of divorced parents; always trying to mend broken relationships. When it comes to her uncle and me, she uses every excuse to force us to talk to each other.

'Jen, how is she really? I mean, how long—?'

'It's hard to tell,' she says, the professional tones of a doctor's voice overtake her words as she relates the prognosis. 'She's weak, but she could still rally or, well, we just don't know. Don't wait too long, Mom.'

'I'm taking the six a.m. bus,' I tell her. 'It should arrive at the junction at nine tomorrow night. Can you pick me up?'

The turnoff from the Trans-Canada Highway is thirty miles north of Atwood. The bus will only stop on that lonely piece of highway if someone is waiting for connecting passengers.

'Of course I'll be there.' Jenny says. 'We can stop in at the hospital and see Gram on the way home.'

'Good,' I say then hesitate. 'I'm going to stay in town at the Alpine Inn though.'

'Why?' she asks. The doctor's voice is gone now, replaced by the whine of a daughter's hurt feelings. 'We have lots of room in our new house, Mom. You haven't even seen it yet.'

'I know, and I will. I will. It's just that I can walk next door to the hospital from the Bed and Breakfast.'

'You can use one of our cars while you're here.' When I don't reply right away she adds with an impatient sigh, 'You can't even see the farm from where we've built our house.'

I know. I know exactly where her new house is.

'Please. Please just understand for now, Jenny. I want to stay in town. Just pick me up, okay?'

'All right,' she says with resignation. 'We can argue about it on the drive into town.' There's a moment's silence on the line before she adds, 'There's something else I need to talk to you about, Mom.'

My empty stomach lurches. I manage to keep my voice even as I ask, 'What is it?'

'Not on the phone.'

Back in bed I am unable to sleep. I am tempted to get up and read to pass the night away. *God, I'm finally turning into my mother.* I wish I had her faith at times like this. And her belief in the power of prayer. But I lost that a long time ago.

Beside me Vern's even breathing fills the quiet while I fight the images of my estranged family.

It wasn't always this way. There was a time when I couldn't imagine my family wouldn't always be together. There was a time when all I wanted was to be with my oldest brother, Boyer, whom I idolized during my childhood. Back then, my favourite part of the day was sitting in his room playing 'penny words' – a spelling game Boyer had taught me as soon as I was old enough to talk. And in the evening lying in bed listening to my mother playing my favourite song on the piano downstairs in the parlour.

When I was young I thought she had made up that song just for me. And whenever I asked her, no matter what she was doing, my mother would always, always, stop and sit down at the piano and play 'Love Me Tender'.

I can almost hear it now as the north wind plays through the branches of the fir trees outside our bedroom window.

The alarm rings. As if he has been waiting for it Vern sits up. He pulls back the covers and swings his legs over the side of the bed with slow deliberate movements. I know he thinks I'm still asleep. This has become our morning routine, Vern getting up first and letting me sleep until after he takes his shower and makes the coffee.

'There's a bus as six,' I say as I climb out of bed. I explain the schedule as I follow him into the bathroom. He offers once again to drive me.

'At least to the Cache Creek junction,' he says as he glances up from the sink. 'It will save you the wait there. This way you can get a few more hours of sleep before you go.'

I pull out my make-up case and begin tossing in toiletries. 'I can sleep on the bus,' I tell him, but even as I say it I know it's not true.

Vern squeezes the tube too hard and white toothpaste spurts into the sink. 'I want to be there for you, Natalie,' he says. 'I'd like to meet your mother before she—' he bites off the word before it escapes from his mouth. 'While I still have the chance.'

I stiffen. 'There's lots of time, I'm sure. I'll call you when I get there. When I know more.'

Vern raises his eyebrows. 'Promise?'

'Promise.'

'Stubborn,' he mutters with a mouthful of toothpaste. But his eyes smile back at me.

I stand at my sink and study him in the mirror while I brush my teeth.

We've been together for almost ten years now, married for seven of those years. He was the one who pushed for marriage. I resisted.

Given my track record, I warned him, I wasn't a very good bet. 'If you don't get married, you don't get divorced,' I told him.

After two failed marriages I wasn't anxious to try a third.

'You just hadn't met the right one until now,' Vern insisted. Eventually he wore me down.

We met while I was living in Vancouver. Early one rainy morning we ran into each other on the Stanley Park seawall. Literally. We were both about to pass slower joggers from opposite directions when Vern's elbow clipped mine and sent me sprawling onto the wet blacktop. After that we began greeting each other on our morning runs. Before long we fell into an easy routine of running together. That led to after-run coffees at Starbuck's on Denman Street and then to dating.

Besides running, we found we shared a passion for reading, sushi, and oldies music. Before long he infected me with his passion for fly-fishing.

Vern was a widower. He had sold his logging company on Vancouver Island to move closer to the clinic where his wife eventually lost her battle with breast cancer. Afterwards he remained in Vancouver to re-assess his life.

When we first met he was in the throes of starting his tree-planting contracting and consulting company.

'It's karma,' he joked, 'from forest-destroyer to forest-restorer.'

Now as I watch him brush his teeth, I am still taken by how handsome he is. Vern is five-foot ten, not much taller than I am, perhaps three inches at the most. At fifty-five he still wears jeans without embarrassment, although lately I have begun to notice a thickening around the waist. He blames it on his too-successful business, which requires him to spend more time in the office and less in the field.

His olive skin, thick dark hair, and black-brown eyes hint of First Nations ancestry somewhere back down the line.

'When I retire, I'll take up genealogy and trace my roots,' he once said with his lop-sided grin.

Vern's mouth is asymmetrical. The thinner left side of his lip rises higher than the right and twitches when he is smiling. It can be difficult to tell if his smile is genuine, or if he is trying not to smirk. And it can be rather unnerving; it would be easy to doubt his sincerity – if it weren't Vern.

I think this little tic adds to, rather than takes away from, his rugged good looks. I can see that I'm not the only one who finds him attractive. Sometimes, when we meet women, or even men, for the first time, I catch that flicker, that what's-he-doing-with-her look in their eyes. Sometimes I wonder myself.

Vern says it was my independence he was attracted to. Now he calls it stubbornness.

He leans over the sink to spit. As he straightens up he catches me studying him in the mirror. 'What?'

I open my mouth, a word or two away from giving into the temptation to accept his offer. How easy it would be to have him come with me, take care of me. But I have never burdened him with my past. It's too late to start now.

I reach up and stroke his cheek. 'Nothing,' I say then turn away to switch on the walk-in closet light.

As I rummage through my underwear drawer I am suddenly startled by the thought of what to wear to a funeral.

My mother's funeral. Vern's unspoken thought is more reality than probability.

The idea of attending a ceremony in St Anthony's Church, of sitting in the front pew while a priest's monotonous voice chants the ceremony and speaks of my mother's life, is almost too much. I stand in the middle of my closet, underpants in one hand, and bras in the other, and hold my breath to stifle the sneeze I feel building between my eyes.

At the downtown bus depot, Vern unloads my suitcase from the back of his pick-up truck. Pink light from the streetlamp filters down through the grey stillness of the early morning air. The smell of pulp, a rotten egg aroma, intensified by the heavy autumn mist, hugs our bodies. Long-time residents of Prince George seem to be immune to the pungent smell from the pulp mill; sometimes even I forget it. But on fall mornings when cold, dense air, presses down on the sleeping city, the odour is so thick I can almost taste it.

As if he has read my mind, Vern wrinkles his nose. 'Mephitic,' he says referring to the noxious odour.

And as clearly as if I could turn around and see him standing in the morning fog, I can hear Boyer's youthful voice saying, 'Well, there's a ten-penny word for you, Nat.'

Inside at the counter I ask for a ticket to Atwood. The sleepy-looking attendant wears a blue-striped shirt with a name embroidered in red on her pocket. Brenda.

'Atwood?' Brenda repeats. It's obvious she has never heard of it. Why should she have? The old mining town, turned ski-resort, with a population of less than three thousand, is not exactly a prime destination. She punches the computer keys, her ink-stained fingers moving with a studied effort. Her eyebrows raise and I assume she's located it. 'One way or return?'

'Return,' I tell her. *Oh, yes, return. Soon, I hope.* Then I realize what soon could mean, and I feel the guilt of wishing to hasten my mother's demise.

'One hundred and forty dollars,' she says and attacks the computer again. She is all efficiency now, back in familiar territory. 'You have a two hour wait in Cache Creek …'

After I purchase my ticket I rejoin Vern outside. He has placed my suitcase in front of the only occupied bus stall. A young couple stands nearby, huddled in the cold, saying their goodbyes. White puffs of breath fill the air between them. The bus doors are closed and I can't see through the blackened windows. I hope the bus isn't crowded. I don't want to have to sit next to anyone and make small talk.

'I want to be there for you,' Vern says again. He takes my hands as he searches my eyes. 'At least promise me you will let me come down and get you.'

I slip the return ticket into my pocket as he takes me into his arms.

'I feel like I'm losing you,' he murmurs into my hair.

'I'm just anxious to get going,' I say and start to pull away.

'Not just this morning,' he says. 'Lately I feel like you're getting ready to bolt.' He releases me, then steps back with a crooked smile. He holds his arms out in an open-handed gesture of surrender. He won't keep me against my will, I know, but he'll do his best to interrupt this dance of leaving.

That is Vern. His strength is what has kept me with him this long, his strength in being able to let go. But he's right. It's just a matter of time. This is what I do. I run. I leave. He's the first man to recognize this, or the first one to place it in the light where we both have to look at it. And he's the first one who will not be surprised when I go.

The bus driver strides out from wherever it is bus drivers hide at these stops. He walks with the swagger of someone who, for the moment, has the destiny of others in his hands. The semantics of his job pull him back to the reality of the morning as he lifts the sliding luggage compartment doors and begins to throw bags into the belly of the bus.

Behind me the bus doors fold open with a mechanical sigh. I put my arms around Vern for a final hug. He hangs on for a moment after I let go.

A part of me wants to tell him I'll call for him when the time comes. That I will cry on his shoulder, lean on his strong body. But we both know it wouldn't be true. Besides, I tell myself, there's no need for him to be there. He only knows my mother from what I have told him. And she doesn't know him at all. My mother gave up on the men in my life after my second husband. And for the last five years she's been too busy dying.

Chapter Six

I PLACE MY hand on the window in a silent wave to Vern as the bus backs away from the Greyhound station. He stands motionless beneath the neon sign, his shoulders hunched in his jacket, his hands thrust into his jean pockets. As his figure recedes into the morning mist I think about long ago summer mornings when I stood watching a bus pull away with my daughter on board. And I remember feeling that same sense of sadness and panic I now read on Vern's face.

When Jenny was ten years old I gave into my mother's pleas to let her spend part of her summers at the farm. I couldn't deny my daughter the chance to know her family. They were all she had besides me. Jenny's father died when she was seven. He had no family to offer her. The men in my life were loving and loved by Jenny, but they had no shared history, no roots. Her uncles, Morgan and Carl, so different, so inseparable, both live on Queen Charlotte Island, off the West Coast. Jenny has seen them only sporadically over the years. Their infrequent visits were filled with laughter, joking and teasing. They bounced their only niece between them, jostling for her attention and adoration during their brief stops. But for the most part, while Jenny was growing up, I was it, the only real family she had. I was not enough.

While I continued to find excuses not to return to Atwood, Jenny became my surrogate. The buffer between me, and Mom and Boyer. And every summer, after I put her on the bus, I began to worry that while she was there she would hear the old gossip. When she returned at the end of each visit I listened carefully as she shared her adventures. I listened and watched for any hint of a change in how she saw me; any sign of disappointment in finding out I wasn't who she thought I was.

The Greyhound bus pulls onto the highway, and just like every time I return to Atwood, I fight the panic I feel rising in my chest. I've only been back twice since Jenny settled there. Both times I stole into town like a thief and stayed cooped up in her rented house by the hospital, hardly seeing the light of day. Each afternoon Jenny brought Mom over to visit – as if I was the one who was the invalid. I ventured outside only for my daily runs.

In the early mornings, in the half-light of dawn, I ran north along the highway, avoiding the streets of the sleeping town. I wore a hooded jacket and kept my head down whenever a car approached. Still, it's unlikely that anyone old enough to remember the Ward Dairy Farm would recognize this lean, middle-aged woman as the chubby farmer's daughter who once delivered milk to their doors. And certainly no one would see any resemblance to the only Wards left in Atwood now, Mom and Boyer; or to the town's newest doctor.

I lean back in my seat and close my eyes. Jenny's words haunt me. What is it that she needs to talk to me about? What can be so important that she can't discuss it on the phone? If it isn't about Mom, then is this finally the conversation I've been avoiding?

I knew someday I would have to fill in the blanks for her – the circumstances that created this fractured family of ours. But the years passed and she has never asked. And I have managed to push aside any temporary feeling that the moment was right. Maybe the time has come to tell her the truths, the secrets, as I know them, or have imagined them. All of it. The forgivable and the unforgivable.

Chapter Seven

THE SHATTERING OF our family did not occur gradually. There was no drawn-out series of events that could be pointed to and blamed. No slow motion accident to be replayed and pondered over. It came suddenly. The irreversible tragedy of errors was accomplished in the course of a few long-ago summer days. It left everyone in our family with their own secret version of what happened. And the rest of their lives to come to terms with it. Whatever conclusion each of us came to, we kept it to ourselves.

If I could go back and rearrange the past, if I could erase that July afternoon, would I? Would I change everything that happened afterward, have it so he never became part of our lives?

I would. Of course I would. But the past cannot be altered; it can only be lived with. Or buried.

On that July afternoon I watched Mom unlatch the gate. For a moment I wondered if she knew when she hired him, that the young man who stood on the other side of the fence was one of those 'long-haired freaks', as my father called them. I wasn't sure if I wanted to be around when Dad, and my brothers, came back with the next load of hay.

Only a few days before, as Mom cleaned her freshly gathered eggs in the kitchen sink, she had mentioned that Dr Benjamin Spock was encouraging young Americans to resist the draft.

My father sat at the table rolling cigarettes. He looked up and raised one eyebrow. 'I wonder what he thinks would have happened if the fathers and grandfathers of those boys had thought that way?' he said to Mom's back.

Mom placed the last egg in the carton, turned and smiled at Dad. 'He just wants to see the babies he helped raise have a chance to grow up.'

My father snorted. 'Those babies have grown up to be a bunch of spoiled, greasy-haired hooligans, who stand under a peace banner because they don't have the guts to fight for their country,' he said. He ran his tongue along the paper of a freshly rolled cigarette.

Boyer, who was twenty-three at the time, sat at the opposite end of the table. He looked at my father over the rim of his coffee cup. In that quiet voice of his he said, 'It's about choices. The very existence of the draft takes away their democratic right to choose. It looks to me like those who are saying no are taking a stand for democracy.' He added, 'At least they have the chance to take a stand on something; to be involved in something larger than themselves.'

And now here was someone walking into our lives who looked as if he had done just that.

He was dressed like no one I knew. Instead of the denim or plaid snap-button shirts my father and brothers wore, a beige Indian cotton tunic hung loose over dark bell-bottom pants. Instead of cowboy boots, he wore leather moccasins. A carved wood emblem – a peace sign, I would learn later – dangled from a leather cord around his neck. His hair, the sun-streaked yellow of a hayfield drying in the sun, hung loose around his shoulders.

But it was his eyes that held me. His eyes were the colour of a blue-green ocean, an ocean I had seen only in my imagination. When he blinked, they closed and opened slowly, almost as if the thick, surprisingly dark, eyelashes were too heavy for his lids. I later heard Mom describe those eyes, saying he had lashes that 'most women would kill for.'

'Bedroom eyes,' our neighbour, old Ma Cooper, would snort after she met him.

The stranger smiled as Mom opened the gate, a smile that crinkled into premature crow's feet around those aquamarine eyes. He set his guitar case down, shrugged the canvas bag from his shoulder, then held his hand out. 'Good afternoon, ma'am,' he said, the 'a' in ma'am stretching out with a hint of a drawl.

'Nettie,' Mom smiled back and took his hand. 'You can call me Nettie.'

'Nettie,' he repeated. Her name slipped from his lips and into the air between us. It came as so much more than a word. It came soft and warm, a musical note.

'And you must be Richard Jordan,' Mom said, her hand still resting in his.

'River,' he said. 'My friends call me River.'

Listening to his voice I knew. I knew right then why my mother had hired him sight unseen. His voice was his recommendation. His voice was hypnotic, mesmerizing, as soothing as a familiar melody.

'River,' Mom repeated. 'I'm happy to meet you.' She let go of his hand then turned to me, 'And this is my daughter, Nat.'

'Natalie,' I corrected her. I wanted to hear him say my whole name. I wanted it to last as long as it could. I wanted to hear it slide from his tongue, onto his lips, and caress my ear the way my mother's name had. I wanted to take it in and keep it in my memory.

He held out his hand to me. 'Well, it's a pleasure to meet you, Natalie,' he said.

And my name fell flat into the still air, thudded, and was gone. No magic, no music, just vowels and consonants. Three flat syllables. Nothing more.

He captured my hand in a firm grasp, where it went limp from the heat of this stranger's skin. I stood there frozen, tongue-tied, suddenly feeling conscious of my childish ponytail, my jeans and loose T-shirt, and my tomboyish looks, of which up until that moment I had been proud. I jerked my hand away and held it behind my back.

My mother hurried to fill the silence. 'Well, now,' she said. 'Well, River, come with me and I'll show you your room above the dairy. You can get settled, put your things away, then come back to the house for something to eat.' Mom's sure-fire solution to everything; fill their bellies and get to know them while they're off-guard.

River picked up his bags and together they headed to the dairy. Buddy followed at their heels, his tail wagging. As they passed the rose arbour I heard River say, 'That's a beautiful garden you have there, ma'am.'

'Thank you.'

'Did you know that Jacqueline Kennedy had a rose garden when she was in the White House?'

'I'll bet she never had to prune it,' my mother replied with a laugh.

Pruning that garden was always an ordeal for Mom. Once a week, from spring to fall, she put on Dad's oilskin mackinaw, leather gloves, and rubber boots. Then she attacked those rose bushes with the vengeance of a warrior. Still, the angry thorns found their way through her armour, leaving tiny tell-tale streaks of blood on her delicate skin.

I often wondered what it was she thought about while she hacked away, muttering under her breath, and arguing with the bushes as if she expected them to talk back.

'Roses, Natalie,' she once stated after emerging from another losing battle, 'are highly overrated flowers.'

That afternoon I watched as my mother and the stranger strolled past the rose garden. An unexpected breeze carried the fragrance of the blossoms through the heat-thickened air. I stood by the gate feeling forgotten, excluded, shut out of whatever it was that made my mother laugh.

As they made their way across the farmyard, it struck me that something about these two together looked familiar. And then I realized that, from behind, River resembled Boyer. The hair colour, the carriage, seemed similar to my brother's. Boyer in hippie clothes. The thought made me smile.

Walking along beside River, Mom looked like a young girl, her hips swaying with a lilt I had never noticed before. For the first time in my life, I resented my body, my inheritance of my father's frame and blunt features. For the first time I felt something for my mother other than adoration.

Chapter Eight

'WE WEREN'T POOR,' my mother often said about that time in our lives, 'we just didn't have any money.'

Whenever we seemed to get a little ahead, according to her, my father went out and bought more cows or equipment. Still, the only thing I remember her complaining about back then was the lack of a 'decent family photograph'.

I keep the results of my father's giving in to her lamentations in an old shoebox along with the stray snapshots that I keep promising myself I will someday put into an album.

The family portrait was taken back in the sixties, by a travelling photographer. Every September or October, a large blue van, a mobile studio, showed up in the empty lot next to the Texaco station on Main Street. It drove Jeffrey Mann, the local photographer, crazy, to see people line up outside that van. Every year he would complain to anyone who would listen, how, 'Those carpetbaggers come into town and pillage all my Christmas business.'

One fall afternoon in 1965, the year before River arrived, my father returned from town and handed Mom a flyer. 'What d'ya think, Nettie?'

Mom took the glossy pamphlet and studied the prices. 'Not bad,' she mused. 'They even have Christmas cards in these packages,' she added wistfully. 'But I just don't feel right taking business away from Jeffrey.'

'It wouldn't be like we were taking business from him if we can't afford it in the first place,' my father said. I watched my mother struggle with the temptation of finally having a family portrait done.

Two days later, under the cover of darkness, we stood outside the parked van, waiting our turn to sit in front of the blue-sky and fluffy-cloud backdrop. Afterward, Mom was plagued with guilt over her perceived betrayal. Whenever the Manns came out for a visit, she snatched the portrait from the piano top and stashed it in her bedroom. But the 'chickens came home to roost', as Mom's friend, Ma Cooper was fond of saying, because my mother, not being a calculating woman, sent out her Christmas cards as usual that year. She was horrified to realize, after she had signed and mailed that year's unique cards, that one for Jeffrey and June Mann had gone along with the rest of them.

Everyone was dressed in their Sunday best for that photograph. Yet every time I look at it I can visualize a scorch mark on the back of Boyer's shirt. And I remember how he found me standing at the ironing board in tears before we went into town that evening.

'I burned your shirt,' I wailed when he came into the kitchen after the milking. I couldn't look at him. I wasn't afraid Boyer would get angry. He was never angry with me. But I hated the thought of disappointing him, and I had just ruined his favourite shirt.

'It's just a shirt, Natalie,' Boyer said gently, 'it's not worth your tears.' He lifted my chin and smiled at me. 'An old shirt could never be as important to me as my girl is.' He handed me his handkerchief. 'Besides,' he added as he turned and picked up the scorched shirt, 'they take the picture from the front.'

Anyone looking at the finished portrait would smile at the hodgepodge of bodies that made up our family. We looked like we were thrown into a blender and came out in a menagerie of shapes and sizes. Mom and I sat on a bench with Dad and the three boys standing behind us. Boyer was twenty-two when the picture was taken. With his blond hair and blue eyes he was the only one of us who truly resembled Mom. Except for his height. He was six foot tall – two inches taller than Dad, who stood on his right.

Dad was bluntly handsome. Like a rugged John Wayne, his looks only improved with age and the inevitable map of laugh lines marking time on his sun-scorched skin. Morgan and I inherited his dark eyes and brown hair – 'mouse-turd brown', my father called it.

Morgan stood on the other side of Dad with the same laughing eyes, widow's peak and strong jaw. But unlike Dad, he was short and stocky. At seventeen Morgan was only five foot six. He would grow no taller. Carl was fifteen years old, all hands and feet that he had not finished growing into. As usual, he stood right beside Morgan, dwarfing his older brother. Carl was the anomaly, with his red hair and freckled skin, a throwback, Dad often teased him and Mom, to some married cousins on Mom's side.

How easily we all smiled for the camera. The smiles of a family who – though they knew no excess of money – were aware their lives were as rich and sweet as Mom's freshly churned butter. I wonder if any of us has ever smiled that openly, that honestly since? Even Mom, who was camera-shy, and usually had to be coaxed to say 'cheese', smiled with a pride barely held in check.

At fourteen, I was already a good two inches taller and probably fifteen pounds heavier than she was. Mom was five-foot two – oh, how she hated that song, or at least professed to. She was tiny, but not deli-cate. It was as if her small-boned body was made of steel. Gracefully strong is the only way I can describe her. She looked like good music should sound. Back then I'm sure I looked and moved like the proverbial ugly ducking, waddling under her mother's beautiful wing.

I wasn't very old when I became aware of the fact I would never be beautiful, never turn heads the way my mother did. I grew up knowing that, unlike her, I would never be on the receiving end of appreciative glances from men, or the tight-lipped smiles of the women by their sides. It wasn't until midway through my teenage years that I too began to covet my mother's beauty. Not until after River. Up until that time I lived in the glow of hers. Even when others carelessly pointed out the difference.

I believed I had grown immune to the shocked expressions that crossed people's faces when they realized we were mother and daughter. But when Mom first introduced me to River on that summer day I was relieved to see no surprise, no hint of secretly comparing us, in those blue eyes. And I was grateful not to hear yet another rude comment about my lack of resemblance to my mother.

The first time I overheard one of those thoughtless remarks I was seven years old. That winter I was chosen to recite a ballad at our school Christmas pageant. The poem about our town's founding father, Daniel Atwood, was written by none other than my hero, Boyer Angus Ward. He coached me every evening for weeks before the concert.

The first time I read the ballad I was sitting wrapped in a blanket at the makeshift desk in Boyer's narrow attic room. 'Won't this make Mr Atwood angry?' I asked. All I knew about the Atwood family was that they lived in a massive brick and stone house overlooking Main Street.

'Don't worry,' Boyer smiled at me from across his desk. 'This is about the first Mr Atwood, old Daniel. Stanley Senior is his son and he's nothing like his father. Stanley could be called a philanthropist.'

'Philanthropist?'

'There's your ten-penny word for the week,' Boyer said and handed me his Webster's Dictionary.

The next day I took the ballad to school as my project for the concert rehearsal. When the teacher asked who had written it, I kept my promise to Boyer. I was pretty proud of that word too. Anonymous.

Boyer and I rehearsed the verses so many times in his attic room that I could repeat them in my sleep. I still can. I know that the composition penned by a fifteen-year-old boy was not literary genius, but it was to me then and I felt a responsibility to do my brother's words proud. The night of the concert I stood on the stage in the Atwood Elementary gymnasium-cum-auditorium and swallowed.

Mom sat in the front row beaming at me as I waited to start. Beside her, my father winked and flashed me his white-toothed grin. Morgan and Carl sat in the back row making monkey faces. Nothing would have pleased them more than to see me trip over the words. But neither the silent jeers of my two brothers, nor having to repeat well-memorized words, would faze me. I focused on Boyer's encouraging smile and began:

'Oh, there are tales they tell at the Atwood Hotel,
Between the card games and the chewing of snoose.
And the stories go 'round, how gold was first found,
By Daniel Atwood, the Old Bull Moose.'

I threw the words out into the air, directly to Boyer just the way he had taught me in his attic room. He nodded at each one as if he had caught it.

His words flowed out of my mouth as easily as my mother's hands danced across her piano keys.

'The legends say Dan was a North Country man,
And so big that they called him Bull Moose.
From Alaska they say, old Dan ran away,
To escape from the end of a noose.

He arrived here by course on the back of a horse,
And stopped to make camp in the cold.
As Daniel stepped down on the harsh frozen ground
He tripped on a huge nugget of gold.

It took Dan no time to dig that first mine,
Before long the first shaft was down.
When the miners all came, old Dan had laid claim
To the land for miles around.

But he put them to work, just digging his dirt,
And he started building this town.
He built a sawmill and store, the hotel and more
From the gold that came out of the ground.

Oh, the miners went down, deep into the ground
Why they did it I really can't say
Dan was generous, I hear, at Christmas each year,
And gave them the day off without any pay.

Old Bull Moose they say worked his whole life away
Just hoarding each cent he could save
Until he fell to the floor of his company store
And became the richest man in a grave.

Now Stanley's the man, the son of old Dan,
With his fortune he plays fast and loose.
He still runs the old mine but spends most of his time
Making up for the Old Bull Moose.

So at Christmas this year, raise a glass of good cheer,
For the gold that came out of the ground,
And to Stan, who they say, now gives it all away,
And to Old Bull Moose who founded this town.'

When I was finished I couldn't tell if the laughter that rippled beneath the applause was at the words, or me, but Boyer's smile was enough.

After the concert, the wise men in their father's bathrobes, the angels with their tinselled halos, Christmas trees, stars, and sugarplums, waddled off the stage. I followed the flow to the back of the now brightly lit room where parents, teachers and performers milled among tables laden with cookies, cakes, and cups of punch. As I grabbed a paper plate I glanced up and saw Boyer at the back of the room by the exit doors talking to Mr Atwood and an auburn-haired boy about Boyer's age whom I had never seen before. As I wove my way through the crowd towards them I heard my name. I was torn between the curiosity of what Mr Atwood thought of Boyer's poem, and wondering why my name had been spoken. I peered over the heads of my classmates and spotted Mrs Royce, the wife of the pharmacist, talking to our neighbours, Ma Cooper and Widow Beckett.

'Yes, that's right,' Ma Cooper said. 'That was Nettie Ward's daughter.' The bun at the back of her head, the size of a cantaloupe, bobbed up and down as she spoke. She was a huge woman, Ma was, the kind of woman who left a wake when she walked out of a room. The only dainty thing about her were her tiny hands and feet. I always thought her feet looked too small to carry her enormous bulk, but every Monday morning she, along with Widow Beckett, walked two miles out to our house.

They looked like a female versions of Laurel and Hardy as they came up our road, Ma rolling along in her rocking gait while the willowy thin Widow hurried along beside her taking two steps to each single stride of Ma's. These two were fixtures in our kitchen each Monday. Along with our laundry, as members of the Catholic Ladies Auxiliary, every week the three of them pressed and mended uniforms for the girls of Our Lady of Compassion.

Although the sign over the oak gates leading to the building next to St Helena's hospital read 'School for Girls', I had yet to see beyond the hedges that surrounded the grounds. And Ma Cooper's many veiled comments only left me curious about the mysterious girls who lived in the dormitories.

There wasn't much going on in town that Ma didn't seem to know about. And she brought all the local news into our kitchen each week. My father called the Monday ladies the 'steam team' because, as he said, 'There's a lot more steamy gossip going on in that kitchen than ironing.'

Mom said it was usually just harmless talk. 'What's more inter-esting to talk about than people?' she asked. But more than a few times I heard her challenge Ma Cooper on the accuracy of the latest rumours while she punched into dough rising in a porcelain tub so enormous she sank into it up to her elbows.

Widow Beckett usually said very little, letting Ma Cooper keep her position as the authority on local goings-on. The widow was never far from her friend though, and could be counted on to agree and encourage her. And sure enough, after the Christmas recital, there she was, standing next to Ma Cooper, nodding at her friend's words.

'Nettie Ward's, daughter? Really?' Mrs Royce replied to Ma Cooper. 'My, she certainly doesn't look anything like her mother, does she?'

Widow Beckett responded with a silent tsk-tsk shake of her head. I moved closer to them as Ma Cooper leaned in, and in a voice that was meant to be a whisper, but was not anywhere near to it, said, 'Homely as a mud fence, that one.' Then she straightened up and added with a strange note of pride in her voice, 'But her teacher says she is brilliant.'

Thanks to Boyer, and his penny words, at seven I already had a large vocabulary. I knew the meaning of lots of words, but 'homely' was not one I had come across. Still, I knew it could not be good when paired up with 'mud fence'. I made my way to the back doors, but Boyer was gone. I stood up on my tiptoes and scanned the room. Suddenly Mom was beside me. 'What is it, Nat?' she asked.

'I'm just looking for Boyer,' I told her. Normally I would have asked Boyer about a new word, hoping it was a ten-penny one, but something told me that this wimpy sounding word had little value. So I asked Mom. 'What does homely mean?'

'Where did you hear that?' she asked, her brows knitting together in a frown.

Afraid I'd stumbled on a forbidden word, I told her what Ma Cooper said. My mother's eyes narrowed for a brief moment, the muscles of her cheeks twitched as she clamped her mouth shut. Then she smiled and touched my face, 'Well, it could mean many things, honey. My guess is that it means you're good around the house. She knows what a help you are to me.'

I wondered for a moment what that had to do with a mud fence, then decided that this was probably one of those Santa Claus fibs. So I chose to believe her. It almost made sense. Later I could look it up in Boyer's dictionary.

Before we left, Mom walked over to Ma Cooper and Widow Beckett. The smile never left Mom's face as she spoke, but Ma's smile melted down. I could not make out Mom's words, so I went and stood beside her in time to hear Widow Beckett say, 'But Nettie, we only meant it in the kindest of ways.'

'There is nothing kind about insinuating,' my mother started, enunciating each word in a voice so brittle, so unlike her, that I grabbed her hand. She stopped and looked down at me, clamped her mouth shut, and squeezed my hand. She then nodded to her friends, spun around and marched away straight-backed with me in tow.

For the next few weeks my mother did the Monday ironing by herself. 'Where's the steam team?' my father asked at lunch on the first Monday Ma Cooper and Widow Beckett were absent.

'I told them not to come,' Mom said. 'They needed a break.'

A few weeks later, on Christmas Eve, they showed up at our door just as all my parents' friends and neighbours did each year. They stood on the enclosed porch stamping snow from their boots and looking a little sheepish. As my mother ushered them in, hugged them, and wished them Merry Christmas, I swear that I saw stern old Ma Cooper blink back tears. Widow Beckett's voice caught as she said, 'We're so sorry, Nettie.'

Mom shushed her and said, 'That's forgotten.' And she meant it. 'Forgive and forget,' that was Mom's credo in life.

'It's okay if you bruise easy,' she often told me. 'As long as you heal quick.'

Chapter Nine

THINGS WENT BACK to normal after that. Monday's ironing and gossip days continued and the incident was never spoken about again. But every time I ran into Ma Cooper, she found some reason to throw a compliment at me, while Widow Beckett nodded agreement. Most of her compliments revolved around the other thing I heard her say about me that night, which was that I was brilliant. Brilliant. That was a word I knew. It felt so good to be called brilliant that I chose to ignore the sympathy I had heard in their voices at the Christmas concert.

The only other person who ever called me brilliant back then was Boyer. From the time I could hold a book my oldest brother was my mentor. But I was not brilliant. I had a good memory. That's all. I could memorize anything: facts, numbers, names, words, and nursery rhymes. 'It's like taking a snapshot, Nat,' Boyer taught me. 'And then you keep going back to it, checking the picture often, until as soon as you see the first word or two, the others will follow like a series of mental dominoes.'

Still, it was not brilliance. It was nothing more than the mental gymnastics I learned from him.

It was Boyer who was brilliant; Boyer who had the analytical mind that craved knowledge. And it was Boyer who saw it as his mission to pass along that love of learning. Mom told me once that after Boyer's first day of school he raced into the house and announced he was going to be a teacher when he grew up.

'A teacher?' Dad laughed. 'You don't need to be a teacher. We're farmers.'

'Boyer's face fell,' Mom said, '"Can't I be both?" he asked. When your father didn't answer I told him '"of course."'

So Boyer began to bring his books home from school every night to practice teaching on Morgan and Carl on the wooden apple crates he hauled up to their shared bedroom.

Not long after, when I was old enough to join Boyer's makeshift classroom, Morgan and Carl started school and lost interest. I never did.

Do all little girls think they will marry their older brothers when they grow up? I did. Up until I was six years old I assumed it was the natural order of things, that one day Boyer and I would be just like Mom and Dad. It was not until a week before I started school that Morgan and Carl put an abrupt end to that childish notion.

Boyer was an altar boy for a number of years. When he was thirteen he began spending time in discussions with our parish priest, Father Mackenzie. They met each week, either at St Anthony's or at our house.

Everyone in our town knew and loved Father Mac: Catholics and Protestants alike. He could often be found sharing a shot or two of Captain Morgan's rum with the locals in the Atwood Hotel. Mom said sometimes she believed he heard as many confessions from his barstool – where he had patience for even the most inebriated souls – as he did in the confessional. But the most trying test of his patience he himself would joke was his friend and bridge partner, Dr Allen Mumford.

According to Mom, the relationship between those two men was the most unlikely of friendships. Dr Mumford, the town doctor and a self-proclaimed agnostic, was the polar opposite of the priest. He was a loud, outspoken, and opinionated man. He fought with his bridge partners so much that his wife refused to play with him. Finally, it was only Father Mac who had the patience to be his partner.

Even though they were both a few years younger than my father, to me they often looked like bickering old men. 'If you would pay as much attention to your bidding as you do to praying for my immortal soul,' Dr Mumford would tell the priest during their spirited debates, 'we might do better at the bridge table.'

'And if you put half as much thought into your play as you do into your disbelief,' Father Mac would reply, 'you might not have need for my prayers.'

They were a strange sight, those two, hunkered over their chessboard in the park, or at the community centre, arguing theology and the other's foolish play between moves. They were fierce competitors and not above a wager on their games. Every once in a while, Dr Mumford appeared at Sunday mass. He sat scowling, his arms folded over his chest, in a pew at the back of the church. He grudgingly endured Father Mac's welcoming of their 'guest to the fold' at the end of the service. Then he made his escape, but usually not before some parishioner asked him, 'Lost another chess game, eh, Doc?'

One evening a month, Mom and Dad went into town to play bridge with them. And on many Sundays Father Mac joined us for dinner.

He had no shortage of dinner invitations. Yet, it was our table the priest chose most often to grace. 'It's my roast beef and Yorkshire pudding,' Mom told anyone who questioned his preference. Dad said it was really because they always watched the priest's favourite television show, *Bonanza*, after the milking on Sunday nights. 'I think Father Mac is beginning to believe what people say about his voice sounding just like Lorne Greene's "voice of doom",' Dad teased.

One Sunday evening, just before I turned six, I stood anxiously in the sunroom doorway. I peered out the window hoping to catch a glimpse of Boyer and Father Mac returning from a walk. Behind me Mom, Dad, Morgan and Carl settled themselves in front of the television. Suddenly I heard Morgan ask, 'Mom, is Boyer gonna become a priest?'

A priest? Boyer a priest? I knew very little about priests, but I did know they lived alone and had no family.

Before Mom could answer, I spun around and blurted, 'Boyer can't be a priest, he's going to marry me.'

Morgan threw himself against the back of the couch and screeched, 'Dummy, you can't marry your brother.' He jabbed Carl in the ribs. Carl rolled on the couch, holding his side, 'What a dummy,' he hooted. 'Marry your brother!'

Mom leaned forward in her recliner. 'Boys,' she said and shook her head at them. I couldn't read the expression on her face as she chastised Morgan and Carl. Beside her, Dad sat in his recliner, a stream of blue smoke rising from the cigarette hanging from his lips. He stared straight ahead at the television, as if the conversation and all the commotion my brothers were making was not happening.

Panicked, I ran to my mother. 'Is it true?' I demanded.

'Well, it's true Boyer is talking to Father Mackenzie about many things,' she said. 'But the decision about entering the priesthood is a long way off.' She smiled and pulled me onto her lap. 'And yes, it's true that brothers and sisters don't get married. But no matter what, Boyer will always be your brother. He'll always be family, and always love you.'

My brothers sat wiggling on the couch trying to stifle their hysteria. Neither of them ever let me forget the foolishness of the idea that I would marry Boyer.

Except for that conversation, the subject of his becoming a priest was never openly discussed in our family. I said nothing to Boyer. I guess I was afraid he would tell me it was true. I couldn't imagine life without him, so I pretended it would never happen.

Then one afternoon in the spring of my first school year, I sat on the steps to Boyer's room while I waited for Father Mac to leave. The murmur of their voices leaked down into the hall. I caught the odd word like, 'commitment', and 'calling'. After a while I heard Father Mac ask Boyer a question. I could not make all of it out, but heard the last few words, '… as an excuse to avoid the real world?' Then Boyer's door opened. Before the priest came down the stairs he said, 'You will have to wrestle with those feelings yourself, my son. But not in the seminary.' His voice was kind, but I heard finality in his words.

At dinner one night a few weeks later Morgan, who held nothing sacred, asked where the priest was these days. Boyer quietly announced he would no longer be an altar boy.

My father could barely disguise the smile that came to his lips. It was harder to read my mother. I wasn't sure if it was sadness, or relief, I saw in her eyes as she nodded silently at Boyer then rose and busied herself cutting bread at the sideboard.

'Does that mean you're not gonna be a priest?' Morgan asked.

'No, Morgan,' Boyer said not unkindly, 'I am not "gonna" be a priest.'

'Guess that means you can marry Natalie now, eh?' Carl chimed in, then poked Morgan in the ribs.

'Good one,' Morgan laughed and pushed him back.

I didn't care about their teasing. I was just relieved to hear Boyer wasn't going away. That everything would stay the same. I stuck my tongue out at my brothers across the table as Boyer ruffled my hair and said, 'Natalie will always be my girl.'

Even after I entered grade one, I continued to go up to Boyer's new room in the attic on rainy afternoons, or snowy winter evenings to read and play his penny word games.

The game started out with spelling simple words for a penny. As I grew so did the words. At some point, Boyer added ten-penny words, difficult and unusual words, words I not only had to spell but define as well. Over the years, long past childish games, it remained a challenge for both of us to find words that the other did not know.

During my childhood I spent most evenings at his homemade desk. With dictionaries open beneath the glow of the lamp he taught me the power of words while the rest of the family sat two storeys below in front of the television.

'Don't lose yourself in that little box, Natalie,' Boyer said when the television first appeared in the living room. His warning was unnecessary. I never learned to love the *Mickey Mouse Club* or *Howdy Doody* shows that Morgan and Carl became so caught up in. What I did love more than anything else then was Boyer.

Sitting in his attic room, surrounded by his books, spelling words for pennies, or reading silently while he studied, was a privilege I clung to. Listening to his voice as he read to me from *The House at Pooh Corner* and *Heidi* meant more to me than any images flickering downstairs in the darkened living room while my brothers jockeyed for position on the lumpy sofa and my parents sat in matching his-and-hers recliners.

Thanks to Boyer, I learned to read long before I received my first yellow copy of *Dick and Jane*. Unfortunately I thought everyone else should be able to as well. One of my earliest memories is of my grade one teacher, Mrs Hammet, asking Bonnie King to read.

Bonnie stood up beside her desk. She stared intently at her open book before she finally stuttered, 'S— s— see, s— Sa— Sally—'

Elizabeth-Ann Ryan sat at the desk in front of me. I admired her – for nothing more than the fact that she had an unheard of box of sixteen Crayola crayons – and I wanted to impress her. I tapped her on the shoulder and leaned forward to whisper, 'Isn't she stupid.'

Mrs Hammet put an end to Bonnie's torturous reading and turned to me, 'Natalie Marie Ward, stand up!'

I thought she was going to ask me to read, to show Bonnie how words were supposed to sound. I picked up my book and stood.

'Now, Natalie, tell us what you just said to Elizabeth-Ann,' the teacher demanded.

The proud smile left my face. I hesitated, then in a shaking voice I repeated my three-word opinion of Bonnie's reading. The classroom filled with titters and giggles. I looked at Bonnie, her face reddened, but she held her chin out and glared at me.

'Come to the front of the class,' Mrs Hammet said, her voice harsh. I picked up my reader still believing there was some hope that I would be asked to read. 'Leave your book,' she said as she walked around to the front of her desk and picked up her wooden ruler.

I hid my hands behind my back as I stood before her with my head down. I could hear the impatient tap of the ruler against her open palm. 'Palms up!' she ordered. Moments later I watched the black blur of the inch marks on the ruler smack down three times on each of my trembling hands while the rest of the class, including Elizabeth-Ann Ryan, snickered behind their books.

Word of my punishment never did reach my parents. But Boyer missed little. That was the thing about my brother. When he looked at me it felt as if he knew everything about me. When we were together I believed there was nothing in the world more important to him than I was. I am certain he made everyone he was with feel the same way.

That evening, as I sat in his room, with a pile of pennies and a dictionary on the desk between us, he reached across and picked up my hands.

His eyes softened as he turned them over, 'What happened, Nat?' he asked.

The fading evidence of the red marks on my palms stung far less than my confession about calling Bonnie stupid.

'The thing about words,' Boyer said when I finished, 'is once they're said, they're like spilled milk, impossible to retrieve. Words are too powerful to use carelessly. You had two chances not to let your words have the power to hurt. When you first said them and then when your teacher asked you to repeat them. Sometimes telling the exact truth is not as important as sparing someone's feelings.'

'A lie?' I gulped back the tears that were threatening. 'I should have told Mrs Hammet a lie?'

'Not exactly a lie, but perhaps if you had used a little discretion, taken a moment to think, before you spoke in the first place,' he said, all the while holding my hands. 'Well, that and a little white lie might have avoided some hurt. For you and for Bonnie.'

Then, as if to take away the sting, he said, 'Then you could have done a few Hail Marys as penance.' He winked. 'Remember, a little white lie, and a little discretion.'

Discretion. For a six-year-old that was a ten-penny word. And a lesson I would take far too long to learn.

Chapter Ten

THE BUS HUMS along Highway 97 South. We pass rolling fields edged with orange and yellow, frost-touched trees. The clear autumn sky is blue, crisp, and clean. I have always loved the open sky of the Cariboo and Chilcotin plateaus, where it takes an honest day for the sun to pass from east to west. Such a contrast with Atwood.

When I was growing up I paid little attention to the fact that the mountains dominated the landscape. I didn't know anything else. I didn't notice the absence of sky. Now I have to brace myself for the suffocating claustrophobia that grips me once I am in the shadows of those alpine slopes.

The mountains, the sheer abundance of them, crowding and blocking the sun for a good portion of the day, can be over-whelming. Each time I return I feel hemmed in, smothered. When I lived there I hardly noticed when the sun disappeared prematurely behind the granite outcroppings and forest-covered hills, pulling its blanket of shadows behind. I gave no thought to the fact that to look at the horizon, I had to look up.

The mountains that loomed over our farm were as familiar to me then as family. I knew their shapes, their locations, their size and elevations. I knew their names. Mostly thanks to Boyer.

From as early as I can remember I rode his shoulders whenever he went hiking through the surrounding woods.

'I'm the queen of the mountain!' I hollered from my perch one afternoon. A weak echo tried to reverberate across the slopes.

'Well, princess, maybe,' Boyer laughed.

He stopped to catch his breath on a mountaintop clearing. We sat side by side in the meadow grass and warmed ourselves in the sun as we gazed down at our farmhouse and the meandering patchwork of fields and pastures cut into the narrow valley below.

Boyer pointed out landmarks and taught me how to orient myself by finding Robert's Peak, which loomed over our farm. 'On the other side of that mountain is the United States of America,' he told me with a note of wonder in his voice. 'Imagine, Natalie, a whole other country just miles away.'

'Is there a line?' I asked.

'Line?'

'Like on the map?'

'No, it's an imaginary line that divides us.' He smiled.

'Are the people there different?'

'Well, there are certainly a lot more of them. But they're pretty much the same. We're fortunate to have them there,' he added. 'It's kind of like living next door to a big brother.'

'Like you,' I smiled.

'Something like that,' he said and hugged me.

Boyer showed me how to locate South Valley Road in the shadows of Gold Mountain and Robert's Peak. Anyone turning off the main highway onto that winding dirt road was either lost, or coming to our farm. Or both.

As Boyer pointed out the boundaries of our land he told about how our grandfather had arrived in the area after the first rush of gold fever. 'It didn't take him long to realize that prospecting wasn't for him,' he said. 'So he decided to make his living from the miners, instead of with them.'

Our grandfather bought two Holstein cows and a bull. Then he began his return to what he knew best, dairy farming. He homesteaded the only usable acreage in the narrow valley south of town. He also laid claim to a good deal of the surrounding hillsides and forests. Four hundred acres of hill and dale, rock and dirt.

'More hill than dale, and more rock than dirt,' I heard my father joke more than a few times.

Even when I grew too heavy to ride on Boyer's shoulders I tagged along with him whenever he went hiking. Morgan and Carl often joined us. He taught my brothers and me how to use the sun and the evening stars to guide ourselves home. 'There's no need to lose your way in these hills,' Boyer assured us. 'If you ever do, just climb higher until you can look down and see something familiar.'

As Boyer shared his love of the forest he constantly reminded us of the hidden dangers in the mountains that toed into our fields and meadows. Both he and our mother made sure we did not forget.

One summer day, when I was five or six, Morgan and Carl and I went with Mom to pick wild huckleberries that grew in the forest behind our farm.

My mother's blue flowered cotton dress swished against her black rubber boots as she walked in front of me. Mom always wore a dress, even in the bush. My father hated to see her in pants.

'Ya look ridiculous,' I heard him exclaim one winter morning when she emerged from the bedroom in a pair of his woollen trousers. 'I'm sorry, Nettie,' he said when he saw her crestfallen face. 'But it's such a shock to see those beautiful legs covered up.' During my childhood I never saw her wear pants again.

Sunlight seeped through the canopy of trees and danced through the branches as we hiked up the mountain that day. The air smelled of dry leaves, mossy bark, and dust. Mom jingled as she moved. Christmas bells, from the horse's halter, hung around her neck. 'We're in bear territory now,' she told us.

'Bears!' I shrieked.

'Yeah,' Morgan chimed in. 'We're gonna get eaten by bears.'

Mom ignored Morgan and Carl's laughter. 'Bears don't eat people,' she said to me. 'They eat berries. Still we don't want to surprise them.' She lifted the bells and gave them a shake. 'We've got to give them fair warning.'

She promised the noise would be enough to keep the bears away. I believed her. But then I believed every word she said.

I followed close behind her, my red lard bucket swinging. My brothers and I ate more of the fat blue huckleberries than we put into our buckets. A few small berries rolled around the bottom of my tin pail, making lonely hollow sounds that were no match for my mother's jangling bells.

I tried to swing my hips, to swish my skirt across the top of my calves, the way Mom's did. My feet became tangled. I tripped over my heavy boots and tumbled to the ground. My pail flew out of my hand and the few berries I'd gathered scattered onto the forest floor. My awkward sprawl sent Morgan and Carl into shrills of laughter. 'Look at Nat. She's gibbled,' they shrieked.

Neither of my brothers wanted to be there. They wanted to be with Boyer and Dad who were cutting trees for our winter's firewood. 'In such a hurry to be men,' my mother chastised them earlier that morning when they tried to talk their way out of going berry-picking.

They were bored with searching for berries; their laughter lasted longer than my unceremonious stumble warranted. 'Well that should keep any bears away,' Mom said. She helped me up, my spilled berries too scattered to retrieve. 'You two sound like a couple of braying jackasses.'

Hearing the word 'ass' come out of her mouth only set Morgan and Carl off into another frenzy. They laughed and poked at each other as we entered a clearing in the sweltering afternoon sunshine. Clicking grasshoppers leapt from the dry overgrown alpine grass as we passed through. Wisps of steam rose like smoke from the black, moisture-laden tree stumps scattered across the hillside.

Back in the cool shadows on the other side, the musty odour of dried lichen and crushed pine needles filled the forest air. In the shade of the overhead trees we came upon a dense stand of bushes, their branches heavy with the purple-blue huckleberries.

'Now, try to get some in your buckets,' Mom told us.

The four of us slowly worked our way through the patch. Even I managed to cover the bottom of my pail. The bushes thinned out as we moved further into the trees. I followed Mom as she meandered back along the edge of the clearing.

Suddenly, Morgan and Carl started to holler. I glanced up to see them scrambling over a mound of rubble, an enormous pile of weathered tree stumps and boulders, overgrown with weeds and vines.

My mother stopped picking and called out, 'Come down from there.' She beckoned me to follow her to the bottom of the pile where she stood and waited for them to descend.

My brothers groaned, then reluctantly backed down. When they reached the bottom Morgan stood back and looked at the heap of tangled debris. 'What is it Mom?' he asked.

'It's a long story,' she said as she ushered us away.

We walked a short distance when Mom stopped and set her pail on the ground. She sat down on a moss-crusted log and stared back at the mountain of rubble as if she could see something we could not. 'It's really your father's story,' she said. She removed the bells from her neck. In the blinking light of the forest she began to speak matter-of-factly, without emotion. I still remember her words.

'It happened in 1927,' she began. 'After the milking was done one fall morning, your father, and his older brother, Emile, headed out with their dog to hunt grouse. Your dad was twelve; Emile was fifteen. It wasn't unusual for the boys to hunt alone. Your grandfather, Angus Ward, taught them early how to handle guns. The same way he taught them to drive the truck and farm equipment when they were still just boys. Things were different back then. Necessity and competency were the only licence they needed.'

The background drone of insects accompanied my mother's voice. 'Grouse hunting was half sport and half serious business. The boys usually returned home with an abundance of birds hanging at their sides, the tiny wings falling open, limp and useless. Their mother, your grandmother Manny, was always pleased to receive their bounty. She plucked and cleaned the small, thick-chested birds with relish, happy for a change from the chicken or beef that filled the platters on their kitchen table each night.

'But as the sun rose above the tree tops that morning, their dog, a blue healer, had little success flushing out their prey. He zigzagged haltingly, sniffing, and whining, through the dew-wet undergrowth. The brothers followed him further up the slopes. The sun grew warmer. They still had no birds tied to their belts.

'When the boys came to an old clear-cut – that clearing we just walked through – the dog ran ahead. Your father turned for only a moment to look down at the farm.

'Behind him the dog gave a bark of discovery and bolted across the clearing. Your father spun around and saw the startled eyes of a young doe. She stood motionless against the backdrop of tree trunks and branches. Then with a flash of white tail she leapt into the underbrush, flushing a covey of grouse as she disappeared. The birds rose in a whirr of flapping wings. Emile lifted his rifle and fired. A wounded bird hung in the air, and then fought against the descent into the thicket. The blue healer bounded into the bush, with Emile close behind. Your dad took up the chase. He knew his brother, an expert with a shotgun, would not miss if he got a second shot. He followed them into the forest. In the shadows of the trees he spotted their dog as it leaped through the air above a fungus-covered snag. Emile ran ten feet behind, changing his shells on the fly; he thumbed a fresh shell into position and snapped the gun shut as he ran toward the deadfall. In the next blink Emile was gone. Gus thought the flickering light was playing tricks with his eyes. He raced toward the log. He saw the gaping hole at his feet just in time. He threw himself to one side, his fingers clawing at brambles and roots as his feet slid on wet grass.'

Mom took a deep breath. 'Oh, what sounds for a young boy to carry with him into the rest of his life,' she sighed. She was no longer speaking to us. 'Those sounds, the commotion, all melded into a single moment: the muffled thuds of flesh against unyielding rock, the receding scream, the dog's furious barking, the clatter of the falling gun, and finally the gun shot, the thunderous shot rico-cheting, echoing, in the depths of the air shaft at your father's feet.

'Then the ringing silence. A silence broken only when the blue healer raised his head to howl to the heavens.'

She told us how, half blind with tears and shock, Dad raced, stumbled, and fell his way down the mountainside. Covered in blood and dirt he made his way home. Deafened by the pounding in his ears, gulping each breath as if it were his last, he could not hear his own voice as he told his parents the unbearable news.

Mom said it took the rescue party, led by my shell-shocked father, until nightfall to retrieve his brother's twisted, lifeless, body. My grandfather himself rappelled down the shaft to carry his son to the surface.

Manny Ward stood in the clearing, apart from the rescue party, stiffening at any attempts of comfort. Her clutched fists bulged in her apron pockets; her thin mouth an expressionless line on her tearless face. She stared straight ahead as the afternoon sunlight passed over the scene; the moving shadows the only marking of time as she waited for her son's body.

'Your father stood in shock and watched it all as if from under-water,' Mom said, 'from another world, a world of silence. He remembered seeing mouths open and close, but heard no words.'

'It took years for him to make his way to the surface,' she added. 'Dad did it alone. His parents offered no words of comfort, no life-line, so deeply were they drowning in their own sorrow.

'For months after, your grandfather spent every free moment of his time carting boulders and felled trees to throw down that mine shaft. He didn't stop when it was full. He piled more on the top, creating this rock and wood memorial for his first-born son,' my mother mused, then added, 'a memorial that looks like a funeral pyre waiting for a match.'

My grandfather continued to search for and fill, or board over, every mine shaft he could find on his land. When he had exhausted his four hundred acres he started on the neighbours' land. Neither my grandfather, nor my father, ever picked up a shotgun again.

I never heard my father speak of his brother, or say anything to us about mineshafts. Perhaps he felt that his father had taken care of them and there was no longer any danger. Still, our mother warned us that day, 'Even your grandfather couldn't be sure he'd found them all.'

It's hard to be certain now how much of the story was actually told by my mother, and how much is my memory filling in the blanks. I only know her words painted a picture so clear it was as if I were watching it play out before me. I saw and heard the tragedy of that long-ago autumn day. But I was only a child then, the sorrow and pain of broken hearts were concepts in fairytales. The sadness lasted as long as the telling. Suffering and grief were not part of that sunshine time of our lives. They were something that happened to others, not to our perfect family.

Chapter Eleven

On a September afternoon, when I was eight, I came into the kitchen after digging potatoes to find my mother and father at the table with a young man I'd never seen before.

I placed the bowl of dirt-covered spuds in the sink, rinsed my hands, then dried them while I stood behind my mother peering over her shoulder. An array of black-and-white photographs, all about the size of my school scribblers, was spread out on the table in front of her. The enlarged photographs were overhead shots of our farm, and one of the entire town of Atwood, taken from an airplane.

As I looked closer at the pictures I experienced a twinge of vertigo. I sat down beside Mom and studied the photographs. I could make out the landmark stone and brick buildings: the post office, the courthouse, even Our Lady of Compassion, School for Girls, next door to the hospital. The town looked neat and orderly from this birds-eye view. It looked nothing like the hodgepodge menagerie of steep-roofed houses that hung on the hillsides.

I was surprised by how flat everything looked. The mountains and forests, the steep winding roads and streets, were rendered harmless by the camera's overhead eye. How perfectly nestled into the valley our home site appeared, as if my grandfather had been guided by a divine plan when he carved out the four hundred acres.

The eager-eyed young salesman watched as we scrutinized the pictures. 'The finished portrait will be hand painted by a water-colourist,' he said as he reached for a huckleberry tart from the full plate in front of him.

No one ever entered our kitchen without staying for the next meal, or at least sitting down for tea and whatever baked goodies sat on top of the large wooden sideboard in the corner of the kitchen. I think my mother would have been horrified if ever anyone left her home without something made by her hand sloshing around in his belly. Family, friends, or strays, they were all treated the same. Hikers and huckleberry pickers, priests and Jehovah's Witnesses, would be invited in to break bread if they showed up at our door. Even the members of the small Royal Canadian Mounted Police detachment often stopped by on evening patrols to share one of my mother's late-night snacks. Travelling salesmen: the Fuller Brush man, the Watkin's man, and the Avon lady, all choked back my mother's black-as-tar tea – 'panther-piss', Morgan and Carl called it – if they wanted a chance at a sale.

Not many went away without at least a small order. There was always some ointment, creme, brush, or bottle of fruit syrup that was just as easy to buy from these wandering mail-order catalogues. Of course, it helped if Mother liked them. And how she liked a good talker. I think this dying breed of door-to-door peddlers entertained her as much as the black-and-white television set in the corner of the living room.

The young salesman at the end of the table that day did not measure up. But it didn't matter. I could see in my mother's eyes that she would have one of these painted aerial portraits no matter how bad the sales pitch. My father too was intrigued, but I could tell by the way his cigarette migrated back and forth, from one corner of his mouth to the other, that he was going to play a bartering game.

At the end of the table the salesman took a slurp of tea, then looked over the porcelain mug and asked, 'Ever seen your home from the air?' A smear of purple huckleberry tart hung at the corner of his mouth.

Certainly neither of my parents had ever been in an aeroplane, but both – though father was trying hard not to show it – were fascinated by the pictures spread out on the table. Mom leaned over them; she ran her fingers slowly, lightly, almost reverently, down the roads, over the fields, without touching the paper. She held her other hand to her chest as if she were having trouble breathing.

'It looks so beautiful,' she crooned. 'So beautiful.' Her fingers found the house, the barn, and the dairy. 'Everything seems so close. Oh, look Natalie, you can see the lake, the old miner's cabin.'

My father leaned forward for a quick glance, trying hard to put on his stern, in-control face. Even to my young scrutinizing eyes, he failed.

'So. How much?' he asked.

'Well,' said the salesman, with the confidence of someone who knew that a sale was in the bag. 'That all depends on size and framing. The portrait size—'

'How long?' my mother blurted.

'Pardon, ma'am?'

'How long will it take to paint, frame, and deliver the large portrait size?'

My father coughed, 'Now wait a minute, Nettie,' he said. 'We haven't decided anything yet. Let's just hear the prices first. Probably cost an arm and a leg.'

Mom was the most patient person I know, but when she made up her mind on something she expected action. She was a worker, a doer, and she thrived on concrete results. Still, she seldom went against Dad, and certainly never in front of a stranger. But she had made up her mind to have this portrait and in that made-up mind I imagined she could already see it hanging in a place of honour above the piano. I saw the determination in the way she sat up and squared her shoulders.

The salesman looked helplessly from Dad to Mom.

Then I saw it in her eyes. The briefest flicker, a movement, a flash, there, then gone. In that fraction of a second she told him, without saying a word, where the sale rested.

'Well, Mr Ward sir, let's see,' the salesman said as he pulled out a letter-size sheet of paper from a flat leather folder. 'Here we are.' He passed it down to my father. 'The price list. The sizes, descriptions, all the prices are there.'

My father crushed out his cigarette and put on his reading glasses. He picked up the paper and leaned back, the chair creaking in protest as the front legs lifted off the floor. The clock over the stove ticked into the silence as my father pondered. After a few moments he laid the paper flat on the table and smoothed it with his hands. Mom's eyes followed his fingers down the list. As he touched each description, I saw her shrug her shoulders as if indifferent to the selection. When he reached the last line, she gave the briefest of nods.

'Well, Nettie,' my father finally said. 'I think this one might do.'

My mother smiled, 'Yes, I think you're right,' she said. 'And the mahogany frame will go nicely above the piano.'

Father handed the sheet back to the salesman. 'All right then, that's the one we'll have.' He flashed a smile and a wink at Mom. 'Now, how long before you deliver it?'

The salesman began writing the order. 'Let's see, large portrait size, thirty inches by forty-two inches, hand-painted watercolour, mahogany frame. Hmmm.'

Forty-two inches wide? The picture would be much larger than any other in our home. It would cover most of the flocked wallpaper above the piano, dwarfing the photographs scattered over the long lace doily on the piano top.

'That should not take more than a few months,' the salesman said directing his words to Mom now. 'You should surely have it by Christmas.'

My mother's mouth opened, her shoulders sagged as if air were escaping and deflating her body. 'Christmas?'

'Let's just put a rush on that,' the salesman said quickly and wrote a note on the invoice. Even strangers could not stand to disappoint my mother. Sometimes I believe she relied on that.

'It won't cost any more,' he hurried to inform my father. He finished writing and tore the sheet from his order book. He gave the carbon copy to my father, who glanced at it then folded it and tucked it into his shirt pocket.

'That will be half now and half when it is delivered,' the salesman said. 'Will that be a cheque or cash?' He pulled out a receipt book. 'That's an even eighty-five dollars for the first payment.'

My father's mouth opened briefly and then clamped shut. I could see his jaw muscles working as he started to rise. 'I'll get my wallet,' he said.

'No.' Mom placed her hand on his arm. 'The egg money is going to pay for this.'

Dad started to protest then sat back down.

'Just a moment,' my mother said to the salesman. She rose and walked out of the kitchen. I heard her go into her bedroom and open the doors to her wardrobe. She returned carrying a folded white envelope. She counted out a stack of one and two-dollar bills while the salesman made up a receipt.

I'd never seen Mom dip into her egg money before. I knew how much she wanted this portrait when I saw those wrinkled bills hit the table. She'd earned them, along with rolls and jars of quarters and silver half-dollars, selling chicken eggs at fifty cents a dozen. It was her dream money. Her dream that one of her sons would go to university. It was not a dream she shared with Dad. His dream was that his boys would take over the farm when it was time. I knew he'd quit school before he finished grade eight to work alongside of his father. So, although the egg money was my mother's, he had no sympathy for its final destination. When she offered to pay for the picture that day, my father let her.

I expect she had her own reasons for paying. I watched the silent messages pass between my parents and realized that somehow Mom had tricked him into buying the most expensive portrait. As my father tried to hide his shock at the price it dawned on me how she had manipulated him. I was stunned to realize their shared secret. My father could not read.

The hand-painted aerial portrait arrived in less than a month. Mother proudly directed Dad as he hung it above the piano in the parlour. I can still see her through the years as she sat at the piano, her fingers deftly finding the keys, her eyes focused on the painting above. She seemed to disappear, become lost in it.

The painting probably still hangs there over her piano. I wonder if Boyer ever looks at it. I wonder if he ever glances up and remembers a time when our lives were as simple, as neat and tidy, as the farm looks in that picture.

Does he look closely? Does he ever think about that old miner's cabin by the lake? Does he ever wonder how different things might have been if he could change what happened in the place that now exists only as a darkened image beneath the faded watercolour?

And does he ever pause to consider the life he may have led if only our father had been a literate man.

Chapter Twelve

WHEN I WAS nine, Boyer left school. Quit. And just like that, on a snowy November day in the middle of his final year, Mom's vision of one of her sons going to university began to fade around the edges.

I never heard my father directly ask any of my brothers to quit school. But it was always there, unspoken. The first time I sensed it was during the days following Boyer's sixteenth birthday.

After the milking each morning Boyer changed into his school clothes as usual and squeezed into the cab of the truck with the rest of us. Every day Dad raised his eyebrows and heaved an exaggerated sigh, but said nothing as we drove into town. He didn't need to speak. The words hung there in the air. *The farm needs you.*

Then there was Jake, the hired man. Whatever Dad wasn't saying, Jake was.

I don't know how Jake ended up at our farm, but he had lived in the room above the dairy for as long as I could remember. Anyone could see he was not part of the Ward family. He looked nothing like any of us. He was all knobby and gnarly, as grey as his personality. His bristled face carried a perpetual scowl. What little he had to say was blunt, sarcastic, or teasing. But unlike Morgan and Carl's good-natured, elbow-in-the-ribs, wink-wink, kind of teasing, Jake's was sharp, cutting. Sort of like trying to tickle a person with a pointed stick. And his teasing always had a point. Behind his back Morgan and Carl called him the Anti-Dad. He was so much the opposite of our father.

Jake was fiercely loyal to Dad. His devotion did not extend to the Ward family. He tolerated us. I stayed out of his way. Mom said his bark was worse than his bite, but I didn't want to test it.

Morgan and Carl held no such fears. Even old Jake wasn't immune to their good-natured taunts. They learned early though that some subjects were taboo.

Jake was a confirmed bachelor. I couldn't imagine him living with a woman, or there being one who would consider living with him. Sometimes Morgan and Carl joked about finding him a lady friend. One evening after milking, they went too far and offered to fix him up with Widow Beckett. As they followed him out of the barn Carl said something about how the Widow 'must be pining for a man to warm up her bed.' Jake's face darkened. He turned around and grabbed Morgan and Carl by the backs of their collars, lifting them off the ground.

'You two little buggers better keep your filthy gobs shut!' He held them up in the air; their arms and legs flailed, gumboots fell into the dust. 'Any more dirty talk like that and I'll tan your asses so hard they'll blister for a year.' He released them. They thudded to the ground, grabbed their boots, and scrambled away.

Neither of our parents had ever 'tanned', spanked, or hit any of us. The idea that anyone would was as insulting as it was frightening. It took Morgan and Carl a while to resume their teasing ways, but in all the time Jake was with us, I never heard them mention women to him again.

Between Jake and Boyer there was a civil respect. Boyer treated him with the courteous regard of a youth for his elder. And Jake seemed to hold a grudging admiration for Boyer's devotion to his family and the farm. At least until after Boyer turned sixteen.

When Boyer seemed in no hurry to leave school, Jake saw it as his duty to start prodding him. He made grumbling remarks at the supper table each night. 'Sure could use an extra hand around here,' he muttered to no one in particular; or, 'I won't be around forever, yer know.'

'You'll not learn anything about dairy farming in those books,' he said whenever he saw Boyer with a novel in his hands.

'The mine is hiring,' I heard him remark one afternoon when Boyer was seventeen. 'With this year's price of hay going crazy your folks could use the extra income.'

The mine? Boyer working at the mine? I looked at Boyer as he opened the door to the stairway with an armload of books. He hesitated for only a second before he started up the steps.

Jake called after him, 'Hey, book-boy, got any girlie magazines in your stash up there?'

Boyer stopped on the first step, turned, and held up the books. 'Would you like them, Jake?' he asked. 'They're my school books. I won't be needing them any more.'

For the first time I could remember, dinner was eaten in silence that night. After the milking, Mom came up from the dairy, went straight to her bedroom, and closed the door behind her. Morgan and Carl washed up without their usual jousting and then, without a word, went into the living room. As I finished the dishes I heard the familiar whip-crack of the *Rawhide* theme coming from the television. I made my way up to the attic where Boyer sat on his bed reading. He looked over the top of his book as I entered.

'What are you reading?' I asked and plunked myself down at his desk.

'*The Catcher in the Rye*,' he said and held up the book so I could see the title.

'Can I read it when you're finished?'

Boyer placed a bookmark in the pages. 'I don't think this would hold your interest right now.' He threw his legs over the bed. 'Let's find you a better one.'

'Did you really quit school?' I asked as he scanned the shelves.

'Yes, I did.' He reached up and pulled a couple of books from the top shelf.

'Why?' I fought back the tears welling up in my eyes. 'Are you going away?'

'No, nothing's going to change,' he said and turned to face me. 'I'll still be here every night.' I could hear the false cheerfulness in his voice.

'It's Dad, isn't it?' I blurted. 'Just because he hated school he expects everyone to.' An anger surfaced with my words that surprised me.

Boyer sat down across from me. He placed the books on the desk. 'No, this was my decision, Natalie. It's just the right thing to do.'

'He can't read! Do you know he can't read? That's why. He doesn't want you to be smart either!' The words rushed out of my mouth as if they could argue him into staying in school.

'What makes you say he can't read?' Boyer asked then handed me a tissue.

As I blew my nose I told him what had happened in the kitchen between Mom and Dad the day they bought the watercolour portrait of the farm.

Boyer sighed. 'Look, first of all, not being able to read doesn't mean a person isn't smart. Dad just never experienced school in the same way as you and I. Things were different then. Farming was all Dad ever wanted to do.

'Secondly,' he said, 'he's a proud man. Promise me, Natalie, you won't say anything to him about the reading. Try to understand how it is for him. Imagine not being able to read.'

I understood now why Boyer's scholastic achievements were not something Mom shared with Dad. All of our report cards were read and signed by her. I remember her joy at my own grades, but her enthusiasm was tempered when she read the yellow report cards out loud to Dad at the table. My father would smile and say, 'Well done, Natalie.' And that was the extent of his interest in my schoolwork.

I don't remember her ever sharing Boyer's report cards with him. Was it because she felt the perfect grades and glowing comments would be too much for him to hear? Or that the pride – a pride I could see in her blushing face as she silently read the teacher's remarks – was hers to cherish, and to bear. I'm sure she confessed this pride with humble reverence each Sunday.

'Promise?' Boyer said again.

Of course I promised.

The next morning, Boyer's English teacher showed up at our door. I heard the insistent knock as Mom and I pushed the wringer washer back into the corner of the enclosed porch. Above our heads, Saturday's wash hung from wooden racks. I opened the porch door.

Mrs Gooding wasn't much taller than I was. Grey hair poked out from beneath her brown felt hat. Her slight frame made her appear frail at first glance, but I shrunk back from the steely determination in her eyes as if I was once again in primary school. The teacher stood on the top step with an air of indignation that seemed to melt the snowflakes on her long woollen coat. Behind her I could see where her resolute footprints marked a path in the snow leading from her car to the house. The fact that she had braved driving to our farm on a day like this was a testimony to the seriousness of her visit. Mom ushered her into the porch where she wasted little time stamping the snow from her boots.

'Let me take your coat,' Mom said once we were inside the kitchen.

'No, I won't be staying long,' Mrs Gooding replied as she placed a package on the counter. 'I promised Boyer I would not speak to his father. So I want to be gone before Mr Ward returns from his milk deliveries.' She sat down on the chair my mother pulled out from the table and held her gloves primly on her lap. 'I doubt that Boyer has told you how I reacted to his announcement yesterday,' she said in her clipped no-nonsense teacher's voice. 'But I don't mind telling you that I am mortified by this waste of a brilliant intellect.'

Mom's mouth opened but before she could form a response Mrs Gooding continued.

'After I got over the initial shock, I made a few phone calls. First I called Stanley Atwood. I swore that if he let that boy go underground I would report him to the child welfare. Apparently my threat was not necessary,' she sniffed. 'Mr Atwood is chairman of the school board and if Boyer wants it, there's a job for him in the bus maintenance yard starting Monday.' A small smile of triumph lifted the corners of her mouth. Mom and I both stood mute by the sink as she went on.

'Then I talked to Boyer's other teachers.' She patted the package on the table. 'These are the text books for the final semester. If Boyer picks up the lessons once a week, we see no reason why he cannot write the exams at the end of the year like everyone else.' She added, 'There's no reason for his name to come off the school roster.'

I heard my mother's intake of breath and knew her dream had been rekindled.

Mrs Gooding stood. 'Although I gave my word not to confront his father,' she said, 'unlike Mr Ward, I refuse to give up on Boyer.'

Mom finally found her voice. 'I'm grateful for what you've done, Mrs Gooding,' she said. 'But I want you to understand that, while it's no secret that we can use the extra income, my husband did not make Boyer quit school. That decision was Boyer's.'

The teacher's raised eyebrows betrayed her disbelief.

'My husband's a good man,' Mom insisted. 'But he's first and foremost a farmer. Dairy farming is all he knows. It's who he is.'

'Yes,' Mrs Gooding replied as she opened the door, 'but it's not who Boyer is.'

Chapter Thirteen

MY FATHER WAS not a complex man. Everything he was could be read on his face. The essence of his personality was etched into those permanent laugh lines at the sides of his mouth, into the V furrow between his eyes.

When my father smiled, his right brow lifted higher than the left. That along with the widow's peak on his forehead gave him a devilish or rakish look, depending on whom he was looking at.

Whenever I try to visualize my father I have difficulty seeing him as the still, sometimes serious-looking man in the posed images of old photographs. I have to imagine him doing something. My father was always moving.

I can picture him, wearing coveralls and gumboots, walking to the barn in the evening twilight, or waving from the cab of his milk truck, his handsome face a flash of teeth and tan beneath his snap-brim hat. I can see him steering the tractor through a field of freshly mown hay, or tinkering on equipment in the machine shed. He seemed to spend half his waking hours with his feet protruding from beneath a tractor or mower.

Mostly, I can visualize him at our kitchen table. Even there he was animate. His arms and hands waved and poked at the air while he ate, or directed the constant table talk. And I see him smoking.

My father always seemed to have a roll-up in his mouth, the thin cigarette moving across his lips as if on its own. The ashtray in the milk truck was always full-to-spilling with butts. Every afternoon he sat in the kitchen with a tin of Export tobacco and Zig Zag papers, his 'fixens', on the table before him. He picked up a piece of the thin translucent paper with a licked finger. Then holding it between the thumb and forefinger of his left hand, he sprinkled on the dry, wormy-looking tobacco. He loaded the paper without even looking, and deftly squeezed and rolled the paper back and forth, back and forth, until, as if by magic, a thin, neat, tube appeared beneath his thick fingers. He ran his tongue across the top of the paper above his thumb – an almost feminine gesture – then laid the finished product on the table. He lined the rolls up, twenty, thirty, at a time and let the spittle dry before he placed them neatly in a small flat silver case.

The cigarette case was a wedding gift from my mother. It was tarnished and worn, but always in my father's left-hand breast pocket. Even while he was rolling, my father had a cigarette in his mouth. When he inhaled, his dark eyes squinted and tightened as grey-yellow smoke drifted into them. I still remember his expression as he sucked in what I thought must be delicious smoke. Except now I know that while this smoke was swirling around it was searching out places to invade, to blacken, and to infest with the cancer that would eventually eat its way from the inside out. But when I was young I saw only that my father looked even more handsome when he smoked.

As I grew older, I noticed that his female customers found him handsome as well. I could tell by the way they looked at him.

On weekends and holidays Morgan, Carl, and I took turns delivering milk with Dad. At many of the houses, women suddenly appeared on their front porches when he arrived, as if they had been waiting behind their doors. They leaned over and picked up the milk bottles, their nightgown or dress fronts often falling open. Or they held a quart bottle in one hand and waved with the other, while the tops of their dressing gowns hung loose against bare flesh. My father would wave back, flashing his famous smile, calling out, 'Good morning darlin'.' Then he would wink at me as he climbed back into the truck and lit another cigarette.

I once heard Morgan and Carl laughing over this willingness of Dad's female customers to expose their breasts. 'Guess they figure with all these cows he's an expert on tits,' they howled.

Everyone knew my father. And they knew I was his daughter. 'Nat, Nat, milkman's brat, butter and cream make her fat, fat, fat.' The silly singsong, skipping rhyme followed me through the playgrounds of elementary school.

There are worse things than being teased. There are worse things than wearing heavy black gumboots in the winter while your classmates wear shiny, fur-lined ankle boots. Worse things than homemade dresses instead of reversible pleated skirts and pastel sweater sets. There are worse things than being called 'heifer', and 'fatty, fatty two by four'. But when you are a young girl it's hard to imagine what that would be.

The only thing that got me through those early primary school days was knowing that when the final bell rang I would spend the rest of my day with my father, my mother, Morgan, Carl, and Boyer. Especially Boyer.

Still, I wasn't above revenge. When I was in grade school I took my revenge in the only way I knew how. I took everything I learned from Boyer and used it to compete with them. And I beat them. I beat them at every spelling bee, pop-quiz, or book report. And I beat them on the playground.

During the winter when I was ten, Boyer and I practiced shooting marbles on the floor of his room. In the spring I carried my purple velvet Seagram's bag with a few pieces of choice ammunition to school. I returned home with the same bag bulging each afternoon. The girls soon stopped playing, but the boys were more determined. They kept moving the shooting lines further back, which only made it more difficult for them. Each night I emptied my winnings out into boxes and hoarded them under my bed. Of course, my abilities did nothing to improve my popularity.

I had a brief respite from my status as the class 'square' in grade five. Thanks to my mother. When I was eleven years old, she came to the school to play the piano for parents' day. She made her way across the stage as if she was called for a command performance. She wore her Sunday go-to-church outfit, a blue duster over her best dress and a little blue boxlike hat on her head. She sat down at the piano and beamed out at the audience. Everyone clapped when she was introduced. Before she started to play she nodded at me and silently mouthed, 'Hello Sweetheart'. I sat up a little straighter. Everyone would know this beautiful lady was *my* mother

'Wow,' I heard over and over that day, 'your mom's really pretty.' For a brief while I was no longer 'Nat the Fat', but Natalie Ward, the daughter of the beautiful piano player. I basked in the glow of the second-hand compliments all the next day.

Even Elizabeth-Ann Ryan couldn't help but comment on my mother's beauty. 'Your mom looks just like a blonde Jacqueline Kennedy,' she said to me as I drank from the water fountain a few days later. I straightened up and wiped the water from my mouth, but before I could respond she added, 'You must be adopted.'

It took a moment for the implication of her words to sink in. I forced the smile to remain on my face. 'Must be,' I said and turned away. Who needed friends? I told myself it didn't matter. But looking back, I realize that my alienation in elementary school was, in large part, my own doing. I did nothing to encourage friendships. I either competed with the other girls or I ignored them. The games that drew them together, the skipping, hopscotch, and Barbie doll fantasies, held no interest for me. I told myself they weren't important. I had Boyer, our word games in his room up in the attic, and books. And when Boyer was eighteen and became the school bus driver, I got to sit right behind him while the other girls watched with envy as my handsome brother, his eyes smiling in the rear-view mirror, talked to me about my day.

Because of Boyer, school for me was only about learning, about soaking up knowledge so I could go home and impress him. By the time I reached grade six I was a serious 'teacher's pet', shunned by the rest of the class. I had no friends, did not know how to make friends, and I didn't care. At least I'd pretended I didn't care for so long that I believed it.

So when Elizabeth-Ann – who was easily the prettiest and most popular girl in school – came to me a few weeks after we entered high school and said, 'Want to come to a sleep-over at my house on Saturday night?' I had no idea how to respond.

Something had shifted over that summer. My long hair was still pulled back and plaited. I still wore the same clothes as last year, yet the teasing had stopped. It was as if the world left behind last June belonged in another dimension and the slate was wiped as clean as the brand new blackboards of our junior high classrooms. The girls who entered grade seven that September looked and behaved far different from the girls who had left elementary school a few months before. Barbie dolls and skipping ropes were forgotten. Poofy hair and nylon stockings had replaced bobby socks and braids.

They had discovered boys. More exactly, they had discovered my brothers. Morgan and Carl were both in grade eight now and as inseparable as ever. Mom swore that Morgan failed grade six on purpose so that he wouldn't have to move on to high school two years before Carl. It wasn't hard to figure out that they were the reason for my sudden popularity.

'Everyone's coming at eight,' Elizabeth-Ann said, smiling at me with a look that said how grateful I should be for this invitation.

'Why?' I asked not sure what kind of joke this was going to turn into.

'Why what?'

'Why would I want to sleep at your house?'

'It's a pyjama party,' she said sweetly, as if she had included me all along and couldn't understand my reluctance. She named some other girls who would be there. 'Come on, it'll be fun.'

'I'll think about it,' I told her before I made my way over to the school bus.

Except for Widow Beckett's niece from Vancouver, Judy Beckett, who visited her each summer, I had no one I could really call a girl-friend. And even Judy only came out to the farm during the day. I had never been away from home overnight, never slept anywhere but in my own bed. It was hard to imagine sleeping in the same room as a group of girls.

'Why, Natalie, that's nice,' Mom said when I told her about the invitation as we set the table for dinner that night. 'Pyjama parties can be fun.'

'What do they do?' I asked trying to sound uninterested. 'Play silly games?'

'Maybe,' Mom smiled. 'Though they probably spend more time talking about boys if sleep-overs are anything like the ones I went to when I was a teenager.'

'You went to pyjama parties?'

'Sure, I was young once too, you know.'

'You still are,' Dad called in from the porch where he was hanging up his barn coat.

So I went. If it was good enough for my mother, it was good enough for me. I was nervous, but secretly I was curious.

Boyer drove me in on Saturday evening. He parked in front of the Ryans' house on Colbur Street. 'Smile,' he said as I opened the truck door. 'You look like you're going to a wake instead of a party.'

I shrugged. 'It'll probably be just as boring.' I grabbed my pillow and a cloth bag that held my flannel nightgown and toothbrush.

'Then I hope you have a book in your sack.'

I groaned. Boyer had long ago taught me always to carry a book with me wherever I went. In the nervous preparations for my first night away from home I had forgotten to pack one. Boyer reached inside his jacket and pulled out a small dog-eared paperback. 'Here, take this one,' he said. 'I think you're ready for it now.' He winked as he handed me *The Catcher in the Rye*.

I tucked the book into my bag and leaned over and kissed Boyer goodbye.

Mrs Ryan answered my knock. Every time I saw her, Elizabeth-Ann's mother looked as if she were on her way to a party. Her angora sweater, tweed skirt, and high heels were in such contrast to my mother's bibbed apron tied over a printed cotton dress.

'Hello,' she said. 'Natalie, isn't it?' she asked as she waved me into a foyer as large as our kitchen.

I nodded.

'The girls are upstairs,' she smiled and gestured to the stairway. She smelled like a cloud of perfume and hair spray.

'Thank you Mrs Ryan,' I said and headed towards the stairs.

As I crossed the foyer I heard the clinking of ice against glass. 'Well, if it isn't the pretty little milkmaid,' Elizabeth-Ann's father called out from the living room.

Gerald Ryan, the owner of Handy Hardware, was the mayor of Atwood. Somehow being called the milkmaid by him did not sound the same as when my father said it.

Unbidden, a forgotten image welled up. An image from when I started helping Dad deliver milk years ago. As I placed milk bottles on his porch early one morning I glanced down and saw Mr Ryan standing at the basement window. At first I felt embarrassed that I'd caught him scratching himself and I hurried away. The following weekend he stood in the basement again, his hand rubbing the front of his pants as he stared out the window. I plunked the full milk bottles down, almost dropping them in my haste. I spun away, but not before his narrow red-rimmed eyes met mine. His lips opened in a leering smile. I didn't tell my father. I still can't say why. Perhaps it was because I didn't understand why it frightened me. But I did ask Dad to change sides of the street with me when we delivered to houses on Colbur Street. Without hesitating, or questioning, he said, 'Okay, Sunshine,' and that was as close as I came to telling anyone. After a while I began to question what I had really seen behind that window. But as Mr Ryan winked at me over his raised glass, I felt the same repulsion I had back then.

'Hello, Mr Ryan,' I mumbled. I kept my head down, but I felt those red, rodent eyes follow me as I hurried up the stairs.

It looked like half of the grade seven girls' class was in Elizabeth-Ann's bedroom. They were sprawled about, lying or sitting on the twin beds, and on the jumble of sleeping bags covering the floor. *Movie Star*, *True Story* and *Mad* magazines were scattered every-where. Even Bonnie King was there. As she flipped through the pages of a glossy magazine I wondered if she still had problems reading.

I noticed eyebrows rise as I walked in. *Who invited you? What's she doing here?* Elizabeth-Ann called from her bed. 'Hi, Nat, come on in.'

A few of the other girls smiled and said, 'Hey, Natalie,' then went back to their magazines.

'Come and put your stuff over here.' Elizabeth-Ann indicated a sleeping bag next to the bed she sat on.

I stepped around the air mattresses on the floor, feeling self-conscious and clumsy.

'Listen to this,' Sherry Campbell shrieked. Sitting cross-legged on the other twin bed, she was wearing pink baby-doll pyjamas and had matching giant pink rollers in her hair. She held a copy of *True Confessions* magazine. An illustration of a movie-star-handsome man, and an equally perfect young woman, her long hair flowing behind her as he held her in his arms, adorned the cover. 'I was a teenage love slave,' Sherry read, her voice an exaggerated stage whisper. The other girls leaned closer and listened, sometimes giggling behind their hands. I sat on the sleeping bag, feeling awkward, fat and separate. But as Sherry read on I was surprised by the effect the unfolding story had on me.

'I felt his hands on my tender breasts, harsh and demanding, as he forced his tongue in my mouth,' she read. There was something deliciously wicked about hearing the forbidden words, something sinful about the warmth spreading through my abdomen, the unexpected tingling. When she finished, Sherry held the magazine to her chest and breathed, 'Oh, that poor girl!'

'Oh, that lucky girl!' Someone else laughed.

'Those stories aren't real,' another scoffed.

'They are so,' Sherry retorted. She held the magazine up. 'See, it says *true* confessions.'

'I want to be someone's love slave,' Bonnie sighed and threw herself back on the bed.

'I want to be Morgan Ward's love slave,' someone cried. I whirled around to see who it was, when another voice said, 'No, Carl's!'

'Yes, yes, Carl's.'

'Is Carl going with anyone?' someone asked.

'What about Morgan? Does he have a girlfriend?'

Everyone's eyes were on me. I was the centre of attention. I turned from one to the other. So it was true. My brothers were the reason I had been invited. I was not surprised. I was surprised, though, at how I felt about all the eager faces waiting for my words. I found I liked the feeling.

I straightened up. 'Morgan and Carl have lots of friends,' I said. It was true. Lately it seemed our sunroom was always full of kids from town who came over to listen to records and dance.

The questions kept coming.

'Do you ride horses?'

'Do Carl and Morgan have their own horses?'

'Of course they do,' I said. Stupid girls, how did they think we went after the cows when they wandered off?

Some of the girls began changing into their pyjamas as the chatter continued. I pulled out my flannelette nightgown, trying not to look at the half-naked bodies, unable to stop myself. The room became a blur of baby-doll pyjamas, bikini panties, and bras. Bras! The only one in the room who needed a bra was me. I had not even considered one until that moment. As the other girls flung their clothes around, I turned my back and stripped down to my cotton briefs and vest, then quickly yanked my nightgown over my head.

'Oh, a granny gown,' Elizabeth-Ann said. 'You look cosy.' She sounded sincere, but at thirteen, who can tell?

The giggling and chatter continued into the night. Once Mrs Ryan called out, 'That's it girls. Lights out.'

Later Mr Ryan's slurred, singsong voice called up from the bottom of the stairs, 'If I hear any more giggling up there, I'll have to come and paddle some pretty little bottoms.'

My stomach lurched. Elizabeth-Ann groaned. She leaned over and switched off the lamp. Much later, when I thought everyone was asleep, I heard her whisper in the dark, 'Natalie, does Boyer have a girlfriend?'

Boyer? Every muscle in my body stiffened. Why would she ask about Boyer? Until that moment I had never imagined him with a girlfriend. The thought of someone else besides our family as part of his life had never occurred to me.

'No, my brother's too busy with his job and the farm.' My voice was tight, protective, possessive, and jealous. Even I could hear it. 'He doesn't have time for girls.'

'Oh,' she sighed.

And he won't have time for you, either, I thought. Besides he doesn't need anyone else. He has us.

The next morning I dressed before anyone was awake. I stood at the top of the stairs and listened before I crept down in the silence and slipped out of the house. I walked to the corner of the street and sat down on the kerb. I pulled out my book and in the half-light under the street lamp I tried to read while I waited for my father. When he finally pulled up to the kerb I breathed a sigh of relief and jumped into the milk truck. The welcome odour of cigarette smoke, barn, and Old Spice gathered me in.

'Well, how was the party, sunshine?' my father asked as he shifted gears.

'It was okay,' I mumbled.

I didn't tell him I had lain awake all night listening to the angry voices downstairs and the strange noises of the unfamiliar house. I kept silent about how I had cringed inside my sleeping bag, pretending to be asleep, when in the middle of the night the bedroom door opened. I peered out from the tiny opening in my bag as Mr Ryan slipped into the room. I thought Elizabeth-Ann was asleep until I heard her hiss, 'Go away, Daddy,' as he leaned over her bed.

I didn't tell my father about the fear I felt as Mr Ryan backed out of the room, the moonlight exposing the gaping front of his pyjama bottoms.

As my father and I finished delivering milk that morning it dawned on me how silly I had been to feel ashamed of him because he couldn't read. I had just found out that some fathers have far worse secrets.

Chapter Fourteen

DURING THOSE TEENAGE years, extra bodies often crowded in at our table at mealtimes. Town kids. Morgan and Carl's friends. They were all willing to carry milk buckets, chase cows or throw hay bales in exchange for the privilege of spending time 'out at the ranch'. They showed up regularly on weekends and summer holidays. It seemed everyone wanted to be at our place during those blameless years. Our table was so full sometimes that, when Jake was still with us, he refused to sit down for dinner. He would slink into the kitchen and scowl at anyone sitting at, or near, his spot at the end of the table.

After I started high school our home was suddenly filled with the twittering noises of young female voices. My new-found friends. They never seemed to know when to go home. During summer months it got so bad that Dad threatened to change the Ward's Dairy Farm sign over our gate to Ward's Home For Wayward Girls. Carl joked, 'Last stop on the way to Our Lady of Compassion.' Dad told him to watch his mouth.

Elizabeth-Ann was the most frequent visitor. The first time she phoned and whispered, 'Natalie, my dad's drunk. Can I come out?' I was unable to turn her down. Before long she stopped asking and just showed up, sometimes even on school nights.

Since the slumber party, I hadn't returned to the Ryan house.

Besides not wanting to run into Mr Ryan, I had no interest in town life. I believed that my family, my home, was far better than anything those neat houses stacked on the hillsides of Atwood had to offer. When she pursued my friendship, I allowed Elizabeth-Ann into my life because I believed that my world was perfect and hers was not.

We became close, I suppose, in the way friends do who need something from each other. Even though I knew Boyer had been the attraction at first, my friendship with Elizabeth-Ann grew, and I began to look forward to her company.

I'm certain that she, like the other girls, thought it was a fair exchange. They got to spend time at the same table as the Ward boys. They got to act coquettish and flirty and pretend they were grown up, away from their parents' eyes. In exchange they gave me their friendship. They tried to teach me the latest beauty tricks; they loaned or gave me the latest style short skirts and sweater sets. If it seemed a fair exchange in their minds, to me at first, it was nothing more than an indulgence, a curiosity. I stubbornly hung onto my tomboyish looks.

Our hayloft became a favourite hangout once we convinced Mom that no one smoked. I followed as they climbed the ladder on the side of the barn and scrambled over the loose hay to the open overhead doors. From this vantage point they spied on my brothers working below, then fell into fits of giggling at the slightest glance their way. Of course my brothers were aware of all this. Morgan and Carl strutted around during those days, posturing like bantam roosters, pretending even to themselves that our little farm was a 'ranch' and as romantic as those mesmerized young girls saw it to be. I watched closely as Elizabeth-Ann tried her wiles on Boyer. At mealtimes she jockeyed her position at the table to sit close to him.

She used every excuse to ask him to pass her something, shamelessly batting her eyes every time she spoke to him.

Boyer was immune to her obvious flirting, treating her with the polite indulgence he showed anyone but family. And every time he winked or smiled at me I felt a smug superiority knowing I was still 'his girl'.

I think each of the girls who came out to our farm had her own dreams of romantic encounters in the hayloft with one of my brothers. I'm sure that for some, it eventually happened. In those early summers though, they had to be content with each other, pretending the thin white arms that held them were tanned and muscled. I watched with an amused curiosity as they rolled around in the loose hay, budding breasts rubbing against each other, in pretence of preparation for the real thing. I even felt something, a small igniting of a spark of interest, when they practised French kissing. Certainly more than any spark I could imagine feeling for the pale-faced boys at school, or any of my brothers' friends. When we started having campfires out by the lake behind the back field and playing spin-the-bottle I prayed that the bottle top would not point to me. Whenever it did I would retreat into the darkness with an equally reluctant partner and whisper, 'Let's not and say we did.' And when I was challenged to act I felt a nauseating shudder as a wet tongue touched my lips. Secretly, I began to believe that I might never feel even a small tingle of excitement or attraction to the opposite sex.

But all that changed after River arrived.

Chapter Fifteen

RIVER JORDAN. HE flowed into our lives as easily as water finding its course. And like water, in time, he would erode the jagged edges of resistance.

Morgan and Carl were the first to yield. They didn't crumble right away. It took them at least a day.

Before supper River came back to the house. He rapped lightly on the side of the screen door as he peered in.

'No need to knock here,' Mom called out from the sideboard where she was cutting bread.

'Just like home,' River answered and stepped into the kitchen.

Mom looked up, her face still flushed from the day's heat. 'Good,' she said with a smile. 'I hope you will come to feel as comfortable here.'

'I'm certain I will,' he said then hurried over and took the stack of dinner plates I was reaching for in the cupboard. 'Here, let me get that, Natalie.'

'Thanks,' I mumbled, sure my face was as flushed as Mom's.

'My pleasure,' he said, his blue eyes crinkling with a smile. He helped me set the table for supper while he and Mom chatted as easily as two old friends. As we pulled the table away from the wall I heard Morgan and Carl out on the porch with Dad.

At the kitchen stove Mom lifted the cast-iron stewpot off the element. She turned at the creak of the screen door hinges. 'Come and meet River before you wash up,' she called out as she leaned over to place the heavy pot on hot pads in the middle of the table. She straightened up and smoothed down her apron. 'Everyone, this is River Jordan,' she said.

I thought I heard a hint of anxiety in her voice as she introduced him to Dad. Maybe it was me. Maybe I was the only one who was apprehensive about how my father would react to this stranger. But I don't think so.

Dad's right eyebrow lifted, either in response to the unusual name, or to the sight of the shoulder-length hair and flowing Indian cotton shirt.

To say River looked out of place in our kitchen would be an understatement. The contrast between his hippie attire and my father and brother's work clothes was glaring. Dad's checkered shirt was sweat-stained, his striped coveralls covered in a film of dirt. Hay dust clung to his hair and darkened every crease and wrinkle of exposed skin. My brothers, in similar dust-covered denim shirts and jeans, reeked of the morning's labour in the fields.

On the other hand, even though River had walked out to our farm in the heat of the day, he smelled and looked as if he had just climbed out of the shower. His clothes, so different from anything we were used to, seemed freshly laundered and crisp. And yet, as he stepped forward and offered his hand, he seemed oblivious to any difference.

'How do you do, sir?' he said. And I wondered if the velvet drawl of that voice sounded as wondrous to everyone else as is did to me.

My father didn't seem to notice. He took the offered hand and gave it a single, firm shake. I thought I saw a quick wince behind River's smile.

'River?' Dad let go of his hand. 'Can't say I've ever heard of anyone called River before.'

'It's not my real name,' River answered. 'Just a nickname. My given name is Richard.'

'Well, Richard,' Dad said, 'these guys here,' he nodded at Morgan and Carl as he headed into the washroom, 'are big on nicknames. This'll save 'em from figuring one out for you.'

'Oh, I'm sure we'll think of something,' Carl said as he took River's outstretched hand. I caught the smirk that passed between him and Morgan and knew that River would not escape the razzing that every new person at our table endured.

'Whew,' River laughed and gave a mock shaking of his hand after Morgan released his grip.

Just then the screen door screeched open once more and Boyer came into the kitchen. While Mom introduced River, I was struck again with the thought I'd had earlier when I'd watched him walk across the farmyard. Even though River was shorter, his features finer than Boyer's, and his eyes much bluer, as their tanned hands came together in a handshake I couldn't help thinking again that they were somehow similar. Seeing them together I realized the resemblance was more than just the colour of their hair. Perhaps it was the reserved nods they exchanged as they acknowledged each other. I knew Boyer was never quick to judge anyone, and something told me River was the same.

I still felt unsettled by my initial reaction to River and I watched closely as Boyer shook his hand.

'Never rely on first impressions,' Boyer once told me. 'One way or another, only time will prove who people really are.' Yet, as he released River's hand I saw a brief smile cross Boyer's face. A smile mirrored in the aquamarine eyes looking back at him.

After everyone washed up, River slid onto the bench at the back of the table beside Morgan and Carl. With the final Amen of the mealtime prayer, Mom reached over to the middle of the table and lifted the lid from the cast-iron pot. She picked up the ladle and began spooning out the soupy mixture.

'Thank you, ma'am,' River said to Mom as she placed the first steaming serving in front of him.

'Ma'am?' Carl and Morgan parroted River's accent. Their laughs were cut short as Mom frowned at them.

'Nettie,' Mom reminded River as she continued serving.

'Yes, ma'am,' River said, 'Nettie.' And he nodded to Mom with a smile so genuine that even Carl and Morgan could not have doubted his sincerity.

After Mom set a plate of stew down in front of Morgan he leaned over and rubbed his hands together. 'Mmmmm,' he said as he breathed in the aroma, 'stewed brains, my favourite.'

Our mother was not a great cook, but she was good enough. Her hamburger stew was hearty and tasty, if not colourful. Other victims of this worn-out joke usually turned pale as they were handed a plateful of the pinkish-grey concoction.

'You like brains, River?' Carl asked as Mom passed along another serving.

River didn't miss a beat. He tucked his hair behind his ears, picked up his fork, and dug in. 'Sure do,' he said after swallowing the first mouthful. 'I especially like them for breakfast, fried up with onions and hot sauce.' He retrieved a thick slice of bread from the platter Mom offered. 'I'll cook up a batch for you guys sometime.' He flashed a conspirator's smile across the table at me as he buttered his bread.

Morgan and Carl's smirks began to fade. A hint of a grin played at the corners of my father's lips, and then disappeared, leaving me to wonder if I had imagined it. Dad was the only one in our family who liked brains. He ate every organ, every part of a cow Mom would cook: the heart, liver, kidneys, and even the tongue. My brothers would never touch 'innards'. Whenever Mom served up these delicacies to our father, they ate leftovers, or sandwiches.

'I have to say, Nettie,' River said, dunking his bread in the anaemic gravy, 'this tastes exactly the same as my momma's stew. She mixes the cow brains with hamburger just like this. If you didn't know, you could never tell they were in there.'

Morgan and Carl looked down at their plates, then back up at Mom. She raised her shoulders in an innocent shrug. The corners of Boyer's mouth twitched. Morgan and Carl poked suspiciously at their stew.

Then Dad began his interrogation. There was no other word for it. Whether he was still annoyed at Mom's taking it upon herself to hire River, or whether he felt a true dislike for this young man, I didn't know. But he began to fire questions like accusations. 'So, how come ya left the States?' he asked.

River swallowed, then wiped his mouth with his napkin. He looked directly at my father. 'Well, sir,' he said, 'I left because I don't believe in the war in Vietnam.'

'A draft dodger,' my father said and took a mouthful of stew.

'Gus!' Mom cried.

'I prefer war-resister,' River said. 'But I guess you're right, draft dodger is probably the label I'll have to live with.'

During dinner conversations, my father had a habit of punctuating his words by pointing his fork as he spoke. He lifted his fork, then thought better of it, and dug into the stew before he spoke again. 'I'll say one thing straight out right now,' he said, 'I believe a man should fight for his country when he is called to.'

I thought I saw an expression of sorrow fill River's eyes as he looked down the table at my father. 'And I respect that, sir,' he answered quietly, 'but I don't see where this war in Asia is my country's war.'

From the calm determination in his voice I guessed that River must have debated this controversy many times before he arrived at our table. I watched his face as he contemplated my father's questions. He thought each through with patience and respect, before he replied without apology. He told Dad he was neither a crusader nor an anarchist. To him it was simple: he could not take part in an immoral war.

'Those are just words,' Dad said. 'Excuses you young people make to avoid your duty.'

I felt an urge to join in the conversation, to say something, anything, to somehow defend this stranger sitting across from me, but I knew next to nothing about the issue and so I held my tongue. Mom felt no such reluctance. 'What if it were our sons?' she asked Dad.

'Alls I'm saying is a man has a responsibility to his country,' my father muttered without looking up from his plate. 'Freedom comes at a cost.'

Boyer, who'd watched the exchange in silence, spoke up. 'I doubt if America's freedom is at stake in Vietnam,' he said, looking straight at Dad. 'Any more than ours is.'

'A man has a duty to his country,' my father responded.

'To his country, yes,' River said. 'But I don't believe that blindly following the orders of corrupt politicians is my duty to my country. I would die for my country, sir. That would be easy. Living with killing people who have done us no harm would not be.'

Dad grunted and continued eating. After a moment he asked, 'And what do your parents think of all this, of you leaving your home, maybe never being allowed to go back again?'

River didn't answer right away. He placed his knife and fork at the top of his plate and nodded across at my mother. 'Thank you Nettie,' he said. 'That was delicious.' Then he turned his full attention to Dad.

'My father's dead,' he told him. 'My mother doesn't believe in this war either. And my grandfather, well, he doesn't agree with my decision to defy the draft. And he never understood my choice to leave university in the first place.'

'University?' Boyer's voice betrayed his surprise. 'If you were in university, weren't you safe from the draft?'

River turned and directed his attention to Boyer at the other end of the table. 'Yes,' he said, 'that's true, if I had stayed. But I couldn't sit back while the war and the bombing was escalating and not stand up against it. I joined the peace movement. When I received my draft card, burning it, leaving, was my only way to protest the actions of a government I no longer believe in.'

'Well, I guess Canada's not as bad as prison,' Dad snorted.

'Being in exile is its own prison,' River said.

There was a silence at the table. Like me, Morgan and Carl had watched the conversation without joining in. I wondered then what they, and Boyer, would do if they had to face the same decisions. I wondered if they too were thinking that it was only an accident of birth, of being a few thousand feet from an invisible line, that made their choices so simple compared to this young American, who in the end, was not so different from themselves. It was Dad who changed the subject. 'So why'd ya choose here?' he asked. 'I understand there's a whole community of your kind in the East Kootenays. Call themselves "The New Family".'

'I didn't come here to live in a little America. Or a commune. When I saw your ad in the paper I thought it was a good opportunity to take some time to think out my next move. And to get to know Canada. Canadians.'

My father glanced at Mom then back to River. 'Have ya ever worked on a dairy farm?'

'I grew up on my grandfather's farm in Montana,' River told him. He didn't tell him the size of that farm, or that it was a modern automated operation that shipped milk out each day in gleaming stainless steel tanker trucks. We would learn that much later.

Dad's chair scraped on the kitchen floor. 'Better grab a pair of rubber boots from the porch,' he said as he headed to the door. 'Those moccasins are about as useless in the barn as socks in a bath tub.'

River smiled. 'Yes, I expect so,' he said and slid out from behind the table.

After I finished clearing up and washing the supper dishes, I went upstairs. My bedroom window looked out over the enclosed porch. Sometimes, when I was alone, I took a book and climbed out the window to sit on the sloped porch roof. From there I could see the entire farmyard, the dairy, and the barn.

That evening I sat with my back against the faded whitewashed siding and gazed down the dirt road that wound past the fenced pasture and disappeared around the bend beyond our gate. The road that had brought this intriguing stranger to us.

Sitting in the shade of the house I listened to the familiar sounds of the evening milking carrying up from the barn: the scraping of bovine hooves on slippery concrete floors; the bawls of protest from the cows locked into their stanchions; the murmur of calming voices, and the suction of milking machines. Before long, Morgan and Carl began carrying the full stainless steel milking machines from the barn to the dairy. Inside the dairy, Mom and Boyer would run the warm milk through the cooler and cream separator. Then they filled the sterilized milk bottles to be stored in the walk-in cooler for the next day's delivery.

From the way Morgan and Carl were hustling it was easy to see that Dad and River were supplying milk much faster than Dad and Jake ever had. Neither Morgan nor Carl had time to notice me watching from the porch roof as they rushed back and forth across the yard.

When the milking was complete River came out from behind the barn. His hair was tied back in a ponytail and tucked into the collar of the green coveralls he now wore. With his arm draped across the shoulder of the lead cow he leaned down and whispered something in her ear. She followed him to the pasture across the road as if she had been doing it every day of her life. He held the gate open and patted each of the cows on the rump as they filed through.

He closed the gate, turned and caught sight of me on the roof. He lifted his arm in a wave. And even from that distance I believed I could see the sparkle of those aquamarine eyes.

Later that night, through the grates in the upstairs hallway, I heard Dad's voice carry up from the kitchen. 'Well, Nettie, the boy does know his way around cows,' he said grudgingly. Then he added, 'But don't count on him too much. His kind's about as likely to stick around as dust in the wind.'

The faint strains of guitar music drifted across the farmyard, and along with the light of a full moon, the notes stole through the open window into my bedroom, where I lay hoping my father was wrong.

Chapter Sixteen

FOR AS LONG as I remember visitors were always showing up at our farm on one pretext or another. They came to pick huckleberries or mushrooms on the mountain slopes behind our house. They came for loads of manure from the ever-present stockpile behind the barn. They came for Mom's eggs or cream, or simply for a Sunday drive. And they always found an excuse to enter our kitchen.

Everyone wanted to spend time around our family back then. Like Mom, I took pride in the fact that others seemed to envy our lives. I had yet to hear the saying, 'Those the gods would destroy they first make proud.'

After River arrived the visitors intensified. As word spread, a steady stream of the curious, young and old alike, dropped by to check out our new hired hand. And without even trying, in his quiet gentle way, River charmed them all. He seemed unaware of his effect on people. He treated everyone with an old fashioned respect. All men were, 'sir', and all women, 'ma'am'. And from the first day, to my joy, he never shortened my name or called me anything except Natalie.

Whenever River spoke to anyone his eyes held theirs with a soft intensity. They never flickered with boredom or darted around to check out the surrounding action. It was so easy for me to believe I was the most important thing in the world when he looked at me.

Easy to see the best of myself reflected back in those eyes. By August I was completely infatuated with River. I am certain everyone was. Except Dad.

He was not rude exactly, but he held something back. Mom, of course, treated River with the same hospitality she shared with anyone who showed up at our door. Maybe more. Did she really laugh more when he was around? Did she really seem younger, prettier? If I thought she did, surely my father must have noticed. Was it possible he was jealous? I know I was.

After the first night's initiation, it was obvious Morgan and Carl were, according to Dad, smitten. The growing length of their hair during the following months did nothing to help our father warm to River.

'You both need to get your ears lowered,' he told the two of them at breakfast one morning. 'You're starting to look like a couple of wacko beatniks.'

'That's hippies, Dad,' Carl laughed, 'hippies.'

That summer, instead of playing 45s out in the sunroom, or cruising the streets of town after the evening milking, Morgan and Carl and their entourage began spending time at night in the room above the dairy. My father shook his head and cringed the first time the two of them came down the stairs wearing muted tie-dyed shirts.

Confused by my feelings, I kept my distance and watched. At first anyway.

One afternoon, a few weeks after River arrived, I climbed out of my bedroom window to sit on the roof above the porch. Morgan and Carl had gone off riding horses with their friends. Mom and Boyer were in town.

I sat down in the shade to read. A few minutes later I heard the clanging of a wrench against concrete followed by my father's groan.

'Every time the sun shines upside down!' Dad's voice bellowed out from the machine shop.

I smiled to myself. This expression of my father's was the closest I ever heard him come to cursing.

'The tractor must be fighting back,' River's voice called out from the yard.

I looked down, startled to see him there. Just as I once was aware of the location and number of every candy or sweet in the house, these days I was usually aware of River's whereabouts. I was surprised I had not sensed his presence.

I gave a startled laugh. 'You've heard Dad's idea of swearing?'

'A time or two.' River stopped at the gate and smiled up at me. It was impossible not to smile back.

'What're you reading?' he asked.

I held the book up and turned it to face him. '*Sometimes a Great Notion.*'

'Seems you've always got your nose in a book,' he said. 'You must haunt the library.'

'Yeah, Boyer's library,' I laughed.

'Boyer's?'

'Come on up, I'll show you,' I offered.

'Shall I climb the roof to prove my devotion?' he asked with a mock-serious voice.

'The stairs are fine,' I blushed.

We met in the upstairs hallway and I led him up to the attic room thrilled at being alone with him. River stood in the doorway and whistled. 'Man, I see what you mean.'

Books filled every available surface and space in Boyer's room.

They lined shelves, covered his desk and the window seat. They filled boxes under the bed and were stacked against the walls all the way up to the edge of the sloped ceiling.

'Do you think he will mind if I look through them?' River asked, a note of awe in his voice.

'He won't mind at all,' Boyer's voice answered from the stairway behind us.

Up until then Boyer had treated River with the same polite indifference he treated anyone but family. But as he came up the stairs that afternoon I saw a look of acceptance as he ushered River into his sanctuary.

'Cool.' River pushed back his hair as he surveyed Boyer's collection. 'Did you raid a second-hand bookstore or something?'

'Something.' Boyer sat down at his desk, leaned back and folded his arms. 'Most of these are from an old high school teacher of mine. Thanks to her, I get the rejects from the town's library.'

'Some teacher,' River murmured. He picked up one book after another then asked, 'You mind if I borrow a few?'

'Any time.'

I leaned against the doorway and watched them discuss different books. Up until then I never knew Boyer to have any outside friends. I mentally patted myself on the back for bringing them together, and I tried to ignore the sudden pinch of envy I felt.

A few days later I heard their voices out in the sunroom after lunch. I went out to find them searching through the record albums.

'You're sure this will work?' Boyer asked.

'Worked for my grandfather's cows.'

Later the two of them headed into town in Boyer's Edsel. They returned with a battered old portable record player from the second-hand store and carried it into the barn.

That night I listened from my perch on the roof as the strains of a Mozart concerto carried up with the sounds of the evening milking. My father scoffed at River and Boyer's project, but before long he had to admit to a significant increase in milk production.

The long hot summer of 1966 produced a bumper hay crop. My favourite memory is of my father and brothers working in the fields. I carry a mental picture of them drenched in the golden glow of the late summer sun. I keep this precious gem hidden deep in the dark closet of my mind, behind all of life's stored clutter. I take it out rarely, cautiously. Like a fragile object stored in opaque tissue, I unwrap it with slow trepidation. I turn it this way and that, trying to see more, to see beyond the faded edges of memory.

There must have been others in the field, there were always extra hands around at haying time, yet whenever I allow this image to surface I see only the faces of my brothers, my father. And River.

One day in the middle of August, in the thickness of the afternoon heat, I carried ice-cold lemonade out to the back hayfield. With Elizabeth-Ann tagging along at my side, I made my way down the dirt road.

I hugged the sloshing jug close to my chest. Condensation ran down the cold glass and dropped like tears into the dust whirling at my feet.

I heard my brothers before I spotted them. Morgan and Carl's voices carried out over the mechanical drone of the tractor and the clanking of the hay wagon. They called out to each other, teasing and laughing, mocking the backbreaking work. River's voice joined in, floating like a song on the summer breeze.

Elizabeth-Ann and I paused at the edge of the hay meadow in waist-high grass. The sweet aroma of drying alfalfa filled my nostrils. Out in the field my father drove the tractor, pulling the hay wagon along neat rows of baled hay. With his right hand on the steering wheel, he peered over his left shoulder at Morgan and Carl pitching bales.

Boyer and River, both stripped to the waist, stacked the heavy bales on the deck of the wagon. Rivulets of sweat streaked through the fine hay dust covering their naked torsos. Their heads turned, as first one, then the other caught sight of us. I smiled at the relief in their eyes. The noise of the tractor engine wound down. The droning buzz of insects filled the sudden stillness of the dust-and-heat-rippled air. I hurried across the dried stubble of the mown field, ignoring the harsh prickles jabbing the bottom of my tennis shoes.

Delivering Mom's thirst-quenching lemonade on these hot summer afternoons was a chore I never tired of. I enjoyed it even more when any of my friends – in particular Elizabeth-Ann – came with me. I secretly relished the envy I saw in her eyes as I passed cold drinks to waiting hands.

'Thank you, sunshine,' Dad said, turning off the tractor and reaching for his tin cup.

'Ah, sweet Natalie, the lifesaver,' River said. He sat down on the back of the hay wagon and wiped the sweat from his brow with his leather glove. The he held up his arms to strum an invisible guitar and began singing 'Aura Lee', an old American Civil War song with the same melody as 'Love Me Tender'. And as he crooned, he substituted my name for Aura Lee.

> As the black bird in the spring,
> 'neath the willow tree,
> sat and piped I heard him sing,
> sing of Natalie.
> Natalie, Natalie. Maid with auburn hair,
> sunshine came along with thee, like swallows in the air.

And the magic of my name filled the meadow and warmed me beyond anything the afternoon sun ever could.

Feigning annoyance, but secretly thrilled, I passed him a drink. He gave a mock bow of his head then raised his tin cup in a toast to me.

I dipped another cup into the jug and Boyer jumped down from the wagon to get his drink.

'This deserves a hug,' he said and pulled me into his arms in a bear hug, deliberately smearing my T-shirt with his muddy sweat.

I giggled and shrieked while I tried to wiggle away, fully aware of the frown that crossed Elizabeth-Ann's face.

Afterward, as we walked side by side back to the house, she said casually, 'Wow, that River sure is mint.'

I stopped abruptly and scowled at her.

Elizabeth-Ann was beautiful. I was not. If she set her sights on River, how could he resist? 'I like him,' I said, a note of warning on the edge of my confession.

'Oh,' she answered, then shrugged. 'Okay. You get River. I get Boyer.'

She had made no secret of her attraction to Boyer. I knew she believed it was just a matter of time before he noticed her. In the beginning of our friendship I fought the stay-away-from-my-brother thoughts that welled up each time she spoke about him. Still, I felt a relief as she put her arm around my shoulder and marched back to the house with me, our childish bargain sealed. Besides, somehow I knew that Elizabeth-Ann's affection for my brother would not be reciprocated.

My relief turned out to be short-lived that summer afternoon. Just as we arrived at the gate, a black Lincoln Continental pulled into the yard.

'What's he doing here?' Elizabeth-Ann moaned as she saw her father's car.

Mr Ryan had never been out to our farm that I knew of. I hurried up the porch steps as the car door opened.

Mom stood at the open screen door wiping her flour-dredged hands on her apron. 'Well, Gerald, to what do we owe this honour?' she called out as I brushed by her. 'We can't vote in a town election, you know.'

I stood behind Mom for a moment and looked over her shoulder.

'Oh, no, I'm not campaigning Nettie.' Mr Ryan puffed up the porch steps. 'Just thought I'd drop by and see what the big attraction is. Seems my daughter here,' he smiled up at Elizabeth-Ann, 'spends more time at your place than at home these days.'

Elizabeth-Ann rolled her eyes and stepped past Mom and followed me as I fled up the stairs. In the upstairs hallway I slid down and sat by the open floor grate. Downstairs, I heard Mr Ryan settle in a chair and accept the lemonade Mom offered.

'Thought I'd take the opportunity to come out and meet this new fellow I've heard so much about,' he said between slow gulps. Although I couldn't see his face, I heard the smirk in his voice.

Mom's rolling pin slammed down rhythmically on the table as she worked the pie dough. 'Well, then I guess you'll have to wait until dinner time later tonight,' she said using the smooth, polite voice she reserved for bankers and inspectors from the Milk Board. 'They'll be haying until the last minute.'

'Why, Nettie, is that a dinner invitation?'

'There's always room at my table,' Mom replied.

I cringed.

'That's hospitable of you,' Mr Ryan crooned, 'and I would love to stay, but I'll have to take a rain check. We're having guests to dinner ourselves this evening.'

I breathed a sigh of relief until I heard him say. 'I hear this young fellow's American. A hippie. Maybe a draft dodger. What did you say his name was?'

'I didn't,' Mom replied. 'Why?'

'Well, I'm just thinking, as mayor, that it's my duty to run a check on him. Make sure he's here legally. Maybe make some inquiries with the FBI. We should be certain he's legit, not running from the law or anything like that. For your family's own protection and the town's.'

'Oh, there's no need to bother yourself with that,' Mom said, perhaps a little too sweetly. 'I can vouch for him. He's family. Richard's my cousin's boy from Montana. Now, you wouldn't want to interfere with family, would you?'

Family? Her cousin's boy? I put my hand to my mouth and choked back the giggle I felt bubbling up.

Elizabeth-Ann mouthed, 'Is that true?'

I shrugged my shoulders and she clasped her hand over her mouth to stifle her own giggles.

We stayed upstairs while the overly polite conversation droned on in the kitchen. Finally Mr Ryan called up for Elizabeth-Ann. She rolled her eyes again. Before she left she whispered, 'Don't worry, I won't tell.'

I waited until I heard Mr Ryan's car drive away before I went down to the kitchen.

I looked at Mom. I had never known my mother to tell a lie. I had no idea she was capable of even a little white lie. And this was a whopper. Somehow I expected her to look different. But she smiled innocently at me and continued filling the pie shells lined up on the table with huckleberries. I remained silent, but I wondered what penance she would have to do. Then I decided, that with all her praying she should have at least a few credits built up.

Chapter Seventeen

MOM AND I spent the next morning pulling weeds in the garden.

Working out in the vegetable garden with my mother was another of my favourite chores. I loved the feel of the soil on my hands, the smell of the earth and the sun-warmed plants. I loved listening to the sound of my mother's soft voice as we chatted across the rows.

I glanced at her over the lacy carrot tops. Mom straightened up and placed her arms at her waist to stretch her back. She threw a handful of chickweed into an overflowing basket. Then she stood, picked up the basket and headed toward the chicken pen.

'Nettie's girls,' everyone called her chickens. Her birds were something of a local phenomenon the way they kept laying, summer and winter. Everyone wanted to know her secret. A few jokingly offered to hire Mom to counsel their hens. They tried her trick of playing a radio in the coops night and day, added eggshells to their feed, but in the end they said, the only difference was Mom.

Dad said the chickens – like everyone who knew her – were in love with Mom. He was certain they each produced an egg a day only to please her. And Mom's egg money kept piling up.

'Hello ladies,' she called out as she approached the pen. The flock turned as one at the sound of her voice. The chickens ran beside her on the other side of the wire fence, their piston heads moving in unison. As soon as she stepped inside the pen they crowded around her legs, rubbed themselves against her boots, and jostled for position to be petted. She bent down and, being careful to give each one the same attention, ran her hands down their white-feathered backs as they crouched to the ground.

Once, when I was very young, I made the mistake of trying to pet one of the birds. While Mom made clucking sounds and spread handfuls of grain in a wide arc to her brood, I bent down to stroke a white back. Before my fingers touched a feather a red-crowned head shot out. A globule of blood appeared where a razor sharp beak struck the back of my hand. Suddenly a flurry of beady-eyes and orange beaks swarmed me. I stumbled backwards, then ran screaming around the pen trying to escape the frenzied attack of beaks pecking at my bare legs.

My mother scooped me up and held me on her hip. I wrapped my legs around her.

'It's all right, sweetheart,' she assured me as I sobbed into her neck. 'They just don't know you.'

It was a long time before I ventured back inside the pen. By then Boyer had added another ten-penny word to my vocabulary: alektorophobia.

'Those birds don't want anyone but your mom near them,' Dad consoled me when he heard about my ordeal. 'They think she's their ruddy mother. I swear those chickens purr when she pets them.'

After Mom scattered the weeds and vegetable tops for her 'girls' in the pen she returned to the garden. She grabbed two long-handled hoes and passed one to me.

We worked side by side hilling potato plants. The midday sun warmed my back. My nostrils filled with the rich aroma of the freshly turned soil, and the heavy perfume wafting over from the rose garden.

The rose garden was Mom's domain. I used to think Mom insisted on tending it alone because it was my father's wedding gift to her. Lately I noticed her weekly excursions looked more like a contest of wills than a labour of love. Sometimes I sat out on the sloped roof outside my window and watched her work below. She attacked the rose bushes with pruning shears, hedge clippers and even a hand saw. She could never keep ahead of the prolific runners and suckers. The bushes grew gnarled and tangled no matter how far back she cut them in the fall – so far sometimes that it looked impossible they would ever regenerate. Yet each spring new shoots sprouted and filled the garden with thick thorn-laden branches and rosebuds once again.

'How come you never pick the roses, Mom?' I asked. Just then I heard the milk truck pull up to the dairy.

Mom leaned her hoe against the fence, 'Roses die too quickly,' she said. She opened the garden gate. 'Besides, flowers in the house only make me think of funerals and death.'

The only person I ever knew who died was my grandmother. I was twelve years old when Grandma Locke passed away. She visited us only a few times, but I never forgot the way she looked at my brothers and me, as if we were to blame for her daughter's lot in life. As if, by merely existing, we held our mother, who was meant for much finer things, captive against her will. And I remember the only words of advice my grandmother ever shared with me. 'Never marry a farmer, Natalie,' she told me. 'Remember it's just as easy to love a rich man as a poor one.' It didn't seem to occur to her, or to bother her if it did, that it was my father who paid her bus fare whenever she came to visit.

I followed Mom out of the garden. 'Why didn't Grandma Locke like Dad?' I asked her, but my eyes were watching River climb out of

117

the truck. His ponytail bounced against his back as he started unloading the empty crates from the truck.

Mom closed the latch on the gate behind us. 'Oh, it wasn't so much him she didn't like,' she said, 'as what he did for a living. And when he called me Nettie. Well, both my parents thought that was barbaric!'

'Ah, yes, the late, great Leslie and Christine Locke,' Dad's voice called from inside the back of the milk truck. 'The king and queen of Victoria.'

'Oh, Gus,' Mom answered. I'd heard her use this expression so many times that, when I was little, I thought it was one word.

'I don't think your folks ever forgave you for marrying a milkman,' Dad replied, passing an empty crate to River. 'And according to them an ill-bred one at that.' Then he added, 'Maybe that was the attraction.'

I hurried to the back of the truck and reached up to take the next milk crate, then followed River into the dairy. He stacked his crate, then smiled at me as he reached to take mine.

'Got a little sunburn there, Natalie,' he said and tapped me on the end of my nose.

I wondered just how much was sunburn and how much was from being around him. No one else had the power to make me blush except River. Although he had been there for a month I was still finding myself tongue-tied around him.

Outside, he gave me a conspiratorial glance as my parents continued to banter back and forth. After the last of the empty milk bottles were stored in the dairy, we followed Mom and Dad up to the house for lunch.

Dad threw his arm around Mom. 'So, Nettie,' he said, 'I hear congratulations are in order.'

'Congratulations?'

'On finding your long-lost relatives,' Dad said slyly. 'We ran into Gerald Ryan this morning.'

Mom stopped so abruptly I almost bumped into her. She turned and looked at River, who was fighting to keep a straight face, then back to Dad. 'Oh, I—' she stammered, a flush rising in her cheeks. 'I didn't— I thought—'

'Yes, thanks for vouching for me, Cousin Nettie,' River drawled.

'I always knew you wanted a large family,' my father said. 'I just didn't realize what lengths you'd go to get it.' He laughed and hugged Mom closer.

I let go of the breath I had unconsciously been holding.

'And that's the only reason I married you,' Mom sniffed and shrugged off his arm in feigned anger. But I could tell she was relieved too.

River rushed up to the gate and, with a mock bow and a wave of his arm ushered her, and then me, past.

'Don't ya believe it,' Dad said to me as he walked by River as if he wasn't there. 'It was love at first sight when your mother saw me.'

'Ha! For you, maybe.' Mom's back was straight and her chin held high as she made her way up the porch steps.

Dad hurried after her and pulled open the screen door. He held it as Mom and I went into the kitchen. Then he followed, letting the door close behind him. River caught it just before it slammed. Inside, Mom and I stood together at the kitchen sink, rinsing the garden dirt from our hands.

'If you could have seen the goofy look on your father's face when he saw me, instead of Aunt Elsie, at her door on my first morning in town,' she said ignoring my father. 'He stood there with a milk bottle in each hand, looking like he had just discovered them, and had no idea what they were for.'

River chuckled. As he pulled the kitchen table away from the window, he asked, 'So what brought a city girl to Atwood in the first place, Nettie?'

Mom thought for a moment then said. 'Well, my father joined the Navy in 1939, as soon as war broke out.'

She retrieved the kettle from the stove, took it over to the sink and filled it as she spoke. 'He left my mother and me in Victoria on Vancouver Island and shipped out. After Pearl Harbor, when the Americans joined the war, Mother suddenly realized that Japan was "just across the water". A week later she sent me to live with her Aunt Elsie here in Atwood.'

'And then she saw me and was a goner,' Dad said. He winked at me before he headed into the bathroom.

'Not exactly,' Mom said over her shoulder. She turned off the tap and lifted the kettle out of the sink.

River hurried over and took the heavy kettle from her hands and carried it to the stove. Mom watched him for a moment, then turned back to the cupboard.

'Tell River about the dance,' I prompted. I had heard the story of how my parents met many times. I thought it was so romantic that I wanted River to hear it too.

She pulled out the cutlery drawer and continued. 'Your father couldn't even stammer a hello that first morning. I'd completely forgotten him by the time he showed up at the Christmas social at the Miners' Hall the next weekend.'

'To the surprise and delight of a number of excited young women there, I might add,' Dad called out over the sound of running water.

'That's true,' Mom whispered.

'Yes, it is,' my father said. He emerged from the bathroom drying his face with a towel. 'I saw all those ladies look up hopefully with their dance cards ready when I came into the hall. But I headed straight across the dance floor to where your mother stood and said, "I believe this is my dance." She glanced down at her dance card, back up at me, put the card in her pocket and said, "Yes, I believe it is."'

As River slid into his seat behind the table, he mouthed silently, '*dance card*?' and we exchanged a secret smile.

'I was never one to make a scene,' Mom sniffed. She was slicing bread at the sideboard. 'It wasn't as if I had many partners to choose from. There was a war on after all. There was a shortage of eligible men and I was new to town. The only names on my dance card were friends of my aunt's. When the song was over—'

'And what was the name of the song?' my father crowed.

'"It Had To Be You".' Mom rolled her eyes at me as we set the table. 'Anyway, when the dance ended I thanked your father cordially, but firmly. Then I returned to Allen Mumford. He was the town's new doctor then. It was his name that was really on my card. As Allen led me out onto the floor, I saw your father leave.'

'*I* was never one to overplay my hand,' Dad retorted.

They were into it now and needed no further prodding from me. I glanced at River and caught the amused expression on his face as I passed him a platter of cold cuts from the fridge. 'The next morning, when I delivered the milk to Aunt Elsie's,' Dad went on, 'her front door opened and out comes your mom. She bounces down the stairs, opens the passenger door of the milk truck, jumps in, slams the door and says, "I believe this is my seat", without even cracking a smile.'

Just who swept whom off their feet depends on which one tells the story. In the wedding picture taken eight months later my father looks a little shell-shocked. He says it was because he still couldn't believe he was standing there beside this 'beautiful stranger', his bride, ten years younger than he was. He had proposed to her on their second date – after more than a few gulps of whiskey from a brown-bagged bottle. When she surprised him by answering 'yes', he walked into the alley behind the Roxy movie theatre and threw up.

Mom says they would have married even sooner except that it took a while to convince her parents, who had to sign for her because she was only seventeen. After she threatened to run off to the States and marry without their consent – a very real threat since the border was only minutes away – her mother and father gave in. If they had realized she would give herself over to the Catholic Church, my grandfather said, he 'would have come here himself and kidnapped her, dragged her home and tied her to her bed until she got over this foolishness.'

'As it was, he found out too late,' Mom said. 'Dad was at sea when Father Mackenzie performed our vows in St Anthony's. Your grandmother realized it was a Catholic church only minutes before the ceremony.'

My grandmother was also not one to make a scene, but anyone in the church that day could have seen that the gulping sobs and tears she shed were not the normal mother-of-the bride tears of joy.

Contrary to my grandmother's belief – a belief she held until her dying day according to Dad – my mother insisted she never regretted becoming a farmer's wife. From the moment she stepped out of the milk truck at the Ward Dairy for the first time, she said her heart was captured.

'It was really the farm I fell in love with first,' she said wistfully, the tea kettle whistling on the stove.

I've tried to imagine what it was she found so compelling when she first climbed out from her shanghaied-seat that winter morning. By December the countryside is usually hidden under snow so deep it's hard to believe there's anything beneath the endless white, or that the fields and gardens will ever be green again. All winter the entire farm and surrounding hills are completely obscured by a heavy white carpet. The cows mill around close to the barn in a brown slush-filled mud and manure pasture. Still, to hear Mom describe the scene it's easy to understand how she romanticized her first vision of the farm.

'It was like a Christmas card,' she said. 'The snow hung heavy on the branches of trees, it rolled off the barn roof like thick icing. Fat, silent flakes fell, dusting the backs of the cows and horses. A stream of smoke curled up from the brick chimney of the farmhouse. It was beautiful ...' she mused. 'In the dairy, the smell of cream, wet cement and bleach was as familiar to me then as it is now.'

'You sure it wasn't the kiss I stole as soon as the door closed behind us?' my father teased.

Mom ignored him as she poured boiling water into the teapot. She knew with certainty, she went on, that as she followed Dad through the maze of shoulder-high snow banks to the farmhouse that it was her future in-laws she was about to meet.

As she placed the teapot on the table, Dad came up behind Mom and wrapped his arms around her waist. 'And that was our lucky day,' he said as he spun her around. 'Underneath those snow clouds, the sun was shining right side up. Eh, Nettie?'

I caught a brief flash of something akin to sorrow fill Mom's eyes as Dad took her into his arms. It was there, then disappeared so quickly, I thought I imagined it. I couldn't tell if River had noticed because when I glanced over at him he was studying his fingernails.

While Dad sang an off-key version of 'It Had To Be You', Mom frowned in mock exasperation.

'Oh, Gus,' she sighed, letting him lead her around the kitchen in an exaggerated swaying slow dance, 'of course it was.'

Chapter Eighteen

Nettie

SHE STANDS AT the gate. A dust-covered truck lumbers up the dirt road and passes beneath the Ward Dairy sign. The flatbed with its hulking cargo pulls into the farmyard. Carved birds-eye maple legs and foot pedals protrude from beneath the quilted packing blankets. Nettie recognizes the piano, a wedding gift from her parents. It's the same piano she grew up with, took lessons on, and played each day, in her childhood home in Victoria.

'Probably could have bought a new one for what it cost to bring it up,' Gus's voice whispers in her ear. Nettie smiles.

Gus places his hands over her eyes and leads her to the side of the farmhouse. His first surprise on this her wedding day. He pulls his hands away to reveal the rose garden. It is not her new husband's wedding gift itself so much as the thought that pleases her. The fact that this pragmatic man secretly worked so hard to produce a romantic tribute to her middle name brings tears to her eyes.

Wedding guests gather behind her.

'Well, he's no gardener by any stretch of the imagination,' Ma Cooper's voice says. 'When Gus started tilling a small strip of soil between the house and the dairy, Manny and I wondered what he was up to. We watched him mix wheelbarrow after wheelbarrow full of manure from the pile behind the barn, with soil. I was beginning to think he had flipped his lid. Finally he came in and asked us what roses to plant.'

'Frivolous,' Nettie's new mother-in-law, Manny, snorts. 'I said it then, and I'm saying it now. Frivolous. I wasn't letting him have any of my vegetable garden to waste on flowers.'

'I told him to go with yellow tea roses,' Ma Cooper's voice continues. 'He planted the bushes along the fence. Once they were in we watched Gus stand back and contemplate the effect. It wasn't good enough. Oh, no. He decided it wasn't quite right and dug a larger strip, tilled, manured and planted the red American Beauties. Then he tilled, manured, and planted again, and again, until what started out as a simple border of tea roses turned into this.'

Nettie stands before Gus's labour of love, a profusion of colours, sizes and varieties of roses in an enormous fenced garden, complete with a cedar trellis and an arbour over the gate.

'Well, I've had about as much gardening as a man needs in his lifetime,' Gus's laughing voice recedes into the dark.

Now she sits on the iron bed in the old miner's cabin by the lake. Gus has fixed up the old one room shack for their honeymoon. Another surprise. She watches Gus blow out the kerosene lamp. He reaches for her in the dark. Nettie's final surprise, in this day of surprises, rings hollow and disappointing.

Nettie wakes, still she hangs on to the images. She wills her life's scenes to play out. She can almost hear the hum of the walk-in cooler in the dairy below as Gus snores beside her. Boyer is born while they live in the room above the dairy. On the day after Gus's father dies of a heart attack, they take their one-year-old son and move in with Gus's widowed mother. Gus adds a downstairs bedroom and a sunroom to the farmhouse. Nettie's dream of her own home disappears.

No matter how she tries, Nettie never grows close to her mother-in-law. Still, they are cordial. Enough so that, as Nettie's family grows, Manny teaches her how to can, to preserve, and bake along with many other skills so foreign to Nettie, but necessary as the wife of a farmer. Nettie even feels some grief when, at the age of sixty-one — after gutting twenty-seven chickens at the kitchen table — Gus's mother lays down for a nap one afternoon and never gets up. Pregnant with her fourth child when she finds her mother-in-law's lifeless body, Nettie fights back the joy she feels at the thought of an extra bedroom. Even now a wave of guilt rises as she allows the scene to replay one last time.

They're all gone now: Ma Cooper, Manny and Gus. Morgan and Carl have moved so far away. And Natalie. Natalie was the first to leave. Nothing is the same any more. Even the rose garden no longer exists. But Boyer is still out at the farm. Boyer and the piano.

Home. She wants to go home, to give herself over to the soothing, healing sounds of music once again.

She sits in the parlour. She will play Natalie's favourite song; maybe the notes will hurry her daughter home. Then she can tell her.

She pushes back the wooden lid and places her hands on the ivory keys. Her fingers deftly find the chords. But no matter how hard she presses no sound comes.

Chapter Nineteen

THE BUS LEAVES me at Cache Creek. I eat my lunch outside the motel restaurant that serves as a bus depot while I wait for my connection to Kelowna. Two hours to kill.

I feel a nagging regret kindling over my stubbornness in not allowing Vern to drive me to Atwood. I try to ignore the meaning behind his words this morning. His unfinished sentence about not having a chance to meet my mother. But he's right. Her dying is more a reality than a probability. A spark of fear ignites in the pit of my stomach. The fear that I might be too late.

I push aside the last of my salad. My notebooks and laptop are spread out on the table top, open, ready, waiting for words to flow from thin air to keyboard, to hard drive. Nothing comes. I am working on a series of articles about northern women for the *Prince George Chronicle*. Inspiration wanes as I travel south.

Before me a swimmer does laps in the motel pool. I watch indifferently as an arm arches up. Water cascades over tanned skin, a strawberry blond head lifts and turns from side to side. Something familiar wakes me to the moment. I am sure the swimmer is Ken.

Kenneth Jones, my second husband. I'm afraid to look too closely. How would I feel if he stood up, removed his goggles, and walked toward me? What would we say to each other? But no, no it can't be.

Still, each time the swimmer's head comes up for air I'm less certain. The features, the shape of the back, the long arms, are all my ex-husband's. But the way this swimmer carries himself is not the way the man I was married to for nine years did. The constantly nervous Ken that I knew would never have glided through the water with such self-control. He would have stopped many times to see who was watching, to flash a timorous smile, as if apologizing for being there, for taking up space. And yet, as I watch him, almost mesmerized by oblique possibility, I am not sure. It occurs to me that perhaps the anxiety, the lack of confidence, was only there when I was. Maybe this is who he is now that I am not in his life, not threatening to leave.

As if I have willed him to, the swimmer stands in the middle of a lap. He pulls off his goggles and wipes a hand over his face and shakes the excess water away. He looks at me, then through me. I am of no more importance in this stranger's life than he is in mine. I don't even see now what it was about him that brought Ken – who I haven't seen for over fifteen years – to mind. The men in your life never really go away; they only disappear. Or you do.

Vern pointed out not long ago that my staying power in marriage seems to be ten years. We were in our basement getting ready for a yard sale when he made the observation. I looked up from the cardboard box I was filling with books. 'Where did that come from?' I asked.

'Just a thought,' he said as he closed one of my photograph albums and replaced it on the shelf.

'You might be right,' I answered and lifted the box of books. 'That's about the time it takes to reach the line.'

'The line?'

'Every relationship has a line. The moment you step over it, love begins to diminish.'

Vern raised an eyebrow. 'What about unconditional love?' he asked.

'Sure, until you cross that line.'

'I don't have a line, Natalie.'

'Everyone has a line. Some are just closer than others.'

I found my family's line when I was seventeen.

Two backpackers interrupt my musing. They throw their bags on the ground beside the next picnic table. The young man sits and leans backward against the tabletop, dreadlocks, nose ring, earrings and all. He stretches his legs and turns his face to the autumn sun. His female companion, wearing a matching army fatigue jacket and baggy pants, joins him. The uniform of rebel youth. They think it's new.

The girl glances at the newspaper stand and shakes her head. 'It's Vietnam all over again,' she says.

I study the faces of two American soldiers staring out from the front page of the *Vancouver Sun* and wonder sadly when the casualties of this war will stop having names and become part of a body count.

While the two backpackers debate America's involvement in Iraq – another war based on lies – I want to tell them that it's not quite the same, one difference being that the soldiers serving in Iraq and Afghanistan are there by choice. No draft or conscription has forced them to choose between armed combat or fleeing their country. Yet.

And that freedom to choose is in large part thanks to young men like River Jordan who defied the system back then. Still, the current events are so confusing. It's a changed world. And harder to hang on to the simplistic '60's belief that, 'if there were no soldiers there would be no wars.'

Chapter Twenty

'It's an ill wind that blows no good,' Mom was fond of saying. But I wonder what she would have called the winds that blew River Jordan into our lives.

'The winds of discontent,' River called them one night when the conversation turned to the protests sweeping through the university and college campuses of America. He told us that for him, those winds began in Washington D.C. the year before.

'On November 2, 1965,' he said, 'beneath Defense Secretary Robert McNamara's Pentagon window, a young Quaker pacifist, Norman Morrison, doused himself in gasoline. Then he lit a match.

'A split second before he exploded into flames,' River went on, his voice growing quieter, 'he handed his one-year-old daughter to a bystander.'

I gave an involuntary shudder as the image of a human fireball flashed through my mind.

River looked up and his eyes met mine. 'When I heard the news in my dorm room at Montana State University,' he said, 'I felt that same shudder in my soul.' He reached into his jean pocket. 'The next day I found this article on the front page of the New York Times.' He pulled a folded newspaper clipping from his wallet.

As he passed it to Boyer I caught the headline; 'Vietnam Foe Burns To Death.'

'It was the word "foe" that caught me,' River said. 'How easily they used that word. I knew it wasn't meant that way, but to me if felt as if to be in opposition to the war made him the enemy.'

While Boyer read, my father cleared his throat and pushed his chair back. He left the table and slipped out the door as the article was passed around. When it reached me I read the fading words.

The protester's widow has issued this statement: 'Norman Morrison has given his life today to express his concern over the great loss of life and human suffering caused by the war in Vietnam. He was protesting our government's deep military involvement in this war. He felt that all citizens must speak their convictions about our country's action.

'Norman Morrison woke me up,' River said after the article was back in his wallet. 'I couldn't ignore what was happening any longer. I wasn't willing to make his sacrifice but I could stand up and be counted.'

He told us that after he left university he began marching in protests, attending rallies and sit-ins across the country. 'I believed I was exercising my democratic right to protest,' he said. 'But with the National Guard and the police attacking demonstrators, the streets and campuses of America don't look very democratic right now.' He sighed then added, 'Even the student movement is becoming militant. When my draft card came it was an easy decision to burn it.'

The table was silent. Neither Morgan nor Carl, or any of their friends, had a witty comeback for River's quiet words that day.

It was obvious from the first that he was different from the usual strays who found their way out to our farm. Like Boyer, River had no need to fill the empty spaces in conversation with words. His quiet maturity made the constant bantering between all the town kids who crowded around our table seem like mindless chatter.

Indirectly, I guess, all those young people could be held responsible for everything that happened after River. If they hadn't crowded Jake out, River would never have come to us.

Like each person in our family, while Jake lived with us he had his customary place at mealtime. He sat on the opposite end of the table from Dad, beside Boyer. Guests either squeezed in on the bench with Morgan and Carl or pulled extra chairs up beside Mom and me. If anyone dared sit in Jake's chair, he grabbed his plate and filled it up before slamming out the door.

Mom blamed our expanding circle of friends for his leaving. 'Poor old Jake,' she said after, 'he just couldn't tolerate all those young people.'

Whatever the reason, out of the blue one day, Jake packed up and said, 'Well, guess it's time for me to move on,' as if he had been there for a few weeks instead of over twenty years. Then he surprised all of us, and the entire town I'm sure, by moving in with Widow Beckett. On the day he left, he and the widow, who had never been known to even talk to each other, much less have a relationship, were married at the town's courthouse. We saw little of either of them after that. On the following Monday, Ma Cooper arrived as usual, for ironing day. She appeared stunned and, for once, at a loss for words.

The loss of her sidekick didn't slow Ma Cooper down for long though. She continued her weekly updates of the local goings-on in our little town each Monday. Her stories were even more embellished when she had an audience. I think she enjoyed shocking the girls who filled our kitchen then as much as Morgan and Carl enjoyed teasing them.

One Monday afternoon, not long after River arrived, Elizabeth-Ann and I sat at the kitchen table helping Mom can peaches. Our hands were wrinkled and stained orange from peeling and pitting. Every once in a while Elizabeth-Ann let out a shriek at the sight of a slithering earwig side-winding its way out of the pits of the over-ripe fruit. The air in the kitchen was heavy with the aroma of baking bread and boiling syrup. Steam hissed from the large blue canning pot as it bubbled and rocked on the stove.

Ma Cooper stood at the ironing board, the loose white flesh of her huge bare arms swayed in rhythm with her heavy-handed ironing.

'It's not decent the way some of those girls are strutting around town,' she said as she pulled a blue smock middy from the board and hung it up.

We all knew 'those' girls were the very ones whose uniforms she was working up a sweat ironing. Like Mom she was a hardworking member of the Catholic Ladies Auxiliary. Her deeds may have been charitable, but her comments about the girls from Our Lady of Compassion seldom were.

Everyone in town knew that the school for girls next to St Helena's Hospital was really a home for unwed mothers run by the Catholic Church. 'City girls,' Ma went on. 'Their families send their bad girls up here when they get caught. Guess they think we don't care here in the sticks!'

I had often heard Ma and other women from the church complain about the idea of these girls walking around town and the influence they might have on their own daughters. But Mom was always ready to defend them.

'They're just kids who've made a mistake,' she said. 'Kids who deserve our "compassionate understanding",' she reminded Ma.

Every week Dad donated milk to the home. And Mom always seemed to find extra eggs or cream to send along with him. Once, when I was young, while Dad was making a delivery, I peeked in through a hole in the thick hedge. The way Ma Cooper talked about those girls, I expected them to have horns. The ones behind the hedge didn't look much different from the teenage girls in our town, with the exception that they all seemed to have various sizes of watermelons tucked beneath their identical blue smocks. They were not weeping or praying, as Ma Cooper seemed to think they should be, but talking and laughing with each other as they lounged on the lawn in the morning sunshine.

'Bold as brass,' Ma went on as she ironed. 'I saw two of them walk into the post office on Saturday. Those girls have no shame.'

'Now, Ma,' Mom said while she opened the oven to retrieve a batch of bread, 'they need fresh air and exercise as much as anyone else. Maybe more.'

Just as Ma's mouth began to form a reply, the screen door screeched open. Without entering the kitchen River leaned in and placed a brown grocery bag on the corner of the counter. 'Here's your lids for the mason jars, Nettie,' he said. His smile took everyone in, then the screen door closed behind him.

'Thanks for picking them up,' Mom called after him as she placed a steaming loaf on the sideboard. She removed her mitts then picked up the bag as she gazed out the screen door.

'That young man is too handsome for his own good,' Ma Cooper sniffed as soon as River was out of earshot. 'He reminds me of the hired man who worked for old Angus and Manny years ago.'

Mom and I rolled our eyes at each other. We knew there would be no stopping Ma. She would tell the story of my grandparents and the farm hand yet again.

'That fella was a hard worker too, but, oh, he had an eye for Manny,' she told us. 'Guess he figured he was too handsome for anyone to resist. Wouldn't stop pestering your grandmother whenever they were alone. She never told Angus 'cause she was afraid to lose the help. She figured she could handle him herself. But he kept at her, making rude suggestions that drove your gramma crazy. Then one day when your grandpa was out delivering the milk, that cocky young man came into the kitchen while Manny was alone. She was standing here chopping meat at this very table.'

Mom breathed an exaggerated sigh as she sliced peaches into jars. We'd both heard this story before and knew where it was going, but Ma was telling it for the new ears in the room.

'He started teasing Manny that they could have some fun while Angus was away,' Ma went on. 'Your gramma told him to git and just ignored him. She kept working. Next thing she knew he was standing right beside her whispering, "I got something for ya, Manny." Before she knew it he'd unbuttoned his pants, flapped his pecker right out there onto the table, saying, proud as punch, "How'd ya like that?" as if it was some gift he was presenting!' Ma stopped for only a moment to catch her breath and retrieve another uniform from the basket.

Elizabeth-Ann stopped peeling fruit and stared open-mouthed at Ma.

'Well, Manny, she kept on chopping that meat, staring straight ahead.' Ma Cooper pantomimed the motions on the ironing board, 'Chop, chop, chop and then, WHAM! The cleaver flew to the side and clean took off half of his … his … well, you know what.'

Elizabeth-Ann gasped. She looked from Ma, to me, then to Mom who shrugged her shoulders to confirm that as far as she knew, the story was true. Elizabeth-Ann thought for a moment, then in a hushed voice asked, 'Did he die? What happened to the … to the … to it? Could they sew it back on?'

Ma Cooper brushed the questions away, a satisfied smile creasing her face. 'Don't know,' she shrugged. 'He just disappeared. Was never heard from again.'

I shivered. Once again the story left me with the image of a faceless man running out of our kitchen door and down the road clutching the remaining stub of his blood-spurting penis. Only this time the image had a face. The face of Mr Ryan.

Ma Cooper unplugged the iron. 'Can't help but notice that Gus takes this here young man on the milk round with him every day,' she said in a coy voice. 'Maybe he's afraid to leave him alone with you, Nettie.'

Mom blushed, then gave a short laugh and said, 'There's no such thing as alone on this farm.'

Chapter Twenty-One

DURING THE TIME he was with us River never sought anyone's company; neither did he avoid it. He seemed as comfortable left alone or spending time with whoever showed up in his room above the dairy.

Once Boyer started spending his evenings there I tagged along. I sat at the chrome table in the corner and listened as Boyer read the poetry of Dylan Thomas, or River played the guitar and sang mournful Bob Dylan songs. The more I saw them together the more I saw how similar they were in their quiet accepting ways. I watched from the sidelines with a growing envy over the time they spent together. I wasn't quite sure if the twinge of resentment I felt was directed at Boyer or River.

By default, Elizabeth-Ann, instead of Boyer, was now my best friend. We became co-conspirators, plotting ways for the four of us to be together. One night, we pushed our way, uninvited, into Boyer's new Ford Edsel, as he and River headed into the Roxy Theatre on Main Street. In the rear-view mirror I saw Boyer's indulgent half-smile as we made ourselves comfortable in the back seat. I knew my brother would deny me nothing back then.

Inside the darkened theatre we followed him and River to the middle seats of the back row. Before Elizabeth-Ann climbed over their knees to sit on the other side of Boyer, she nudged me to sit down beside River. Not nearly as bold as her, I plunked down and stared straight ahead, but not before catching the amused smiles on both my brother and River's faces. Elizabeth-Ann and I could pretend all we wanted that this was a date, but it was obvious it was not. Still, I enjoyed the looks of envy when our high-school friends waved hello.

The movie was *Cool Hand Luke*. Morgan and Carl had seen it three times before they convinced Boyer and River to go. I don't remember much about the story – I was too aware of the closeness of River's body to concentrate on the show – but I do remember thinking how much he resembled Paul Newman. Morgan and Carl thought so too. They talked about the movie and for weeks after, compared River to Cool Hand Luke. Mom chased them out of her kitchen one afternoon when she caught them about to boil up dozens of her eggs to see if River could beat Cool Hand Luke's record.

If either Boyer or River minded the two of us shadowing them, neither of them let on. Like everyone else we were always welcomed when we showed up in River or Boyer's rooms.

Folk songs, poetry and talk of world events, would only hold Morgan and Carl's attention for so long though, before they headed back to the house to dance to rock and roll 45s out in the sunroom. On many evenings Elizabeth-Ann and I had to choose between following the gang to the sunroom, or out to the lake, or staying to listen to poetry and songs of protest that we didn't quite understand. For me there was no contest.

Every summer my parents held a barbecue at the farm on the Labour Day weekend. Half the town showed up. Mom loved those get-togethers. I'm sure it was the highlight of her year, and as close to a family picnic as she could get. She worked for days preparing. Everyone who helped with the haying was rewarded with thick steaks, endless potato salad, Mom's fresh baked bread and platters of steaming hot corn-on-the-cob drenched in her fresh-churned butter. And, of course, huckleberry everything – pies, tarts, and cobblers. Mom hardly sat down the entire day. She kept plates full, and drinks refilled, while my father and the men played horseshoes and the women sat in gossip circles on the lawn. I noticed she danced expertly around, or ignored, any questions and references to River being family.

With all the extra hands, the evening milking was done early, leaving my brothers and their friends free to head out to the small lake by the old miner's cabin. It was their concession to River's presence. Before he came, on hot summer evenings we all piled into the back of the pick-up truck and headed down to Blue Lake, ten minutes on the States side of the border. Both the American and Canadian Customs officers were so used to seeing one of my brothers at the wheel of the old blue farm truck loaded with teenagers, that they usually nodded us through. We stopped going down after River came.

As we all headed up the road to the lake that day, I turned to wave at Mom. She sat in the shade by the side of the house, between Dr Mumford and Father Mac. I noticed the expression in her eyes as she watched us walk away. I knew that look, the look of an uninvited child, left behind to endure the droning conversation of adults, while everyone rushed off to play. It made me want to stop and call out, 'come on with us'. But, of course, I did not. I turned and joined the laughing crowd of young people hurrying up the road with towels and bathing suits hanging from their shoulders.

It was not much of a lake, more of a pond, but large enough for swimming. Lily pads and weeds floated around the muddy edges.

Years before, Morgan and Carl had built a wooden raft. As kids we used long poles to push it around the lake. That summer someone anchored it in the middle.

Everyone took turns changing in the abandoned log cabin by the lake. The old miner's shack had been there long before our grandfather homesteaded this land. When we were children, Morgan and Carl and I used it for a playhouse, dragging out bits and pieces of old furniture. If I had paid attention, I might have noticed Boyer checking out the cabin. But I was too busy being aware of River's every move to notice Boyer's interest in the old shack.

I think most teenagers from town must have been at the lake that day. They splashed in the water, lounged out on the raft, or on towels spread in the meadow grass. Every once in a while Elizabeth-Ann snapped a picture with her new Instamatic – another one of the many trinkets her father was forever buying her.

She caught Carl and Morgan wearing girls' petal bathing caps on their heads and towels wrapped around their waists like skirts. They hold their arms up in a clowning hula dance. Behind them Boyer leans against the doorway of the cabin, his head almost touching the top of the low frame. I don't know who talked Boyer into coming with us to the lake, but when Elizabeth-Ann showed me her pictures the following week, I noticed him in the background of each photograph. Even in the one of River.

I kept that picture, folded down the middle, tucked inside my wallet, or whatever book I happened to be reading. Boyer's image showed on the front, with River's hidden away on the other side. I took the photograph out when no one was around and turned it over. I studied River's face secretly, memorized it, and, just as any adolescent might do I supposed, I sometimes even kissed it.

Elizabeth-Ann's camera caught River sitting backward at the

141

picnic table, his guitar in his arms. He is aware of the camera's eye on him as he strums. His smile flashes carelessly into the future. A smile I pretended was for me.

Boyer sits on the ground leaning against the trunk of an old apple tree.

The tree, an accident of a windblown seed, or planted by whoever once inhabited the cabin, was gnarled and ancient. It grew so close to the cabin it seemed to be a part of it. Branches had rotted, dried, then broken off. It couldn't have had much life left in it. Still, each spring it sprouted random blossoms and in the fall yielded baskets of translucent green apples. We used the fruit to make pies and apple butter. During those summers the fallen branches provided wood for our campfires, but until I saw the photograph of Boyer sitting beneath the shade of that craggy and twisted old tree, I had given no thought to its beauty.

In the picture, Boyer's elbows rest on his knees; a book is in his hands. He's not reading though. He's gazing over the top of the pages at River. Unlike River, Boyer is unaware of the camera catching this moment. The usual detached indifference is gone from his face, replaced by an expression I could not read.

When I first saw the photograph, I was struck by the contrast between River's open smile, and Boyer's intense focus. I was blind to the similarities in those unguarded expressions.

That day, I watched from shore as everyone swam in the lake. The girls resembled huge flowers bobbing in the water in their brightly coloured petal bathing caps, which Morgan and Carl found so hilarious. Some soaked up the dying rays of the sun out on the raft. They leaned back in their two-piece bathing suits, trying too hard to look like the swimsuit models of their teenage magazines. No snapshots were taken of those poses.

The boys did posturing of their own, diving and racing, competing for the admiration of female eyes. Morgan and Carl seemed unaware of the contrast between their tanned torsos and their pasty white legs as they performed cannonballs off the raft, sending showering sprays of water over the screaming girls drying in the sun there. Boyer and River swam leisurely out to the raft and back – enough to cool off – then retreated. Boyer to his book, River to his music.

I was certain Elizabeth-Ann had warned the girls off, because there was surprisingly little flirting with Boyer or River. The girls concentrated their attentions on Morgan and Carl and their friends.

'Hey Nat,' Carl hollered from the raft. 'Com'on in.'

I ignored the calls as I set out desserts and drinks on the table where River sat picking at the guitar strings and singing softly. I still can't hear Dylan's 'Love Minus Zero/No Limit', without thinking of River and that summer day. As I listened to River singing the confusing lyrics about a lover who speaks like silence, I fantasized it was me he sang about.

I discovered that summer that being in love changes you. It makes you want. I wanted to be nice. I wanted to be pretty. I allowed Elizabeth-Ann, who wanted to be a hairdresser, to cut my hair into a pixie. I still was not ready for the teased bouffant hairstyles all the other girls were wearing.

And I wanted to be thin. Not long after River arrived, I began to eat nothing unless it was first drowned in vinegar, another trick taught to me by Elizabeth-Ann. By September I was no longer the pudgy milkmaid. No longer 'Nat the Fat'.

Still, I was reluctant to change into my bathing suit. I knew my new lean body looked more like a boy's than like the bronzed bodies of the girls in the water. My skin was as pale as my brothers' skinny legs. Swimming in Blue Lake with my brothers and our friends was one thing, but wearing a bathing suit in front of River was quite another.

I still wore my pedal pushers and a T-shirt. My bathing suit, wrapped in a towel, lay on the counter in the cabin. The basket of desserts and drinks was my excuse to avoid putting it on.

River looked up from the guitar and swung his head to flick his wet hair back. 'Just like your mom,' he grinned at me. 'Always feeding the masses.'

I didn't mind being compared to my mother. In any way. Especially by River. I felt my heart swelling at the softness of his voice, the intensity of his eyes.

'You'd better start eating some of that though,' he said, nodding at the food I was placing on the table. 'Or there won't be anything left of you.'

'Com'on, Natalie,' Morgan's voice taunted across the water. 'If you don't come in, we'll come and get you.'

I continued to ignore them, until he and Carl dove in and headed to shore. The dark waters roiled as others followed, laughing and calling out warnings that I was going in with my clothes on.

'Better to go in on your own than be thrown in,' River warned me while he continued to strum his guitar.

'Right,' I said and headed to the cabin. I knew I had some time before Carl and Morgan would reach shore. None of us Wards were strong swimmers.

Inside the cabin I changed in the dark. Once I was back outside I hurried to the lake, anxious to be hidden by the water. By the time my feet sunk into the muddy bottom, everyone was arriving at the shore. They splashed and teased as I waded in. Suddenly I stood frozen, the hidden muck oozing between my toes.

'Grab her feet,' Morgan called to Carl. 'I'll get her arms.'

I was surrounded, trapped, more afraid of making a scene, having the attention on me, than of the water. It felt as if the mud was quicksand, as if my lungs were drowning in the air. I began to hyperventilate.

'Wait,' River called out. 'Let her go in on her own.' He laid his guitar on the table, then joined me in the water. He moved backwards in front of me. I lifted my feet out of the sucking mud and followed. When he was waist high, he said, 'Now lean forward.' His voice was gentle, easy, for me only. 'Just lay on top of the water and let it take you.'

I followed him as he moved backward slowly in the water. 'Keep breathing,' he said.

'Yeah, it's kind of essential,' I tried joking, lowering my torso into the water and paddling toward him. River laughed and lay back. He backstroked to the raft, rolled under and came up beside me. His arms made clean, sure strokes through the water as we swam side by side. He lifted himself up onto the raft, water streaming from his body. He held his arm out to me, then pulled me up onto the wooden boards.

I don't know why I felt such triumph in that moment, why I no longer cared about my pasty, exposed skin. I only know I felt safe being there, on that raft, alone with River. It was enough. It was everything. On shore we were forgotten. Everyone was caught up in another bout of splashing and screaming. I barely heard them. And even though the mountains had claimed the last rays of the evening sun, I felt warm, exhilarated. The shore seemed far way, another world.

Then I noticed Boyer still sitting under the apple tree. Watching us. He peered over his book with an expression I did not recognize.

For a moment I felt an involuntary shiver as if a rude wind had interrupted the serenity of the lake.

I lifted my arm and waved.

Either Boyer did not see my wave or he ignored it. Bending his head down, he went back to reading his book.

Chapter Twenty-Two

GHOSTS DANCE ON the edge of my vision. They follow me, stalk me, then vanish when I take notice. I turn quickly when I see them flirting with daylight in the corner of my eyes, but I am too slow. Or they are too quick. The teasing shadows evaporate before I can catch up to the blurred movements. But I know they are there. And I know who they are. I just don't know how to make them go away.

Even here, sitting on this bus that is speeding into the past, I catch a sudden dark movement in my peripheral vision. I know if I look up from my laptop it will go away. I cannot resist. I turn and see him sitting in the seat across the aisle. My father. He is wearing his dark blue Sunday suit, a red poppy pinned to his lapel. He feels me watching and turns his head.

An unfamiliar face stares back at me. A questioning smile forms on his lips. 'Do I know you?' the look asks. The face is that of a stranger. There is no Sunday suit. But the poppy on the tattered black windbreaker is real. I have been caught again, played with by the shadows and the tricks of the afternoon light flashing through the bus windows.

It was the poppy that did it. It's only mid October. Far too soon for this Remembrance Day flower. My father was the only person I knew to wear one this early. Every year in the middle of October he took last year's poppy down from the visor in the cab of his truck. He pinned it to his lapel and wore it until the Legionnaires appeared on the streets with boxes of new ones strapped around their necks. My father was always one of their first customers. Only then would he discard last year's dusty felt flower, replacing it with the new one purchased from the old soldiers. After the Remembrance Day ceremony, he removed the poppy from his lapel and stuck it on the visor, where it stayed, ready for the same ritual the following year.

I never questioned this yearly switching of poppies. By the time I wondered about it, it was too late to ask.

My father never went to war. Like Dr Mumford he was denied enlistment. I once heard him joke that delivering babies, and delivering milk, were equally essential to the home war effort. Knowing how he felt about guns, I often wondered if his regret over not being allowed to fight for his country was feigned. Still, every November 11, my father started the milk run early, finishing in time to attend the annual Armistice Day parade.

The last times we went as a family was during the years River was with us.

My father still had not warmed up to River by that first November. Yet, one afternoon I came into the kitchen to find the two of them huddled together at the table.

'It wouldn't cost much,' River was saying as he scribbled notes on a series of diagrams. 'We can use a lot of equipment parts you already have.'

I peered over Dad's shoulder at the intricate plans spread out on the table. He said nothing. He lit a cigarette and let a small stream of smoke escape from the corner of his mouth. I watched as River went over the diagrams and written instructions. Then I noticed that, as he explained the automated system for removing manure from the milking stalls, he had stopped using written notations and was drawing more detailed sketches.

The following week, the system was built and installed in the barn. 'Shoulda' thought of this years ago,' Dad said when he stood back and watched as an oil drum, cut in half length ways to form a carrier, attached to overhead pulleys, slid neatly above the concrete floor. Not long after that River began to go with Dad on the milk route even on weekends.

Whatever the reason Dad took River with him on the milk route, I didn't care. For me it was a relief. It meant I didn't need to worry about the chance I might have to deliver milk to the Ryans' house. I wondered if River had ever seen Mr Ryan behind the basement window. Had he ever caught sight of the image I thought I remembered from years ago? Somehow I knew he had not.

At breakfast on Remembrance Day, however, Dad asked me to come along on the milk route. Mom, Morgan and Carl would come in with Boyer to meet us for the services. I grabbed my coat and followed Dad outside, excited at the thought of sitting so close to River.

River was waiting for us by the dairy. Even though he had told us that wearing poppies was no longer a tradition in the States, a red felt flower was pinned to the left side of his jacket. When we reached the truck, Dad said, 'No need for you to come, Richard. Natalie's helping me today.'

I felt a pin prick into my nervous excitement. Dad opened his door. 'We're all headed to the Remembrance Day ceremony afterwards,' he said. 'I'm sure you're not interested in that.'

River opened the passenger door and motioned me in ahead of him. 'Well, if it's all the same to you, sir,' he said, ignoring Dad's caustic tone. 'I'll come along on the milk run. Then I'd like to attend the ceremony with you all.'

My father hoisted himself into his seat and muttered, 'A pretty strange place for a pacifist isn't it?'

'Well, I don't know about that, sir,' River replied, climbing into the truck, bringing the scent of freshly shampooed hair with him. 'But isn't Remembrance Day here much the same as Veterans Day, at home? Isn't the purpose the same? To remember the horrors of war, and to honour those who died? I've attended both Veterans Day, and Memorial Day services with my mother and grandfather every year for as long as I can remember.'

'What for?' Dad grumbled. 'I thought you were against war.'

River banged the truck door shut. I felt the heat of his body as he settled in the seat beside me. 'Yes, sir,' he replied, 'I am. But, for me, today isn't about protest.' Then his voice became even quieter. 'It's about my father and my uncle,' he said slowly. 'To remember them. They both died in the Battle of Okinawa, three months before I was born.'

There was silence for a moment. Then my father reached down and threw the truck into gear.

It doesn't take long for the small procession to march down Main Street in Atwood each November 11. That morning, with the smell of burned leaves and the promise of snow in the crisp autumn air, we stood on the sidewalk and watched the silent parade make its way to the Cenotaph.

A handful of aging veterans, wearing tight-fitting uniforms, which wafted the scent of mothballs in their wake, came first. They marched in stoic and proud rhythm, staring ahead to some place those of us on the side of the road could not see. A Scottish piper, his bagpipes held ready and silent on his arm, followed – the pleats of his kilt swaying to the beat of the lone drummer. Then the young cadets with serious faces brought up the rear. They marched by, slow, solemn, reverent. There was no hurry this day. The dead would still be dead when they reached the granite war memorial at the end of Main Street.

I looked over at River standing erect as the procession moved down the street. I thought about his words, about his father, and uncle. For the first time, I felt the reality, the sadness of this memorial to fallen soldiers.

After the small troupe filed by, those of us watching began to fall in behind. The wives and mothers of soldiers, present and gone, joined in. Then, as they did every year, my father followed behind with his three sons. Before Dad started marching, I saw him turn and wave at River to join them. Mom and I brought up the rear.

At the end of Main Street, the crowd gathered around the Cenotaph, a looming monument honouring Atwood's fallen sons. During the ceremony, a number of women, including Widow Beckett, stepped forward to place poppy wreaths below the brass plaque, which bore the names of those lost in both world wars. Following two minutes of silence, gunshots broke through the air. They echoed through the streets and the sound bounced off the mountain tops around us. As each shot rang out, I saw my father's body flinch as violently as if he had been struck. And, on either side of him, I noticed both Boyer and River's shoulders jerk with the identical involuntary spasm.

After the service, as we did every other year, our family headed to the Atwood branch of the Royal Canadian Legion to join the local veterans for lunch. As we strode down the street I spotted Jake up ahead with Widow Beckett at his side. My father called out and they turned to wait. It was the first time I had seen Jake since he left the farm. I did a double take, surprised to see that he could actually smile.

While Mom and the Widow Beckett greeted each other with hugs, my father shook Jake's hand. 'So, looks like married life agrees with ya,' Dad said. Each of my brothers greeted Jake and shook his hand. Then Dad gestured to River and said, 'Jake, I'd like ya to meet our new man, Rich … er, I mean, River. River Jordan.'

After lunch, I climbed into the cab of the milk truck with Dad and River. Once again I felt the electric thrill of sitting so close to River. As we drove home I noticed two poppies pinned to the overhead visors.

Chapter Twenty-Three

THE HEADLIGHT BEAMS stab through the blackness, cut it wide
open and leave a gash of white-lined highway as we plunge into
the night. They're out there. I can't see them, but I can feel the
mountains as we speed from summit to summit through the
rugged Cascades.

The roads are bare; the snow hasn't arrived yet. Still, I am certain
that if the invisible peaks looming over us are not dusted in white,
they soon will be. Before long snow banks will flank the highway.
Banks that can grow to heights taller than this bus.

Snow was a constant in our lives for four to five months of the
year while I was growing up. Every winter our farm became a
labyrinth of trenches between the house and the outbuildings. Most
mornings Dad had to clear the yard between the barn and the dairy
with the tractor; the plow blade pushing the mountains of snow
into the front pasture.

The snowfall was unusually heavy the year River came.

'Man, I've never seen so much white!' River called out to me as he
trudged his way through the fresh powder after the first overnight
storm.

'Ha! Just wait,' I puffed. I lifted my shovel and tossed a load of
snow from the walkway over my shoulder.

'Here, let me do that for you,' he said and reached for my shovel.

'No, I like this job,' I leaned on the handle and nodded at the porch. 'Get your own,' I laughed.

'Ah, a women's-libber,' he grinned. 'Good for you.'

Fat flakes fell silently onto his wool cap and shoulders. They landed on his cheek and thick lashes where they melted from the heat. And I felt myself melt as he reached over and brushed off my face with his woollen mitten. Even in the cold I could feel the blush rise. I lowered my head and dug my shovel in while River turned and ran up the porch steps. Then just as quickly he was back. We worked side by side on the path as the snowfall thickened, making a mockery of our progress.

Over the months I had become used to River's presence. More than used to it. I couldn't imagine my life or my family without him. I saw him almost every day and except for the times he went on his juice fasts – 'to clear body and mind,' he said – he shared most meals with us. It was hard to remember a time when he didn't sit across the table from me.

After we reached the gate River looked down the road. 'Good thing the milk truck's four-wheel-drive,' he mused. 'Or we'd have to hook up the horses to pull us into town.'

'It wasn't so long ago that we did just that,' Dad answered him from the porch. 'And sometimes we still do. Eh, Nat?'

Before I had a chance to respond, Dad called out to River, 'Looks like ya missed breakfast.'

'That's okay,' River answered as Dad came down the steps. 'Natalie and I like this job.' He grinned at me, then handed me his shovel so that he could take the thermos and a brown paper bag from Dad.

'Toast,' Dad nodded at the bag. 'Can't have my co-pilot starving.'

I watched as they walked together over to the truck, the sound of fresh snow crunching under their boots with each step. River peered into the bag and said something I couldn't hear. Dad threw his head back and laughed out loud. They looked so at ease with each other that it made me smile.

Lately I had noticed that River and Dad took longer and longer to deliver the milk each morning. Morgan and Carl had noticed too. Dad brushed off their teasing. He told them that when he stopped to pick up his newspaper at Gentry's they stayed for coffee so River could get to know the locals. River never disputed this explanation, but I had a hard time imagining Dad leaning over his paper at the counter, pretending to read, while River chatted it up with Mrs Gentry or the other patrons.

Yet, even though Dad told River he could take the weekends off, each day the two of them went together on the milk route.

Except at Christmas. Early Christmas morning Mom and I carried quilts and blankets down to the front of the barn as my brothers harnessed up the horses. Like every other year Mom would ride along in the milk truck with Dad for the Christmas Day deliveries, while my brothers and I followed behind in the flatbed sleigh.

I threw the blankets onto the loose hay on the sleigh when the door above the dairy opened.

'What's this?' River stood at the top of the stairs, tucking his long blond hair into his wool hat. He looked from one of us to the other while our entire family stood waiting with smirks on our faces. We had deliberately kept this part of Christmas a secret to surprise him. We all knew he was missing his mother and grandfather and hoped our Christmas morning tradition would take away some of the sadness of not being with them for the holidays.

'Merry Christmas,' I sang along with everyone, excited at sharing this day with him.

River looked up at Boyer, who stood up on the sleigh, holding the leather reins. 'So what's happening?' River asked.

'Hop on and you'll find out,' Boyer called down.

'It's a hay ride,' I added needlessly, then felt my face redden.

River's blue eyes crinkled into a smile as he glanced over at Mom standing beside the passenger door of the milk truck. 'What about the milk route?' he asked.

She smiled back at him and sung out, 'This is my seat today, River. You go with the kids.' Before she climbed into the cab she looked up at the sky. Stars still twinkled in the grey morning light. She took a deep breath of the crisp air, 'It's going to be a perfect day,' she said and climbed into the cab. As the truck pulled away she leaned out the window and called, 'Don't fall off now.' She said that every year.

Boyer clicked his tongue. The horses leaned into their harnesses and strained forward. River reached under my shoulders and boosted me up, then threw himself onto the sleigh as it began to move.

He crawled up beside me and rested back against the empty wooden boxes stacked at the front of the sleigh. 'And what are these for?' he asked.

'You'll see,' I said.

The horses tossed their heads, fighting the first taste of the bits. Clouds of white vapour puffed up from flared nostrils. Rows of silver bells attached to their manes jangled when they surged forward. As we picked up speed leather harnesses creaked and shifted against horsehide while the sleigh runners glided along soundlessly on the hard-packed snow.

The warm musty fragrance of horse sweat and the sweet smell of hay cut the sharpness of the morning air.

'This is my favourite part of Christmas,' I shouted above the bells.

'And now it's mine too,' River shouted back. He put his arm around my shoulder and hugged me to him. And despite being bundled up I imagined I felt the warmth of his body through my heavy woollen coat.

When the sleigh slowed down on the first hill, I felt a sudden shove from behind. The next thing I knew I was tumbling into a sea of snow, Morgan and Carl's laughter following me. I surfaced and blew out a mouthful of powder as River landed next to me. He rolled over and laughed. He laid back and stared up at the clear sky for a few moments. 'Wow,' he breathed. 'Neat.'

As the sleigh crested the hill he sat up and offered me his hand and we pulled each other up. Like snow-crusted penguins, with arms straight out at our sides, we tottered back to the sleigh. Before we jumped on, River nodded to me, and by unspoken agreement we pelted Morgan and Carl with the snowballs we had hidden in our mitts.

When we pulled off South Valley Road, we all huddled together beneath the quilts as the sleigh glided along the empty highway.

In town, the horses trotted behind the milk truck as Dad and Mom made deliveries. The whole town appeared to be sleeping under a thick white blanket. Yet, at every house we stopped doors flew open. Dad's customers, many in dressing gowns and pyjamas, greeted us with choruses of Christmas wishes. Handshakes and hugs were shared as the sun rose in a clear blue sky. Hot toddies, Christmas cookies and presents were pressed into our hands. By the time we'd finished the bottom half of town the wooden boxes on the sleigh were brimming with gifts and Christmas baking.

Hand-knitted mittens, caps and scarves filled an entire box. Fruit cakes, cookies, squares, homemade jams and preserves filled the others.

River laughed out loud as Morgan and Carl sorted through the bounty and offered up treats. 'Man, all this on top of your Mom's mountains of Christmas baking? Whatever will you do with it all?' he asked as he popped a butter tart into his mouth.

'You'll see,' I answered.

When we reached the end of Main Street, Boyer took off his gloves, cupped his hands together and blew into them. Then he turned the reins over to an eager Carl. I rode between River and Boyer as the horses started the climb to the top part of town. We sat with our legs dangling over the side while River talked about Christmases growing up in Montana. I listened, mesmerized by his voice, as he shared his memories.

'You're so lucky to have a large family,' he told us. 'Pretty hard for an only child to go on a hay ride. But what I did love about Christmas was going carolling. Every year on Christmas Eve, Mom and Granddad and I went from farm to farm visiting and singing Christmas carols.'

'We can do that,' Morgan called and started singing, 'We wish you a Merry Christmas'. Everyone joined, even Boyer, our voices ringing out in song as we glided along the snow-covered streets of town. I wanted the moment never to end.

But it did. As soon as we turned onto Colbur Street.

We stopped in front of the Ryan house. Elizabeth-Ann came hurrying out, carrying a tray of mugs and calling, 'Merry Christmas everyone!' Her mother followed with a steaming jug. Mrs Ryan chirped her season's greetings while she poured hot chocolate into the mugs her daughter held up.

'Well, if it isn't the famous Wards.' Mr Ryan called out from the open door where he stood in his dressing gown. 'Atwood's favourite family. And their long lost American … uh … nephew isn't it?'

'Cousin!' Morgan and Carl cried at the same time, then laughed.

'So,' Mr Ryan asked coming out onto the porch, 'does that make you kissing cousins then?'

I shivered and shrank back between River and Boyer.

River looked from me to Mr Ryan. 'Well, by gosh, sir. I guess it does,' he said in an exaggerated drawl. He turned and smiled down at me. I saw his eyes flicker for an instant over to Boyer, before he took my face between his mittened hands and planted a loud smacking kiss on my cheek.

Morgan and Carl hooted while I sat there momentarily stunned at the touch of River's cheek.

'Well, although I'm sure the ladies like the new milkman here,' Mr Ryan's slurred voice continued, 'I must say I miss the pretty little milkmaid coming to my door.'

Mrs Ryan finished pouring the last mug and glared up at her husband as he stood on the edge of the porch steps, a drink in his hand. She shook her head. 'Go back inside, Gerald, before you catch a cold,' she sighed. 'Or fall down,' she added under her breath.

At the same time both River and Boyer placed their arms protectively around my shoulders. Before the sleigh jerked forward Elizabeth-Ann passed me the last mug and said, 'You're such a lucky duck, Natalie Ward.'

I recognized the envy in her eyes as we pulled away. And as the cocoa and the heat from my brother and River's bodies warmed me, I snuggled even closer.

When the milk route was completed, when the wooden boxes on the sleigh were full-to-bursting, we came to a stop before the building next to the hospital. Mom and Dad climbed out of the truck. They came back to the sleigh where Morgan and Boyer handed them each one of the full boxes. I jumped down and reached for one too.

River passed the box to me, his eyes watching Mom unlatch the heavy wooden gate between the hedges. 'Our Lady Of Compassion, School for Girls', the sign above the gate read. But by then, even River knew what the stone building next to the hospital really was.

'Is this all going here?' he wondered out loud.

'Yes,' Boyer told him as he pushed more boxes to the edge. 'Every year we take most of our Christmas haul from Dad's customers to the home.'

Morgan snickered and said out of the side of his mouth, 'Yeah, kind of ironic given how everyone in the town gossips about this place.'

River jumped down and grabbed a box. Boyer did the same. When they started to follow us Dad glanced at Mom with a cocked eyebrow. Mom hesitated for a moment, then continued through the gate. 'All right,' she called back. 'But just to the front doorstep. Even that will probably throw the nuns into a tizzy. But I'm sure the sight of a few handsome young men will give the young ladies peeking out the windows some Christmas cheer.'

Carl stayed at the reins. When Morgan made no move to leave the sleigh, River called back, 'Aren't you going to come along to add to the young ladies' Christmas thrill?'

Morgan shrugged his shoulders then said, 'Why not?' He jumped down and grabbed a box from the sleigh. He hurried after us, his out of tune voice rising in another round of, 'We wish you a Merry Christmas'.

We all joined in the singing while we deposited box after box on the front steps of the school.

Chapter Twenty-Four

ONE NIGHT IN January, Boyer announced his intention to fix up the old miner's cabin by the lake. I looked up from my plate. No one at the table seemed surprised. Except me.

'What for?' I asked.

'To live in,' he said. 'I'm going to move out there.'

'No!' I blurted without thinking. I glanced quickly at River, wondering how childish I must have sounded.

Boyer ignored my outburst. 'I'm almost twenty-four,' he stated. 'It's time I had my own place. It's less than a ten-minute walk, Natalie. Besides, it's not as if you won't still see me every day.'

The thought of Boyer not being upstairs in the attic room left me with an empty feeling. Yet, for the rest of the winter I became caught up in the plans formulated at our kitchen table. In the spring I joined the work bees along with my brothers, Dad and River. After school and on weekends there were more than enough spare hands busy with hammers and saws. Before long a framed addition with a small bedroom and bathroom was added onto the side of the log cabin.

In April, Boyer moved in. I sat in the cab of the pick-up truck between him and River on the day we drove out with the final load. As we crossed the meadow in the afternoon shadows I thought that the ancient apple tree, which stood so close to the cabin, looked like a sentry keeping guard. Branches curled over the roof like gnarled fingers, possessive of their charge. When I was a child it wouldn't have taken much to convince me that this moss-covered dwelling on the edge of the forest belonged to some witch or wizard of my bedtime fairytales. But it was Boyer's home now. Over the last few months he had turned the old shack into as cozy a nest as his sanctuary in the attic.

As we pulled up to the door, ebony wings rose from the branches above the roof. Harsh voices barked with annoyance at the interruption as the flock of crows took to the sky.

Boyer looked up through the windshield. 'Corvine?' he challenged me.

'That's easy,' I scoffed. I spelled the word out, then said, 'An adjective, pertaining to the crow.'

Boyer opened his door and climbed out of the truck. He shoved his hand into his jeans pocket and came out with a dime.

'I'm too old for that,' I said, suddenly feeling embarrassed at having played this childhood game in front of River.

Boyer tossed the silver coin to me, 'Too good, maybe,' he said, 'but not too old. Never too old.'

River gazed up and began counting the crows as they winged through the sky above the lake. 'Seven crows for a secret never to be told,' he said quoting the last line of the old nursery rhyme.

If I believed in omens I might have shivered at his words. But at the time, if I shivered at all, it was at the thought of my own delicious secret, my feelings for River, which had only grown over the winter.

'I'm sure this old shack has many untold secrets,' Boyer said as he pulled down the tailgate and started to unload the truck.

Inside, he lit the gas lamps. 'Propane will do until I can afford to bring out hydro lines,' he had said when he installed the propane lights and stove.

I've heard it said that cars come to look like their owners. Well, to me, Boyer's new home already looked like him. More exactly, it felt like him, warm, comforting, and safe. The glow from the yellow light reflected on aged wood. I'd spent hours beside Boyer cleaning and re-chinking those square-hewed logs, only to have him place bookshelves against most of them.

As I unpacked and organized the array of novels, which filled most of the boxes, it occurred to me that Boyer had created this space as much as a home for his book collection as for himself.

The heavy wooden door closed and River came in. Over the winter I had watched with envy as Boyer and River's relationship developed into a quiet friendship. Up until that time I'd never seen him spend so much time with anyone except our family and Father Mac.

'That's the last one,' River said placing the box on the table. He breathed an exaggerated sigh and picked up a hardcover book from the top of the box. He looked at the front cover then turned it over to study a photograph of President Kennedy on the back.

'It's hard to believe that in November it will be four years since he was killed,' he mused, then handed *Profiles In Courage* to me. 'I'm curious,' he said. 'What was it like up here – for Canadians – then? How did the news affect you when he was assassinated?'

'I was only twelve,' I said, conscious of River's eyes on me as I spoke. 'I don't think I really understood it then.' I thought for a moment trying to recall how I felt that day. 'I remember our principal coming into our classroom and announcing that President Kennedy had been shot. We were let out of school early. Mostly what I remember was the shocked, even frightened, expressions on the faces of all the teachers huddled outside while we waited for the bus.'

And I remembered Boyer's grim face as he drove everyone home. The following days were the only times I ever saw him spend hours in front of the television. We all sat solemnly in our living room and watched the events in Dallas play out over and over again.

Boyer pulled a chair up to the table and sat down. 'I was stunned,' he said quietly. 'Like most Canadians, I think, I knew we had lost a friend. I remember his visit to Ottawa in 1961. Fifty thousand people gathered on Parliament Hill, trying to catch a glimpse of him and Jackie. I think many saw him as a cross between royalty and a movie star, rather than as a politician. When he died, we mourned him as if he was one of our own. It *felt* as if he were our own.'

The hiss of the propane lights filled the silence. After a moment River spoke. 'I was in my twelfth grade history class when the announcement came over the PA system. Our teacher laid his head on his desk and waved us from the classroom. The halls were eerily silent as we filed out. No one spoke. Even locker doors were opened and closed carefully, silently.'

The shadows grew in the room as River continued. 'That night I met with three of my buddies, Ray, Frankie, and Art. Before Ray's father left for work he placed a bottle of whisky on the coffee table. The four of us sat in front of the TV until the test pattern came on. Then we sat in the dark trying to make sense of it all. Which, of course, couldn't be done. It was surreal. None of us wanted to accept that he had been murdered so easily. We were convinced it was the Russians. We all wanted something bigger to blame than the skinny little man they arrested. As the night wore on, and the whisky bravado grew, talk turned to the possibility of war. And to enlisting. Ray and Art already planned to join up as soon as they graduated. They saw it as a career choice. But neither Frankie, nor I, had any intention of becoming universal soldiers. Yet, the strange thing was there was a moment, a moment when I thought the Russians were behind it – that it could have really meant war – when I imagined myself in a uniform, with a gun in my hands.' He shook his head slowly at his admission.

'Half of us ended up wearing that uniform,' he said. 'Ray was no surprise. But Frankie? Frankie was such a gentle soul. His family had a chicken farm only a few miles from ours. He wasn't going on to university, so he talked to his priest about refusing the draft on religious grounds. The priest convinced him to serve. As a conscientious objector, in a noncombative role. Sure, noncombative, but you still go through boot camp – learn to carry a gun.' River leaned forward and studied his hands. His hair hung loose around his face.

'I got a letter from Ray last spring,' he said without looking up. 'Three days after Frankie arrived in Nam, he and Ray ended up together on a medical supply boat on the Mekong River. They were caught in a sniper attack and ordered to take arms. As Frankie shouldered his gun he begged, "Please God, don't let me kill anyone." As the last word came out of his mouth, a bullet hole appeared in the middle of his forehead. Ray wrote that as Frankie slumped to the deck he was smiling.' River sighed then said, 'I guess his God answered his prayer.'

He looked up and tucked his hair behind his ears. 'Ray's still over there,' he said. 'He'll probably come through this unscathed – come home a hero. I hope he does anyway. He deserves it. Anyone willing to risk everything, to die for what they believe in is a hero. Frankie was a hero. The boys – men – over there are all heroes. It's the politicians, the leaders willing to sacrifice young men for their own political games, who are the cowards. Thank God we still have Robert Kennedy to stand up to Johnson and his lies. When Bobby's president, he'll put an end to this war.'

The room grew silent once again. After a few moments Boyer asked, 'And your other friend?'

'Art?' River smiled. 'He tried to volunteer. He failed his medical. An inner ear problem. He cried like a baby when he was denied enlistment,' he said. 'And then there's me. I hid away in university. Nice and safe in classes. Until Norman Morrison lit that match.'

Unconsciously River again reached into the box on the table. He pulled out a small cloth covered book and let it fall open in his hands. I recognized the yellowed pages of *A Book of Treasured Poems*. Boyer's favourite.

Boyer shifted in his chair. 'Have you ever regretted your decision?' he asked.

River studied the pages in front of him. 'I don't regret protesting the war,' he said, then looked up and met Boyer's eyes. 'But, of course, I'm sorry I had to leave my home, and that I had to give up my education.'

After a moment he let his gaze return to the book. He started to read out loud:

> And great is the man with the sword undrawn,
> And good is the man who refrains from wine;
> But the man who fails and yet fights on,
> Lo! he the twin-born brother of mine.

'"For Those Who Fail", by Cincinnatus Miller,' Boyer added without a moment's hesitation. 'Poet laureate, Oregon. Early nineteen hundreds.'

River shook his head in wonder. 'Do you know every poem in this book?' he asked.

'Yes, he does,' I answered knowing Boyer would never acknowledge this.

But my brother quickly changed the subject.

'So what are your plans?' he asked. 'Do you think you'll ever go back? To university, that is.'

I was startled by the question. Up until that moment I hadn't thought about River leaving, but suddenly it made sense. Of course he would not stay forever. I waited nervously for his answer.

'I have a trust fund from my grandmother that matures when I am twenty-four,' River said. 'When I first came up here I thought I would get to know Canada by travelling around doing odd jobs. But I'm content to stay here if your family will put up with me until then. When I come into my trust I guess I'll apply to university in Vancouver or Calgary.' He smiled at Boyer. 'Which one do you think is best?'

Boyer shrugged. 'I haven't given it much thought.'

As they spoke I did a quick mental calculation. River was twenty-one. In three years I would be finished high school. For the first time I considered going to university.

But it was Boyer to whom River directed his question. 'Well, why don't you? Why don't you think about coming with me?'

'That's not an option.' Boyer attempted a laugh.

River stared intently at Boyer as if he were weighing his thoughts. After a moment he said quietly, 'You once asked me how I could deliberately give up a university education. But isn't that exactly what you're doing?'

'It's not the same thing,' Boyer said looking taken aback by River's remark.

'Isn't it?'

Boyer avoided his eyes. 'All the education I need is right here,' he said and waved at the books surrounding us.

'And the real world is out there,' River nodded toward the window. 'Just be certain you're being honest with yourself, man. That you're not using the farm – or your father – as an excuse to avoid that world.'

Chapter Twenty-Five

I SMELL IT in the air.

In Kelowna, I waited inside the bus depot for my connection and still I could not escape the clinging odour of smouldering forests. Now, as the bus pulls away from the Okanagan town heading east, I can still smell it. I avoid looking out of my window. I don't want to see the destruction caused by the recent wildfires.

It seemed all of British Columbia was burning this summer. The yellowed skies were heavy with the smoky haze for months. Now I am unwilling to look out at the evidence of destroyed forests, naked black skeletons dotting a desolate landscape. I don't want to deal with my own memories of charred and blackened buildings.

It's a strange feeling to travel on a bus, like being in a humming vacuum, a separate world, a time machine, carrying me – in slow motion it now seems – back to my past. Why do I always take the bus home? It's more than my aversion to flying. I could drive. I drive everywhere else. Except when I go back to Atwood. Is it because once I'm on the bus I'm not in control? Cannot change my mind? Cannot turn back?

The first time I travelled by bus was when I left home in 1969. The next time was after my father's funeral.

I remember an elderly couple on that bus. They must have been in their eighties, or more likely their nineties. I found myself feeling irrationally impatient with them at each stop as they climbed on and off the bus with the careful slowness of old age. I felt an irritating resentment, even anger, at the unfairness of it all. They got to live, to be old. And my father did not. He was too young to die. I'm startled by the sudden thought that when my father died he was only four years older than I am now.

In the end it was not the cancer that killed him. It was the farm. My father died on the cold concrete floor of the machine shed, underneath his Massey Ferguson tractor.

Morgan called to tell me. I took the first flight home.

Jenny and Vern tease me about my fear of flying, but they wouldn't if they'd seen me on that flight. They have no idea the extent of my phobia. I hadn't either until I strapped myself into an aeroplane for the first, and last, time. As soon as the stewardess pulled the cabin door closed I nearly bolted from my seat. My hands gripped the tiny armrests. I felt the perspiration run in rivulets under my sweater as the plane began to taxi down the runway. I forgot how to breathe. Then, as we lifted into the air, it was all I could do not to scream out to be let off. I kept my eyes squeezed shut until someone tapped my shoulder. I looked over to see the woman in the seat beside me hand me an air bag. Just in time.

The airport shuttle-bus delivered me, shaken and weak, into Atwood. As we arrived on Main Street I was startled to see the old milk truck angle-parked in front of Gentry's – the small magazine store and soda counter that served as the bus depot. Behind the dark windscreen of the cab, I glimpsed a familiar silhouette. My father! The amber glow of a cigarette hung from his mouth. I sat frozen in my seat and watched as his head turned and a half-finished cigarette came flickering out of the window. It sailed, end over end, through the air before falling to the dark asphalt. The cab door opened and he climbed out of the driver's seat. Morgan.

The awkwardness of returning home for the first time was lost in the need to bury our father. My brother took me into his arms without a word. Behind his welcoming smile was a steely determination not to shed tears. I was grateful for that.

On the drive home, he filled me in on the details of Dad's accident. 'The jacks slipped,' he told me. 'The tractor engine landed in the middle of his chest. His silver cigarette case was actually imbedded in his chest. Her gift broke his heart, Mom says.' He shook his head and continued. 'He must have been pinned there for quite a while. Carl and I were out working in the wood lot. Mom and Boyer were in town, so there was no one there.'

'Oh.'

'Yeah, I can just hear his final words.'

'Every time the sun shines upside down!' we murmured the words together. Morgan smiled, his Adam's apple going up and down in a swallow. I wanted to reach over and touch his face, his face so much like our father's. Instead I turned and stared straight ahead while I held back my own tears. And the sneezes.

'How have you been?' he asked.

'I'm okay.'

'You're working at a newspaper I hear. Gonna be a famous reporter, eh?'

'No.' I tried a laugh. 'I'm just selling advertising. But it's a start.'

The truck slowed down as we turned onto South Valley Road. 'How's Mom?' I asked.

'Oh, she's, ah, well, she's Mom. You know. Busy feeding and comforting everyone who shows up to offer sympathy.'

While Morgan parked the truck in the carport beside the dairy, I walked up to the house. I stood in the shadows of the enclosed porch. And I smelled him there. My father. The musky scent of Old Spice and tobacco wafted from his barn jacket which still hung by the screen door. How could he be dead when the scent of him was so alive, so warm? I wanted to lean my face into his coat and inhale him.

Then, through the mesh screen, I saw my mother. She stood at the kitchen table, her back to me. Exactly where she was standing the last time I saw her.

She turned at the first creaking of the screen door. Over two years had passed since I last saw my mother's face. Her eyes took me in as if it was only yesterday. Her smile was open, warm, vulnerable, and naked with love.

'Natalie,' she rushed over and threw her arms around me. And just like every hug that Nettie Ward has ever given any of her children, she hung on a little too long, a little past the point of comfort, and then she kept hanging on, until you gave into it.

I stood there, stiff and remote. My unyielding arms hung at my side, still holding my suitcase and an oversized book-bag. A part of me wanted to melt into the hug – as I always had as a child – to melt into the love, the acceptance, the arms of home. But I could not. I could not, even in that moment of shared sorrow, let go of my resentment. The unnamed resentment I'd carried with me out the door the day I left. I carried it every day, like some animal clinging to my back that wouldn't let go because I kept petting it, stroking it, enjoying the perverse pleasure of letting it hang on.

'I'm so sorry, Mom,' I heard myself say.

'Hush, darling. There's nothing to be sorry about.' She said it as if she thought I was apologizing.

I'm sorry. It's what you say, a greeting, when someone dies. Those words fill the empty air. She couldn't brush them away as if they were an unwanted apology. What did she think I was apologizing for? Sorry for? What did she mean, 'there's nothing to be sorry about?' Of course there was. I was sorry my father was dead. I was sorry her husband of twenty-nine years was dead. For the way he died. I was sorry I wasn't there, that I hadn't seen him for over two years. Sorry I would never, ever have the chance to be with him again, to talk to him again. And I was sorry I did not have another chance to tell him I love him. To tell him I was sorry.

And I was sorry our family was even more broken.

Mom reached up and brushed the hair from my face. Her eyes filled. She pulled a tissue from her pocket and pressed it to her nose. After three quick sneezes, she squared her shoulders. 'Just look at all this food.' She waved at the table and counters. Every available space was covered with casseroles, cakes, and pies. 'Burnt offerings,' she said, then cringed at the thoughtless words. 'Whatever will I do with all this food?'

'I'm sure you'll see that it all gets eaten,' Boyer's voice came from the doorway to the parlour. I had not seen him through the film of tears I was blinking back. Cowardice stifled them. I avoided looking at him, just as I have avoided thinking about what I would do when the eventuality of this moment arrived.

'Hello Boyer,' I said. 'Good to see you.' But it was a lie. I looked anywhere but his face.

'I'm really tired, Mom,' I said. 'I'd like to lie down for an hour.'

'Of course, dear,' she said. 'Go on up to your room. It's exactly as you left it.'

'The wake is at seven o'clock tonight,' Boyer said, a tired resignation in his voice. 'We should head into town at six-thirty.'

He withdrew back into the parlour. I heard the murmur of hushed voices coming from the living room and wondered which neighbours, which of the few friends we Wards had left, were gathered there. There was no other family to come. We were it: Mom, Boyer, Morgan, and Carl. And me. Our entire family – such as it was.

I slept. I slept in a bedroom that was, as Mom said, exactly as I had left it. My books still lined the shelf above my bed. The patchwork quilt she made for my tenth birthday lay on my bed, fresh, clean, and inviting. My knitted slippers waited under my bed along with forgotten boxes of marbles. Everything right where I left it. The family photograph, taken four years before I moved away, still sat on my desk. A jar of pennies, silver dimes scattered amongst the copper, sat next to it. The room had the appearance of a dead child's bedroom. It was.

'Natalie?' I woke to the soft knock at my door and Carl's voice calling my name.

In the late afternoon darkness, it took a moment to realize where I was. I reached over and switched on the bedside lamp. The door opened and Carl leaned in.

Beautiful, sweet-faced Carl. He was the first one to cry in front of me. He sat down on the bed and put his arms around me.

'I've missed you, you brat,' he teased. 'And I miss the old beggar too,' he attempted a laugh, failed and wiped at his tears.

Then he asked, too wistfully for my teasing brother, 'When did it all start to go so wrong?' He sighed, 'I expected it to last forever, you know, the way it was when we were growing up. What did we ever do to deserve this?'

I stared at him, not knowing how to answer his rhetorical question.

Then I reached up and touched his face. 'Nothing,' I whispered. He had done nothing to deserve the way things had turned out. But I had.

The drive into town is not long, but it stretched out in the silence that day, each of us lost in our own private memories of our father. I sat on the padded red leather seat, between Morgan and Carl, in the back of Boyer's Ford Edsel.

I watched the familiar road through the right hand window, not wanting to look straight ahead. Not allowing myself, even accidentally, to look at Boyer, to catch his eyes in the rear-view mirror. He sat stiff and formal behind the wheel of the only passenger car our family had ever owned.

Before we reached the highway, Mom shifted around and said to me. 'This accident may have been a blessing for your father.'

I was stunned by her words. I couldn't imagine any blessing in dying pinned under a tractor, with the motor crushing your chest.

'When they did the autopsy, they found he was full of cancer. Allen Mumford told me it was a wonder he was still walking around at all. He said your Dad couldn't have lasted much longer without feeling it, if he wasn't already.'

I don't remember my father ever missing a day's work, even when sick with a cold or flu. He had no patience for illness. And a strong aversion to hospitals.

'They smell of death,' he always said. 'All the antiseptic and chlorine in the world can't get rid of that smell.'

He refused to enter St Helena's Hospital to visit friends, or to take any of us in with childhood ailments. My father, who could plunge his bare arms up inside a birthing cow, then turn and pull out a stuck calf while the blood, slime, and mucus gushed over him, cringed whenever he pushed through the hospital doors with Mom when she was about to give birth. She let him off the hook. She sent him away each time saying she couldn't stand to see him so green around the gills.

'God spared your father from suffering a long and painful illness,' she said as she turned back around in her seat. Then, as if it gave reason to his bizarre death, she added. 'It would have killed him to be in the hospital.'

I put my fist to my mouth to choke back the sudden unexpected urge to laugh.

'You know,' she added wistfully, 'he took his monthly bath the night before.'

That did it. I lost control. The repressed giggle burst through my fist. On either side of me I felt Morgan and Carl's bodies shake. Suddenly the car filled with choking laughter. Even Boyer and Mom's shoulders started to shake.

Boyer stopped the car on the side of the highway before we reached town so we could compose ourselves. It took more than a few moments for the fits of hysterical laughter to quiet down, the tears to be wiped away, and noses to be blown. As the car started again I shrunk back in the seat and avoided Morgan and Carl's eyes in fear that the inappropriate giggles, or sobs would start up again. I pressed my tissue to my nose. My muffled sneezes were echoed in the front seat by my mother.

We parked in front of St Anthony's. Yellow light spilled from the windows of the stone building next to the church. Suddenly I didn't want to leave the car. I had no desire to go inside to meet the old strangers and new friends gathered there. And I did not want to see my father lying in a casket. Reluctantly I climbed out after Morgan. I stood outside the church with my brothers and my mother and mentally put myself on autopilot. I would follow their lead. I steeled myself to get through this, unemotional and detached.

Boyer took Mom's arm. She was only forty-six, but for the first time I had a glimpse of what she would look like as an old woman. Shrunken, smaller, worn down by time, yet still strong.

I followed behind with Morgan and Carl. Inside the chapel solemn faces turned to greet us. Some I recognized and some I knew I should. Ma Cooper hugged Mom and murmured something to her as Widow Beckett and Jake, red-eyed and grim-faced, stood waiting to offer comfort. Boyer too waited at Mom's side as she accepted hushed condolences. Then they continued making their way toward the wooden casket at the front of the room. The small crowd parted and let them pass.

Morgan and Carl followed. I held back. The coffin, surrounded by flowers, seemed surreal. The heavy fragrance from the blossoms repulsed me. No wonder Mom never liked cut flowers in the house.

Somehow my legs carried me forward, my feet floating as if on their own, towards the polished mahogany casket. The open casket. I stood behind Mom. She whispered something to Boyer. Then she leaned down to kiss my father.

But the waxy face enfolded in cream satin resembled no one I knew, least of all my father. There had been a mistake. This was not my father! This was not even a person. Just a hard wax dummy. Why was my mother kissing this apparition? Now touching it, as she murmured soft words that only she could hear? Tears slid down her cheeks and dripped from her chin as she caressed the sunken face. Then she patted the folded hands, just as she patted my father's hands every time she poured his coffee at the kitchen table. But she was patting the wrong hands. Couldn't she see that?

She reached over and put her arm around my shoulders, urging me closer. 'Kiss your father goodbye, Natalie,' she said, as if I was a little girl who needed to be coerced into kissing someone who was leaving for a short while.

I recoiled, almost fell, as I tried to step back. She took my hand and placed it on the chest of the impostor. I felt the scratchy wool of my father's Sunday suit. But underneath was a hollow hard nothingness. *This is not my father! This is not my father!*

'It's okay, Nat.' Morgan took my arm. Had I said it out loud?

Behind me I heard the rising whispers. 'What's Natalie Ward doing now?'

Even here, even now, they would talk. Talk about me. Talk about Boyer, our family. I bristled. I would not make a spectacle of myself, my family. I leaned over and kissed the cold, grey cheek of the stranger, who at one time must have been my father.

That evening, the next day, the funeral, all passed in a blur. I was there in body, but like a swimmer caught too far out I was treading water, watching my breathing, trying not to panic. I slept so deeply in my childhood bed that Carl or Morgan had to come in the morning to wake me.

I dreamt of my father. He flashed a smile at me as he climbed into the cab of his truck. I reached over and placed my hand on his face. It felt warm and soft. Then suddenly it was Boyer's face. It melted like wax and ran down onto my father's Sunday suit.

The morning after the funeral, Carl shook me awake.

'Natalie, come and look at this,' he said. He hurried across the room and threw open the window.

I climbed out of bed, wrapped myself in my quilt and joined him. I followed his gaze down to the rose garden. It took me a moment to recognize the hulking figure there. It was Mom. She had on our father's canvas jacket and woollen pants. My mother was wearing pants! The shock of seeing her in them was almost as startling as the state of the garden. All around her lay pieces of thorny branches and chunks of rose bushes. The last of the autumn blossoms lay scattered and crushed in a profusion of colour. Mom stood swinging an axe over a half-felled yellow rose bush. Chips of barbed branches, thorns and petals flew in the air with each swing. I glanced at Carl, then open-mouthed, we both watched as Boyer and Morgan approached the garden. They moved towards Mom cautiously, as if afraid they might be the next to be attacked. 'Mom?' Boyer called tentatively.

It looked as if she had not heard him. She gave no reply. She dropped the axe, then leaned over, picked up a handsaw, and began working at the gnarled branches at the base of the bush. The scene was so bizarre I wondered for a moment if I were still asleep.

'Mom?' Boyer called again, as if her name was a question that needed to be answered.

'What?' She kept on sawing.

'What— What are you doing?'

'What does it look like I am doing?' she answered with a quick glance up. 'I'm getting rid of these old bushes.'

Boyer surveyed the destruction that lay at their feet. 'But, your rose garden—'

'It was never my rose garden,' Mom said punctuating each word with a saw stroke. Then she dropped the saw and kicked at the severed plant with her rubber boots. 'This garden was always your father's.' She grabbed a shovel and jammed it into the roots. 'He doesn't need it any more.'

Boyer and Morgan remained motionless, unsure what to do next.

'Don't just stand there gawking.' She stood on the shovel blade and wiggled it into the earth. 'Either grab a shovel and help,' she puffed. 'Or go away.'

I felt, rather than saw, Carl step away from the window and leave the room. I remained there, riveted, unable to pull myself away.

For the rest of the day, wrapped in my quilt, I sat on the window seat and watched the four of them dig up the garden. They took wheelbarrow after wheelbarrow load and dumped them beside the compost heap. The twisted and snarled roots, tangled branches, sharp hooked barbs and thorns, all lay in an angry-looking pile in the fading afternoon sun. After Mom raked up the last remnants of pastel and blood red petals, she took Dad's silver Zippo lighter from his jacket pocket and held it to the dried branches. The air filled with the smell of pungent smoke, mingled with the aroma of freshly turned earth, and the sweetness of crushed petals.

Mom stood and leaned against her rake watching the smouldering fire. 'Peonies, now there's a nice soft plant,' I heard her say. 'In the spring we'll plant peonies. They don't bite back.'

I smiled at her words. I knew she was not speaking to anyone standing there.

Chapter Twenty-Six

Nettie

GUS'S FACE FLOATS before her. She lifts a weighted arm and reaches out to touch him. Her eyes open. She tries to focus, to search the room for him. But the room is bare. Hospital bare.

'I'm coming, Gus,' she whispers.

But death is taking its merry time. She fights the dark spectre, not willing to surrender at the first assault. She coughs, then clutches the sheet. It is near now, close enough to whisper promises. She agrees to take its hand, welcomes it as a trusted friend. But first – first, there is something she needs to do. What is it?

Natalie's name comes to her lips. Where is she? There is some-thing she must tell her. It's more than goodbye. But what?

She hears the hum of machines; the nurses' hushed voices in the hallway, and the laboured breath of someone in the room. No, it's not someone else's breathing she hears; it's her own. The morphine is wearing off.

The afternoon light is fading. Night is coming. It's not the pain she wants to avoid; it's the night. The night is not her friend; it never was.

The pain begins to seep in. She feels it creep relentlessly through her wasted body. She does not resist it; with the pain comes a lifting of the fog. She holds back the moan she feels rising in her throat. She doesn't want the nurse to come in and check her intravenous feed of oblivion. She opens and shuts her hands, the only part of her body she can move now without the pain. She wants to clear her mind, to be able to think, to find her way back to memories.

She closes her eyes searching for visions of summer fields, yellow with drying hay. Of winter days, brilliant with the sounds of her children's laughter and sleigh bells jangling on the harnesses. She wants to bring forth images of the autumn brushed onto the treed hillsides above her home. She concentrates until she sees once again the colours so bright she had to remind herself to breathe when she first looked up and saw them on a crisp fall morning after a hard frost ran wild through the forest.

And the spring. She longs for visions of springtime. Of days when the farm was alive with the sounds of new life. She pictures fluffy yellow chicks chirping madly as they ran willy-nilly under a heat lamp, wobbly-legged calves bawling as their mothers licked off the after-birth, a new foal under the belly of a mare, sucking greedily from swollen teats. She smiles at the memory of her children's faces, faces still young enough to be as awe-struck as she was at these miracles.

She allows the memories to flow, free from the blur of morphine, memories awash in the light of time, the daytime.

Her eyes open to see the darkening sky through the window. And she suddenly remembers long ago nights and shudders.

It was only during the night times that she had lost her way. Only as she lay in the dark beside a snoring Gus, that she wondered. She would try to drown her thoughts in lists of chores, meal plans, and prayers. Yet too often, like the nauseating perfume of the roses, the voices bullied themselves back in. Until she reached for the book always waiting on her night table, and left her bed.

Sometimes she believed her reading was a curse. Sometimes she thought it would be a blessing to be like Gus, to never have read a novel in her life, to be unaware of what she was missing, to be ignorant of the possibilities. She was certain that all of Gus's carnal knowledge came from observing the farm animals. His lovemaking was as business-like, and over as quickly, as any barnyard mating.

Only once did she shed her shyness and try to put into words what she was feeling. But she quickly learned that for all his public displays of affection, her husband could not, would not, discuss the intimacies of their bedroom. So she pushed back the unnamed and unspoken yearnings on those nights when the only relief was the weight of her husband's body falling away from hers. And then, in the mornings, as her family surrounded her at the breakfast table, the family she had longed for all the years of her only-child youth, she wondered how she could question her life. In the light of day, she felt foolish for her night-veiled thoughts. And so in the dark of their room she stifled the sneezes into her pillow and was grateful for the fullness of her life in the daylight. Until River.

River? Now she remembers what she needs to tell Natalie.

Chapter Twenty-Seven

SOMEWHERE IN THE back of the bus a child cries, probably from the pressure of changing altitudes. I swallow to pop my ears.

We're getting closer, almost there. I see nothing except my blurred reflection as I try to peer out the side window. But I don't need to see to know we are nearing the turnoff to Atwood.

The bus driver glances at me in the rear-view mirror. 'Going home?' he asks as he catches my eye.

'Yes,' I answer automatically, and then wonder why. Atwood has not been my home for over thirty-four years.

Home. Such a simple word. What does it really mean? Where is it exactly? I think of the line from the Robert Frost poem, 'The Death of the Hired Hand', once one of Boyer's favourites:

> Home is the place where, when you have to go there,
> they have to take you in.

And they would take me in. No one sent me away or shut me out. My exile was self-imposed.

But there's really no 'they' left there any more. Only Boyer. Now that Mom is in St Helena's, Boyer is the only member of our family who still lives out at the old farmstead.

Even the farm is not the same any more. The year after I moved away, shortly before my father died, the barn was automated and the milk sold in bulk to the large pasteurizing dairies. And not long after that Morgan and Carl moved to the Queen Charlotte Islands.

The bus begins to slow. As the air brakes release their long-held breath, a flurry of conflicting emotions grips me. For a moment I feel nauseated. I push the anxiety back down and begin to gather my belongings.

We pull to a stop at the side of the wide junction. Parked beneath the highway sign is the old Ford Edsel. *Boyer?* Boyer has come to pick me up? My body goes rigid with sudden panic. Oh, God, alone with Boyer for the forty-minute drive into Atwood? I have not spent one minute alone with him in thirty-five years. What will we find to talk about? Why would he come? Where's Jenny? Then I feel the heat rise to my face. *Mom?* Maybe I'm too late.

But it's not Boyer who climbs out of the car's driver's seat as I stand waiting for the bus door to open. An involuntary sigh of relief escapes from my throat as I step off the bus and into my daughter's arms.

Through our tearful hug, Jenny assures me that Mom is all right. 'She was sleeping a bit fitfully when I saw her earlier tonight,' she says, 'but she has some fight in her yet.'

The sharp mountain air bites my face as we load my suitcase into the trunk. The bus tail lights recede. Darkness enfolds us. I'd forgotten how suddenly blackness snaps on in these mountains.

'I was surprised to see you with Boyer's old car,' I tell her once we are settled inside.

'My car,' she says, a note of pride creeping into her voice. 'Uncle Boyer gave it to me. I'm just taking it out for the last spin before the snow flies.' The dashboard lights cast green shadows on her face as she pulls onto the highway.

We drive in silence for a few miles, then without taking her eyes off the road Jenny says quietly, 'Tell me about River.'

I am momentarily stunned at hearing his name. A name from another lifetime. A name I haven't given voice to for years. My mind races trying to give meaning to the simple question.

'Mom?' Jenny glances at me then back to the road. 'Who was he? Tell me what happened to him – what happened between you and Uncle Boyer.'

So there it is. This is what she wanted to talk to me about. I've always known this day would come.

I have always known that when I told my version of our family's story to Jenny, I would have to begin before that summer of my sixteenth year. I need to tell her about who and what our family was before it all happened. I need to tell her about the 'before River', and the 'after'. I want her to understand just how much had been lost – left behind.

Still, I am startled at her request, not ready to speak it all out loud. I always thought the telling would be in writing. It would be so much easier to put it down on paper than to hear the truth falter in my voice. But now? I'm not ready now. Not while my mother is dying. I cannot deal with both these traumas at the same time, and I tell Jenny so.

'But now *is* the time,' she says, her voice firm, but kind. 'Now, while Grammie is still with us.'

'How do you know about River?' I finally ask. There, I've said his name. I've let it out into the small universe we inhabit within the interior of this car, where his presence still remains in the wooden peace sign hanging from the rear-view mirror.

'Gram,' she says. 'She's said some pretty strange things in her delirium. And I've talked with Uncle Boyer. He said if I wanted to know more, I had to ask you.'

I concentrate on the highway before me, on the darkness unbroken by oncoming headlights. If I could see out the passenger window, if it were daylight, I know I would be looking over a vista of treed mountain tops rising like islands out of a sea of clouds. I shiver, but not from the cold.

I recall how, on other trips home, my imagination ran away with thoughts of the bus losing control and careening off one of the sharp corners, plunging into the steep chasm below. The vision, the idea, of the fiery end on the tangled forest floor, was not without its morbid appeal then. Everything would be beyond my control – not my fault that I couldn't make it back to Atwood. I would not have to deal with the reality of my past. But not tonight. Not with my daughter in the car.

Jenny's questions create mixed emotions. Would it be a relief to finally unburden those secrets? Can I tell them all to this person whom I love more than I fear the past? The only other person I have ever felt that temptation to tell is Vern.

From the start, Vern and I resisted the urge to play the 'tell-me-something-you-have-never-told-anyone' game all new lovers seem to play. I realize with a start that the real reason I don't share my past with him, why I avoid bringing him to my childhood home, is I do not want him to see how much devastation I am capable of.

I wonder now how much of the truth a daughter should hear about her mother? How much does Jenny already know? What have Mom and Boyer told her? Have they told her about that long ago summer night? The night it all started to go wrong?

They couldn't have. They weren't there.

Chapter Twenty-Eight

No one was home that night except me. And in the room above the dairy, River.

June 8, 1968. The date is easy to remember because two days earlier Robert Kennedy had died. It was the only time I ever saw River cry. On Thursday night, he sat with Dad and Boyer in front of the television set in the living room. Silent tears spilled from his eyes and rolled down his cheeks while the image of the senator lying on the pantry floor of a Los Angeles hotel – his life seeping out in a dark pool of blood beneath him – played out in the news.

'He was our hope to end this war,' River said, his voice almost inaudible, as he left the room.

On Saturday afternoon Boyer drove to Kelowna for the School Board to take delivery of a new school bus. He would stay in Kelowna overnight and drive the bus back to Atwood on Sunday morning. Morgan went along to drive his car home. Of course Carl wasn't about to let Morgan go on an excursion to the 'big smoke' without him. The three of them would be back the next day.

That Saturday evening was unusual to begin with. There were no town kids at our place. Not even Elizabeth-Ann. Well, perhaps it was not so unusual since the main attraction was two hundred miles away in Kelowna.

After supper I worked with Mom in the dairy and River took over Morgan and Carl's job.

The sadness of mourning had not left River's eyes. Still, he made attempts at humour as he ran the milk from the barn. 'Ah, now I know your secret, Nettie,' he said as he came in with the first load and caught Mom smearing her hands with translucent yellow cream. 'Can't fool me with that baby-smooth skin.' He emptied a stainless-steel milk container into the separator.

Mom tried to look innocent as she pulled rubber gloves onto her greased hands. She couldn't deny that every day she applied the same salve to her face and hands that Dad used to soften the cow's teats. She'd taught me to use udder balm from an early age. I still use it and, whether it's that, or good genes, my skin is one thing I thank my mother for. We thought it was our own little discovery.

'The milkmaid's salvation, according to my momma,' River said as he pushed open the door to leave. 'But don't worry, your secret's safe with me.'

River had been with us almost two years that June. His teasing was as harmless and easy as Morgan and Carl's. He was like a part of our family. Much more than Jake ever was.

There are those who would say later that they had thought the affection between Nettie Ward and River Jordan was more than it appeared to be. Even I wondered for a moment when I saw the flush of her cheeks as he called back, 'And my momma's skin is just as beautiful.'

But as quickly as the thought entered my mind, I let it flutter away. I could not imagine there being an attraction between my mother and River, other than the affection of a young man who is missing his own mother. Besides, all our friends fell in love with Mom. Why should River be any different?

Without my brothers the milking took much longer that evening. After Mom and I finished hosing down the dairy, we strolled together across the yard. The surrounding hillsides were losing the final rays of a blazing sun, which had turned our little valley into an oven that day. The evening air felt still and heavy. Billowing white clouds boiled up over the mountains behind the house. Distant rumbling in the skies warned of thunderheads that could not be far behind.

Mom sniffed the air. 'We could use a good rain,' she said. But there was not a breath of wind. It looked as if the brewing storm would skirt our valley.

After Mom and Dad took turns washing up, I filled the claw-foot tub in the bathroom. As I lay soaking, I heard them leaving for their monthly bridge game with Father Mac and Dr Mumford.

'Don't forget to bring in the rest of the wash, honey,' Mom called out before the screen door slammed.

I finished my bath and pulled on a cotton nightgown. As the sky outside darkened, I sat at the kitchen table studying for my grade eleven final exams.

The house felt strangely empty. Sounds I had never noticed before, the ticking of the kitchen clock above the stove, out of sync with the mantle clock in the dining room, the hum of the refrigerator, moths hitting the darkening windows, all seemed amplified in the silence.

The soft aroma of sweet peas wafted in through the window screen. The delicate blossoms, which climbed up the trellis outside the kitchen window, danced in the breeze. Like the flowers, I felt restless. I was finding it hard to concentrate. My mind was not on the books spread out on the table. My mind was in the room above the dairy.

I stared out the window. The last colours of the day shadowed, and then darkened, as heavy black clouds rolled in. The leaves on the aspen trees across the yard turned their backs to the rising wind. The Pearson windows began to rattle when I suddenly remembered the wash.

Outside the clothes snapped in the heightened wind. I stepped out onto the laundry platform and began to pull shirts, socks, pants, and underwear, wooden pegs and all, from the line. I tossed everything into a wicker basket while the commotion of wind and dust swirled around my bare legs.

Then I glanced up and saw him in the window above the dairy. River.

He stood there, backlit by the soft glow from his room. He raised his hand and waved. But I saw what I wanted to see. I do not even see the truth in memory. I have replayed that gesture many times over the years. My memory will not let it play any different. I saw him beckon for me to come to him.

I finished yanking the laundry from the clothesline and carried the last basket into the porch. I grabbed a shirt from the top of the pile and pulled it on over my nightgown. The cotton shirt smelled of fresh air, aspen trees, and Boyer. I wrapped it around me and skipped down the porch stairs. The night sky was now black with the fury of roiling clouds. The only light in the yard was a circle of yellow from the bulb over the dairy door, and the glow in the empty window above.

If anyone had been watching as I hurried across the yard, if any of the promised thousand-eyes-of-the-night had been paying attention, they would have seen no hesitancy in my steps. They would have seen a confidence that propelled me forward, as if I believed in what I know now – what I knew then – was an imagined gesture.

When I was halfway to the dairy, a lightning flash lit up the night. Seconds later thunder ripped through the air. At the same moment the sky opened up, as if the crashing thunder had cut through the thick black clouds, unleashing their heavy load. A deluge of rain spilled over me. By the time I reached the bottom of the stairway at the side of the dairy I was as drenched as if I had swam there.

The faint sounds of guitar music came from River's room. I had to knock twice before the quiet strumming ceased and the door opened. River stood in the dim light dressed only in a pair of cut-off jeans. The expression on his face was more curiosity than surprise, as if he were trying to focus, to figure out just who this half-drowned creature standing in his doorway was. Then, startled, he exclaimed, 'Natalie, man, you're soaked.' He ushered me inside and sat me down on the bed. He disappeared into the bathroom and returned with a towel and began to rub my head.

Three fat candles burned on the night table next to the bed, filling the room with a soft orange light. The air smelled of melting wax, the spice of incense, and the heady aroma of sweet smoke. The thrill of being alone with River, the pressure of his fingers through the towel, the tingle on my scalp, felt invigorating. I became bold. 'Can I try some?' I asked when he laid the towel on my shoulders. I nodded at the thin cigarette resting in an ashtray on his guitar case.

'Oh, no,' River laughed. 'I promised your father. None of my wacky-tabacky, as he calls it, for any of his family.' He reached over and pinched the tip of the marijuana butt, extinguishing the tiny glow.

We sat together on the iron bed with pillows propped up at our backs and watched the storm play out in the picture window across the room. Outside the wind was working itself into a frenzy. The storm wrapped itself around the dairy, isolating us, cocooning us. Torrents of rain pounded a hard-step on the tin roof. Every few minutes lightning flashed, illuminating the canopy of heavy black clouds. Roars of thunder relayed through the night sky.

It felt somehow magical, otherworldly, being caught in a storm with River. It was easy to believe the world was distant, as if only the two of us existed, while nature swirled around us. It felt as if that moment in time was separate, unconnected.

I picked at the threads on my grandmother's patchwork quilt while I pretended there was nothing unusual about sitting beside River in my nightgown, while his naked torso reflected the golden glow of candlelight.

But inside I was weak with the thrill of it. My whole being felt his nearness; the fine hairs on my arms and legs lifted as if pulled by the static electricity of his body. I wondered if he could hear my heart pounding.

After a while he reached down to retrieve his guitar from the foot of the bed. Melancholy strumming filled the air, while guttering candles created dancing shadows in the corners of the room.

I don't have the luxury of being able to say I was seduced to excuse what followed. It's difficult to explain how a young girl as naïve about sex as I was could be the seducer, but that is what happened. Until that night, other than what I read in books, my only experience with the opposite sex was a few awkward kisses during spin-the-bottle games held by the glow of campfires out at the lake. And yet there I was, alone with River, sitting on his bed knowing there was nowhere I would rather be, and nothing I wanted more than to have his naked body pressed to mine.

I pulled my legs up and wrapped my arms around them. I rested my head on my knees and watched him as he played. The candle glow cast a warm light on his face. His eyes were closed as if he were asleep, but his hands caressed the guitar strings with the knowledge of a lover. As he strummed, his heavy lids raised, and his blue eyes slowly crinkled into a smile. A smile so tender I ached to reach over and stroke his face. Instead, I touched his bare shoulder, feeling the heat from his skin run up my arm. 'Teach me,' I said. 'Teach me to play.'

He passed his guitar to me and slid over to my side of the bed. 'I'll show you three easy chords you can use to play almost any song,' he said, adjusting the instrument in my arms. 'Even,' he added with a warm smile, "Love Me Tender".'

To say I was paying attention to anything other than River's closeness as he placed my fingers on the frets would be a lie. I don't know how much time passed as the storm played itself out in the night while I pretended to be interested in his patient instructions.

In the end it was me who put the guitar aside. I bent down and placed it on the floor next to the bed. Then I straightened up, leaned into River and tentatively placed my lips on his. I took his lack of response as surprise. And suddenly I was pressing harder. But the hunger, the heat in that first kiss was all mine. I was the one who laid back, pulling him to me. I felt the rigidity of his body, but I did not stop. With a certainty that was beyond my experience, I caressed his face, his neck, his naked chest. My fingers explored his body, undid the snap-button, then the zipper of his jeans. My hands reached down and pushed up my nightie to expose my naked body. My hips lifted to his, guided him to me, while he lay with his face buried in the bunched-up shirt on my shoulder, barely there. I ignored the robot-like response of his body, believing, wanting to believe, that he was holding back because he didn't want to hurt me. In the end, the coupling that took place, the joining of our bodies, was all my doing.

I knew – even then I knew – the part of River I wanted was not there. The whimpering coming from his throat was not that of passion, but of sorrow. He was still in mourning I told myself; his grief was for Robert Kennedy, for his country. Still I held on to him, unwilling to let go, to believe what my heart knew.

The pain that I had read about, the searing pain of the 'first time' that girls had whispered about in the hayloft, did not happen. I felt only a warmth at the first thrust, then the heat spread through the core of my being as I clung to him.

Even though I've played that scene over endlessly in my mind, reliving and embellishing our hurried encounter, it could not have lasted more than a few minutes before River pushed himself away, as if he had suddenly woken up. 'Oh, God,' he moaned as he rolled off me. 'This is wrong.'

'It's all right,' I murmured and tried to pull him back.

'No, no, it's not,' he cried. 'This is so wrong, so wrong.' He threw his legs over the end of the bed, and leaned over, his face in his hands. 'God! I'm so sorry, Natalie.'

'I'm not,' I sat up and pulled my nightie back down. 'I love you,' I whispered.

He looked up at me with glazed-over eyes, 'And I love you too, Natalie, but not like this.'

Outside the wind was winding down. The rain had stopped. Through the window I saw stars appearing between the parting clouds. Then I heard the crunch of tyres on gravel as Dad's truck pulled into the yard.

Suddenly there was nothing to say. The world turned back on. River grabbed his cut-off jeans and retreated into the bathroom.

I couldn't leave. I knew I was stuck there until my parents settled in for the night. I curled up on the bed while I waited. I closed my eyes and tried to ignore the muffled sounds of retching coming from behind the bathroom door.

Chapter Twenty-Nine

I GLANCE AT Jenny as she drives and I sort through memories. I take my time, picking and choosing which details to keep, which to discard or ignore, and which to share before I say anything. Then I lean back and in a detached voice I tell her about how River came to us, became part of us, how we all fell in love with him. And I tell her briefly about the night I went to his room.

It all sounds so banal, so commonplace – a young girl, who was so blinded with what she believed was love, that she lost sight of reality. A child lost in the moment, believing that her desire made her an adult.

I don't bother telling Jenny that 'nice' girls didn't do 'it' in those days. I don't say that what happened in that room all those years ago filled me with guilt and remorse. It did not. Not then. That came later.

That night I lay curled up in River's bed, hugging myself and hanging on to his words. *He said he loved me!*

He thought I was too young for him, that was all, I told myself. I was sixteen. River was twenty-two. My father was ten years older than my mother, I would remind him. She was seventeen when they married, and look at them. In less than two months I would be seventeen; six years wouldn't seem so much of an age difference then. I could wait. We could wait. I drifted off to sleep convinced he would see that too. He would wait for me, everything would work out, would be all right.

Except, of course, it would not.

I don't know how long I slept. I woke to a gentle hand on my shoulder. 'Natalie, wake up.' I opened my eyes to find River standing over me. 'You should go back to the house,' he said not unkindly.

He was fully dressed in jeans and a shirt, as if it was the morning instead of the middle of the night. The fragrance of Ivory soap radiated from his body. His hair, still wet from a shower, dripped onto the shoulders of his cotton shirt.

He picked up his journal from the nightstand and went over to the chrome table beneath the window. The candles were extinguished. Bright light from the open bathroom door spilled into the room. River sat hunched over the table, his back to me. Through the window, I saw the storm had passed. Whole patches of starry sky showed through the breaking clouds. I climbed off the bed and took a step toward him. 'Go home, Natalie,' he said without turning around. It was more of a plea than a statement.

'Everything will be okay,' I said. I wanted him to feel the same joy I did. I knew he did not.

'We'll talk tomorrow,' he said with a sigh.

I didn't want to leave, but the promise in those words moved me. I leaned over and retrieved my wet shoes from beside the bed. At the door I turned back and whispered, 'Good night.'

There was no response. At the table in front of the window, River sat bent over his journal, a pen in his unmoving hand. He stared out into the night. Then his shoulders sagged and his head dropped as if in defeat. I wanted to run to him, to beg him not to be upset, but instinct held me back.

I hesitated only a moment before I quietly closed the door behind me. I stood at the top of the stairs. Across the yard the house was dark, except for the whitewashed siding, which seemed to glow in the growing light of the moon. As I looked at the darkened windows of our house, I felt a shiver that was not caused by the cooling air. In that moment I suddenly knew what Ma Cooper meant when she said, 'a goose just walked across my grave'. I pulled Boyer's shirt tighter around me and shook off the feeling of sorrow as I climbed down the stairs.

I did not hurry. I stepped carefully through the gravel- and mud-puddle-strewn yard. As I made my way past my mother's rose garden, the air was heavy with barnyard aromas and the perfume of rose petals bruised by the heavy rain. To this day, I cannot smell the earthy fresh-ness after a rainstorm without being transported back to that night.

When I reached the porch, I opened the screen door slowly, stop-ping when it squeaked, then held my breath until the silence returned. I closed the kitchen door behind me and stood in the darkness for a moment. Grateful for the childish games of blind walking, I tiptoed up the unlit stairway, counting each of the eighteen linoleum-topped steps. In the narrow upstairs hallway, I turned left and counted six steps to my door, then felt my way across my room to my bed.

Even as a child, the dark had held no fear for me. No bogey men or monsters ever lurked in my closets. I never looked over my shoulder to see what might hide in the shadows. Perhaps if I was not so at ease with the night, perhaps if I was timid in the dark, I would have cast furtive glances around, or paid more attention. Maybe I would even have felt the eyes watching me as I crossed the yard. Then I may have glanced back over my shoulder, or turned around and looked behind me. And perhaps I might have seen her there – my mother standing in the shadows beneath the dairy stairs.

Chapter Thirty

Nettie

EVEN IN HER dreams the perfume haunts her; the heavy fragrance drifts into her sleep. Like smoke it seeps through her body. Her stomach – so used to the upheaval of nausea from failed chemotherapy – now lurches at the invasion.

Nettie's eyes open. She turns to the bedroom window, but no lace curtains lift in a night breeze.

Her eyes search the darkened hospital room for the offending blossoms. Have they forgotten she does not want flowers in her room? Especially roses. And there are none now. Yet the pungent aroma that stole its way into her dreams was so real. The memory of it still lingers.

She cannot escape it. She cannot get up and leave her bed like she did on long-ago nights at home. Nights when she lay in the dark feeling empty and used, trying to quiet the voices dancing in her head. All those nights blend together in her memory. Except one. The memory of one June night remains clear.

Gus insisted they come home early. He feared the lightning might knock out the hydro as it often did in the heat of a summer storm. He needed to be there to start the gas generator for the cooler. So after their bridge game they left Dr Mumford's before the usual midnight snack.

The storm's fury was spent by the time they pulled into the yard. Nettie noticed the flicker of candlelight in the room above the dairy, but the yard light and kitchen lights in the farmhouse were on.

'No power outage here,' Gus said, relieved, as they made their way up to the house.

Nettie picked up a laundry basket beside the screen door. She smiled. She could always count on her daughter. She did not stop to wonder why the baskets had been left out on the enclosed porch, or why in the kitchen Natalie's books were still spread out on the table.

Gus switched off lights as he followed her through the kitchen. 'I don't remember the last time the house was this empty on a Saturday night,' he said. He took her hand before they reached the bedroom door, 'While the mice are away, the cats can play,' he whispered.

In the silence of their room, before their nightly prayers, he lifted the bedroom window. 'Leave it closed,' Nettie said.

'It's so stuffy in here,' Gus told her, then slid the window halfway up in concession. But no breeze lifted the curtains to enter the room.

In their bed, in the darkness, his hands reached over and lifted Nettie's cotton nightgown. In all the years of her marriage, she never refused her husband.

She lay there and waited for it to be over.

Later, a satisfied Gus patted her on the hip – as if she had enjoyed it as much as he – then rolled over. Nettie turned her face into her pillow. She tried to sleep. As the demons of the night overcame her, she rose. She pulled on her dressing gown in the darkness then left the room, quietly closing the door on her husband's snores.

She slipped through the shadows of the silent house. Out on the porch the battered wicker chair creaked in protest as she sat down.

Through the window screens she watched the last of the storm recede over the mountains.

Even on the porch Nettie's sensitive nose detected the roses. But before long the odours of the farm took over. She inhaled the heady fragrances, separating them in her mind: the pungent smell of the barn radiating from the coats hanging by the door; the crisp scent of aspens, wet with rain; and her favourite, the sweet-smelling hay.

The warm scent always brought the memory of lying in a sea of loose hay, watching her young children bouncing in the spongy fullness of the loft, while barn swallows scolded and dove at them from the rafters.

These days the hay was stacked and stored in hard bales.

But it was not the aroma of the hay, or memories of lost summers that tugged at Nettie's mind as she sat looking out across the farmyard. It was River.

It was the image of River climbing up to the loft earlier that day to throw bales down to the calving pen. He was halfway up the rungs on the side of the barn when she looked up from where she stood hanging the wash on the clothesline. Her hands stopped mid air as she spotted him. Except for leather gloves, he wore nothing from the waist up. His blond ponytail bounced on his tanned shoulders. When he reached the top, he swung around and glanced back. Even from across the yard she saw the melancholy look that had taken over his face since the news of the death of another Kennedy. She felt the heat on her own face rise as his eyes met hers. He waved and called, 'Hey Nettie,' as if it was perfectly natural for her to be standing there frozen, with a pair of longjohns dangling in front of her.

She willed herself out of the trance and finished pegging her husband's wet underwear to the line. She half raised her hand to wave back then glanced around to see if anyone had caught her staring so brazenly.

As she finished hanging the wash she tried not to compare River's tanned body to her husband's red farmer's tan, which ended at his elbows and at the V of his neck. She pushed away the betraying thoughts of the 'chicken skin' appearance of Gus's torso under his longjohns and refused to let her eyes stray back to the loft.

But in the loneliness of night, in the darkness of the porch, Nettie allowed those visions to play out. She allowed herself to wonder what it would feel like to touch River's bare skin, what it would feel like to have his touching hers.

From somewhere in the distance came the relaying echo of dogs barking in the valley. From under the washtubs, hiding from the storm, Buddy whimpered in his sleep, but did not wake. The border collie, getting too old to run except in his dreams, offered no company.

Nettie stared up at the window above the dairy. The flickering golden glow of candlelight was gone. Yellow light from the bathroom clicked on and River's silhouette moved across the room. She felt less alone in the night knowing he too was awake. The light remained on. River reappeared and sat down at the table in front of the window.

Nettie pushed herself up. She moved across to the porch doorway, down the steps, and across to the yard gate as if sleepwalking. The last of the rainwater ran down the tin roofs, the heavy drops splashing in the mud puddles below, as she unlatched the gate. In the lean-to beside the barn, horses shifted in their stalls. From the rafters above a barn owl questioned Nettie's passing. She barely heard. Her slippered feet carried her over the gravel path, past the rose garden, and across the farmyard to the bottom of the stairway at the side of the dairy.

As she placed her foot on the bottom step she realized her slippers were soaking wet. She hesitated. Suddenly, the door above opened. With her hand on the railing, her right foot in the air above the second tread, Nettie froze.

The sound of Natalie's voice whispering, 'Good night' stunned her into movement. Nettie quickly backed away, then ducked into the shadows underneath the stairs.

Moments later she watched as her daughter, dressed only in her nightgown and what looked like one of her brothers' shirts, came down the stairs. She passed so close that Nettie could have reached out and touched her through the wooden steps.

And as she passed, Nettie smelled it. Above the odours of the barn, the night storm, and the roses, wafted the unmistakable musk of sex.

Chapter Thirty-One

THE NEXT DAY, I woke to sunshine streaming in through my bedroom window. It was not morning light.

I had slept in.

The house was silent, empty. The alarm clock on my night table read ten o'clock. Except during a few childhood illnesses, I never stayed in bed that late. It felt strange to be getting up at that hour. Stranger yet was the fact that my mother allowed it. I should have recognized this as the first warning sign that things had changed, and would never be the same again. But I didn't see it then.

Downstairs, the breakfast dishes still sat on the kitchen table, along with my schoolbooks pushed to the side. I found a note on the counter from my mother telling me – as if I wouldn't know where she would be on a Sunday morning – that she'd gone with Dad.

'Natalie, please start lunch,' she wrote. 'Your brothers should be back from Kelowna some time this morning.' My mother's handwriting went on to remind me Father Mac would be joining us for supper that evening. The Sunday roast, leaking red at the bottom of the brown paper wrapping, was defrosting in the sink.

After I washed up my parents' breakfast dishes, I spent the rest of the morning pretending to focus on the war of 1812.

If my mother behaved differently, if she was quieter, more subdued when she and my father returned from town that day, I barely noticed. If she seemed distant while we set the table for the noon meal, like my father, I put it down to her worrying about my brothers on the road.

Right on time, as if they'd heard a dinner bell ring, Morgan and Carl blew in the door in a whirlwind of excitement and travel fatigue.

'You can relax now, Nettie, your boys are home,' Dad teased. But I was too lost in my own thoughts to wonder why she still seemed distracted. I was too wrapped up in reliving the images of the previous night, feeling the changes in my body, too certain that my delicious secret must be obvious to everyone. I was too busy looking into the faces of my family to see if they noticed any change in me, to be able to see a change in her.

As I watched the door, anxiously waiting for River to come through, I let the imagined promised conversation run through my mind. But lunch passed and no River.

Later, at Mom's insistence, I reluctantly went with her to afternoon mass. I assumed she had gone to mass earlier. It never occurred to me that my mother had delivered the milk with Dad that morning.

In St Anthony's I went through the service by rote. I knelt when Mom knelt, crossed myself when she did; I mouthed the responding chants, but my mind was elsewhere.

Following mass my mother went to confession. I sat out on the cold marble steps in front of the church and waited for her.

My mother went to confession once every week, sometimes twice. I often wondered what she – a woman whose most damning sin surely existed only in her mind – could possibly have to confess that would take the amount of time she spent kneeling in that little booth. When I was very young I thought she must make things up, like I did in my first confessional.

As a small child I wondered what lurked beyond the small oak door my mother disappeared behind each week. Once, when no one was looking, I peeked inside the forbidden box. What I believed I saw was a black abyss that would swallow me whole if I did not do things right. By the time I made my first communion, I shook at the thought of entering that suffocating place. My carefully memorized Act of Contrition, *'Oh, my God I am heartily sorry for having offended thee and I detest my sins ...'* dissolved the moment I knelt in the shadows and heard the rough slide of the wooden slat. With the appearance of the priest's silhouette behind the screen, I blurted out, 'I didn't eat my peas!' and burst into tears.

At six, the concept of sin was too abstract. I am not sure it is any less confusing now, but as a teenager I was pretty certain I knew which acts the church considered sins.

After my mother emerged from the church doors she said to me, 'Natalie, aren't you going to confess?'

I was momentarily surprised by her words. I refused to meet her eyes. I stood and hurried down the steps saying, 'Not today.' I could not imagine what a priest, who would give a frightened six-year-old child five Hail Marys, and four Our Fathers, as penance for not cleaning her plate, would expect from a sixteen-year-old seductress.

We ate at the dining room table that night. We always did when Father Mackenzie joined us for dinner. The best china and silverware came out. It was the only time, except at Christmas, that we had wine, supplied by the priest, with our meal.

Neither River nor Boyer showed up for supper. Boyer had arrived home from Kelowna late in the afternoon and went straight to his cabin. I was not surprised by River's absence. He never joined us when Father Mac visited. Perhaps it was simply because River was not Catholic, but I believed it was because he could not forget the priest who advised his friend to enlist. Whatever the reason, the only evening meal River did not share with us was on the Sundays when Father Mac came out.

I was anxious to see River, but a part of me was relieved he was not there. I was certain that even if no one else noticed the change in me, Father Mac would see the lust in my heart just by looking at my face.

Although everyone was on their best behaviour when the parish priest sat at the head of our table, Father Mac was not a stern man. I found it hard to imagine this flesh-and-blood being, who joked and gossiped with my family, as the same apparition that heard and knew all our sins, the one whose voice doled out penance without hesitation in the darkness. It was as if he left the judgments and the knowledge of our transgressions behind when he left the booth.

That night, after Father Mac said grace, Mom began passing the steaming platters around. As the priest forked up slices of meat he said, 'Well, Nettie, I think you need to confess the real reason you left our bridge game early last night.'

Mom, usually so attentive to guests, had seemed distant, preoccupied. She looked as if she had not heard his words and was trying to catch up to what he had just said. His steel grey eyes held hers. When she seemed at a loss for a reply, he let her off the hook. 'You were down two games,' Father Mac said. 'You escaped before we thoroughly trounced you.'

'You caught me, Father,' Mom replied.

'Ha!' Dad interjected. 'We were just getting warmed up. If that storm hadn't blown in, you wouldn't have stood a chance.' My father and the priest argued bridge while the rest of us pretended to listen.

As he helped himself to another slice of Yorkshire pudding, Father Mac said, 'It looks certain that we will be closing down Our Lady next year, Nettie.'

That got Mom's attention. 'Closing it down?' she asked, startled. 'Whatever for?'

'Unfortunately, or fortunately, depending on how you look at it, there is less and less need for it,' the priest answered between mouthfuls of mashed potatoes.

'Less need?' my mother said. 'There will always be girls in need.'

'The home has ten dorm rooms,' Father Mac went on. 'There has been as many as thirty girls staying there in the past. Lately there are fewer than ten. Right now we have only four girls with us.'

'Well, I'm sure it's no thanks to the church's stance on the birth control pill.'

Movement at the table stopped, forks stayed in mid-air after my mother's words. My father stared open-mouthed at her. I expected him, or the priest, to ask what got into her; it was so unlike Mom to question the church. But Father Mac sighed and said, 'Now, Nettie, you know I spoke out in favour of liberalizing the church's policy on contraceptives. But since the pope has reaffirmed the church's traditional teachings in the papal encyclical, I have to respect that decision, even if I was disappointed in it.'

'Of course,' she murmured. 'I'm sorry, Father.' Then, as if she could not stop herself Mom added, 'But obviously many Catholic girls are taking the pill anyway. I'm glad that it's lessened the need for places like Our Lady, but now those same girls are condemned for committing a mortal sin just by putting that pill in their mouth.'

'Well, as it is,' the priest said, in a voice that clearly meant he was done with this discussion, 'by this time next year, you and your "steam team" will never have to press another uniform again.'

After supper Father Mac took off his jacket and rolled up his shirtsleeves. My father protested, as he always did, that there was no need for the priest to help with the milking. And as always he followed my father out the door saying, 'I can always carry a few buckets. A little physical work is good for the soul.'

I knew there would be no opportunity to see River that night.

The next day passed in a blur of exams and studying. Again River did not show up for meals on Monday. No one questioned his absence. Perhaps they thought he was still in mourning, or on one of his periodic cleansing fasts. I knew this was not one of those times. By that evening I was in a state of panic.

After supper, after everyone had gone to the barn and Mom to the dairy, I hurried through the dishes and went upstairs to my bedroom. Instead of climbing out on the roof I stood at my window and watched. I watched as Morgan and Carl finished carrying the last milk containers to the dairy. I listened to the clanking of the stanchions as the cows were released, the stumbling of hooves on slippery concrete as they were herded out the back doors. I heard the blasting spray of hoses washing down the stalls. I watched as first the lights of the barn went out and then the dairy. From behind my window I saw Boyer get into his car and drive up the road to his cabin. Morgan and Carl made their way to the house, their steps subdued, displaying none of their usual jostling or rushing to get into town. Mom and Dad followed behind, looking relieved another workday was done. But still no sign of River.

I waited. I waited, while the surrounding hills lost the last of the orange rays. I waited, while the water pipes whined and complained as everyone took turns in the bathroom. I waited, while my brothers' footsteps echoed down the stairway, while Morgan's pick-up truck started and rumbled down the road. I waited until the only sound in the house was the staccato canned laughter coming from the television set in the parlour. Then I crept downstairs, and out the kitchen door.

I hurried across the yard and ran up the dairy stairs. The rap of my knuckles on the wooden door sounded hollow. I opened the door and looked inside. My grandmother's quilt still covered the bed; a lonely Curier and Ives calendar still hung on the wall. But there were no books on the nightstand or the grey chrome tabletop. No guitar leaned in the corner. His absence filled the room.

I ran over and pulled open the closet door. No green duffel bag waited inside, no clothes hung there smelling of him. I don't know what I expected to see when I frantically threw open the bathroom door only to be greeted by the institutional cleanliness of the white fixtures, the sterile odour of Old Dutch still clinging to the air. What did I expect to find when I turned and knelt to look under the bed? There was no trace of life in this room, no trace of his presence. It was as if the two years he had spent here did not exist. I fled from the empty room, and ran down the steps and across the yard. I stopped at the gate. Up on the porch Mom stood in the shadowed doorway as if she was waiting for me. She was waiting for me. *She knew*!

Somehow she knew, and she had sent him away!

I rushed up the path and stood at the bottom of the porch steps. 'Where is he?' I demanded, the panic in my voice leaking out, accusing, begging.

'He's gone,' she answered, her voice flat.

'Why?' I yelled. 'Why?' I felt my foot stamp with each 'why.' I was outside myself, watching myself having a childish temper tantrum. And I could not stop.

'It's for the best,' my mother said, her eyes focused beyond me, beyond that time and place. Then, for the first time in my life, my mother turned her back on my tears.

Chapter Thirty-Two

I PULL MYSELF out of my private thoughts as the Edsel slows down. We have reached the outskirts of Atwood. Here and there a solitary light from a hillside home appears and disappears as we pass.

'I once heard Jodie Foster say during a television interview that a moment comes in every young girl's life when she hates her mother so much she can feel it in her toes.'

'Did you ever hate me like that?' I ask Jenny as she drives. 'I mean a hate so deep it penetrates your bones?'

'No,' she answers without hesitation. 'Not really. Oh, I remember as a teenager, whining along with my girlfriends about our mothers. Sometimes those conversations seemed like competitions over whose mom was the biggest bitch.'

'Was I in the running?'

'Only when you wouldn't let me triple pierce my ears,' she laughs. 'No, I didn't really feel any of the animosity some of my friends seemed to feel for their parents. But then we didn't really have that type of relationship, did we?'

It was true. Except for the summers, Jenny and I spent most of her teenage years alone. Just the two of us against the world. Like the old Helen Reddy song. We experienced very little conflict, were more like friends than mother and daughter. But then Jenny, like her Uncle Boyer, had always been mature for her age – an old soul.

'What about you?' she asks. 'Did you ever feel that way about your mother?'

'Briefly,' I tell her. 'Only briefly.'

And I see myself standing at the bottom of our porch steps on a warm summer night.

I watched my mother's back disappear into the house. And in my foot-stomping fit of frustration, I felt the searing heat of rage seep through every part of my body. *She sent River away! Somehow she knew, and she sent him away!*

I spun around and ran out of the yard. *Boyer! I need to tell Boyer!*

I fled up the dirt road, past the silent machine shop, past the alfalfa field behind our house. Sparrows scattered off fence rails in a confusion of wings as I ran by. Clicking grasshoppers leapt from the tall grass on both sides of the road. I swatted blindly as they hit my body. I ran on, stumbling on sun-dried hard dirt ridges and wiping the tears and mucus from my face with the back of my sleeve.

Boyer will fix it! Boyer will fix it! I kept telling myself. Exactly how he would do that was not part of my hysterical mantra.

Shadows darkened the edge of the woods beyond the field. A canopy of branches and leaves covered the narrow road that led to the lake. The only sound I heard was the pounding of blood in my ears and the echo of my laboured breathing as I raced under them and into the meadow.

In the grey light, Boyer's cabin looked empty, abandoned. From the outside the only hint that anyone lived there at all was the new shiplap siding on the addition. And Boyer's Edsel parked at the side.

Oh, how I wished I had sensed the danger, the harsh unwanted knowledge that lay behind that heavy wooden door, before I rushed up and, without knocking, pushed it open.

I stood in the doorway, catching my breath and squinting into the dim interior. I heard a muffled sound and turned towards the bedroom. There was a sudden blur of movement on Boyer's bed. As my eyes adjusted, my mind could not keep up with what I was seeing, could not comprehend what was happening in the murky light of that small room. A flash of bare buttocks, a muscled back, naked arms and legs tangled. At first I thought I had caught Boyer sleeping. I was about to turn away from his nakedness when I saw the surprised face staring back at me was River's. And beneath him, raising his head off the pillow, was Boyer.

I stood frozen. The scene in front of me, the rumpled bed, the clothes strewn on the floor, River's canvas duffel bag in the corner, his guitar case leaning against the wall, I took it all in. But it made no sense. The relief of finding River there conflicted with the truth of what I was seeing. I heard Boyer's voice groan, 'Oh, God, Natalie.'

On the floor, at the end of the bed, two pairs of jeans lay crumpled, accordioned down as if they had just been melted out of. Both Boyer and River scrambled for them. They hurried to pull them up over their bare legs. Still, I did not turn away. Even in my shock, some place deep in the back of my consciousness noticed how beautiful they both were. Then, as suddenly as light snapping into a room, it hit me what I had just witnessed.

I watched Boyer and River in the other room and felt my stomach sour and rise to the back of my throat. I cupped my hands to my mouth to stifle the moans that rose with the bile.

'Oh, no! No!' I could not stop the rush of confused words that

spilled through my fingers and out into the room. 'Shit! What …
why … you can't … what are you doing?'

River slumped on to the edge of the bed, his shoulders rounded,
his elbows on his knees, his head down, as if he were faint.

Boyer came through the bedroom doorway. He lifted his arm and
reached out to me. His eyes did not avoid mine. They were weary,
sad, but I saw no shame hidden there, just hope, hope that I would
understand, that I would accept this unimaginable truth.

I twisted away from his touch. 'No, this is wrong, wrong. You
can't do this,' I cried. I looked past him. 'River … River … I thought
… you said you loved me!'

River raised his head. In his eyes was the same plea for understanding. 'I do love you, Natalie,' he said. 'But not that way.' His
face softened. He looked up at my brother. 'I love Boyer that way,'
he said.

'But … but … what about us …' I stammered as if I could argue this
all away, as if it were an argument I could win. 'We … we made love.'

At my words, they both seemed to stop breathing. Boyer turned to
River. 'What? You what?' His voice was a hoarse whisper. Suddenly it
was as if I was not in the room. The looks that passed between them
needed no words. Boyer waited for the denial he knew was not
coming; while River's eyes confirmed the horror of the truth.

'It was a mistake.' His voice was barely a whisper. 'A terrible,
terrible, mistake. I'm so … so sorry.'

'A mistake!' I cried. 'I'm a mistake!' But no one was listening to
me.

Boyer leaned down and grabbed River's boots and socks. He
flung them through the bedroom doorway where they landed at
River's feet. 'Get out,' he said, his voice barely audible. 'Take your
things and leave.'

'Please, Boyer,' River pleaded, 'I was going to tell you. Should have told you.' He looked to me, 'Natalie?'

I knew what he wanted, what he was asking of me. Even in the half-light of the bedroom I could see the panic in his eyes, the silent plea for me to explain, to say the words that would make Boyer understand. I would not give them to him. 'Yes, go … go …' I spat, 'both of you go. I hate you! I hate you both!'

I backed out of the cabin, tripped on the doorsill and stumbled. I reached up and grabbed the doorframe to straighten myself. 'Oh, God,' I moaned. 'I wish I was dead.' I turned and ran out, leaving them both hurrying to retrieve their clothes as I screamed back ugly words of hate. Words that came out of a frightened hysterical place, a cruel place that I did not even know existed inside me.

I heard Boyer call, 'Wait, Natalie. Don't go.' Concern for me filled his voice, as if he hadn't heard my condemnations.

I fled across the meadow grass in the fading light. I hurried, not down the dirt road that led home, but up. Up to the ragged edge of the woods. I looked over my shoulder and saw my brother rushing out of the cabin, hopping on one foot, while trying to pull on his other boot.

Shadows wrapped around me as I entered the trees. The forest was giving itself up to the night. Dried pine needles and twigs crunched under my feet as I scrambled up the slope. Branches scratched at my bare legs. I wished I wasn't wearing a mini-skirt – a new outfit that I had put on earlier that day hoping to impress River. Below, I heard arguing as they struggled to get dressed.

'Leave! Just leave,' Boyer shouted, as he ran out the door. 'I'll go find her.'

I glanced back over my shoulder. Through the trees I saw River rush out of the cabin after Boyer. 'I'm coming with you,' he shouted back as he followed Boyer up the hillside. The fury of their frustration rose with their voices in the night air and carried up the mountain.

It's impossible to get lost in the forests and hills that surround our farm Boyer once told me. 'If you ever get lost,' he said, 'ever lose your way, just climb higher until you can look down and see the fields and the barn.' He taught me how to use the North Star at night as a guide to lead me home.

But I wasn't heading home. Halfway up the slope, I turned north and began traversing the mountainside, stopping only a moment to catch my breath and get my bearings. A full moon rose in the starlit sky, casting lacy shadows through the trees. I heard the scurry of small feet in the undergrowth.

Our mother instilled in us a healthy respect for the wildlife of the forest. The more noise I made, the safer I would be. Below, Boyer and River's voices created enough noise to keep any nocturnal animals far away. Their hollers carried through the woods. I heard Boyer once again yell at River to leave, then both of them calling my name repeatedly in the darkness.

As they came closer, I pulled myself up into the crotch of a giant cedar tree. Bark scratched my bare thighs; mosquitoes attacked exposed skin. I concentrated on being still as their shouts came closer. Just before they reached the tree where I sat crouched, they veered in the opposite direction.

I waited and listened as their voices receded. Then I climbed out of the tree. In the glow of the rising moon I fought my way through the thick underbrush. I continued along the slope until I came to the edge of the gravel pit. I lost my footing in the loose gravel and slid down to the bottom, where I picked myself up and scurried across to the dirt road leading to the highway. To Atwood.

Chapter Thirty-Three

ALL MY LIFE I have wrestled with the question of why I did what I did. What ridiculous, needy part of me led to such a foolish decision? There's no explanation that makes sense.

Even as I ran through the streets of Atwood, I knew I could have – should have – gone home. I should have climbed into my bed, pulled the covers over my head, and sobbed out the confusion, hurt, and anger, until I had come to my senses, to the truth, to acceptance.

Instead, I ended up standing, panting and out of breath, on the porch of the only friend I could think to run to. Elizabeth-Ann opened the door to my pounding.

'Natalie! What is it?' she cried. I opened my mouth, but no words came. And in that instant, that millisecond of time, and forever after, I asked myself why I was there. Although Elizabeth-Ann had become my closest friend I had not been on this porch since her pyjama party years ago. I started to back away as my eyes frantically searched for signs of Mr Ryan. But when Elizabeth-Ann reached out and pulled me into the entry foyer and up the stairs to her room, I let her.

She closed her bedroom door behind us and led me to the canopied bed. Pink light from a ruffled-skirted lamp reflected the worry on Elizabeth-Ann's face as she sat down beside me. Concern shone in her eyes. My friend, my best friend, held both my hands in hers and asked in a hushed voice, 'What is it Natalie?'

'Boyer,' I sobbed, gasping to catch my breath, 'Boyer and River!'

'Boyer?' Panic flooded her face. 'Did something happen to Boyer? Is he all right?'

And without a thought I choked out the story. With the serious faces of the Beatles looking down from the posters on her wall, I told Elizabeth-Ann how I had found Boyer and River together, in each other's arms. *Lovers! God! They were lovers.*

Elizabeth-Ann remained silent, her full-lipped mouth half open, as my stream of words, barely connected, but forever betraying, told all. I hardly noticed the change of expression on her face as I went on spilling my confusion in a verbal barrage of bitterness. Then I saw it, the slight lift of the corners of her mouth as she fought to control a smile. *A smile*! She looked beyond me, through me.

'Ohhh,' she said, the word stretching out as understanding took hold. 'Oh! So that's it. That's why.'

'What? Why what?' I stammered, already realizing that I had released something that could never be retrieved.

'No wonder he wasn't interested in me. He's a *queer*!' She spat the word out – the word I had not even allowed myself to think – as if it burned her tongue.

Her eyes narrowed and once again focused on me, the smirk on her face complete now. I knew that look.

'Oh, poor Natalie,' she said, her voice a little too sweet. She pulled her hands from mine and wiped them on her skirt.

And just like that I was once again 'poor Natalie', farmer's daughter, 'Nat the Fat', waiting like the unwanted pick for baseball in front of the school's most popular girl.

'A queer!' Elizabeth-Ann giggled, then pressed her hand over her mouth. The giggle turned into a laugh, a laugh that I imagined following me as I fled down the stairs, out the front door, and into the street.

What have I done?

I fled through the streets of town. There was nowhere else to run, nowhere else to go. Except home.

I retraced my steps out of Atwood. At the end of Main Street I turned south and hurried down the empty highway. Suddenly the glare of headlights cast long shadows on the road before me. The car approached slowly from behind. I increased my pace as the black Lincoln pulled up beside me and the passenger window whirred down.

'Let me give you a ride home, Natalie,' the familiar voice called, the car keeping pace with my steps. I glanced quickly into the window. Mr Ryan leaned over from the driver's seat to open the passenger door with one arm as he held the steering wheel with the other.

'It's okay. I want to walk,' I said, moving faster and staring straight ahead.

'Don't be silly,' he said. 'Get in the car, and I'll have you home in a few minutes.'

I edged closer to the ditch, pretending I had not heard, hoping he would leave, but the car moved with me.

'I can't let you walk home in the dark,' he called out. 'Especially not while you're so upset.' When I didn't respond, he said, 'Natalie, I heard what you told Elizabeth-Ann.' He let his words sink in then called out. 'Now imagine what will happen if the wrong people find out. Think of Boyer's job, your father's business?'

Suddenly it was hard to breathe, as it struck me how much pain my careless words could bring. My lack of discretion.

'Now if you don't want the whole town knowing about your brother, I suggest you get into the car,' Mr Ryan demanded.

I can't explain why I thought I could undo the damage, somehow protect Boyer, by getting into that car. I can't say why, when every instinct within me warned me not to. I stopped walking, and let Mr Ryan push open the passenger door for me.

I felt his pink-rimmed eyes watching as I climbed in and pulled the heavy door closed.

'Thanks,' I said in a small voice, but I kept my hand on the door handle.

The car interior smelled of leather and new car, the smell of authority, the smell of careless power.

'Well, that was quite the story you told Elizabeth-Ann,' Mr Ryan said as the car gathered speed along the highway. 'No wonder you're upset.'

I remained silent wondering how much he had heard, how I could fix it.

'Seeing those two boys – men – like that,' he sneered, 'Well, that's pretty disgusting.'

My betrayal was complete.

'Please, don't tell anyone, Mr Ryan,' I begged. 'I was lying. I didn't really see anything. I was mad at my brother … I just wanted to hurt him. None of it's true,' I ranted. 'I was lying to Elizabeth-Ann. It's not true.'

'We both know it is true, don't we?' he said, ignoring my outburst. 'We're going to have to be very careful about who else finds out,' he said his voice now that of the mayor of our little town, the mayor concerned about the morality of his citizens. The Lincoln slowed and turned off the highway.

'No, wait, this isn't my road,' I said. 'South Valley is the next one.'

The car continued.

'We'll just turn around up here,' he said and pulled into the gravel pit, the same abandoned pit I had walked through less than an hour before.

The crunch of tires on gravel sounded hollow in the interior of the car as we swung a slow wide arc. But instead of driving back to the road, back to the highway, back to safety, the car rolled to a stop. Mr Ryan leaned down and reached under the seat with one hand.

'I have to go home,' I said, clutching at the door handle. The lock snapped down.

'Oh, what's your hurry?' A silver flask appeared in his hand. 'You shouldn't go home like this.' He unscrewed the cap and held the flask up to me. 'Here, have a sip of this. It'll calm you down.'

'No, no thanks.' Even in my growing panic, the need to be polite to an adult remained. 'I can walk from here,' I said, keeping my eyes on him as my fingers searched for the lock on the door.

'We have to talk,' he said, ignoring my words. 'We have to think about how we can keep your brother and his boyfriend's dirty little secret.' He put the flask to his lips and took a long drink then held it up to me again. 'Come on.'

I shook my head and pulled back, trapped. I shrunk against the door, pulling on the handle, which snapped back, useless.

'You know what I think you need, Natalie?' Mr Ryan said as he pulled the keys out of the ignition and slipped them into the pocket of his sweatpants. 'I think you need a real man.' He lunged across the padded leather seat, reaching for me.

He shoved his face against mine. Stale alcohol breath assaulting my nostrils. Wet lips sought mine. His hands, his hands were every-where, reaching, groping, finding their way inside my shirt, up my skirt, while mine blindly searched the passenger door for the lock and frantically yanked at the handle.

'Please, no,' I sobbed.

Somehow my shaking fingers found the silver knob on top of the door and pulled it up. At the same time my other hand yanked on the handle. The door flew open. I tumbled out backwards. My head landed heavily, momentarily stunning me. As I tried to push myself up, Mr Ryan's hand gripped my ankle.

'Oh, no you don't,' his voice a harsh growl. 'You're not going anywhere.'

Twisting and kicking, I pulled my foot from his grasp and managed to get to my feet. I bolted away. After a few steps my head snapped back. In a blur I felt myself flung around and slammed face first onto the hood of the car. Hard fingers tangled in my hair. I was held pinned by his body, my right arm caught under my stomach. My left flailed in the air.

'Like it rough, do you?' His free hand grabbed my arm and bent it across my back. He yanked my head back from the hood. I felt his lips against my ear. 'We'll just call this payment for keeping your brother's secret, won't we, Natalie?' he whispered.

When I continued to struggle he pulled harder on my hair while he pushed my twisted arm farther up my back. Pain burned though my skull. I wasn't sure which would snap first, my neck or my arm.

'Won't we?' his harsh voice insisted.

'Yes,' I choked. And I let my body go limp.

'That's better,' he said, breathing heavily. 'We'll just have our own little secret.' And still hanging onto my hair, he released my arm. I could feel him fumbling with his pants. A knee pushed between my thighs and forced my legs apart. A hand, harsh and probing, tore at my underpants.

I focused on the burning pain of hair being torn from my scalp and tried to ignore the assault to my body. The grunting thrusts seemed to go on forever as he slammed into me over and over again from behind. While I pretended I wasn't there.

When it was over, when he was finally finished, he shuddered and slumped against my back with a groan. In that moment his hand relaxed its grip on my hair.

I moved quickly. I spun my body around and, with every ounce of energy I had left, I lifted my knee and slammed it into his exposed crotch. With a grunt he slipped down while his hands, too late, tried to protect himself. I lifted my knee again.

His folded body crumbled to the gravel as I stepped away. I started to run, but first I reached down and grabbed at his sweatpants gathered at the bottom of his bare legs. As I yanked them from his writhing body, one of his moccasins caught in the leg. I clutched pants and slipper to my chest and carried them away with me as I fled.

Behind me I heard his groans turn into curses as he struggled to get up. I ran out of the gravel pit, through the trees, not daring to look back, expecting at any moment to feel a hand grab my hair.

Screaming words of rage followed me as I stumbled through the undergrowth. When his roar became a fading noise, when I was sure he was not behind me, I slowed down. I skirted a moss-covered deadfall. In the moonlight I leaned over to stuff his pants and slipper in the hollow end of the log. The car keys fell from his pocket. I picked them up, lifted my aching arm, and flung the keys into the darkness. I heard them hit branches, then fall to the forest floor.

I hurried through the trees along the edge of the highway. The headlights of passing cars splashed on the road then disappeared leaving the comfort of darkness once again. I was done with running, done with crying. After a while I came to South Valley

Road. I stayed in the brush and followed the road home, unafraid of the dark. The worst that could happen in the blackness of the night had happened.

Somewhere in the distance the lonesome cry of a train whistle sounded. It relayed through the mountains and dissipated down the valley, reminding me that other people moved carelessly through the night, their lives unchanged, while my life had just come apart at the seams.

Chapter Thirty-Four

I KNEW BEFORE I reached home, before I stumbled through the bottom field, weaving through the hulking forms of sleeping cows, their black and white hides reflecting the light of the full moon. Before my bruised and battered body climbed over the snake fence onto the road, before I saw our porch light burning. And I knew before I crept into our dark, empty, house and locked myself in the bathroom. Mr Ryan was right. I would never tell.

I was forever bound to him by our shared secret. I would tell no one, not my mother, my father, my brothers, or the police. I would never feel the relief of revenge. I would never whisper words into the darkness of a confessional to the waiting ears of a priest who would grant absolution from a forgiving God. My penance would be to carry this ugly secret alone.

And even after all these years I still cannot tell my daughter.

'Mom?' Jenny's voice calls me back. 'Mom. We're here.'

I look around. While I was lost in my dark memories, we had entered town, driven through a silent Main Street and up the hospital hill. We are parked in the wide circular driveway in front of the Alpine Inn.

The Alpine Inn. Such a ridiculous name for this regal old two-storey stone and brick building. Surely they could have come up with something more original, more fitting for this place that at one time was Our Lady of Compassion, School For Girls. For years now it has been a bed and breakfast. The dormitories, which once housed the too-young expectant mothers, have been divided into a number of separate rooms, each decorated in paisley and gingham country charm. The enclosed walkway, which once led to the hospital, is gone now. The privacy hedges no longer exist. Except for the Virginia creeper vines reaching up to the corners, the building stands bare and exposed to the street, no longer needing to hide its existence from the world.

Next door, the hospital, a larger version of this building, stands unchanged on the exterior. But inside, nuns no longer glide up and down the halls in wimples and silent efficiency. There is no maternity ward, no surgery floor. Due to the government's centralization of health services the hospital is mostly offices, extended care, and emergency now, not much more than an outpost, a first-aid station.

I look up to the third floor windows to where my mother sleeps. My heart lurches. Suddenly all I want is to see her. Until now I have managed to ignore the nagging thoughts that I might not make it in time, that I could be too late. Now I need to see her, to touch her, to be certain.

'I want to go up and see Mom before I check in,' I say. 'Do you think we can go in this late?'

'There's a night buzzer,' Jenny answers. 'I've already warned the nurse that we're coming.'

We leave the car and cross the lawn that separates the two buildings. 'I wish you'd change your mind,' Jenny says, taking my arm in hers, 'and stay at my house.'

'I want to be close to the hospital. Besides, I already have a reservation at the Inn.' I squeeze her arm. 'Just let me get through this, Jenny.'

She shakes her head, but says nothing as we approach the front doors of the hospital.

'So, when are Morgan, Ruth and Carl getting here?' I ask in an attempt to change the subject.

'Some time tomorrow. They're all staying out at the farm with Boyer and Stanley.'

Boyer and Stanley. She says those names as easily as if she were talking about an old married couple. And, in fact, of course she is. Jenny has always accepted her uncle, his partner, his homosexuality, as naturally as her love for him. And why shouldn't she?

But I wonder if she can possibly imagine how different it was for our generation. Does she realize homosexuality was a criminal offence in Canada up until 1969? Would she be surprised to learn that as late as 1965 a Canadian man was sentenced to life in prison, simply because he admitted to being homosexual? Or, unbelievably, that it was not until June of this very year, 2003, that a United States Supreme Court decision finally and full decriminalized homosexuality across America.

Unlike Jenny, I did not grow up in an era of acceptance. I had to learn it.

Chapter Thirty-Five

IN THE HARSH bathroom light I filled the deep claw-foot bath with steaming water. I pulled off my torn clothes, clothes that must never be allowed to find their way into the laundry for my mother's eyes to read. I tossed them into the corner. I would hide them in the crawl space under the eaves in my bedroom until I found a chance to burn them in the basement furnace.

I lowered myself into the hot water and scrubbed my body until it was numb in a frantic attempt to wash away the evil, the memory, and let it swirl down the drain with the dirt and the blood. I sat hugging my knees as the bath slowly emptied. Then I turned the water on again and lay against the sloped porcelain back. I let the water fill to the overflow, let it slowly crawl up and cover my entire body until only my nose and closed eyes were above water. I lay immersed, allowing my body to float suspended, in a world without sound, without light, without hurt. I wanted to stay there forever. I wanted to sink down and let it claim me.

I pushed away the visions and the cries of outrage that wanted to bubble up. I could not, would not, give them voice. It was all I could do, all I must do, to live with the torture of this secret eating at the lining of my stomach, my throat, trying to find a way out, to scream to the world, 'Look! Look what has happened to me, what was "done" *to me.'* I refused to give the beastly act a name. I would keep it caged, locked up in darkness, give it no voice to whimper in self-pity. And I would give no one the right to look at me with eyes filled with sympathy while they hid their revulsion, and their curiosity, for the imagined acts of violence they allowed themselves to visualize being committed on my body.

No I would not be a victim – his victim.

I even allowed myself to fantasize for a moment, to indulge in the bittersweet thought of making him a victim. Before I locked myself in the bathroom, when I was certain that the house was empty, I had picked up the wall phone by the fridge. The dial tone sounded loud in the silence of the dark kitchen; the clicking of the rotary dial seemed to take forever for each of the four numbers of the local Royal Canadian Mounted Police detachment.

At the sound of a voice on the other end of the line, I whispered, 'Check the gravel pit,' and then quickly put the phone back on the hook. Yes, I would keep the secret, but as I lay in the bath I imagined Mr Ryan trying to explain his half-naked condition to the police. But even these thoughts brought no comfort. I sunk lower totally submerging myself and concentrated on the ringing silence in my water-filled ears.

The bath water had cooled when I felt vibrations ripple through my watery cocoon. I lifted my head. Footsteps pounding up the porch steps, the kitchen door opened, more footsteps followed. 'Natalie?' my mother's voice called out. Her knuckles rapped on the bathroom door, 'Natalie, are you in there?'

I tried to find my voice, not sure what tortured sound would escape and find its way up into my throat and out of my mouth. I was surprised to hear the flat normality of the 'yes,' that finally came.

'She's home.' I heard the relief in her voice. Heavy footsteps hurried from the kitchen.

Behind her my father asked, 'Where's she been? Doesn't she know everyone's been out looking for her?' The anguish of worry hardened his words.

'It's okay, Gus,' my mother soothed him. 'You go with Boyer. I'll talk to her.'

'What was she thinking, running off in the dark like that? Letting everyone chase after her.' A mumbled trail of his words disappeared behind the slamming of the screen door.

'Are you okay?' Mom asked from the other side of the bathroom door.

'I'm fine,' I answered. 'I'm – I'm just taking a bath.'

I wanted her to go away – I wanted her to come in and sit on the edge of the bath and talk to me like she did when I was young, our shared femininity an island in a house full of males.

I wanted her to leave me alone – I wanted her to take me upstairs to bed and tuck me in like a child, tell me everything was going to be all right, then lay beside me until I fell asleep, the heat from her body keeping me safe and warm.

'Do you want a cup of tea?' she asked.

Tea. My mother's solution to every crisis. Oh, how I wanted that to be enough. To sip milk-and-sugar-laced tea once again in our exclusive ritual of 'girl' time, to have her read leaves that told of only good things. But the time for that was passed, was part of another life.

'No, thanks. I just want to go to bed,' I called out, hoping she would leave the kitchen.

I waited a while, then pulled the plug and climbed out of the bath. I took my time, rubbing myself dry, ignoring the complaints of my aching body, while the water drained. I cleaned the bath, making sure there were no traces left there to cause wonder. Then, wrapped in a bath towel and clutching the bundle of clothes close to my chest, I opened the bathroom door. My mother sat at the table waiting, a teacup rising to her lips.

I could not bring myself to look into her eyes. I reached for the handle of the stairway door. 'Good night,' I murmured and pulled it open.

The china teacup clinked into the saucer. I expected her to ask where I'd been, or why I had run off. The questions never came. Perhaps Boyer had told her everything, or perhaps, as she always seemed to, she just knew. Or perhaps she was too relieved to care. Or too worried, because the words she did say, the words that cut through my feigned apathy were, 'River's lost.'

Lost, how could he be lost?

'From what I understand they got separated when they were searching for you,' Mom said. 'When Boyer finally returned to the cabin, River wasn't there. But his things still are.'

I watched Mom's face as she spoke, looking for signs of anger, or even surprise, that instead of being gone, as she told me he was, River had been at Boyer's cabin. But I only saw worry in her eyes.

'Boyer was certain that eventually you would come home,' Mom said, 'but River isn't as familiar with these mountains – doesn't know every ridge and gully the way we do.'

I didn't know what to say. Nothing. There was nothing I could say. There was no accusation in her voice, but I knew, as I was certain she did, that if anything happened to River, it would be my fault. I was the reason he was lost. 'Boyer and your father are going back out on the horses to search for him,' she told me.

A few minutes later, I watched from my bedroom window as Dad and Boyer led the saddled horses from the barn. Mom hurried out with a thermos and a first-aid kit. Dad stuffed them in his saddle-bags, and then he and Boyer rode up the road towards the back field and out of sight.

I crawled into my bed. Curled up in a ball under blankets and quilts, I lay shivering while Mom sat alone downstairs.

I prayed. I prayed for River to come back safe. Somewhere in my prayers was the beginning of acceptance. I realized I could not stop loving River, any more than I could have stopped loving Boyer when I was six years old and learned that you can't marry your brother. I would just have to learn to love River in the same way.

Before long I heard Morgan and Carl arrive home from town. 'We'll go help search,' they said simultaneously after Mom had told them about River.

'No,' she insisted. 'No you won't. We don't need anybody else wandering through the bush tonight.' Her voice was firm. 'Someone has to be here to do the milking in the morning.'

'Oh, he'll show up by then,' Morgan assured her.

But he didn't. There were no answers to my prayers, all our prayers, that night. Before dawn, Dad came home. Alone. He joined Morgan and Carl in the barn. Full udders will not wait while emergencies are resolved.

Downstairs my mother took refuge in routine. I dressed quickly in a flannel shirt and shapeless pants and joined her. We cooked breakfast in silence. Breakfasts that would grow cold on platters. Uneaten bacon wrinkled in filmy white fat, and eggs congealed and hardened, while my brothers rushed off to join Boyer in the search. I went with Dad to deliver the milk.

We rode into town without speaking, both of us lost in our own thoughts. It had been so long since I had gone with him on the milk run. Would my father remember our routine on Colbur Street? How could I ask him to deliver to the Ryan house? How would I find the strength to walk up onto that porch?

I didn't have to worry. When we pulled up in front of the Ryans' house it was dark, all the curtains closed. A piece of white paper was stuffed into one of the empty milk bottles on the step. I knew what the note would say before I dashed up onto the porch and grabbed the bottle then hurried back to the truck and slammed the door.

No more milk!

Two members of the Royal Canadian Mounted Police detachment stood in our kitchen talking with Boyer when I came in after we returned from the milk run. I froze at the sight of them, but they hardly noticed me as I edged past them.

These were the same fresh-faced policemen who often found their way out to our table for afternoon or midnight snacks with our mother. They stood now with their hats in their hands, their faces serious beneath identical white-scalp crew cuts.

'It's too early,' the taller RCMP officer was saying.

'Too early?' Boyer said. 'He's been missing since last night.' He sat on a kitchen chair lacing up his hiking boots. Mom stood beside him staring at the officers, her arms folded.

'Well, he's a grown man,' the officer answered. 'Now if it was a child that would be different. But an adult? An adult has to be missing forty-eight hours before we can organize a search. Who knows why he took off? Maybe—'

'He's lost,' Boyer interrupted without looking up. 'He's in trouble.'

'Isn't he a draft dodger?' the other officer asked.

'Conscientious objector,' Boyer sighed as he tugged at his laces.

'Well, maybe he went back to the States. Maybe he decided to slip across the border and go home.'

'His things are still here.'

'Okay,' the taller officer said brushing the non-existent hair back from his forehead. 'If he doesn't show up by tomorrow, we'll bring in a tracking dog—'

'It could be too late by then,' Boyer said. He stood up and stalked out of the kitchen, the screen door slamming behind him.

Dad caught him on the porch. Through the screen, I saw him put his hand on Boyer's shoulder, 'Go get some sleep, son,' he said. 'I'll go out with Carl and Morgan after we grab some lunch.'

While Dad and Boyer spoke out on the porch the two officers stood, caps twisting in their hands, looking out of place and uncomfortable in the heat of our kitchen. Mom walked over to the sideboard in the corner and turned her back on them as if they weren't there.

'Must have been quite a full moon last night,' the shorter one said, searching for words that would return our kitchen to a place where they had often found respite from the tensions of their job. 'People traipsing through the bush, wandering around in the dark. You wouldn't believe who we picked up skulking around last night with his pants down – literally.'

My stomach lurched. I glanced over at Mom. She stood at the sideboard slicing bread with the determination of withheld anger. The remark had no effect. She was in no mood for local gossip. She spun around, pushed her way past them, and slammed the plate of bread on the table.

'Look, Mrs Ward,' the taller officer said. 'As soon as we call a search, as soon as we put out a missing person's report, we have to notify Customs, the authorities in the States, the FBI, and, well, do you really want to alert them if this fellow is trying to sneak home for a visit?'

'He's not,' she said. She moved to the stove, her back once again to them, dismissing them.

It was the first time I witnessed my mother not invite someone who was in our kitchen at mealtime to join us.

The gossip vine of a small town has its advantages. When the word spread that River was missing, a few people came out to help search. Very few. Mom always said you can tell your friends by those who show up in a crisis. Even more telling are those who don't. She wondered aloud about all the young people, all our friends who had come out to ride horses, to party at the lake, to dance out in the sunroom, who practically lived at the farm on weekends and holidays. Where were they all now?

Jake came, though not to search. 'I'm too old to be climbing these hills,' he grumbled, but he quietly took up the slack helping with chores and milking.

Even while the search continued, the routine of the farm had to be kept. Cows had to be milked and the bottled milk had to be delivered daily. The following morning more empty milk bottles waited on porches with notes instead of quarters inside. By the end of the week we would lose ten more customers.

On Thursday afternoon, Morgan went into town to pick up the grocery order. When he came out of the Super Value, he found written in the dust on the side of the truck the words HOMO MILK! and FAIRYLAND!

The next night someone climbed up on our gate and spray-painted the words FAG FARM! onto the Ward's Dairy sign. In the morning, Dad took the sign down and burned it. It was never replaced.

The anonymous phone calls started that evening. I cringed the first time I heard a muffled voice promising us 'hell and damnation'. Each time Mom answered the phone only to slam it back down, I knew she was hearing similar threats. And still there was not one word spoken in our house about the root of those rumours. As we rushed past each other, frantically doing what we could during those days, no one questioned the accusations about Boyer's sexuality. No one asked how and why the rumours started. No one questioned my part in all of it.

As the rumours spread, rumours that I knew could only have begun their ugly web of gossip from one house in town, there were those who ignored them.

Before the RCMP finally began an organized search, Mr Atwood and his son, Stanley Junior, showed up. They arrived with two three-wheeled ATVs on the back of a flatbed. I heard Jake tell Dad there had been an announcement at the Bull Moose Mine that any man who joined the search would be paid overtime wages.

Ma Cooper, strangely silent for once, and Widow Beckett came and worked with Mom to feed the small group of searchers. I begged to join the search, but Mom insisted she needed me at home. I was kept busy between the dairy and the kitchen.

The police notified River's family. His anxious mother confirmed that neither she, nor his grandfather, had heard from River and had no reason to expect him. Mom spoke on the phone with her every day while the search went on.

By the following Sunday they had turned up nothing. There was no sign, no clue, to lead them to River. Convinced that he had found his way around Robert's Peak and across the border, the RCMP announced that they were calling off the search.

In the next few days almost everyone else gave up as well,

believing or wanting to believe, that the police were right and River was back in the States, safe and hiding somewhere in his own country. Even Dad, Morgan and Carl began to question if that might not be the case.

Only Boyer and I were certain it wasn't true. Boyer and I, and perhaps Mom.

Boyer kept searching. He went further and further into the mountains each day. He was exhausted. I could see the hope had drained from his eyes. Still, he would not let me search with him. He'd hardly spoken a word to me since Tuesday night. I knew he saw the ugly words splashed onto our sign before Dad burned it. He must have known that only my thoughtless tongue, my lack of discretion, could have started the rumours. The morning Dad removed the sign I had caught Boyer on the porch. 'I'm sorry—' I started.

He held up his hand to halt my mumbled apology. But I couldn't stop the rushed words. 'Please, please let me come with you,' I rambled on nervously. 'I know these mountains, I can help in the search.'

'Just stay and help Mom,' he said, dismissing me as easily as if he was waving off a fly.

The next day I stood peeling potatoes at the sink, my mind numbed in the security, the sameness of routine, when the screen door screeched opened. Boyer stood silent and darkened by the backlight in the doorway. 'I found him,' he said.

At the stove my mother's hand rose to her mouth. She stood frozen, the unasked question not making it past her eyes. I stopped breathing. The paring knife fell from my paralyzed hands.

Boyer shook his head, his silent answer filling the room. He slowly made his way across the kitchen and picked up the wall phone beside the fridge. The metal dial clicked and whirred back at each number.

The crows led Boyer to River, Morgan told me later. He followed the crows as they circled above the trees and blackened the branches of an aspen grove, a choir of hoarse-throated mourners keeping vigil.

Boyer untied the rolled tarp from the back of his saddle. He swatted away the carnivorous black-winged scavengers and the haze of iridescent bluebottle flies. Then, he gently covered what was left of the body he had found lying on the edge of a shallow mine hole. He needed to call the police. And River's mother. It was the last thing he could do for him.

While Boyer waited in the kitchen for the RCMP to arrive he gave in to his exhaustion. He sat down and laid his head in his arms on the table. His shoulders heaved with muffled sobs. Mom stood behind him with her arms wrapped around him as if she could curb the shaking. She leaned over and kissed the top of his head. Silent tears ran down her cheeks into his hair as she mumbled something I could not hear.

'God!' Boyer moaned. 'I sent him away.'

But I was the one responsible. I had sent him to his death. *I killed River.*

'A freak accident,' the police would say when they concluded their investigation. River had stumbled over the mineshaft in the dark. The hole was so shallow it shouldn't have killed him. But his head snapped back and struck bedrock when he landed. The officer who brought the report out shook his head with sympathy before he left and said, 'He would have been able to crawl out if he'd survived the fall.'

As it was, a wild animal, a bear or cougar, dragged his body out.

So the hunters came. The same hunters whom my father had

always denied access to our land. They scoured the hills, using the senseless accident as an excuse to track down and kill a cougar, two black bears and a lynx. By the time they rode by our house with their trophies slung across their fenders, the Ward family was beyond caring.

Chapter Thirty-Six

WHILE BOYER LED the police to River and Mom murmured mournful words of comfort to his grieving mother on the telephone, I went out to Boyer's cabin to do the last thing I could do for River.

I peered over my shoulders into the bush as I hurried out alone. Every movement in the shadows held terror for me now. And every time I closed my eyes during the long sleepless nights since the assault, the horrors played out again.

Still, I forced myself on. I knew the police wanted River's personal belongings. I would make sure no prying eyes read his private journals. I would get rid of any marijuana hidden in his duffel bag. The gossipmongers had had enough of him. I would let them have no more.

In the cabin I sorted through his things. Tears rolled down my cheek as I undid the zipper of the duffel bag and lifted out the clothes that smelled of him. At the bottom of the bag I found his journals and a small plastic bag of rolled smokes and matches. I wiped my eyes on the sleeve of my sweatshirt as I placed the journals on the table. Then I opened the small plastic bag and removed a thin cigarette.

Was it really just over a week ago that I had sat in his room over the dairy with the sweet aroma of marijuana smoke hanging in the

air? I placed the cigarette between my lips and struck a match. I'd
never even tried to smoke before, but I wondered if this sweet-
smelling drug would make me not care for a while. I wondered if
that was what he had felt when he inhaled this fragrant weed; what
he had felt on the night we were together. I wanted to understand
why he had allowed himself to be with me for even those few brief
moments that night. I thought I might find some glimpse of that
understanding in the smoke and in the journals.

But I found no answers in either. I felt nothing from the marijuana except nausea. I tried to smoke the only way I knew how,
dragging on the cigarette as I'd seen my father do for years. I sucked
the smoke into my mouth then blew it out in cloudy blue streams.
I found it difficult to keep the thin cigarette lit. When it went out, I
lit another and pulled at the embers in an attempt to create the
billows of smoke that came so smoothly out of my father's mouth.
Three cigarettes burned down in a saucer between my short puffs
and coughing fits, while I sorted through River's journals. Still, I felt
only slightly light-headed. Finally, with my throat burning, I gave
up and concentrated on finding the order of his entries.

River's journals were dated from before he left the States. I started
reading about his difficult decision to leave his country, his family.
I skimmed through the pages trying to find any reference to our
family, to me. But as I read his daily entries I found myself strug-
gling to concentrate. My attention was on the rounded
handwriting, the beauty of the script on the page. I shook my head
and tried harder to focus. But I found it impossible to hang onto the
meaning of his words for anything more than a few seconds.
Through the haze of my sleep-deprived mind I wondered if this was
what if felt like to be high? I closed my eyes for a moment.

The night had crept up and dimmed the light in the cabin when

I reopened my eyes. I forced myself to reach through the fog of my brain. I flipped through the pages of the last journal. Half-asleep I recognized the angst of a gentle soul trying to seek meaning for his feelings, his sexuality, his attraction to Boyer. Then I came to the final date. *June 8.* The night I was in his room. I felt the pain in his words as he chastised himself for his lack of judgment.

What have I done? By trying to deny the truth of who I am I have destroyed everything. I have betrayed her, betrayed everyone. And myself. For what? A thoughtless moment of curiosity? How inadequate the word regret is.

Scribbled on the very bottom of the page, barely legible, as if he had been trying to force all the words into the space, was his last entry. Stunned, I read the words telling how, as he looked out of the window as I was leaving his room, he saw my mother duck under the dairy stairs.

My mother? My mother was there?

So it was true, she knew I was in his room that night. But why was she there?

Was it possible that she too …? No, that couldn't be. But what was she doing there? My mind raced with unthinkable thoughts. I recalled anonymous whispers on the phone, ugly accusations about everyone in our family, about our free love commune, about River. My mind whirled in confusion.

Suddenly headlights flashed in the window. Boyer was home. I jumped up and dumped the ashes, spent matches, and butts, along with the rest of the marijuana in the rubbish under the sink, then quickly rinsed the saucer. I rushed to gather the journals.

Boyer came through the door, defeated, tired, somehow looking smaller, as if a part of him had been cut away. He sniffed at the air and shook his head wearily. Then he spotted the journals.

'These belong to River's family,' he said reaching for them. As he picked them up he said quietly, 'Come on, I'll drive you back to the house.'

In the past I would have argued that I could walk that far, that I was not afraid of the dark, and he would have let me. But not that night. We drove the short distance in silence, both of us surely thinking of different dangers lurking in the night.

'Are you sure we should give those journals to River's mother?' I said before I climbed out of his car. My tongue felt thick as I rambled on. 'I mean, do you think he would want her to read them? To know … to know all this?'

'His mother knows,' Boyer sighed. 'A mother always knows.'

Chapter Thirty-Seven

MOM'S NOCTURNAL WANDERINGS saved Boyer's life that night. She smelled it first. The hint of smoke drifted across the alfalfa field behind the house and in through an open window in the sunroom. Her sensitive nose turned to the scent carried on the night breeze. She peered past her reflection in the darkened window. Above the trees behind the field, she saw her ominous fear of fire manifested in a pink glow in the sky.

I pulled myself up from my drugged sleep, at the sound of her screams ripping through the house, 'Gus! Gus! Get up. There's a fire! Oh! God! Hurry! Hurry! It's Boyer's cabin!'

As I jumped out of bed, I heard Morgan and Carl rush out into the hallway and thunder down the stairs to the kitchen. I ran behind them in my nightgown. Through the kitchen window, I saw my father, still wearing his longjohns, run across the farmyard and into the machine shed.

I flew out of the kitchen and leapt down the porch steps. My shaking fingers fumbled with the gate latch. I forced it open and bolted up the road towards Boyer's cabin. Up ahead Mom ran along the backfield, her dressing gown flapping behind her, Morgan and Carl close behind. I raced after them in my bare feet. The roar of the tractor sounded behind me as I stubbed my foot against a root and tumbled to the side of the road. I threw myself back against the fence as the steel forklift prongs on the Massey Ferguson passed. I scrambled up and ran behind the tractor, dodging clumps of dirt thrown up by the tyres. The grinding metallic screech of changing gears rang through the night as my father stood over the steering wheel, urging more speed from the old machine, the screaming protest of the engine matching the hysteria I felt shrieking in my head.

I caught up with, then passed, the red taillights. I ran ahead of the tractor, down the seemingly endless road, through the trees, and into the meadow. I rushed into the clearing and stumbled towards my brother's cabin, trying to make sense of the scene in front of me.

At first I thought the lake was on fire. Orange light, angry and alive, lit up the night. The shining reflection of flames leaping from the log cabin created a mirrored blaze in the dark waters of the lake. Sparks flew from the shake roof and exploded into the sky, then disappeared into the darkness. Hungry flames escaped from the open kitchen windows. Greedily they reached out and fed on the branches of the apple tree. I stifled the screams rising in my throat as the ancient tree, which had sheltered the cabin for over half a century, burned like a giant torch in the night sky.

Blistering heat radiating in waves distorted the strange dance being performed in the flickering shadows. In front of the cabin, Morgan and Carl, on either side of Mom, struggled to hang onto her arms, to hold her back. She fought viciously to pull away. She kicked and twisted like a mad woman as she strained towards the cabin door. A voice I barely recognized screamed at them, demanded, threatened, and begged them to let her go, to let her go to her son.

I whirled around and ran to the side of the cabin, to the addition, to Boyer's bedroom window. I threw myself up, clawing at the wood, my feet trying to climb straight up the side as I too screamed my brother's name. Strong hands grabbed me and pulled me back. I scratched and bit at Morgan's arms as I fought to escape his hold. The tractor roared behind us. Morgan dragged me further away as our father rammed the front-end of the Massey Ferguson into the side of the cabin. I slowed my struggles as I saw my father's determined face, illuminated by the red glow. He backed up the tractor to take another run at the frame walls. As he willed the tractor forward again and again, the forklift prongs tore into the siding and plywood wall until it ripped apart, leaving a gaping hole into Boyer's bedroom. The fire inside, fed by the fresh oxygen, exploded through the opening.

It took a moment before I recognized that the fireball that shot out and landed at our feet was human. It was Boyer.

Chapter Thirty-Eight

I BARGAINED WITH God. As my parents rushed Boyer to the hospital, I knelt on the linoleum floor in the parlour. I promised untold penitence in return for my brother's life. As the hours passed, I pleaded to, and then in anger, threatened, a nonchalant God, a God who allowed so much tragedy to strike our family. Still, as I waited for a phone call I did not want to answer, I held little hope that the body that Mom and Dad wrapped in wet towels and laid on quilts in the back of the pick-up truck, would return to us as Boyer.

Before dawn, as the shadows of the night pulled back over the mountains, Morgan and Carl, soot-covered and tired, returned home from Boyer's cabin. The three of us sat at the kitchen table. Coffee grew cold in mugs cupped in still hands. My brothers spoke in hushed voices about how everything was lost in the fire. Boyer's books, River's journals, all ashes. I listened, mute with guilt, while they speculated over what caused the fire. 'Must have been the propane gas,' Carl concluded and Morgan nodded.

Just before five o'clock, my mind numb, I followed them outside. As we headed across the farmyard to let the cows into the barn, Dad drove up. He climbed out of the truck. He looked hollow, older. He stumbled by us as we stood waiting for news.

'Dad?' Morgan called after him, his voice gentle but insistent.

Our father stopped and turned slowly. He looked at us with vacant eyes, as if dimly aware of our presence.

'They're taking him to the airport by ambulance, then air-lifting him to Vancouver,' he said, his voice oddly flat. 'They've done everything they can for him here. Your mother's going with him,' he added, then headed into the barn.

The police investigation lasted all of two days. At first, the police, like my father, suspected the fire was deliberately set, but there was no proof. The same two RCMP officers, who had spoken to Mom and Boyer about River, showed up a week later with the final report. I stood slumped behind the bathroom door with a molten lump of guilt lodged in my throat and listened to them report to my silent father that the fire had started somewhere at the front of the cabin from 'unknown causes'.

Mom was gone for two weeks. It would be another five months before Boyer came home. River's mother and grandfather came and went. They took away what was left of their son, and grandson, in a pine box. There was nothing else to take. I knew if my mother had been there, if Boyer had been there, they would have found the right words of comfort to share. I tried. I took his mother over to the dairy and showed her where River had lived. I told her about his time here with us, about his words of love for them in the burned journals; they deserved at least that as Boyer said. But in the end they went away with only their sorrow.

And through it all, our daily routine continued. There were times when I heard Morgan and Carl curse the farm and its never-ending chores, but it was that necessary routine that kept them moving during those months.

While Boyer fought to recover, enduring the endless skin grafts and surgeries in the Vancouver Burn Unit, we went through our days like shell-shocked survivors. And the gossip went on. Rumours about River and Boyer turned into outright lies. We received a poorly-written letter, condemning Boyer for trying to commit suicide over the death of his lover by setting himself on fire. 'Like those damned Budda monks protesting the Vietnam War that draft dodger was too yellow to fight in,' one of them read.

Lewd suggestions about Morgan and Carl's relationship were uttered on the phone too. They stopped going out in the evenings and the few friends who tried to come back were sent away. My brothers wanted nothing to do with town now, only going into Atwood when necessary to pick up the mail or groceries.

I went to the high school and cleaned out both Carl's and my locker. I was finished with school for the year. Carl was finished with it forever. It was just as well he refused to go back. At least he did not have to see the ugly words scratched into the green paint on the metal doors of both our lockers.

By the end of the month almost one half of Dad's customers had cancelled deliveries.

That summer, a summer I had looked forward to with such foolish romantic anticipation, dragged on, a monotonous heat-filled season. Something more than Boyer was missing from our family. We each moved through our days in solitary worlds. Our connectedness, the glue that had held us together, had vanished. Stilted conversations, either about the business of the farm, or of Boyer's progress, became our method of communication.

While Mom was in Vancouver, we fell into the habit of eating only when we were hungry, each of us grabbing leftovers from the picked-at meals I prepared each day. Grazing, Mom called it when she came home and put a stop to it. She insisted we all sit down at mealtimes. 'We need to get back to normal,' she said. But we never would.

Our family became isolated. Except for a few old friends, we were shunned. The only guest who ever joined our table during those days was Father Mackenzie. And starting in October, Ruth.

Ruth was one of the girls from Our Lady of Compassion. She would become the last resident there before the home closed down. Morgan and Carl began keeping company with her after Morgan bumped into her in front of the post office, almost knocking her to the granite steps, as he rushed out one afternoon.

Tall and willowy, it was hard to tell that she was an expectant mother, except for a small bulge under her blue smock. Morgan walked her back up the hospital hill that day and their friendship began. Both he and Carl escorted her to the Roxy Theatre every week. Then they began to bring her home for dinner. It wasn't long before everyone in our family was drawn to the dark-haired girl from Queen Charlotte Island. I suppose she gave us something to focus on outside of our own miseries. We were all aware of her sadness for carrying a child she would not be allowed to keep. Still, she charmed us all with her quiet acceptance of life. Even I, who had become so guarded, began to look forward to her visits.

Back at school after the summer vacation I ignored the huddled groups watching as I walked the hallways. The looks of pity cast my way were as hard to take as the whispered gossip that reached my ears. I pretended not to see, not to hear. I pretended I wasn't there and hid behind shapeless sweatshirts and baggy pants.

When I wasn't in school, or with Dad on his dwindling milk round, my existence was limited to the house and the dairy. In the hours in between, I slept. I slept and I ate. While the rest of my family lost their appetites, I took comfort in food.

Some weekend mornings Dad insisted I come along with him on the milk run. He certainly didn't need me, and I suspected it was just to get me out, but I couldn't refuse him. Each time we approached Colbur Street I felt myself start to hyperventilate.

I knew that sometime during the summer Elizabeth-Ann and her mother had left town. Ma Cooper graced us with the latest gossip.

'Seems the mayor's wife and daughter ran off on him,' she told Mom. 'He came home from work one night and found the house emptied. Don't know how she got a moving van in and out of there without him knowing about it. Everyone else did.'

And even though Ma Cooper reported that Mr Ryan had disappeared shortly after I couldn't shake the panic that rose up every time we drove by the empty house.

She stood by us, Ma did, and so did the Widow and Jake. They weren't the only ones who refused to turn their back on us during those months. There were the fine ladies from the church.

The delegation of three showed up on our porch that fall. I was finishing the breakfast dishes at the sink when I heard the knock on the screen door. No one, except salesmen and strangers, ever knocked at our door. Everyone else just came in.

Mom glanced up from the enormous ball of dough she was kneading to see the three women standing out on the porch. They looked like triplets dressed up in their Sunday-go-to-meeting clothes. Identical pillbox hats sat on their heads; purses hung primly from folded arms.

'Well, well, to what do I owe this honour?' Mom asked. She wiped her hands on her apron as she glared at them through the screen. I was surprised when she didn't open the door and invite them in. Perhaps she recognized the Christian determination to grant redemption in their eyes.

'Hello, Nettie,' Mrs Woods said, ignoring Mom's sarcastic tone.

Gertrude Woods was the president of the women's auxiliary. I was sure she must have been missing Mom's active participation in the good deeds of that benevolent group.

'We have had a meeting,' she said, her voice smooth. 'And we have decided that Boyer – well, Boyer was surely led astray by that American fellow – that heathen draft-dodger. We agreed that God has punished Boyer enough for his unholy acts and that he is surely repentant.'

'You did, did you?' Mom said and folded her arms across her chest.

'We felt it was our Christian duty to come here today,' Mrs Woods went on. 'We have come to offer our support to you and your family. To see if there is anything we can do to help in your time of need.'

The hum from the refrigerator droned on while Mom stood unmoving. 'Why yes,' she finally said, 'there is something you can do.' Her eyes narrowed. 'You can get the hell off of my porch.'

Hell was not much of a swear word even then, but it was one of a very few I'd ever heard come from my mother's mouth. The shocked gasps that followed were not only from the three crows perched on our porch. The same gasp came from me.

'Now, Nettie,' Mrs Woods sniffed. 'We know that it's the sorrow talking, and we have no doubt that God will forgive you.'

'The question is,' Mom said, 'will He forgive you?' She calmly pushed the door closed and went back to her bread dough. 'That's not the church talking,' she said to me, 'that's just those old biddies brewing up trouble.'

I was not sure if Mom was trying to convince me, or herself.

'This town is like a flock of your baby chicks,' I heard Ma Cooper say to her later. 'All fluff and innocence until they detect some weakness. Just let them spot a speck of blood, then watch them turn on one of their own, and peck it to death.'

But in October, after Morgan started keeping company with Ruth, Ma Cooper could not keep her mouth shut.

'It's none of my business, Nettie,' she said, 'but you have enough troubles in this family without Morgan parading around town with a pregnant girl, and an Indian at that.'

'She's Haida,' Mom corrected her.

Ruth's mother was part Haida from the Haida Nations Indian Band on Queen Charlotte Island. Her father was a commercial fisherman there. It was her strict Irish Catholic father, Ruth told Mom, who had sent her away to have her baby when she got into trouble.

'You're right, Ma,' Mom said in her no-nonsense voice. 'It *is* none of your business. And if Morgan and this young lady,' she continued, 'find comfort in each other's company, I'm happy for them. And I'm not interested in the foolishness of wagging tongues.

'This town should be ashamed,' Mom added sadly. 'The people here have been tested and failed. It's obvious that there's no tolerance for anything different.'

I will say for Ma Cooper though, that when she saw how strongly Mom felt, she held her counsel and stood by us once again. And even Ma, after she came to know her, fell in love with Ruth.

Beautiful Ruth with the sparking dark eyes and shy smile. She became the lifeline to our floundering family. And on the day when Boyer finally returned, it was only Ruth who could look into his face without flinching, without shock, without fighting back tears.

Snowflakes drifted down from the grey sky on the late November day Boyer came home. We had all been warned about the scars that were still healing but, except for Mom, I don't think any of us was truly prepared.

I stood trembling behind the porch window and watched as Mom and Dad climbed out of the car. Mom opened the back door and leaned down to help Boyer. As he carefully stepped out then straightened up, I saw the patches of pinto-like skin creeping up the side of his neck. I breathed a sigh of relief. Then he turned.

I gripped the window ledge as the devastation on the other side of his face was revealed. His face! It was as if the whole left side had melted. Somewhere under the angry red scar tissue was where his ear, his cheek and the left side of his mouth had once been.

As Mom slowly led him up the path to the porch, I fled into the kitchen. I tried to look past the scars, tried to find Boyer in the eyes, when he finally came through the door. There was nothing there. He looked back at me for less than a heartbeat and then through me, beyond me. It was as if I had disintegrated, as if I didn't exist. I slunk back into the corner as he passed.

I don't know how long it would have taken my brothers to speak if Ruth hadn't stepped up and held her hand out to Boyer. 'I'm so happy to meet you,' she said in her gentle voice. 'I'm Ruth.'

We had all been warned that Boyer was still having trouble speaking because of the tracheotomy performed on his smoke-damaged throat. And even though it was healed, Mom said it was still painful for him to talk. He slowly raised his hand. Ruth took it and held it cupped gently in both of hers.

Morgan and Carl, usually so quick with words, stood there gaping, as if they'd lost their voices. Finally Morgan found his. 'Hey. Welcome home. Have we missed you!'

Boyer nodded to them and then walked through the parlour into the sunroom.

Mom said he was still in shock, still needed time to heal, that it was normal for burn victims to retreat inward, to feel anger. I don't remember who she said that to or why, but it wasn't to me.

For the next few months, Boyer slept out in the sunroom. The stairs were too difficult for his stiff, recovering body. He healed in private, keeping his scars and his pain to himself.

I confined myself to the kitchen, the bathroom and my room while I tried to be invisible. Late at night when the rest of the house was asleep, when I was sure Mom was not up, I began to sneak downstairs and carry food back to my room. I stayed awake as long as I could, reading and eating, stuffing myself with words and food hoping to ward off the images that came with sleep. Still, every night the visions came – dreams of tendrils of smoke rising from under the kitchen sink in Boyer's cabin. Because no matter how many times I heard Mom tell someone that the police suspected that the fire was arson, or Dad say he believed it was deliberately set by the same hands that painted our gate sign, I knew who the arsonist was. And every time I closed my eyes I could see the embers from marijuana butts that I had so carelessly emptied into the trash, smoulder – smoulder and ignite while Boyer slept.

Chapter Thirty-Nine

I DON'T KNOW how Boyer and I lived together in the same house that winter. Yet during the months after he returned from the burn unit, we somehow managed to avoid each other.

When I wasn't at school or doing chores, I hid out in my room. Boyer lived between the sunroom and the kitchen. An entire world away. Sometimes I caught glimpses of him passing through the kitchen on his way to the bathroom. It was as if a stranger had taken over his body. I couldn't see Boyer even in the relatively normal right side of his face. Certainly it could not be my brother who sat for hours on end in Dad's recliner in front of the television set.

Mom became his keeper. She protected him from the curious eyes of visitors and even from us. She took meals out to him in the sunroom. Each morning she ran his bath, tested the water, and then led him like a reluctant child into the bathroom. She rubbed his thickening scars with oils and insisted he keep mobile. Every few hours, she took him by the arm and led him on short walks, first around the house, then venturing outside, his temperature-sensitive skin bundled up against the cold.

The snow came early that winter. I watched from my window as drifts covered the fence tops in the yard. I watched the snow plough come up our road in the early morning, the giant blade sending great waves of white up onto the snowbanks.

No matter how deep the snow became we were never allowed the luxury of being snowed in. Like the mail, the milk must go through. South Valley Road was the first road to be cleared each day. But except for the milk deliveries and necessities, we rarely went to town. We became as isolated as if we were snowbound. Mom still attended church each Sunday morning, the only one of us who went on a regular basis now. I refused to go at all. No one challenged me.

Before Christmas a few of Dad's old customers tried to renew. He ignored their requests while Mom argued we couldn't afford to be proud. 'I'll sell some cows in the spring,' he argued. 'Well it's either that,' Mom threatened, 'or sell the milk in bulk to the commercial dairies.' That was a solution my father said he'd rather die than see happen. He almost got his wish.

Our dairy was one of the last operations in the province to bottle and sell raw milk. 'Those suits from the city want to sterilize every- thing,' he used to say. 'If they have their way, pretty soon there won't be any goodness, anything natural, left in anything. We'll all just swallow little plastic pills instead of eating real food.' That winter the inspector from the Milk Board began to show up on a regular basis to do random quality checks.

'Someone's looking for an excuse to shut us down,' Dad complained each time they showed up. The tests always came out clean.

During Christmas break it was harder to avoid Boyer. Whenever I wasn't doing chores I retreated to my room. One afternoon, my mother called after me as I plodded upstairs. 'Go to Boyer's old room and bring down some of his books,' she told me.

The attic bedroom had been empty ever since Boyer moved out to the cabin the year before. Neither Morgan nor Carl had any inclination to move up there, both of them content to remain roommates.

Most of Boyer's books were lost in the fire, but some still remained stacked in his old room.

It was not only the chilled, damp air that held me back as I trudged reluctantly up to the attic. There was more than a bed and desk missing from the room. It was as if it was the room of a ghost. I hesitated for a moment before I entered with a shiver and began to search hastily through the piles of books. I carried an armload to the kitchen and placed them on the table for my mother's inspection. She lifted one, then another, as if choosing tomatoes in a store. They were all familiar novels, classics, which I was sure both she and Boyer had read a number of times. Finally she chose *A Tale of Two Cities* and shoved it at me.

'I want you to read this to Boyer,' she said.

I stepped back, recoiling from the book, 'But— but, I can't,' I stammered. She had no idea what she was asking of me.

'Yes, you certainly can,' she insisted. 'It's too difficult for him to hold a book for any length of time.' She nodded towards the parlour. 'Now go in and sit down beside him and just read.' She pushed the book into my hands. 'It will do you both good.'

In the parlour Boyer lay in Dad's recliner, his eyes closed. On the television screen the Galloping Gourmet chopped onions. I walked over and switched off the set. Graham Kerr's tear-stained face shrunk to a tiny white dot on the screen. When I turned back Boyer was sitting up. I could feel his eyes following me.

'Mom said, she said I should read to you.'

Boyer said nothing. He may have nodded. I don't know. I stared at the book in my hand, at the oval rag rug at my feet, anywhere but into that face.

I sat down in Mom's chair on his right side and turned to the first page. I found my voice and began to read. 'It was the best of times, it was the worst of times ...'

I read the words, but I heard, felt, none of them. I kept my eyes on the pages while my monotone voice droned on. We must have appeared a strange pair, the two of us sitting straight and rigid in our parents' chairs, ignoring each other's presence. Boyer, who taught me to read, who taught me to pay attention to the rhythm, the music of the words, stared straight ahead.

When I was a child, he would listen closely as I read, then interrupt me in the middle of a sentence if he couldn't 'hear the passion', as he said, 'the truth', in my voice for the words on the page. That Boyer would never have endured my lifeless reading. He would have stopped me after a few lines and insisted I let him hear the beauty of the words, or he would have repeated them from memory, giving them the life they deserved. But this Boyer said nothing.

When I finished the last sentence of the first chapter, he stood up. The voice of a stranger said, 'Thank you,' a harsh gurgle sounding in his throat. He retreated to the sunroom.

I held the sleeve of my sweatshirt against my nose to stifle the sneezes and the tears I felt building. Those two words were the first my brother had spoken directly to me since the night of the accident.

The accident. That's what my family had come to call it whenever they spoke of the night of the fire, which was seldom. I never spoke of it at all. But I ached to blurt out the truth. The next afternoon I sat down beside him to read again. But before I started, I decided I would tell him. I must tell him. I set the book unopened on my lap, and took a deep breath as I searched for the words. 'The fire, Boyer, I ...'

I felt him wince as he leaned back in the recliner. 'Not now,

Natalie, I'm tired,' the raspy voice of a stranger dismissed me. I fled to my room.

When I came downstairs later to help with dinner, I heard Dad's voice coming from the parlour. I peeked in to see him sitting in Mom's chair beside Boyer. My father held a Dr Seuss book in his hands and was reading out loud from it. I backed into the kitchen and turned to my mother. 'When did Dad learn—?' I whispered.

For the first time since summer, his name passed between us. 'River,' she said. 'He was teaching him. That's why he went on the milk round. They stopped for lessons at a booth in the back of Gentry's every day.'

I went back and stood in the doorway. My father was concentrating on the words while Boyer, who was laid back in the recliner, listened with his eyes closed. A smile lifted the right side of his lips. I turned away but not before seeing the trickle of moisture move down the smooth skin below his right eye. From the kitchen I listened to my father read those simple words about green eggs and ham as if they were the most important in the world. At that moment they were.

Something changed for Boyer after that. Every afternoon he and Dad sat together in the parlour while Dad read to him. Before long they moved to the kitchen table with books spread out in front of them. By the end of January, my father was reading the newspaper for real.

Boyer moved back up to the attic room. He took his place at the table for meals again and started working with Mom in the dairy. And the more he joined the world, the more I retreated.

Once again, most nights I refused dinner and would later sneak down to raid the kitchen while everyone slept. One night in mid February, I loaded my plate by the light of the refrigerator.

'How long can this go on, Natalie?' My mother's voice startled me. She stood in the parlour doorway in her nightgown.

'What?' I asked and shut the fridge door.

Mom sighed and switched on the kitchen light. She came to me, put her hands on my shoulders, and spun me around to face the oak-framed mirror on the kitchen wall. I didn't need to see the image, the tangled hair and swollen face. I knew what I looked like standing there in a baggy, food-stained shirt and sweatpants, clothes I had been living in night and day. I didn't care. I twisted away from her and headed towards the stairway door hunched over a plate piled high with buttered bread, hunks of cheese and a wedge of apple pie.

'Boyer is learning to live with his scars,' she said wearily. 'Why can't you?'

Because those scars are my fault, I wanted to scream. I wanted to tell her then, all of it, but I remained silent, sullen. How could I tell her? How could she still love me if she knew the truth?

Later that same night I woke to the sound of my own muffled moans. A few minutes later, I heard Boyer's voice. He pushed open the door, 'Are you all right?' he asked from the doorway.

I could feel him standing there, just as he used to when I was a child and had wakened from a nightmare. For a moment it was if everything was the same again.

'Yea, I'm okay,' I said. 'I must have been dreaming.'

'I could hear you from my room,' he said. 'Are you sure you're all right?'

'Just a stomach ache,' I said. He came in and switched on the bedside lamp. I saw his scarred fingers reach across the crumb-filled plate – evidence of my once again stuffing myself until I was uncomfortable – on the night table.

'Turn it off,' I wailed as I rolled away. After he left, I pulled a pillow to my stomach as another cramp twisted my abdomen.

I drifted in and out of sleep on waves of pain. Sometime later, I woke to Mom leaning over me, her hand on my forehead. Boyer stood in the doorway behind her.

'It must be her appendix,' Mom said.

'Does your side hurt?' she asked. Before I could answer, she lifted my shirt to feel my right side.

'Dear God!' she said as her hands touched me.

I pushed her away. She turned to Boyer. 'Can you drive us to the hospital?' she asked.

Growing up on a farm means knowing where things come from. Living close to raw nature means nothing is secret. You know the water you drink comes from a mountain spring because you helped your father repair the lines. You know the bacon and ham came from the sow that was once a piglet you were foolish enough to name. You know the eggs and drumsticks are from the same yellow puffballs you watched grow into beady-eyed hens. When platters of sliced roast beef are set on the table, you give no thought to the sudden whoosh of mucus that blew out of the steer's nose as his knees hit the ground at the moment of death. Still you know. You know where it all comes from. You know birth and death, the realities of life.

And yet, I still cannot explain how unprepared I was for Dr Mumford's words in the sterile silence of the emergency room. 'We'll take her up to the delivery room,' he said as he removed his probing hands from my stomach.

Delivery room? What was he talking about? Delivery room? I tried to sit up on the examining table but another pain gripped me. I felt the firm touch of a nun's hands insisting that I lie back down. As the grim-faced sister wheeled me away, I heard Mom's voice repeating the questions that had formed in my head.

'Delivery room? What?'

'She's about to give birth, Nettie,' Dr Mumford told her. 'Surely you knew that.'

For the rest of my life, I would wonder how I could not have known. How I could have carried life inside my body for almost eight months and not know of its existence. But until that moment I had no idea. And yet, when I heard Dr Mumford say those words to my mother, my heart recognized the truth in them.

I gripped the icy stainless-steel side of the gurney as another pain ripped though me. And suddenly I was back in the gravel pit pressed against the black metal hood. The same searing heat assaulted my body promising to rip me apart.

Since that June night, I'd managed to stay detached, numb. It was as if the horrors of that night, and the tragedies that followed, had shut me off. In the months since, I had walked around in a world removed. I acted on direction, doing what was asked of me, following where I was led when I had to, but unconnected from the life around me. With each wrenching pain, it was as if my body was waking up, being reborn against its will.

I fought to stay numb. I didn't want to return. I wanted to stay in the empty vacuum that had become my existence.

As the elevator doors closed, I heard the nun's firm voice. She was the first to say it. 'You must have known,' she said.

In the cold white light of the delivery room, I twisted my head away from the gloved hand holding a black rubber mask to my face. I fought against inhaling the suffocating fumes, but after a few gulping breaths, I welcomed the darkness, the pulsating rings of light sucking me into their vortex, leaving the pain behind.

Chapter Forty

OUTSIDE ST HELENA'S hospital, Jenny leans into the intercom. 'Jennifer Mumford here,' she says. The intercom, like the ramp leading up to modern glass doors, is a recent addition. The marble entrance, the wide steps worn smooth at the edge by a century of footsteps, remains the same.

A buzzer signals the unlocking of the door. Inside, Jenny ushers me to the stairway. 'It's faster to take the stairs than that old elevator,' she says.

I am visiting my mother here for the first time. The last time I was in this hospital, I left behind the lifeless body of a baby born too early. I've been running from that memory ever since. Tonight my need to see my mother is stronger than fright. I follow my daughter up the steps.

Every time I visit Mom I wonder if it will be the last time I see her. Yet each time I leave knowing there are things left unsaid. Things left unsaid by both of us.

Keeping secrets is a lonely business. The longer you hold them, the harder it is to let them go. I knew that my refusal to tell anyone, especially my mother, what Mr Ryan did to me that night in the gravel pit, was a useless sacrifice. He never kept his end of the bargain and I protected no one by remaining silent. Yet once the events that followed began – River's death, Boyer's accident – how could I add the horror of rape to my family's sorrow? I let my mother, my family, everyone, believe that the stillborn child was the result of my night with River.

Between Mom and me, there had been some kind of unspoken agreement to avoid discussions about that time in our lives. What good would it do to drag up the past? It happened. Shared memories would change nothing. But sometimes, sometimes, I long to unburden myself, to confess my part in all of it, to say out loud how it all came about, where it could have been changed.

Sometimes I want to discuss the 'what ifs' with her just once. What if I hadn't gone to River's room that night? What if she hadn't seen me? What if I hadn't run to Boyer's cabin, not seen him and River together? And mostly, what if, instead of running off into the forest that night, I had simply gone home? How different would our lives have played out then?

But I can never say these things out loud to her. I can't tell her of the many moments when I could have made other choices, choices that would have left our lives intact. What would be accomplished? What would be the point? Because I'm certain that she already knows most of it, that she has always known.

What she doesn't know, what no one but me knows, is the real cause of the fire in Boyer's cabin. And I wonder if my guilt would be any less if I tell her?

Guilt is a stern taskmaster. It requires you to always be on guard, always watch what you say. So I resisted the temptation to unburden myself, the temptation that crept up every time I looked into my brother's face.

And I avoided him. The last time I stayed out at the farm, the last time I was forced to fight my demons head on, was at my father's funeral.

When my brothers went to bed after the services that night, my mother put away the teacups and set a bottle of wine and two crystal glasses on the table. I sat across from her in the dining room while she talked about my father. I asked her how she fell in love with someone so different from her.

'Your father was easy to fall in love with.' She smiled and took another sip of her wine. 'I was very young, and perhaps a bit too romantic. When I looked into your father's eyes I saw what I wanted. I married your dad because I knew he would make a good father. I guess we all want what we didn't have when we were growing up. What I didn't have was family. I knew the farm and your father could give me that.'

She began to talk about her disappointment in the intimacy of their marriage. It was as if she had been waiting to let it out, to tell someone about the barrenness of that part of her life. 'Sometimes it left me feeling so empty,' she said. 'So lonely.'

Listening to her reminisce, I felt uncomfortable, as if I were eavesdropping. I resisted the temptation to voice the questions I had wondered about since River's death. Why was she outside his room that night? Did she go up to him after I left? Had River comforted her too? But her answers would not change anything. I knew about secrets; I would let her keep hers. Instead I asked her why she stayed with a man she couldn't be intimate with. She seemed to come back from wherever her reverie had taken her and said, 'We really did marry forever back then you know. We didn't try it on for size then throw it away when it didn't fit. Our faith and the times did not allow it. Besides, I loved him.'

The next morning I watched from my window as she destroyed the rose garden, which to her represented an unfulfilled promise. While my bewildered brothers stood by gaping and thinking she'd gone crazy with grief, I understood.

The hospital corridors are dim on the third floor. The nurse at the night station looks up. 'Doctor,' she nods and acknowledges Jenny as we walk by. The odour of death and ailing bodies is heavy in the air. My father was right, all the talcum powder and alcohol rub in the world cannot mask that smell. Jenny seems immune to it, and I know that in a few minutes I will not notice it either. But at first it is so overpowering that I have to stop myself from covering my nose.

The door to Mom's room is open. A night-light glows on the wall behind her bed. We tiptoe in, not wanting to wake her. She looks so tiny, so lost in the white sheets.

It started in her lungs. My mother, who never smoked a cigarette in her life, would pay the dues my father escaped. Yet even now, with this disease eating her from the inside out, her skin is that of a much younger woman, a healthier woman. At seventy-eight, my mother is still beautiful.

At first she appears to be sleeping peacefully. Then I see the rapid movement of her eyes beneath translucent lids, as if she is fighting her dreams. I take her hand in mine. I feel the warmth as it wraps around my fingers and hangs on like a baby's reflex.

On the other side of the bed, Jenny flicks at the IV tube with her finger. 'She's out of morphine,' she whispers. 'I'll go get the nurse.'

My mother's eyes snap open. She reaches up and clutches Jenny's hand. 'No.' Her voice is weak, but she holds on to both Jenny's hand and mine. I'm surprised by the strength of her grip.

Her eyes focus on me. 'Natalie,' she smiles up at me. 'I've been waiting for you.'

As if summoned, the nurse appears at the door, a syringe in her hand. 'She didn't want any more morphine until you came,' she whispers. She approaches the bed and smiles down at Mom. 'Oh, you're awake, Nettie,' she says. 'This will start working in a few minutes.' She deftly inserts the syringe into the stopper of the IV tube.

'Wait,' Mom says. She takes a laboured breath. 'I heard—' a mucus-filled cough breaks the words in her throat. She catches her breath and murmurs something unintelligible. Jenny motions for me to lean forward and listen.

'I heard the baby cry,' Mom whispers into my ear.

'The baby?' I am not sure I understood her.

'Oh,' the nurse muses, 'there are strange noises in this old building all the time. Some of the residents think it's the nuns hiding in the closets. Your mother hears babies crying.'

'It's okay, Mom,' I croon to her as I stroke her forehead. 'It's okay, there are no babies here anymore.' But she becomes agitated and pulls me closer.

'No,' she breathes into my ear. It seems to take every ounce of energy she has left. 'No, Natalie,' she says. 'I heard *your* baby cry.'

Chapter Forty-One

Nettie

SHE FELT IT. Nettie felt it the moment she put her hand on Natalie's stomach. Instead of the yielding flesh, the layers of fat she expected, her fingers felt the taut skin, the hardened muscles of a swollen abdomen.

Still she told herself, just as she told Boyer and her husband, 'It's her appendix.'

During the slow drive into town, as the truck tyres crunched through fresh snow, she held her daughter in her arms and told her the same thing. By the time they reached St Helena's Hospital she believed it herself.

In the glare of the empty emergency room she breathed a sigh of relief as Dr Mumford, wearing operating room scrubs, rushed in. His unkempt hair stuck out from beneath a green cap. A surgical mask hung at his neck. He looked as if he had been up all night.

Nettie repeated her diagnosis to him.

Wordlessly, his expert fingers probed Natalie's right side, then he held both of his hands cupped to her extended abdomen.

Nettie was aware of the hum of the silent hospital, the constant white noise of the machines, the whisper of a nun's soft shoes as she glided into the room, her daughter's laboured breathing.

272

Even as Dr Mumford glanced up at her, the surprise obvious in his arched eyebrows, Nettie was not prepared for his words. Delivery room? Birth? Those words brought images of her own pregnancy, the birth of her own children, blue serge uniforms and lost girls. They had nothing to do with her daughter, her baby girl, who was being wheeled away by the stern-faced nun.

Dr Mumford put his arm around Nettie's shoulders and led her back to the reception area. Boyer stood as they came into the waiting room. 'Go home, Nettie,' Dr Mumford said. 'I'll take care of this.'

But she refused. She wanted to be with Natalie. The doctor appealed to Boyer. He, too, refused to leave.

'Then wait here,' Dr Mumford said and rushed out of the room.

Boyer took Nettie's arm and led her across the foyer to the hospital chapel. Inside they knelt together in the candlelight and prayed. They prayed for Natalie, for the child. For River's child, though neither of them would say it out loud.

They waited. When she could bear it no longer, Nettie left Boyer in the waiting room and made her way through the sleeping hospital, up the stairs to the third floor.

The corridors were dark, as if abandoned. No night nurse sat at the reception area of the maternity ward. Nettie rubbed her chilled arms, then remembered this unit was being shut down. Our Lady of Compassion would be no more. From now on, maternity cases would be sent to the larger, regional hospitals.

At the end of the darkened hallway, the delivery room doors pushed open. Dr Mumford hurried towards her pulling his mask aside. In the eerie emptiness of the silent ward, he once again put his arm around her, and gently turned her back to the elevator.

'The baby came too soon,' he told her in a quiet voice. 'He was stillborn.'

And with his words, an unexpected flood of sorrow for the lost child – her grandchild – a child she was not even aware of a few hours earlier overwhelmed her. She stopped moving and tried to pull away. 'Natalie,' she said. 'I want to see Natalie.'

'I had to put her under anaesthetic,' Dr Mumford said. 'She won't be awake for hours. Go home now. Get some sleep. Come back and see her in the morning.'

'The baby. He needs a priest, we need Father Mac.'

'I'll take care of that,' he said as he gently steered her down the empty hallway. 'Look, Nettie, there's no need for anyone else to know about this. No one has to find out.'

'But, the priest?'

'Your family has been through enough. We can keep this confidential. Let me look after this for you.'

And she let him. She let him lead her back to the elevator. She allowed him to gently push her through the open doors. She stood obediently inside as he pressed the button. And she convinced herself that the sound, the tiny cry she heard as the elevator doors closed, was only her imagination.

Chapter Forty-Two

GOSSIP SPREADS IN a small town like germs on a warm wind. It doesn't matter if it's true or untrue; it infects and contaminates just as quickly.

This time the rumour mill did not need Elizabeth-Ann or Mr Ryan to get it started. Who knows who began it this time? Someone at the hospital, a nurse, or maybe even a nun? Perhaps it leaked over the grapevine of shared telephone party lines. Perhaps Dr Mumford confided in someone, who confided in someone? Wherever it originated, it leaked and spread as unstoppable as the water over a dam. Within a few days everyone in our town would hear about how the milkman's seventeen-year-old daughter had gone into the hospital for an emergency appendectomy and delivered a baby. It wasn't hard to imagine the thrilled whispers.

'*Didn't even know she was pregnant!*'

'*No! She must have known.*'

'*No, really, she had no idea.*'

'*Impossible!*'

So now our family had one more thing to not talk about. And the town had another juicy story to feed on. Even though I was hidden away in a private room on the abandoned third floor, by the time I left the hospital everyone knew that it was more than a useless appendage I had left behind in St Helena's.

The next morning I lay in the hospital bed and tried not to think about the baby boy who the nuns said was born too soon. I pressed down on my tender abdomen and felt the wobble of loose stomach muscles. Was life really growing there all those months? How could I not have known? I tried to think back on missed monthly periods. How could I have not paid attention?

I refused to give the baby form in my mind. I would not allow it a place in my heart. I felt nothing, I told myself, except relief.

And yet an unexplained yearning, an unknown longing, tugged at the core of my now empty abdomen as if connected to some invisible cord.

A nun appeared soundlessly with a breakfast tray. She glided in and out of my room as if on cushions of air. My mother came on the soles of determination.

I recognized her footsteps, winter boots on tiled floor sounded in the empty hall. She paused for only a moment before she pushed open my door and breezed in, a smile set on her face. She was carrying a Tupperware container filled with cookies. She leaned over the bed to kiss my cheek. 'Morgan and Carl send their love,' she said. 'Dad too of course.'

'Do they know?' I asked. 'Does the whole town know?'

'No one but our family needs to know anything other than you had your appendix out,' she said as she busied herself fussing with my bed. 'Dr Mumford will take care of that. All you need to do is just get better.' She chatted on as if it really was an appendectomy I was recovering from.

She sat on the end of the bed and lifted the lid on my breakfast tray. 'You've got to eat, darling,' she said when she saw the untouched porridge and toast. I pushed the tray away.

'Ruth had her baby last night,' Mom announced. I noticed she didn't say too.

I recalled an image of someone being wheeled past me as I was pushed into the delivery room. Ruth.

'I guess she will be going back to her home in the Queen Charlottes soon,' Mom sighed. 'The boys will certainly miss her. Especially Morgan. I think I'll just pop over to Our Lady and visit her before I go home,' she said.

And not talk about her baby too, I thought.

It struck me then, that it was always that way with my mother. She knew everything; she talked about nothing. This event in my life, our lives, was just another thing to be swept under the carpet. We would all know it was there, but we would carefully step around it. That was fine with me. I had no desire to talk about it, to let it out into the daylight and give it life.

Mom never asked who the father was. I would let her go on believing that the birth we were pretending didn't happened was a result of the night she watched me leave River's room. She could mourn that child, I could not. For I felt certain that the baby boy who lay lifeless somewhere in the building was Mr Ryan's child.

The door to my hospital room opened. Boyer stuck his head in. He must have driven Mom in to see me. I was surprised. Except for last night, he had not left home since he returned from the burn unit. For a brief moment I wondered what it must have cost him to appear in town in broad daylight, to endure the stares of the curious and the rude. Yet, when he asked, 'Can I come in?' I pulled my blanket around me and turned away.

Back at home my isolation became complete. Through the grates I heard Mom tell Dad and my brothers that I would come around eventually, but I wondered how I would ever be able to look any of them in the eye again knowing the destruction and shame I had caused.

From my upstairs bedroom, I watched as the last days of February vented their fury on the countryside. The days lengthened and grew milder. Gigantic icicles outside my bedroom window wept great tears, then shrunk and disappeared. The snow and ice on the roads began to recede turning our farmyard into a spring sea of mud and manure.

All the while my mother brought trays upstairs and left them outside my door. She stopped trying to talk me out of my room, stopped pressing me to return to school. I didn't know if I was relieved or saddened by her silent acceptance.

But often in the evening I heard her at the piano. I buried my head in my pillow as the music floated up through the hallway grate and seeped under my bedroom door.

Once again I began to creep downstairs in the middle of the night, or whenever I was alone in the house. But now it was not for food. I walked around the rooms memorizing the familiar objects of our home. As ritualistic as my mother fingering her beads, I touched all the things that once defined our family. My hand ran along the linoleum-topped kitchen table, the marble sideboard in the kitchen, the wooden bread bin that always gave off the aroma of baked bread, the china cabinet in the parlour, the oak dining room table, and the piano. All the reminders that I was once a part of this family. I stood in the dark staring up at the painted portrait of our farm, and at the smiling faces in the family photograph sitting on the piano top below. Then I carried the feeling back upstairs with me and tried to pretend everything was still the same.

'She can't stay up there forever,' my father said one night in March, his voice rising up through the hall grates to find me.

A week later I sat in the cab of the milk truck as we drove away from the farmhouse. The warm winds of a spring storm danced through the swaying trees, blowing the last of the snow through the branches. The swirling wind created a commotion of white on the road before us. I resisted the temptation to turn and take one last look at my home. I was already gone. I had left my home as surely as if I was already on the bus my father was delivering me to. The bus that would carry me away from this place, from my family, from my life, into the unknown abyss of the city.

Widow Beckett came up with the solution. I said nothing when Mom sat down on my bed and told me about the offer. I'd heard it all from my room.

'For Natalie's sake, for your whole family,' the Widow told Mom. 'You have to get her away from here.'

I'd heard the telephone calls to Widow Beckett's brother and his wife in Vancouver.

'They have a huge home,' Widow Beckett explained. 'They take in foster children all the time, one more in that house won't even be noticed.'

Mom's carefully hoarded egg money would pay my room and board. 'It's only for the rest of the school year,' she told me. 'You have to catch up or you won't graduate.' I shrugged my acceptance.

On the day I left, she stood at the kitchen table, her back to me, when I came downstairs with my suitcases. On the table, pie plates lined with dough waited to be filled. A bowl of frozen huckleberries, Boyer's favourite, thawed in the sink. Mom slammed the rolling pin on the dough round as if life depended on it.

I hesitated for only a moment before I pushed open the screen door with my suitcase and walked out. She did not come after me. I did not turn back. Neither of us was willing to give in to that awkward moment of goodbye.

'It won't be for long,' she'd said the night before as she left my bedroom. I think we both knew it wasn't true.

Dad and I rode in silence to the highway turn-off where we waited for the Greyhound bus. We both stared down the road as if we could will the bus to come sooner.

'Well, this will be an adventure, hey, sunshine?' my father finally said. 'Off to the big city, eh?' He reached inside his jacket pocket, then glanced up at me as he opened the silver cigarette case. I tried to return his crooked smile. He leaned into his cupped hands to light his cigarette, but not before I read in his eyes the toll the fight to keep the farm was having on my father's spirit.

He rolled the window down and blew out a cloud of smoke. 'Your mother and I want you to know that when you want to come home – that is, whenever you are ready – well the minute you think you can come back, you just phone us and we'll have you on the next bus.'

I wondered if he really believed I would ever be ready to come back and face the gossip, the town, Boyer's broken life, the ghosts. Or even if he really wanted me to.

I wanted to go. I wanted to spare my family the constant reminder of the havoc I had created. Yet as the bus pulled away, as I watched my father's truck grow smaller, I could not stop the overwhelming grief that washed over me. For at that moment I believed I would never see my father, or hear him call me sunshine, ever again.

I was right.

Chapter Forty-Three

THE CITY SWALLOWED me whole. It was easy to disappear, to become invisible, swept away in the throng of students who streamed through the hallways of the high school whose population was as big as the entire town of Atwood. It was not so easy in the Beckett home.

The Beckett family lived in a two-storey wartime house in East Vancouver. It was one of the many look-alike houses built by the Canadian government in the fifties for the growing number of families of World War Two veterans. Her brother's home was not quite as large as Widow Beckett believed it to be, but it did have four bedrooms. Four bedrooms and one tiny bathroom, hardly big enough to turn around in, for six children and two adults. And then me. I slept on a cot in the girls' upstairs room.

The two sisters, Judy and Jane, bickered every waking moment. Their bedroom was divided into territories by an invisible line, which ran down the middle of my cot. I was either the object of a tug of war, or ignored.

The four boys ran amok. Unlike my brothers, they had no chores, no routine to guide them. Like frenzied ferrets, night and day they chased each other up and down stairs, in and out of slamming doors.

The house was a constant riot of noise. Doors, cupboards and drawers were never closed quietly in that home, but banged shut, often double slammed as if in defiance of the surrounding mayhem.

Whenever both Mr and Mrs Beckett were home at the same time, swirling cigarette smoke and angry sounding words filled the air. The normal mode of conversation was top-of-the-lungs yelling, the hurried words lost in the rush to be heard.

Meals were an eat-where-you-are affair, most often gobbled down in front of the constantly blaring black-and-white television set in the tiny living room. Whenever two or more people occupied the same room, which was most always, everyone spoke at the same time, each unable to hear the other in the frantic attempt at getting in a say.

I didn't dislike the Beckett children, they were just different. They felt it too. Like animals, we sniffed at each other to find that we were different species. They found the farm odours, which they told me permeated everything I owned, offensive. I didn't mention that they all smelled of the mildew of their perpetually damp city.

I neither avoided them nor sought them out. It was impossible to feel a part of a family who were constantly bumping into each other in the narrow hallways, yet all living completely separate lives. And even though there were no empty corners to get lost in, it was easy to be lonely in that house.

I tried not to compare their lives with those of my own family. Because I knew, for me, that way of life no longer existed. At night I would lie in my small cot and try to choke back the homesickness that threatened to overwhelm me. In time I would stop hearing the noise of the house, the city, the constant hum of traffic. I would stop looking up at the sky at night hoping to glimpse the same brilliance of the star-filled sky of home. And I would stop waking to the imagined sounds of piano music.

Every week a letter from my mother slid through the mail slot in the front door with chatty news of people and a town I would rather forget. I smiled when she told me Morgan was corresponding with Ruth, who had returned to Queen Charlotte Island. 'I think he writes more now than he ever did in school,' Mom said.

I cringed when I read:

The local gossip never ends. Yesterday Ma Cooper said she heard your friend Elizabeth-Ann Ryan and her mother are living in Calgary. Her father returned to Atwood alone, but no one sees him. He's become a complete recluse, cooped up in his house, night and day. Groceries are delivered to his doorstep. And alcohol. Drinking himself into oblivion, the grapevine reports. Imagine that, from town mayor to town drunk. I have to say I'm not surprised. I've always thought there was something not quite right about that man.

He's no longer mayor, but he's still causing trouble. Apparently his last act before he left was to start an order in council to revoke our business licence. Mr Atwood and his son, Stanley Junior, along with Dr Mumford, held a protest at city hall when they got wind of it.

Dad won the fight to keep his licence to deliver unpasteurized milk, but eventually he gave in and sold to the large dairies. I'm glad I wasn't there to see my father the first time the stainless-steel tanker trucks arrived.

'Perhaps it's for the best,' Mom wrote. 'I think the boys might even be relieved. With the automated barn and direct bulk sales now, there certainly won't be enough work to tie them all down here. Maybe Boyer can go to university after all,' she added cheerily. But I knew she saw it as just another event in the chain of tragedies that was tearing her family apart.

It wasn't Boyer who left in the end. Not long after Dad died, Morgan went on a fishing trip to the Queen Charlotte Islands. And to visit Ruth. When he returned, he announced he was moving there.

'Morgan's going to work on a fishing boat for Ruth's father. It seems more than fish were hooked on his trip. Morgan has fallen in love with the West Coast, the ocean, and most of all with Ruth. I'm happy for them. I adore Ruth. But it's such a long way away.' Mom added that she was sure it would be just a matter of time before Carl moved there too.

And, sure enough, shortly after Morgan left, Carl followed. They've all lived there since. Morgan and Ruth are married, but ironically, considering how they met, childless.

'Ruth got two husbands for the price of one,' Mom wrote. 'Although Carl doesn't live with them, his home is a pebble's throw away. Close enough to share most meals with his brother and his wife.'

Ruth doesn't seem to mind though. The few times I've seen them over the years, her shy, oval face portrays only love and acceptance; although I once caught a look of longing cross her eyes as she watched Morgan and Carl playing with their young niece, Jenny, when they visited us.

I often wondered whether Ruth ever tried to find the child she had given up at birth. Not wanting to dredge up unwanted memories or embarrass her, I once asked Morgan if they had ever searched for her baby. He told me that he'd wanted to but she had refused. Maybe, as Mom always says, it's for the best. You can't go back and repair the shattered parts of your life.

In Vancouver, I threw myself into school. And every afternoon I dropped a dime into a clinking glass box on the Hastings Street bus and rode downtown to the public library. I did my homework there, appreciating every moment of the hushed silence, the familiar smell of books. Then I would sit and read until closing time. After a few months, somebody must have either taken pity on me, or thought that if I was going to spend so much time there I might as well be working. I was offered an after-school job. I accepted. For the rest of the school year, I slept at the Beckett house, but the library was home. When summer came, I told myself, and my parents, that I would rather be cataloguing books than delivering milk.

After I graduated from high school I went to work for a small community newspaper, then moved on to *The Vancouver Sun*.

I married the first man who asked me, before I realized I didn't need to be rescued.

Chapter Forty-Four

THE OXYGEN TANK drones on in the stillness of my mother's room. I sit by her bed and watch her breathe.

'Mom,' Jenny's hushed voice breaks into my trance. 'The morphine has taken hold,' she whispers. 'Gram's probably asleep for the night now. Why don't we go and get you checked in next door.'

Now that I'm here I'm afraid to leave. But I nod and let my daughter lead me away like a reluctant child.

In my room at the Alpine Inn I sit down and take a sip from the glass of sherry in my hand. In the matching blue paisley wingback chair across from me, Jenny waits while I settle. I lean back and close my eyes.

'Do you remember much about your father?' Jenny's father, my first husband, died before she was eight.

She considers the question. 'Yes and no,' she finally answers. 'Sometimes I think everything I remember about him is what you've told me over the years, and from our old pictures. I do remember his hands were always ink-stained when he came home from work. And I remember him reading to me at night. But I have trouble picturing his face.' She is quiet for a moment, then asks. 'Did you love him?'

I open my eyes and smile at her. 'You know I once asked your grandmother the same thing about my father. Yes, I think I did, as much as I was able to at the time. I was so young, looking for a saviour. I probably half fell in love with the illusion of who he was. He was older, the editor of a newspaper. And very handsome.'

'He looked like Uncle Boyer,' Jenny says.

He did? Yes, I suppose in a way he did. Funny I never thought about that before.

'So did Ken,' she says, 'and Bert.'

I am startled by her words. With a jolt that is physical I realize the truth of the observation. All of them, all the men in my life, except Vern, have had some resemblance to Boyer. And to River, although she can't possibly know that. The implication of what she is saying is not lost on me. Is that what I do? Leave them, run away, when I realize they're not Boyer – or River?

And Vern? What does this say of him? Vern with his brown eyes and thick dark hair. He is nothing like the others, in any way. He's not a teacher, an editor, or a writer. Like my father, Vern wears the dirt of the earth under his fingernails. And I have been with him the longest.

I'm too weary to think about this now. I drain the last sip of sherry, set the glass on the night table and push myself up.

'I know about the baby,' Jenny says quietly.

So this is it. This is what she couldn't talk about on the phone. I sink back into my chair. 'How long have you known?'

'I heard the rumours years ago,' she says. 'It's a small town, Mom.'

'Why didn't you say anything?'

'I thought that if you had wanted me to know, you would have told me.'

'There was no reason to, the baby didn't live.' No reason not to either. Why hadn't I? As a doctor I'm sure Jenny has heard far more shocking confessions. But not from her mother.

'I didn't even know I was pregnant,' I tell her now. 'And when the baby was stillborn it was as if it was nothing more than a miscarriage.'

'Really?'

I open my mouth, close it, then say, 'No.'

'It was that baby Gram was talking about tonight, wasn't it?' Jenny asks.

'I don't know what she was talking about,' I sigh.

Mom had become incoherent while I tried to soothe her. She mumbled something about Father Mac and Dr Mumford before the morphine took hold. It makes me sad to know my mother is still haunted by my mistakes. 'Your grandmother and I have never talked about it, about the baby. But she couldn't have heard him cry. The baby was born too early, never took a single breath. It was stillborn.'

'No,' Jenny's voice is soft, almost a whisper. 'No, he wasn't.'

I feel as if a hot boulder has thudded into my chest.

'What? What are you saying? Of course the child was stillborn. Dr Mumford, the nuns, they said—' I shake my head. 'No, the baby didn't live.'

Jenny leans over, takes both my hands in hers, forcing me to look into her eyes. 'Mom, listen. You know there were two babies born that night. The other baby, Ruth's baby, was the one that didn't live.' Even though her voice is gentle, I can hear the urgency, the plea for understanding, for belief. 'I don't know how else to tell you, but it's true,' she says.

Confused, my mind races to make sense of her words, and to find denial as I pull my hands away. 'No! That's not right,' I stand up quickly, then sit down again. 'That's impossible – how can – after all these years? How?'

'There was a request for the medical records of the mother of a baby boy born on February 12, 1969,' she says. 'But when the records were searched, something wasn't right. There were two births recorded for the date, both to the same mother. Both to Ruth, hours apart. The clerk brought the records to Nick and me. Nick confronted his grandfather. At first old Dr Mumford said it was a mistake. He insisted there was only one baby born that night. He refused to acknowledge the discrepancy. But he finally broke down and confessed. The baby who lived, your baby, was given to the adoptive parents who were waiting for Ruth's child.'

There's not enough air in the room. I cannot fill my lungs. I don't want to hear any more. I stand again and turn to push open the window and gulp the cool air. 'No,' I insist with my back to her, 'that can't be right. The nuns! The nuns told me! They wouldn't lie.'

'Did the nuns actually tell you your baby had died?' she asks gently.

Born too soon. I have never forgotten the nun's no-nonsense tone as she said those words the next morning. '*A baby boy, born too soon.*' And suddenly I relate them to Boyer's childhood lesson about discretion, about using carefully chosen words to avoid the truth, the hurt.

I spin around and face her. 'That's enough!' I say, fighting the hysteria that rises with my voice. 'I don't want to know any more. This conversation is over.'

'But you need—'

'No! No, I don't. That child was dead to me thirty-four years ago and he's dead to me now. Why drag up the past? Why would you tell me this now?'

But I know the answer before the words are out of her mouth.

'Because he's coming, Mom,' she says. 'He'll be here tomorrow afternoon.'

Chapter Forty-Five

Nettie

THEY CAME TOGETHER.

Nettie heard the hesitancy in their steps. Their shoes shuffled, scratched, barely lifted from the tiled hospital floor. They came into her room so close together they could have been one dark messenger with two heads.

They have come to mourn me, Nettie thought. She had been back in the hospital for over a week now. The stays are getting longer. This will be the last.

But this was a good day.

Boyer stood at the head of her bed, which he had just adjusted for her comfort. Nettie lay with her head cushioned in pillows, watching as the two visitors approached the end of the bed. For a moment she imagined them as two old crows, both garbed in raven black, hovering over the foot rails.

Age had not cowered Dr Mumford. At eighty-five, his posture was still determinedly straight, but she noticed the slight tremor of his hands before he wrapped them around the metal bars.

She looked from him to Father Mac. The years had not been so kind to the priest. His shrunken frame was lost in the bulk of his great wool overcoat. His neck disappeared into his clerical collar.

The greetings were brief. Nettie was relieved her visitors did not ask how she was doing. They knew. Neither of her two old friends was about to waste time on polite lies and reassuring words. The priest spoke first. The timbre in his voice belied his diminishing body. Father Mac placed an arm on Dr Mumford's shoulder. 'Allen has something to say to you, Nettie.'

She saw the doctor bristle as the priest urged him forward, but he made his way to the side of the bed, next to Boyer.

He took Nettie's hand, then asked Boyer. 'Could we have a moment please?'

'It's all right, Allen,' Nettie said. She paused for a moment, concentrated on breathing from the oxygen tubing in her nose, then went on. 'There's nothing you have to say to me, that my son can't hear.'

'Nettie,' Dr Mumford began, but his voice cracked. Something inside him seemed to crumble. His shoulders sagged. Boyer pulled up a chair and the doctor slumped into it. 'I don't know how to tell you,' he said. 'Years ago … Natalie's baby …'

Nettie's heartbeat quickened as the stream of words came tumbling out of the doctor's mouth. She listened in silence as he confessed to how he played God the night she brought Natalie to him. How he had lied about the child not surviving.

'There was a family waiting for the baby – Ruth's baby – it was so easy,' he said when he was finished. 'So easy. I thought it was the right thing.' He lowered his head and wept onto Nettie's hand. 'I'm so sorry, so sorry.'

'I heard the baby,' she whispered.

And she recalled the sound coming from behind the delivery room doors. The tiny cry she convinced herself later was Ruth's child. But as the doctor sobbed his remorse at her side, she remembered. She remembered feeling the strong pull at the core of her being at that cry. It was the same overwhelming tug she had experience at the birth of each of her own children. The memory rose to the surface, a memory buried so deep, she'd never had to face the truth.

She searched the priest's eyes. Although she'd never confessed this one sin, she had lived her life doing penance for her part in Natalie's baby being condemned to purgatory. 'The baby,' she asked between strained breaths. 'Did Ruth's baby receive Last Rites?'

As the priest nodded, Nettie closed her eyes and felt relief wash through her.

She opened her eyes as Boyer asked, 'And Natalie's child? Where did Natalie's baby go?'

'The hospital didn't keep the adoption records,' Dr Mumford said. 'Our Lady of Compassion and the Church handled that.'

Nettie's eyes shifted to Father Mac.

'I'm sorry,' the priest said, 'I can't give you that information. Adoption records are confidential. But,' he went on, his words slow and measured, 'we had a written request from an agency searching on his behalf. I've spoken with a representative from the agency. The young man, she told me, is not looking for his birth mother. He doesn't want to intrude on her privacy. But because he has a family of his own now he would like access to family medical history.'

His frail hand reached into the deep pocket of his overcoat. 'What I can give you,' he said, 'is this.' He held up a folded paper. 'It's the contact number of the agency that was inquiring on his behalf.'

Nettie watched as Boyer reached out and took the paper from the priest's hand.

Chapter Forty-Six

THE AMBER GLOW from the bedside lamp reflects on Jenny's face. A moth is trapped between the bulb and the shade. I hear the muted thuds as it throws its body back and forth in frantic attempts to escape. I know the feeling.

'And me?' I ask, my voice shaking, as I stand frozen by the window, my arms folded. 'Why didn't someone call me, tell me? You had no right! No right to search for him, to find him.'

'He found us,' Jenny says. I can see the excitement growing in her face as she rushes to explain. 'Uncle Boyer sent him a message through the agency that was searching for his birth records. He called back right away. Uncle Boyer explained the circumstance of his birth. Told him how sick his grandmother—'

'Didn't anyone, anyone, stop to think to ask me if this is what I wanted?' I demand. The heat of fear turns into shivers of anger. I whirl around and slam the window shut. 'You had no right to decide for me.'

'I know. We know. But it all happened so fast. There really wasn't time. He called yesterday to say he was flying up from Vancouver tomorrow. Boyer, none of us, wanted to tell you on the telephone,' she says. 'Gram wanted to tell you herself. That's what she was trying to say tonight.'

I face Jenny and feel my eyes narrow. 'Well, I won't meet him. I won't! I don't want to know his name. I don't care ...' I'm rambling, but unable to stop myself. 'You have no idea what you're asking of me!'

I read the disappointment that floods her face. Of course she would have expected my shock, but this – this aversion to meeting my own son – she cannot understand. How could she? She believes, they all believe, that this is the child of my teenage crush. They are each ready, eager, to accept him as family. If only it were that simple. If only he were what they believe him to be – River's son.

Suddenly I am very tired. 'I don't want to talk about this any more.' I turn my back on her and reach for my suitcase. 'It's been a long day. I'm going to bed.' I know my voice has gone flat, devoid of the conflict of emotions that wage a silent war within me.

Behind me, I hear Jenny stand. 'His name is Gavin,' she says wearily. 'He's an airline pilot.'

When I don't respond, she goes to the door. 'He's your son, Mom,' she says. 'But before you decide, for whatever reason you aren't saying, that he means nothing to you, remember he means something to us. He's the brother I never had. The grandson Gram never had. And the nephew your brothers and Aunt Ruth never had. And he's the son of the man, who, from what I understand, is someone you all once loved. Is whatever stopping you bigger than that?'

Now. Now is the time to tell her.

Before the door opens, Jenny adds, 'Uncle Boyer's picking them up at the Castlegar Airport tomorrow afternoon.'

'Them?' My voice is shaking.

'Yes. He has a family. A wife and three-year-old daughter.'

The door closes. As I listen to Jenny's footsteps fade down the empty hallway, I realize with a deep sadness that I'm letting history repeat itself. I'm doing exactly the same thing my mother and I did. I am allowing the unspoken, the things I'm not saying, to create a wedge between my daughter and me.

A sudden flurry of delicate moth wings hammers against the light bulb and they turn to dust behind the lampshade. Like the moth, I am trapped, trapped between the heart-swelling excitement of my daughter's revelation and the frantic need to flee. And, like the moth, this time for me there is no escape.

Chapter Forty-Seven

SLEEP ELUDES ME. I toss and turn in the strange bed while I fight back the faceless image of a son I can't help wondering about. Jenny said he was flying in from Vancouver. Did he grow up there? Had I ever walked by him on some unremembered street? Who adopted him? Was he happy? What – who – did he look like? And did he ever wonder about me?

I dream of crows. The dream is so real that I am certain I'm awake and have sleep-walked in the night. I stand in the clearing by the lake behind our farmhouse. I have visited this place many times in dreams. And each time I wondered how I got there. Do my feet know some magic path my mind has forgotten?

Before me a carpet of black-feathered birds spreads across the meadow and along the shoreline. They fill the branches of the trees and look down from the moss-covered roof of Boyer's cabin. Thousands of ebony eyes watch as I begin to move. They part as I approach and leave a pathway to the cabin door.

The forest has almost reclaimed the burned-out shell. Tangled Virginia creeper vines, their orange and red leaves withered, crawl up the charred logs. My feet carry me soundlessly to the door. It looks so solid, so real. I wonder what will happen if I reach through the vines and push it open? Will I find his ghost waiting inside after all these years, ready with accusations, explanations, forgiveness?

My hand lifts slowly and finds the iron latch. As my fingers touch the cold metal, the door, the walls, the roof, all turn to dust and collapse in a cloud of ethereal smoke, while the crows rise as one to the sky.

In the darkness of early morning I make my way through the empty streets of Atwood. Pink glow from the streetlights sifts down through the thick mountain mist. The rhythmic pounding of my runners rises from the pavement. When I reach Main Street I shiver, not from the crisp autumn air, but from the memory of last night's dream, and the vision of a face rising in the dust of the disintegrating cabin. The face that appeared was not the one I expected. Instead of River's face, I saw the scarred, unsmiling face of Boyer.

When I awoke it was still dark. Unable to find my way back to sleep I laid awake wrestling with the past, and with the present. My body and my mind felt cramped, sluggish from yesterday's journey on the bus, and through memory's corridors. I got out of bed and pulled on my running clothes.

When I was seventeen, after I moved to Vancouver, I started running every day. At first it was an excuse to escape from the house, to have a few hours of solitude. It started as a way to numb my mind. It became a way of life. I've been running ever since – running from guilt and shame, from memories and secrets, from relationships. And from myself.

But this morning I'm running towards something. Unlike last night's dream, I know exactly where my feet are taking me. I know what I must do, what I must face.

I hasten down the deserted street, past the familiar old buildings that now house unfamiliar businesses. Ski and snowboard shops have replaced the small bakery and butcher shops. Quaint coffee-houses and antique stores that cater to the influx of tourists who flock to the nearby ski hills each winter, now fill the storefronts.

As I approach the edge of town, headlights cut through the lifting fog. I remain resolute and continue running, my shoulders squared, as the car passes and the sound of its motor disappears behind me. At the highway intersection I resist the instinct to turn north, away from Atwood, as I usually do. Not this time. I take a breath and turn south, towards the border.

It's called Eaglewood now. The name, carved into a massive cedar log at the entrance, heralds its existence. The old gravel road has been paved. Overhead streetlamps light up sidewalks and driveways. I turn off the highway and run into the empty streets of the subdivision.

Through the trees I see shadowed outlines of timber-frame houses and Swiss-style chalets. This development, of one- and two-acre lots, was carved out of the farm by Boyer and his partner Stanley Atwood. According to Jenny, the seasonal owners of most of these homesites are Americans who have discovered our little piece of heaven here in the Cascade Mountains. I wonder briefly if any of the homes belong to the young men who, after being pardoned at the end of the Vietnam War, returned to the United States to become bankers and stockbrokers. I'm certain they don't belong to any of the leftover hippies who stayed to become farmers, shop-keepers and artists.

My heart pounds in my ears. I push forward, past driveways, courtyards, decorative ponds and the dark houses set back in the trees. I turn a corner and suddenly I am there.

Even though everything is changed now, I know this place. I slow to a walk at the entry to a wide cul-de-sac. Across the way, in the middle of the other side of the street circle, a tree-lined driveway leads to a new post-and-beam home. I stop and stand panting while I stare across the invisible barrier.

Somewhere a single crow calls out. The raucous voice echoes through the silence of the morning. A sudden gust of wind carries a flurry of dry autumn leaves through the trees. They flutter to the ground and skitter across the cobblestones and into the driveway of what was once the old gravel pit.

I take a deep breath and start walking. I resist the urge to look back over my shoulder, to flee. I am determined to erase this fear, to face it head on. I focus on the glowing porch light on the house at the end of the driveway and let it pull me forward.

I am no longer running but my heart races as I make my way across the vast expanse of the cul-de-sac and up the driveway. And then I am there. I have made it through. I stand at the bottom of the steps and look up at the house.

I don't know what I expected to find after all these years, what demons I thought I would confront. There is nothing here, no evil lurking in the shadows. No phantoms of the past wait for me. This is just a place. The gravel pit, which has haunted me all these years, no longer exists. It has been replaced by this beautiful home.

The cedar and stone house appears warm and inviting. It looks like a home in the country should look, as if it had grown there. Light spills from the kitchen bay window as I climb the granite porch steps.

As my hand reaches up to knock, I have to force back the thoughts that still try to push through. The gravel pit may be gone, but not the memory, and the dark secret buried with that memory. Now all the years of protecting that ugly secret are wasted. In a few hours I will be forced to face the results of the horrors of that night. And eventually the young man, too, will have to know the truth of his existence. *How can I tell them? How can I tell him, that he – 'my son' – is the child of rape?*

I let my gloved hand rap on the wooden door. I hear footsteps inside. The door flies open. And Jenny reaches out for me.

'What time did you say they were coming?' I ask.

It's time to start filling in the blanks.

Chapter Forty-Eight

THE HOSPITAL CORRIDORS are decorated in the colours of autumn. Picture cut-outs of turkeys, pumpkins, and scarecrows, cover the walls of the third floor of St Helena's. This could be the hallway of any grade school. Except for the odours. No scent of waxy crayons or sweaty running shoes here. Only the institutional smell of Lysol, urine, and boiled turnips, and decaying bodies.

In front of the stairway door a silver-haired woman, hunched over a metal walker, lifts her slippered feet and slides them slowly one behind the other. On the other side of the hall a man, shrunken into a wheelchair as if he's a part of it, pulls himself backwards along the railing with his one good hand while, with a determined independence, he pushes with his foot.

Still in my running clothes, I wait patiently for this camphor and talcum-smelling traffic jam to clear. An unexpected calmness has overcome me since my uncensored disclosures to Jenny earlier. I am still surprised at the relief I felt at letting go of the secrets I had guarded for so long. Even my footsteps feel lighter as I make my way to my mother's room.

The hospital-green drapes are open, her room flooded with morning light. Mom lies back in her raised bed, her eyes closed, her mouth half open. Even though Jenny told me that Mom is now down to seventy-nine pounds, I am surprised by the frailty of her body evident under the white sheet. Her thin arms are nothing more than skin over bone. 'There isn't much left, but spirit,' Jenny had told me. 'But that counts for a lot.'

I stand at the door and stare at Mom's birdlike chest until I am certain she is breathing.

Her eyes snap open and dart around the room the moment I enter. 'Is he here?' she asks as soon as she sees me.

I thought she had been waiting for me, but it is him that she has put off dying for. I can hear the urgency in her voice.

'Soon, Mom,' I tell her as I lean in to kiss her, 'he'll be here soon.'

My lips touch the delicate skin on my mother's cheek and she lifts her hand to my face. 'I heard him cry,' she whispers. 'The night he was born I heard—'

'It's okay, Mom,' I say and take her hand in mine and press it to my lips. 'It's okay.'

Her eyes focus on me. 'I'm sorry, Natalie,' her voice gurgles and she clears her throat. 'I heard him …' she continues, somehow her voice gaining strength. 'I should have … should have insisted that I see him. I walked away … I should have known.' Her eyes fight to hold mine, pleading as she struggles to get it all out. 'Forgive me.'

'There's nothing to forgive. We all believed – wanted to believe – what Dr Mumford told us.' The steady pump of the oxygen tank fills the empty space between our words. I feel the feather touch of her fingers on my cheek before her hand falls away and her translucent lids close. I sit beside the bed and stroke her forehead, while I breathe with the rise and fall of her chest.

As I gently push a strand of grey-streaked hair behind her ear, her lids flutter open again. Her thin lips part, then lift, in a weak smile.

'He'll come back to us,' she manages to whisper. 'Everything will be all right now.'

A saviour. That's how she sees her grandson. She sees him as someone who will bring this family back together. Someone to wash away the guilt that has kept us apart. She imagines he is the silver lining to the cloud that has hung over our family. She sees him as the proverbial good that comes after an ill wind: River reincarnated.

And I can't – I won't – take that away from her. The speech I rehearsed on the way back from Jenny's, disappears. The imagined conversations and confessions will not take place. I search her milky eyes, so full of hope, so close to death, and realize it's too late to burden her with my dark memories and secrets. I will let my mother leave this world believing her grandson is River's child.

'I should never – sent – away,' she murmurs.

'We all sent River away, Mom,' I say, believing she has once again read my mind.

'No, not River.' Her breathing is laboured. Every word has its cost. 'You. I should never have let you go away.'

'It's all right, Mom,' I say trying to soothe her. 'I couldn't have stayed in Atwood.' It's not just words. It's true. Still, I remember the depth of the sadness I felt on that windy March day when I drove away with my father for the last time.

'I didn't know what to do with your grief,' she says now. 'It was too deep.'

I had come to her, prepared to unburden myself, but it is she who gives voice to her regrets. Her hand closes around mine. 'You and Boyer were both suffering so deeply. His pain was more obvious. But yours,' she sighs, 'I just didn't know how else to help you heal.'

A feeling harboured in some deep part of me suddenly surfaces. As it rises I momentarily remember the resentment I felt the morning I walked out the door while my mother stood with her back to me at the kitchen table. I thought she knew! I expected her to know. She knew everything else. Why didn't she know about my pain? I had done such a good job at keeping my silence, of hiding the horror, and the guilt. I had made it look like anger but it had turned into resentment. Now that resentment surfaces, it surfaces and dissipates with her words.

I reach up and brush away the tear making its way down the side of her face into her hair. 'It was the right thing, Mom. The right choice. I would never have survived here.'

For many reasons. Reasons she need never know.

'I'm sorry I wasn't a better mother,' she says now.

And my heart aches.

'You were always a good mother. The best. To all of us.'

Her hand relaxes in mine. Her eyes close. I think she has fallen into sleep until, without opening her eyes, she asks, 'Have you seen Boyer?'

'No, not yet.'

Her breathing quiets as sleep claims her, but suddenly she whispers, 'Are you ever going to forgive your brother, Natalie?'

Boyer? Forgive Boyer? I am startled by her question. 'Forgive him for what?' I say, but she cannot hear. I lean closer and listen to her breathing. My mother is asleep.

I sit by her bed and wonder at the sense of relief that flooded through me at the thought of blurting out the answer to her question. Was I really about to tell her that it is me, Natalie, who needs to be forgiven? That I cannot look into my brother's face without remembering that I'm responsible for his scars.

While she sleeps I lay my head on the bed beside my mother's hand. Her fingers instinctively stroke my hair.

The sounds of hospital life grow familiar. I begin to recognize the distinctive footsteps of different residents who pass the door on their slow relays up and down the hall. From somewhere the repetitive clanging of winning bells on a TV game show ring out, followed by the rush of canned applause.

I don't know how much time has passed when I look up to see Jenny sitting on the other side of Mom's bed. She smiles across at me. A smile full of understanding.

Our conversation earlier this morning has gone a long way to bridge that gap of understanding.

'Uncle Boyer was just here,' she whispers to me. 'He didn't want to disturb you. He's on his way to the airport now. They should be back in about two hours. While Grammie sleeps do you want to go to your room to shower and change before everyone gets here?'

I nod, then sit for a few more moments studying Mom's face while she sleeps.

This is the face of death, I admit to myself. The skin stretched across her high cheekbones reveals the skeleton structure of her skull. Still there is a calmness in her breathing and a flush on her cheeks. Something is holding her back, giving her strength. She has something left to do. And so do I.

Chapter Forty-Nine

'ARE YOU SURE about this?' Jenny asks as the Edsel turns onto Colbur Street.

'No,' I answer, my voice unsteady. 'But everything I've read, about victims of rape, says healing starts when you confront your abuser.'

Victim?

'You know,' I tell her as she pulls up in front of Gerald Ryan's house, 'I spent so many years denying, refusing to be his victim, that I've become just that – by not allowing myself to talk about it. Today was the first time I've ever spoken it out loud.'

In her kitchen, early this morning, I told Jenny everything about that night in the gravel pit. Our tears flowed unchecked as I cleared the cobwebs from the memories and exposed them to the light of day. Jenny listened without comment, but obviously feeling my anguish, as I relived the nightmare. Afterwards we held onto each other until our tears were exhausted.

When we had gained control, Jenny asked quietly, 'Mom, why are you so certain that the baby was Gerald Ryan's? If you were with River a few nights before isn't it just as likely that he could be the father?'

And there it was, the crack in the rock solid belief I had clung to all these years. Could I allow it to open and let hope seep in?

'I've always been so certain,' I sighed. 'Perhaps that was my way of coping. Maybe it was just less painful to accept that a stillborn baby was a result of rape, than to consider he may have been River's son.' I blew my nose. 'No,' I said as I shook my head. 'No matter how many times I imagine that night with River, I can't believe he could be the father. It only lasted minutes.'

'Still,' Jenny insisted, 'it's not impossible.'

'Perhaps. But not likely.'

Jenny turns off the motor and I force myself to look up at the old Ryan house. The once immaculate yard is overgrown with weeds. Railings are missing on the sagging porch; the paint is cracked and peeling. This morning Jenny confirmed that as far as she knew an ailing Gerald Ryan still lived in this neglected house.

Jenny reaches out and touches my shoulder. 'Do you want me to come with you?'

'No, I have to do this myself.'

'All right. But remember he suffers from alcohol-induced dementia. He may not know you.'

'It doesn't matter, I will know him.'

Before I turn to open the car door, Jenny says, 'There's something else, Mom.'

She hesitates, opens, then closes her mouth, as if she is uncertain over what she is about to reveal. 'You must not have been the only one,' she finally says. 'He's been mutilated. It looks as if at one time, years ago, someone went after his penis with a butcher knife.'

I take a moment to recover from this information. Then I push the car door open and get out in one quick movement.

I square my shoulders and feel myself drawing on my mother's strength. As I walk towards the porch I refuse to let my eyes stray to the darkened basement window. Yet I can't help imagining him standing there in the shadows. My feet feel heavy as I trudge up the creaking steps. It takes everything I have to make my way over to the door and lift my shaking hand. I hammer on the door before I can change my mind.

The house is dark, silent. I hear no movement inside. I knock again, this time more insistent. Minutes pass before I hear a faint shuffle. I move back as the door begins to open and an eye appears in the narrow crack. It looks me up and down, blinks heavily, and then the door opens fully, revealing a bloated, heavy-set woman. A threadbare pink velour pantsuit stretches across sagging breasts and stomach rolls. Stringy grey hair hangs, limp and unkempt, around a swollen face. Suddenly I recognize something behind the blank stare.

'Elizabeth-Ann?'

Her eyes narrow. 'Natalie Ward,' she says finally, pulling her top around her and hugging it to her body.

'I didn't expect …' I stammer.

From somewhere inside a man's feeble voice calls out, 'Elizabeth-Ann?'

Unable to stop myself, I head into the house. Elizabeth-Ann steps back into the hall as I move past her toward the sickeningly familiar voice.

'Elizabeth-Ann?' The voice's repeated query has a whining urgency to it. And then I see the hunched form sitting in front of the silent television set in the living room. Like a frightened animal I stop, frozen, trapped, unable to move, hypnotized by the red-rimmed eyes – rodent eyes – that are looking, not at his daughter, but at me. A palsied hand lifts into the air and reaches out towards me.

Beside me Elizabeth-Ann slouches against the door to the living room. 'He thinks everyone is Elizabeth-Ann,' she says in a monotone voice. 'Everyone, except me.'

I can't pull my eyes from the withered remains of what was once my tormentor. A plaid, food-stained dressing gown does not hide the cloth restraints that lash him to a pink vinyl chair. Yellow parchment-like skin and tufts of transparent hair cover a splotched skull. Catheter tubing coils down from beneath his dressing gown to a full bag of urine hanging off the side of the chair.

'Elizabeth-Ann?' he pleads. Bulging eyes stare back at me. They look at me, through me, but do not see. There is no one behind those eyes, no one to connect with; no one left to hate. He is reduced to DNA.

How do I tell the son that I will meet in a few short hours that this is his legacy?

I turn away. The plaintive call follows me as I retreat. At the front door, I stop abruptly. I whirl around and cross the foyer once again. In the living room I stare down at the apparition that is now nothing more than an empty husk with eyes.

'I am not Elizabeth-Ann,' I say in a voice that is surprisingly calm. 'I am Natalie Ward. Remember me Mr Ryan? Mr Mayor? I am the milkman's daughter. I am the girl you raped in the gravel pit thirty-five years ago.'

Behind me I hear Elizabeth-Ann's sudden intake of breath, but I can't stop now. All the black poison I have kept inside boils to the surface. It spills out like vomit with my words. There is not a flicker of understanding in the milky eyes below me, but I don't care. These are words I need to say. 'You think you took something from me? You think you got away with it? Well, you took nothing.'

I don't tell him what I thought I had come to tell him. That I have something to show for that night of terror. That I am about to meet the son who he will never, ever, know. A son he will never see, never even understand exists. Because he no longer exists himself. I lean down and whisper directly into his ear. 'You're nothing.'

I turn away, shaken, weak, but somehow purged. Like the old gravel pit, the fear I have lived with, run from for so long, begins to disappear.

Elizabeth-Ann follows me to the front door. 'You too?' she says, her voice flat. 'I should have known. I'm sorry.'

'Yeah, we're all sorry,' I say walking out.

Out on the porch I turn back to her and search her face. 'After all he did to you,' I ask, 'why? Why are you here? Why are you looking after him?'

Her face is blank. She shrugs. 'He's my father.'

Chapter Fifty

JENNY AND I rush down the narrow hallway of the Alpine Inn. 'I can't believe I fell asleep,' I say as we hurry down the stairs.

'You needed it,' Jenny pushes through the front door and out into the autumn sunshine.

I feel like the world is spinning again. Everything is happening so fast. I was completely drained when I returned to my room after confronting Mr Ryan. Drained, but already beginning to feel the healing balm of letting go. I showered and changed, then lay down on the bed for just a moment. It was three o'clock when I woke to Jenny's knocking.

'They're here,' she said breathlessly when I answered the door. 'Boyer called from the Gold Mountain Motel. He's bringing Gavin over to the hospital now while his daughter has a nap.'

After the hospital doors close behind us, Jenny asks, 'Do you want to wait in my office or up in Gram's room?'

I follow her across the foyer toward the stairs. The main floor of St Helena's is quiet, mostly reception and offices now. It still has the chapel. I stop before the wide oak doors. 'I want to wait in here.'

Jenny turns with a questioning look. 'Oh, okay,' realizing I mean the chapel. 'Do you want me to wait with you?'

'No, I need a few moments to myself. Will you bring him here? I'd like to meet him alone first.'

'Of course,' she smiles. 'I understand.'

She reaches out to take me in her arms. 'Are you all right?' she asks.

'Yes,' I reply as she hugs me. And just like her grandmother, Jenny hangs onto the hug far longer than expected. And I melt into it.

The inside of the hospital chapel is narrow and dark. It smells of wood, musty with time, and aged linseed oil. The heavy door closes slowly behind me. I stand for a moment and let my eyes adjust to the light. At the front of the room votive candles illuminate a crucifix above the altar. I sit down in one of the two wooden pews. While I wait I let my eyes wander up to the cross, to the blue alabaster statue of Mary, to the candle flames dancing at her feet. Once again I feel a surge of envy for my mother's faith; for the strength she has found in her religion, her church. The church I turned my back on years ago. Still, I pray to whatever no-name God, whatever power in the universe, will listen.

Please, please, don't let him look like Gerald Ryan.

The flickering candles cast shadows on the wall while I beg a God I do not believe in for this favour.

I feel, rather than hear, the sound of the oak door moving behind me. My heart begins to race. I turn around, in slow motion it seems, as light spills into the room.

And he is there. His darkened form silhouetted in the doorway.

I stand up on trembling legs as he begins to move towards me. Neither of us speaks while he approaches. I don't know what to say – hello seems so inadequate. The door silently closes behind him, and he is lost in darkness for a moment. Then suddenly he stands before me. I search his face as the candlelight exposes his features.

And my prayers are answered.

The dark eyes reflecting back at me, Ward eyes, smile with a familiarity that only family can recognize. In those eyes I see my father and Morgan. The fair skin, the brown hair, widow's peak, even the flash of perfect teeth as he attempts a nervous smile, all have passed down from his grandfather.

An ember of radiant warmth begins to grow in my chest. It spills through my body, filling an empty space, a space I did not know existed until now. And nothing else matters. Nothing except that this is my child, my son, and the longing for him that I had denied is now filled with love. Where, or who, he came from means nothing compared to this.

He lifts his right hand and offers it to me. 'Hello,' he says. 'I'm Gavin.'

And I hear that voice!

My legs turn to liquid and my knees buckle. He reaches out to catch me. With his arm under my elbow he helps guide me back to the pew.

'Are you okay?' he asks as I slump down.

The voice! There's no mistaking the voice. The memory of a sun-filled summer day floods through me. The familiar voice fills the musty air of the room with the same music, the same magic that River's voice had on that long-ago day.

I nod, not trusting my own voice for the moment. He takes my shaking hands in his while he waits patiently for me to recover. I search his face for any signs of resentment directed at a mother who would give him up at birth. There is nothing but a gentle concern there. With a bitter-sweet acceptance, I feel the full impact of sadness for the circumstances that kept us apart all this time. 'They told me you were dead, stillborn,' I finally say.

'Yes I know.'

I can't drink in enough of him as he quietly answers my flood of queries about his life. I listen in wonder at the magic of his voice as he talks about growing up in West Vancouver. I am relieved to hear about his childhood, about the parents who raised him, who were responsible for this beautiful young man in front of me.

'I'm not looking to replace them,' he says with candid sincerity. 'They've been wonderful to me and I love them both very much. They always encouraged me to find my birth family. But I never really felt the need to. And I always believed that my birth mother must have given me up for a good reason. I didn't want to impose on her – on your – life. But when Molly was born, my wife, Cathy, and I began to wonder about my genetic background. Cathy encouraged me to search for my birth parents. That led to my conversation with Boyer a few days ago. He explained the circumstances of my birth. When he told me about your mother, my grandmother, being so ill, I began to feel an urgency to come. Fortunately, I have access to a small plane. And the weather forecast was good for the next few days. So, well, here I am.'

'Yes,' I say in wonder. 'Here you are.'

The guttering candles burn down as we talk on. I hear the pride in his voice when he talks about his daughter, Molly. Then my heart fills with warmth as he refers to her as, 'your granddaughter'.

Before we get up to leave he says, 'I don't know exactly what to call you.'

'Natalie would do just fine for now,' I tell him as he helps me to my feet. 'Can you do that?'

His right eyebrow lifts with the same lopsided grin as his grandfather, a grin that once entranced so many Atwood housewives.

'All right,' he says. 'Natalie.'

And it comes off his lips like a forgotten melody.

Chapter Fifty-One

Nettie

Gus stands beside her bed. She strains to see his handsome face. It's the face of the young Gus Ward she had fallen in love with on a snowy winter day of her youth. The one in whose eyes she had seen her future, her family.

'Have you come to take me home?' she asks.

But her daughter's voice answers, 'Mom, are you awake?'

Nettie remembers that Natalie was sitting at her bedside, holding her hand, before she fell asleep. Now her daughter stands next to this apparition, this phantom of her dead husband. Nettie expects him to disappear with her sleep, but he stays. His ghost is as stubborn as he was.

'This is Gavin, Mom,' Natalie is saying. 'My son. Your grandson.'

'Gavin,' Nettie repeats. She smiles. She wants to touch him, to make sure he is real. She reaches towards him. He takes her hand in his. She pulls him closer to search his face. Such a beautiful face. The face of his grandfather. And yet, and yet, behind those dark eyes she sees the gentleness of his father, and the determination of his mother. This is Natalie's son. Nettie would have known him anywhere. His familiar voice erases the sound she denied the night of his birth. The tiny haunting cry fades, and dies.

She caresses his cheek. 'I've been waiting for you,' she says.

Boyer and his partner Stanley appear on the other side of her bed. Jenny and Nick stand nearby. Behind them, Carl and Morgan and Ruth enter the room. Nettie's prayers have been answered. Her family, everyone, is here.

She holds tight to her grandson's hand. She will not let go, even while he is meeting the rest of his family. She has missed his entire life, and now will only have time for goodbye.

'I want to go home now,' she tells Boyer as he leans to kiss her. 'It's time for my family to all come home.'

Boyer looks across the bed to Natalie.

Nettie sees the unspoken question in his eyes. She turns to her daughter.

'Yes,' Natalie smiles back at her brother. 'Let's go home.'

Chapter Fifty-Two

THE TELEPHONE ON the other end of the line rings four times. I prepare to leave a message on the answering machine when I hear Vern's voice.

'Natalie?' he says out of breath, as if he has run to grab the phone.

'Yes, it's me.' I sink down in the paisley chair by the bed. My packed suitcase waits beside me.

Next door at the hospital, Boyer, along with Jenny and Nick, are making arrangements to bring Mom home in the ambulance. Boyer's partner, Stanley, has taken Gavin back to the motel and is now waiting downstairs to drive me out to the farm. Later this afternoon, after Molly finishes her nap, Boyer will bring Gavin and his family out for dinner.

Gavin's daughter! My granddaughter! I still can't believe I have a granddaughter.

I am still reeling from the emotional reunion in my mother's hospital room. The awkwardness of the hushed introductions were overshadowed by Mom's request to be taken home. We all knew what that meant.

'How's your mother?' Vern asks.

So much has happened since I last heard my husband's voice, since I watched him disappear into the morning fog at the Prince

George bus station. Was that really only yesterday morning? So much has changed. There are so many things to tell him, so many things I want to say. It's hard to know where to start.

'Can you come?' I ask. 'I want you to meet her, to meet my family.'

'Of course,' he says. The relief in his voice carries over the static. 'Are you all right?' he asks.

'Yes, yes, I am,' I tell him. 'I just need you.'

'I'll wrap things up here and leave tonight.'

I give him directions to the farm. 'South Valley Road is not hard to find once you've found Atwood,' I tell him. 'Just follow it until you come to the end of the road.'

'I'll be there,' he says.

'Hurry.'

Chapter Fifty-Three

WE PULL INTO the farmyard and park by the yard gate in front of the house. 'I thought you and Boyer might build yourselves a new home like the ones in your subdivision,' I say to Stanley perhaps a little too heartily.

He glances at me quickly from the corner of his eye, but my question is sincere. He smiles. 'No. None of those new houses have the charm of this old place.'

We stroll together up the path to the front porch and I notice the changes have kept that charm. The siding, windows, and trim are all new. The house looks straighter, stronger.

Inside the enclosed porch a gleaming new front-load washer and dryer have been built into designer cabinets. Wide windows stretch across the back wall, looking into the modernized kitchen.

Before I go upstairs Stanley proudly shows me the rest of the renovations. An addition – a new master bedroom with bathroom – now stands where the rose garden once grew. The sunroom at the back of the house has been turned into a suite for Mom. A hospital bed, placed to overlook the back field, is ready and waiting for her.

Upstairs my bedroom looks the same, only smaller. In my memory, the room I grew up in was much larger. The linoleum floor and the floral wallpaper are unchanged. But even though I have grown no taller since the last time I was here, I feel like a giant invading the space of a child.

I set my suitcase down by the dresser and stand gazing out the window. Yellow poplar leaves drift onto the paved road. The barn has been updated too and painted, but otherwise the view is unchanged. I have a sudden urge to lift the window and climb out on to the roof. Only time stops me. Time and a few stiff joints.

Soon they will all come up this familiar road. The first time our entire family has been together in this house – together anywhere – since my dad died.

Downstairs everything is quiet. Stanley is the only other person in the house for the moment. And even though this is the first time I have spent any time with Boyer's life partner, I know that he is as much a part of our family as Ruth is. During the drive to the farm in his pick-up truck, I wondered aloud why I had never met him when we were kids.

'Well,' he told me, his green eyes crinkling into a smile, 'I was in university by the time you recited your poem about my father and grandfather.'

'Boyer's poem,' I laughed. 'You heard about that?'

'I was there.'

I remember the auburn-haired boy talking to Boyer in the gymnasium that night. That hair has faded to a strawberry blond but there is still a boyish look to the rounded face.

'I was home for Christmas and went to the school that night with Dad. He loved Christmas concerts. I wasn't much of a fan then, but I do remember the poem. My father loved it.'

And I like this man, I thought as we shared a memory.

'I did come out here a few years later,' he added tentatively, 'during the search for River.'

'Yes, I heard that you and your father came to help. I didn't see you. I didn't see much during that time.'

I turn from my bedroom window at the sound of footsteps in the hall. Stanley pokes his head in my door.

'Can I show you something?' he asks as he beckons me to follow him. We make our way up the new hardwood stairs to the attic.

As unchanged as my room is, this one, Boyer's old nest, is unrecognizable. The narrow space has been converted into a study. The bottom half of the sloped walls are still lined with books, but now they are all neatly organized on maple bookshelves. A bay window with a cushioned window seat has replaced the tiny Pearson window that once looked out at the familiar view of fields and mountains.

The fading sunlight comes down through the slanted skylight. It shines down on the wall at the end of the room. The only flat wall in the attic. The framed arrangement hanging above the desk gets my attention. I look closer. Each picture frame holds a magazine or newspaper clipping. The entire wall is covered with clippings of my articles, stories and book reviews.

Someone – Boyer – has carefully mounted and displayed a history of my career. Even my very first article, published by the newspaper where I worked selling advertising, is there.

Stanley sits himself down on the chair in front of the desk. He watches while I study the display. After a few moments he slides open a drawer and pulls out a file-folder thick with papers. Without a word he hands it to me. Inside, I find reams of handwritten poetry. Boyer's poetry. I sit down on the daybed and read through some of them while he waits.

'These are beautiful,' I say as I take them in. 'Beautiful. I'm so glad he kept writing.'

'He misses you, Natalie,' Stanley says quietly.

I look up at him, 'And I miss him too.' I force a reply, trying to keep my voice from breaking. Oh, if he only knew how much I miss my brother. I feel his absence from my life every day, as if a part of me is missing. I carry on constant imaginary conversations with him, but each time I see his face the words I want to say die on my lips. I swallow. 'I can't believe he saved all these old pieces,' I wave at the wall display.

'He's so proud of you,' Stanley says.

I search his face with my eyes. It's the face of a kind man. The creases of time etched around his eyes show only concern.

'It was because of Boyer that I became a journalist, you know,' I tell him. 'He was the first one to pay me by the word.' I picture the jar of pennies on the windowsill in my bedroom. 'I get a bit more than a penny a word now.' I laugh. 'Not much though!' Even to me my laugh sounds forced.

'Are you ever going to forgive him?' Stanley asks. His words startle me. This is the same question that Mom asked me only a few hours ago. *Boyer? Me forgive Boyer?*

'Forgive him for what?' I ask.

Stanley's gentle eyes hold mine, but he says nothing.

Then I tell him what I have always wanted to tell Boyer. What I wanted to tell Mom today. 'I'm the one who should beg his forgiveness.' My shoulders sag in resignation. Stanley shifts over from his chair and sits down beside me.

'I stay away because I can't face him. I don't deserve him. I don't deserve to be around him. It was my carelessness that ruined his life,' I tell him, and as simply as that it all comes out. My guilt, my shame, my betrayal – all are given voice in the quiet of Boyer's old bedroom.

I tell him how my thoughtless words started the evil avalanche of gossip, which would shatter Boyer's, and our family's image, in the community.

'And River,' I whisper. 'If I hadn't run away that night, River would never have become lost, never have been killed.'

Finally, as unchecked tears slide down my cheeks, I tell him about the marijuana butts thrown carelessly under the sink in Boyer's cabin. I confess it all to this virtual stranger. 'I can't look at him without knowing I caused the fire, his scars.'

Stanley gently puts both of his arms around me. Nothing about having this man, who I have just met today, hold me, feels strange. I understand now some of what my mother must have felt in all those years of sharing her burdens in a confessional.

He pulls a cotton handkerchief from his shirt pocket. 'You were sixteen years old,' he says as I wipe my eyes. 'A child. Such a burden to carry alone all these years, Natalie. It's you who needs to find a way to forgive that sixteen-year-old girl.'

'The fire—' I start.

He takes my face in his hands and forces me to look into his eyes. 'The fire was arson.'

'I know the police suspected that, but—'

'No, they knew it, but couldn't – or didn't want to – prove it. There were anonymous calls claiming a group of boys had doused the logs at the front door with gasoline and set the fire. Your father found a gas can washed up at the lake shore the following spring.'

'Who—?

'We'll never know. Kids playing a stupid prank or someone with an ignorant vendetta.'

'All because of my foolish words.'

'No, all because of prejudice,' Stanley says quietly, and I wonder what he and Boyer have had to endure over the years just to be who they are. 'But does it really matter now?' he asks. 'After all these years, does it matter how, or why, any of it happened? Is it worth not having your brother in your life to hang onto your guilt?'

When I don't answer he continues. 'What a waste,' he slowly shakes his head. 'This family never fights, never uses words as weapons. They use silence. And it hurts just as much. All of you let what is haunting you, what you are not saying to each other, come between you. Both you and Boyer harbour guilt over River's death. But you never speak to each other about it.'

Momentarily numbed by the enormity of what he is saying I nod silently, then stand up.

'Talk to him Natalie,' he says before I leave. 'Don't underestimate his capacity to love. And to forgive.'

Later, alone in my room, I think about Stanley's words as I search for something to give my granddaughter when she arrives.

I look at the jar of pennies by the window. It won't be long before she's old enough to start playing the penny game. A penny isn't much these days, I know, but then it's not about the pennies. It was never about the pennies.

I lean down and push open the door to the crawl space under the eaves. My joints protest slightly when I get down on my hands and knees. Perhaps there are some old toys in here. I was never much for dolls, but maybe Jenny has left something.

Cobwebs brush my fingers as I reach into a wooden box to pull out a lumpy purple Seagram's bag. I wonder if kids still play with marbles these days.

Behind the box of marbles I feel another box full of books. I drag it out and pick up the small book on the top. I flip through the pages of A. A. Milne's *When We Were Very Young*.

Perfect.

I close the book at the sound of cars coming up the road.

I push myself up and hurry over to the window. My fingers grip the windowsill as I watch Boyer's Jeep pull up in front of the house. A parade of vehicles, Morgan's pick-up truck, the ambulance and Jenny's Edsel, follow slowly behind.

Gavin climbs out of the passenger side of the Jeep. A smile forms on his lips as he takes in his surroundings. The back door opens and a young woman climbs out. She leans back in and lifts a small blonde child into her arms. A black-and-white border collie, astonishingly similar to our old cow dog, Buddy, bolts out from under the porch. He clears the fence and joins the group. The girl leans from her mother's arms and tries to reach down to pet the dog, who, with tail wagging, leads them up the path to the porch.

It's hard to imagine River, frozen in time and in my mind still age twenty-three, as a grandfather. But the three-year-old girl, whose aquablue eyes I recognize all the way from the window, the child who looks up and shyly returns my wave, can only be his granddaughter.

Chapter Fifty-Four

IN THE SUNROOM Jenny hooks up the intravenous while Nick takes care of the oxygen. I can see the trip has taken its toll on Mom. After she is comfortable I adjust her blanket as I stroke her forehead.

'It's good to be home,' Mom sighs and attempts a smile.

I sit down by her bed and take her hand in mine.

'Go visit with everyone, Natalie,' she says, her voice fading, 'I'm going to sleep for a bit.'

On the other side of the bed Jenny nods at me and adjusts the morphine feed. I can feel Mom relax as the morphine begins to work.

Before dinner Ruth and I go over to the dairy together to get the room upstairs ready for Carl.

I switch the gas heat on in the chilled room and we turn the mattress on the iron bed. I reach up and pull linen from the closet shelf then stare down at the quilt in my hands. My grandmother's quilt. And it strikes me that this was where Gavin was conceived.

I walk over to the window and think about the night of the storm. Mom is right again. There are no ill winds. And there's no need to wonder what good she thinks the ill winds of that summer blew into our lives. Gavin. But somewhere, somewhere between those winds, and the good that came from them, a lot of time has disappeared, wasted in keeping useless secrets.

I turn to look at Ruth. As she takes a load of towels into the bathroom I wonder how all this was affecting her, how she felt to find out it was her baby who had not lived.

Determined not to let silence be part of this family's communication any longer, I turn to her. 'Ruth, your baby – I'm sorry,' I say quietly as she brings extra hand towels and flannels to put in the nightstand.

'It's all right.' She speaks deliberately. 'I grieved for him a long time ago. He stopped moving inside me days before he was born,' she tells me. 'When I woke up after the birth I couldn't feel anything. I signed the papers Dr Mumford gave me, but I knew my son's spirit was not in this world.'

I cross the room and wrap my arms around her. We stand holding each other for a few moments.

'But Gavin is,' she says warmly. 'And he, and his family, have returned to us.' She turns to place the towels inside the nightstand. She bends down, looks inside, then tugs at something wedged at the back of the cabinet. 'Natalie, look at this,' she says as she straightens up.

An involuntary gasp escapes my lips as I realize what she is holding. She lets the black hard-covered notebook fall open then hands it to me. I sit down on the bed, unable to believe what I hold in my hands: one of River's journals. I thought all of them had burned in the fire.

I read the date at the top of the first page. *Monday June 10, 1968.* The day he left.

I feel as if I have re-entered the past. Even after all these years I recognize the neat rounded handwriting. Once again I read the remorse in his words for his failure of judgment in allowing himself to be carried away by curiosity, by grief, and in denying the truth of who he was the night I came to him.

Nothing excuses what I've done, I thought I knew who I was, what I stood for, and now I see I don't know anything.

I'm leaving this morning, before Gus gets back from the milk route. Before Natalie comes home from school. Before Nettie comes to the dairy. And before Boyer returns from work. Can I leave without seeing him? Without facing the truth? Without finding out if my truth is also his?

And then I see my mother's name.

Nettie came in without knocking and closed the door. She held her hand up to silence me before I spoke. She walked over and sat at the table across from me. She told me not to say anything, that she just wanted to sit there until Natalie was settled in the house.

But it was Nettie who broke the silence. 'I don't want to know what happened here tonight,' she said after a few moments. 'I just want to remind you she's only sixteen years old.' Once again she held up her palm to silence any reply from me.

She replaced her hands in her lap and stared down at them. Without raising her eyes she resumed speaking, her voice barely audible. 'You young people have it all wrong,' she said more to herself than to me. 'There's no such thing as free love. There's always a cost.'

We sat for what felt like hours in the silence after that. At the sound of morning birds outside the window, she looked up and said, 'You know you have to leave, don't you.'

I nodded.

She stood and walked over to the door. With her hand on the knob she stopped, waited, then turned to look back at me. In a voice so low that I almost didn't hear her, she said, 'Take Boyer with you.'

I let the journal fall open in my lap. And there, lodged in the centre pages is another part of the past. I pick up the old photograph. One I thought was lost long ago. River must have found it. I study the folded black-and-white snapshot. River's face smiles out through time. I carefully unfold the photograph to search for the face I know is on the other side. And there he is: a young Boyer, sitting leaned up against the trunk of the old apple tree, gazing over the top of his book. He is looking at River. And in that look I see so clearly now the love I had failed to recognize then.

Chapter Fifty-Five

FOR THE FIRST time in over thirty-four years our family eats dinner together in the parlour. Before we all sat down we went into the sunroom and stood around Mom's bed and prayed with her. I held her hand and felt the strength return as, with her eyes closed, she began to repeat the rosary.

When we were finished Mom opened her eyes and pulled Boyer closer. 'Now don't let them get all maudlin and morbid,' I heard her whisper. 'I want to hear my family's laughter fill this house.'

At Mom's request the sunroom door is left open. I hope that even in her drug-induced sleep she will feel the comfort in hearing the noisy chatter of her children at the dining room table once again.

My brothers hold nothing back. They all sit in their same old places. The smell of the ocean radiates from Morgan and Carl's clothes, and mingles with the aroma of the farm that clings to Boyer and Stanley. I wonder what odours I bring to the table.

Gavin's wife, Cathy, sits next to me. It was so easy to like this self assured young woman. When Gavin introduced us earlier, she held out her arms and hugged me with no hesitation. I hugged her back and told her how grateful I was that she had encouraged Gavin to search for his birth parents. And that she had brought Molly to us.

'More people to love Molly can only be a good thing,' she replied with a smile.

I can sense Cathy looking around the table now and appreciating just how many people that is.

As I sit and watch this family, old and new, interact, I notice a new glow on Jenny's face as she chatters uncharacteristically across the table to Gavin. There is an obviously eager, almost childlike, acceptance of this older brother. For a brief moment I feel a pang of regret that she was denied this gift for so long.

Jenny catches herself and takes a breath from her hurried words. She laughs, 'Oh, just listen to me. I am a Chatty Cathy aren't I?' A look of confusion crosses her face as Gavin glances at his wife and they both burst into laughter. Jenny blushes beet-red as it dawns on her what she has just said.

'Chatty Cathy, Chatty Cathy,' Molly repeats.

'I'll probably never hear the end of that one,' Cathy laughs. And the laughter of a family ripples around the table joining Molly's giggles. Any awkward moments in the last few hours seem to have been smoothed over by this child's presence.

Molly sits between her father and Boyer. Earlier Carl watched as Boyer set up a makeshift highchair for her. He eyed the thick encyclopaedia under the cushion. 'Uh-oh, better watch out,' he warned Gavin. 'Boyer can get a little ambitious when it comes to words.'

Over the dinner conversation I hear the constant hum of the oxygen tank in the sunroom. My eyes stray every now and then to the open sunroom door. Even though she sleeps, our mother's presence fills the room. And my brothers oblige her every request.

As if no time has passed, Morgan and Carl hassle Boyer about the automated barn and the contractors who now run the farm. 'Hands-off milking for gentlemen farmers,' Morgan teases.

'Wish there was automated fishing,' Carl snorts.

The good-natured bantering goes back and forth throughout dinner, but it's obvious that Morgan and Carl are glad that the farm, although a scaled-down version now, is still intact.

I know they have accepted Gavin when they begin to tease him about his career.

'Must be pretty nice, flying all over the world. Tough job, eh?' Carl grins as Ruth passes him another helping of chicken.

'Yeah, but someone's got to do it,' Gavin accepts their teasing as easily as they deliver it.

'Must pay pretty well too, owning your own plane,' Morgan adds.

'Well, I don't exactly own the Cessna we flew up on,' Gavin replies, as he wipes up the milk Molly has just spilled. 'I own a one-tenth share. So we get to use it a few times a month.'

'A busman's holiday,' Cathy interjects playfully.

'You love it, too,' Gavin says and Cathy smirks back at him.

I see satisfied smiles pass between Boyer and Stanley as they watch the exchange.

Suddenly, Molly tilts her head and studies Boyer's profile. I hold my breath as her chubby fingers reach towards his face. 'That an owie?' she asks.

Gavin opens his mouth to speak, then decides against it, as Boyer leans closer to Molly.

When he is at eye level, Molly reaches up and strokes the mottled skin on the left side of his face.

'What's zat?' she asks with a frown.

'It's a scar,' Boyer tells her. 'A long time ago someone wasn't careful with fire and my skin got burned.'

'Oh.' Molly thinks for a moment then asks, 'Hurt?'

'Not any more.'

'Good,' Molly smiles and satisfied turns her attention to the bowl of ice cream Ruth has placed in front of her.

'Hey, where's mine?' Morgan asks, and once again Carl and Morgan fill the empty space with their kibitzing.

As I look around the table, I'm suddenly anxious for Vern to get here and be part of this. If he leaves tonight, he should be here sometime before tomorrow afternoon. Gavin and his family are planning to fly out at two o'clock. They will have to leave for the airport with Stanley before one. I am hoping Vern will arrive in time to meet them before they go.

Boyer pushes his chair back and gets up from the table. He goes into the kitchen and returns with the coffeepot. As he leans over to fill mugs he asks, 'How long can you stay?'

I'm not sure who he's asking, but I answer without hesitating, 'As long as she needs me.'

Across the table, my brothers and Ruth nod in agreement.

'Good,' Boyer says.

Chapter Fifty-Six

SOMEONE IS PLAYING the piano. The familiar melody floats up through the hallway grates. It seeps under the door and into my slumber. I lie in darkness and wonder if I am still sleeping, if this music is part of a dream I've forgotten. Even though this is my second night here, it takes a few moments to remember where I am, to believe I am lying in the double bed of my childhood bedroom. My eyes focus on the illuminated hands of the alarm clock on the night table: fifteen minutes before five in the morning.

I got little sleep the first night Mom was home. I didn't care. Since she came back to the farm Mom has slipped deeper and deeper into that in-between place between living and dying. I wanted to be near her, and so spent most of the first night in her room. I only went up to my room when I had to relinquish my chair to Ruth. And even with Vern here last night I was reluctant to go to bed.

So much has happened in the last seventy-two hours. A lifetime caught up to us all. It will take time to sort it out.

Although Gavin appears to be taking it all with a quiet accept-ance, I am sure it is a bit overwhelming. Boyer has given him the information about his paternal grandmother who is still alive. 'Guess we'll be flying to Montana,' was Gavin's simple response to the news.

I am not surprised to learn that Boyer has kept in contact with River's mother all these years. I can only imagine how her life too will change with this unexpected gift.

Yesterday morning Gavin and I sat with Mom until Morgan came to be with her. Then we went for a walk together before Vern arrived. Aspen leaves fluttered around us as we stopped at the end of the log snake fence behind the back field. I waved at the house in case Mom was awake and watching us.

'It's so beautiful here,' Gavin said as we strolled into the clearing by the lake.

I smiled as his gaze took in the mountains and the forests, still clinging to the last of autumn's colours. I looked around, trying to see through his eyes, to see this place without the lens of memory. A thin skiff of ice covers the surface of the lake. The forest has crept closer to the grassy place where Boyer's home once stood.

There's no trace of the old cabin now. A new apple tree stands in the same spot where the tree that had burned like a torch, signalling to my mother on that long-ago night, once stood. Planted there by some unknown hand, or raised from the ashes, it too has grown gnarled and twisted with age. A few stubborn apples cling to the unpruned branches; dried leaves click in the wind. Windfalls and decaying leaves litter the ground below; the dank sweet odour of fermenting fruit fill the crisp fall air.

In the morning sunshine, I pulled River's journal from my jacket.

Earlier I had taken it, along with the folder of poems, and gone to search for Boyer. I found him at his desk in the attic room. I knocked on the open door. When he turned to me, I held up the folder.

'Stanley let me read these,' I said. 'They're incredible. They really should be published. Can I show them to my editor?'

Boyer smiled and took the outstretched folder from my hand. 'Oh, I think one writer in the family might be enough.'

'I'm just a glorified reporter,' I said. I pointed to his folder. 'Those are the words of a writer.'

Before Boyer could answer, I held up the journal. 'And so is this,' I told him. 'I found it in the room above the dairy. It's River's last journal. I think you should read it. His words explain what I should have told you about the night he and I were together.'

'Natalie,' Boyer's voice is gentle as he opened the drawer to file the folder. 'I don't need to read it. I came to terms with all that a long time ago.' Then he turned to me. 'The problem was we all thought River was perfect,' he added. 'But, like the rest of us, he was human. With flaws and frailties. I forgave him, and myself, a lifetime ago. Give the journal to Gavin. It will help him understand who his father was.'

I hesitated. 'Yes, I intend to, but I just wonder if he really needs to know all this?'

'If I've learned one thing,' Boyer said, 'it's that secrets cause more damage than truth. Give it to him Natalie. He'll understand. He can handle it.'

'Yes,' I said. 'You're right.' I turned to leave.

'He's a beautiful young man,' Boyer called after me.

I stood in the doorway and smiled. 'Yes, he is, isn't he? He looks so much like Dad and Morgan, doesn't he?'

'No, Natalie,' Boyer said. 'He looks just like you.'

'This is for you,' I said when I handed the journal to Gavin at the late. 'It was your father's.'

The few short pages would tell him more about who his father was than any of us ever could. It's all there, in River's own words: his beliefs, his dreams, his sacrifices, and his loves. All of it told with the honesty that was River.

As Gavin took the journal it fell open in his hands. 'That's your father,' I said when he pulled out the photograph.

He carefully unfolded the old black and white picture. 'Which one?'

I looked down at the two beautiful young faces. I had forgotten how much alike they were.

It was easier to fall asleep with Vern by my side last night. He pulled into the farmyard before noon yesterday, had driven straight through. He made it in time to meet Gavin and his family before they left.

Beside me Vern stirs in his sleep. His body presses closer to mine. Yesterday afternoon, after he arrived, after he met Gavin, I led him to my mother's room. I thought she was asleep but her eyelids lifted when I made a hushed introduction to Carl, who was sitting at her bedside.

'Mom, this is Vern,' I whispered and pulled him closer to her. He leaned down so she could see him.

She looked up into his face and smiled. 'Oh, yes,' she said, her voice barely audible. 'You're the one.'

Her lids closed and her face softened, became younger somehow, as she drifted off.

It was easy to see that my mother was now at peace. She did not struggle against the inevitable. 'I'm ready,' she had told me last night.

Father Mac had come and gone. Mom would leave this world with the grace that had carried her through her life. In the end, she told me, she had what she prayed for, all her children and their families, finally together, in this house filled with memories.

Last night and yesterday we all took turns sitting with her, each of us cherishing the moments we knew could be our last with her.

As Vern and I sat together beside Mom's bed, I began to tell him my family's story. I watched my mother's face as I talked, convinced that even in her morphine-induced sleep she could hear each word.

After Vern and I went upstairs, he held me in his arms in the dark of my room and listened patiently while I told him more. Tomorrow I will begin to tell him the rest. All of it.

All day yesterday I watched him talking and joking with my brothers as if he had known them for years. *How easily he fits in.* I thought and felt a tug of remorse at having waited so long for him to know them.

Yesterday afternoon, while Ruth sat with Mom, the rest of us gathered around Boyer's Jeep before Stanley drove Gavin and his family to the airport. Vern and I stood arm in arm while Gavin belted Molly into her car seat.

Before he got into the Jeep, Gavin turned and asked me, 'Do you ever get down to Vancouver?'

'Vern and I drive down for a few days once or twice a year.'

'Well, maybe you'll visit us sometime in West Vancouver when you're down,' he offered.

Vern squeezed my shoulder.

'Yes, I'd like that,' I said. 'And perhaps someday you'll come up to Prince George.'

'I'm sure we will,' he smiled. 'And when we're there, maybe you'll let me take you and Vern flying.'

I saw the quick sideways glance pass between Jenny and Nick. Morgan and Carl each gave a choked laugh. I felt Vern hold his breath before I returned his squeeze. 'Yes,' I said. 'Maybe I'll do just that.'

*

Downstairs the piano music continues. Like a lullaby the notes carry me to the edges of sleep. But the familiar song tugs at chords of memory and pulls me back. I know that song. It's the same one my mother used to play for me when I was a child.

Who could possibly be downstairs playing that old melody? Surely it can't be Mom. She can't have found the strength to leave her bed. But whoever is playing the piano now plays exactly as she had, with the same inflection, the same tempo, and the same love, as if the song was once again being played for me alone.

Lying in the bed of my youth, I wonder if I am imagining the music. Is memory that strong?

I ease myself out from under Vern's arm. Enveloped in darkness, I find my way into the hallway, and then down the eighteen steps that I still know by heart. I feel for the doorknob at the bottom of the stairway and open the door. Like a sleepwalker, I follow the music. Soft and haunting, the familiar melody lures me through the kitchen and into the parlour.

The gooseneck piano lamp shines down on the ivory keys below. Scarred hands move fluently across them. I lean against the doorway and watch my brother at the piano. I had no idea that Boyer could play, but then he's had plenty of years to learn, and she's had plenty of time to teach him.

The door to the sunroom is closed. Through the glass I see that the nightlight is turned off. The room is dark, quiet. No hiss from the oxygen tank rises over the gentle strains of the music that plays my mother home. I don't have to be told. And I don't try to hold back the tears that well up.

I wish I could say that the last words my mother spoke to me had been enlightening, or a profound revelation. But I can't. I thought she was talking in her sleep as I leaned close to kiss her good night when Boyer came in to sit with her a few hours ago. I barely heard her. Her final words to me, the words I will take with me into the rest of my life, were simple – and they were enough.

'Life is messy, Natalie,' she whispered from the fading fringe of consciousness, 'but it all comes out in the wash.'

The last notes of 'Love Me Tender' hang in the air now as Boyer finishes playing. From upstairs comes the sound of stirring. Soon the rest of the family will join us. And we will begin the process of sharing our grief. This time we will do it together.

At the piano, Boyer slowly turns around on the bench and his eyes find mine. For the first time I see, not the scars, but my brother's beautiful face. And I do not look away. I will never look away again.

A half-smile forms on his lips, but reaches beyond. It reaches up to his liquid blue eyes. Those eyes are the soul of my mother, in the face of my brother. There is so much I want to say, to tell him. And I will. But not now.

Now I smile back at him and say, 'I've always loved that song.'

'I know,' he says.

Epilogue

Atwood Weekly September 30, 2004

Monument to American Draft-Dodgers Sparks
Cross-Border Controversy.

Nelson City Council has passed a resolution to announce its non-involvement in the proposed memorial to Vietnam War resisters.

This small West Kootenay town, until now better known for its pristine surroundings and alpine ski slopes, has become the recipient of insults and threats of boycott from enraged Americans.

The privately-funded monument was conceived to pay tribute to the approx. 120,000 Americans who fled to Canada between 1964 and 1977. The proposed bronze sculpture would depict two Canadians holding out their hands in welcome to an American draft-dodger.

'This will mark the courageous legacy of Vietnam War resisters and the Canadians who helped them resettle in this country during that tumultuous era,' an organizer of the project said.

Since the announcement, the city of Nelson has been blasted with a deluge of e-mail from outraged Americans promising to boycott the area. One enraged writer from Knoxville, Iowa called Canada a country of 'cowards', and wrote, 'We are smarter than you are, tougher than you are, and we will kick your inbred asses.'

The national commander of the Veterans of Foreign Wars, John Furgess, has urged President Bush to express his displeasure over the proposed memorial, calling it a 'tribute to cowards'.

Not all communications were negative. Many writers expressed encouragement for a monument to men of peace, and drew parallels between the Vietnam War and the current events in Iraq.

Project organizer Isaac Romano said in a press release Monday that for now the project was on hold.

In a separate press release the city of Nelson distanced itself from the issue. 'The city's involvement,' said one council member, 'would spell certain economic disaster for members of our local business community that trade with or rely on American tourist dollars.'

A warm April wind drifts north across the Canada/US border. A gentle air stream lifts and carries it through the forests and valleys of the Cascade Mountains. In the town of Atwood, a swirling dust devil topples a child's empty milk container. The child watches unconcerned as the small plastic bottle is carried away, turning end on end, across the schoolyard.

The wind rises and changes direction. It blows south again, swirls around mountainsides, through trees and meadows, until it touches down on a small alpine lake. The still water begins to ripple as the wind skates across the surface. Leaves rustle in the tree at the water's edge. White apple blossoms lift and swirl, then fall gently towards the ground. Like snow they land upon the heads and shoulders of the brother and sister standing hand in hand beneath the branches. At their feet, at the base of the tree, is a newly-laid bronze plaque. The raised letters read:

IN MEMORY OF RICHARD ADAM JORDAN

'RIVER'

1946–1968

'AND GREAT IS THE MAN WITH THE SWORD UNDRAWN'

Acknowledgements

I wish to acknowledge the many people who have shared this journey with me. To those who were with me from the beginning and those I have met along the way. I extend my deep gratitude. In particular my dear friends Verena Berger and Joyce Aaltonen who were there from the very first tentative steps. Thank you both for patiently reading or listening to draft after draft and then having the grace to call it a privilege.

Thanks also to my daughter Tanya LaFond, son Aaron Drake, sister Diane Jonas, mother Gloria Jonas, as well as Kim Corless, and Leanne Schultz. You all in your own way helped to keep me on the path that would lead me to the door of Gregory and Company. My thanks to all the good people there who welcomed me in, especially Jane Gregory, and Emma Dunford. Thank you Emma for reading your slush pile and for your positive and professional guidance through the edits.

Finally, to my husband Tom Milner, who first opened the door and outed this closet writer. Thank you for your unwavering faith and encouragement. I love you. You are my constant beacon home.

Donna Milner